·*· BEETLE & THE HOLLOWBONES ·*·

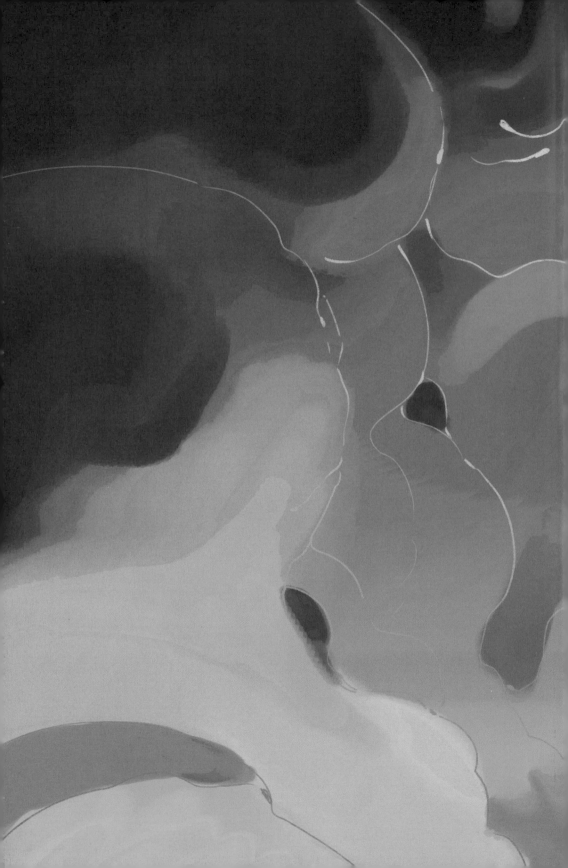

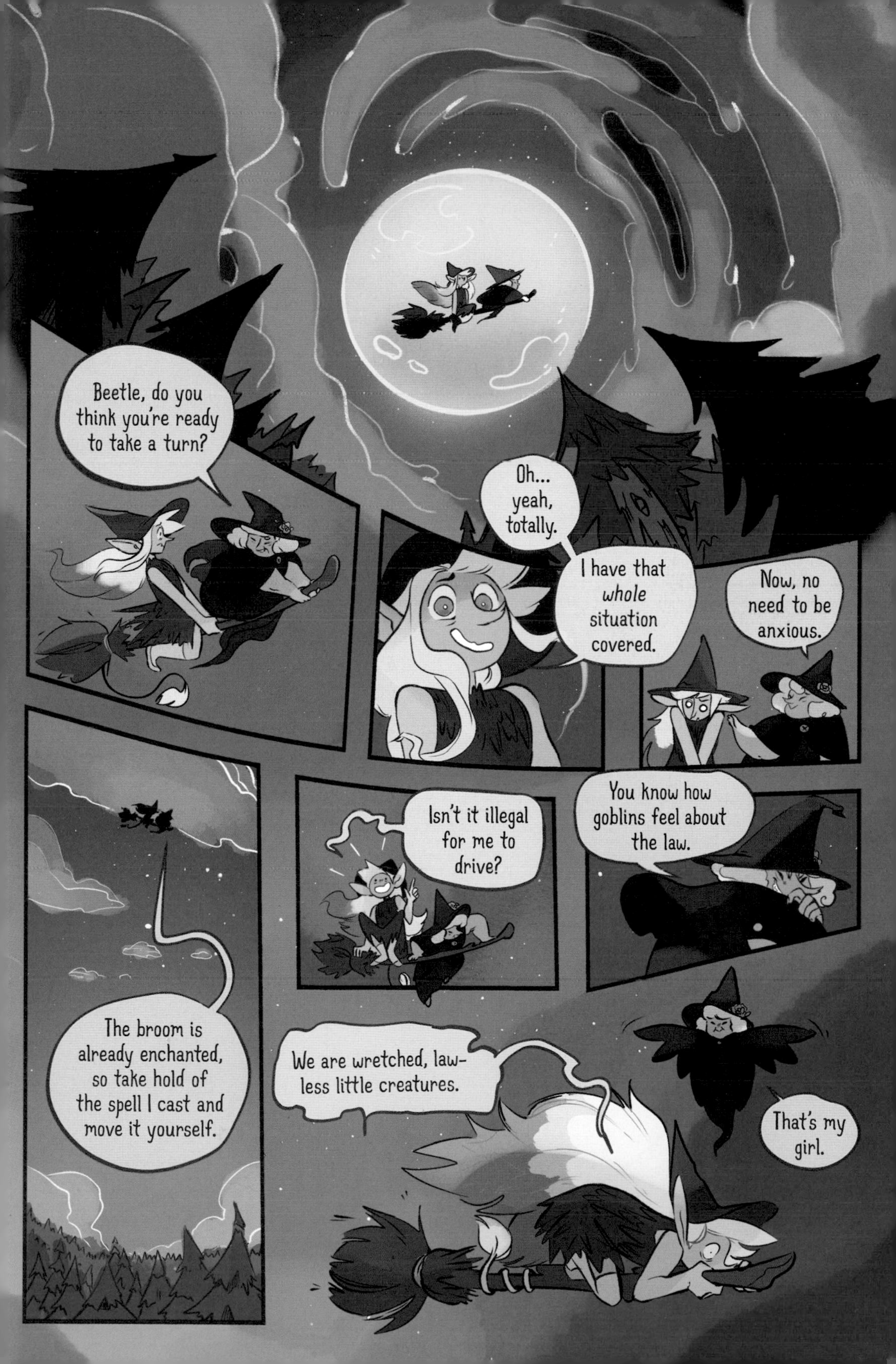
Beetle, do you think you're ready to take a turn?
Oh... yeah, totally.
I have that *whole* situation covered.
Now, no need to be anxious.
The broom is already enchanted, so take hold of the spell I cast and move it yourself.
Isn't it illegal for me to drive?
You know how goblins feel about the law.
We are wretched, lawless little creatures.
That's my girl.

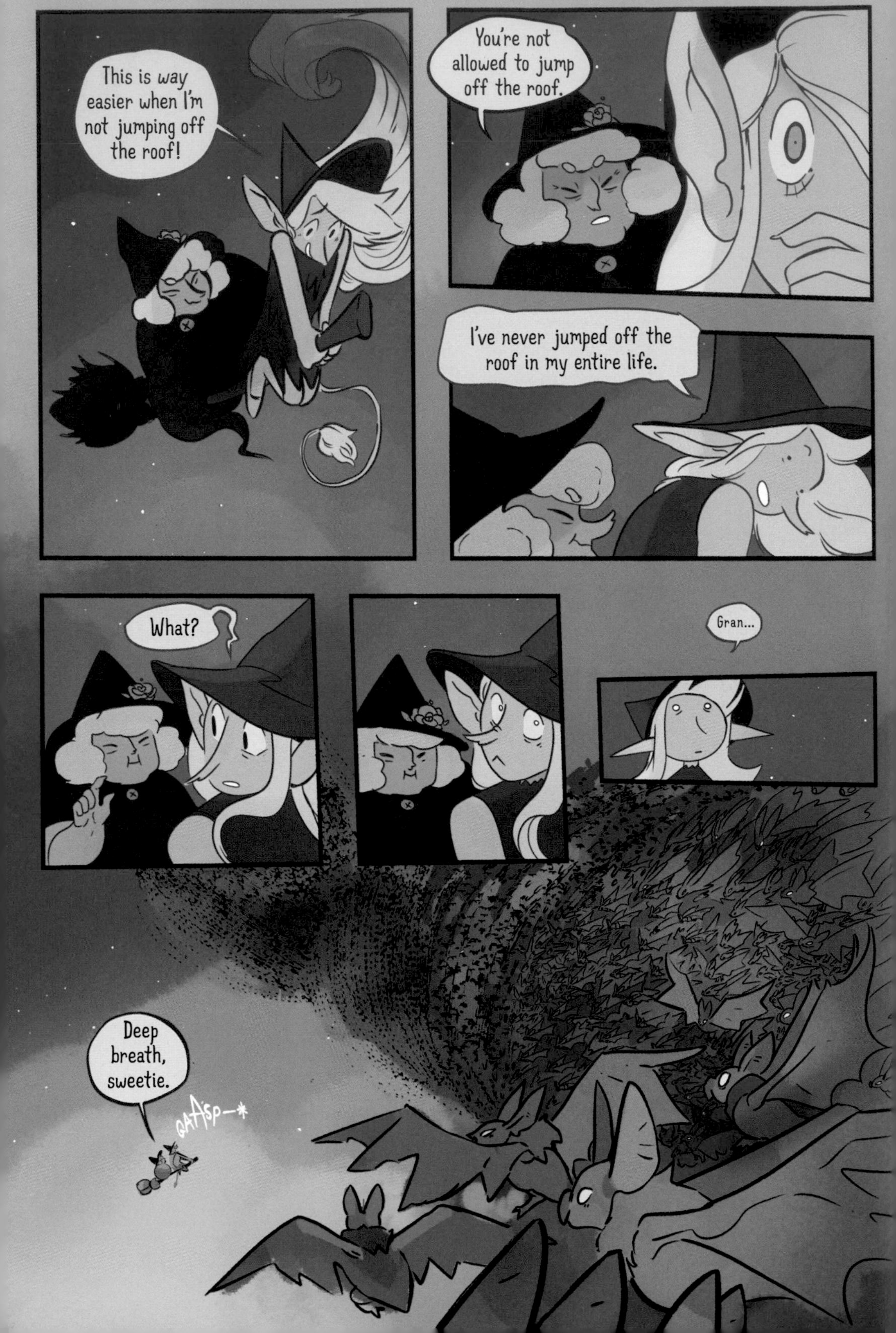
This is way easier when I'm not jumping off the roof!
You're not allowed to jump off the roof.
I've never jumped off the roof in my entire life.
What?
Gran...
Deep breath, sweetie.
GAAASP—*

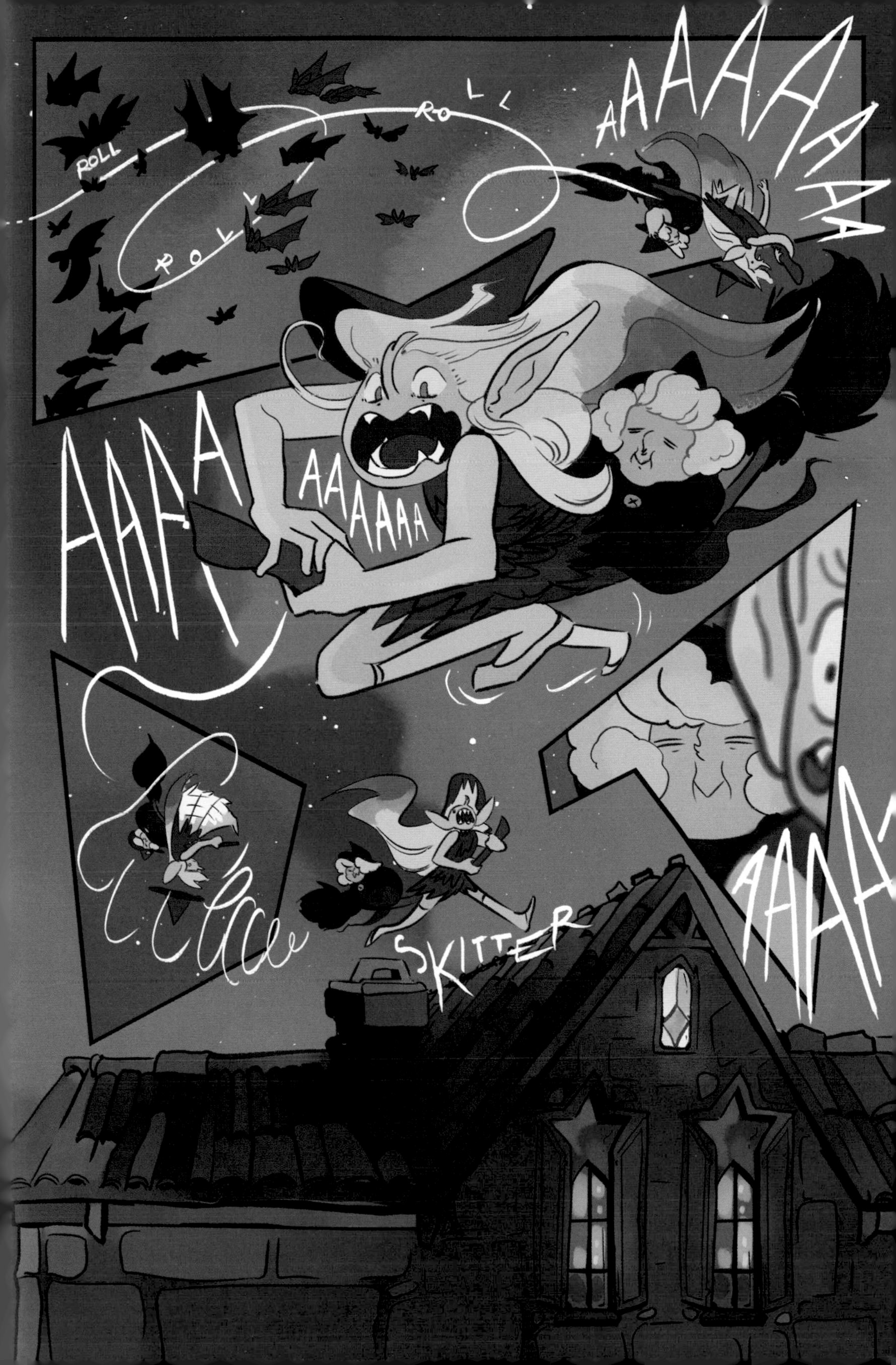
ROLL
ROLL
ROLL
ROLL
AAAAAAAAAAA
AAAA
AAAAAAA
AAAA
SKITTER

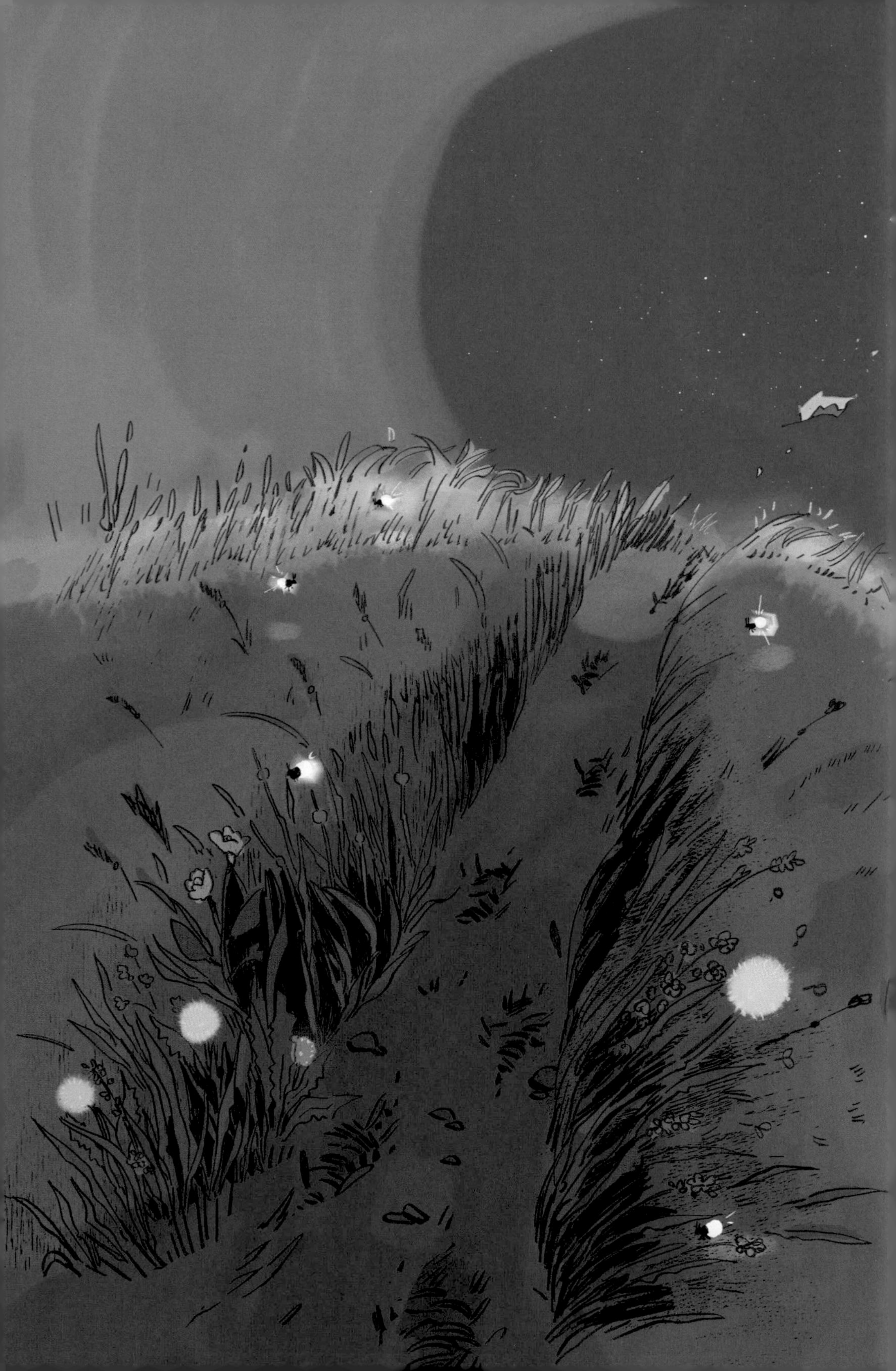

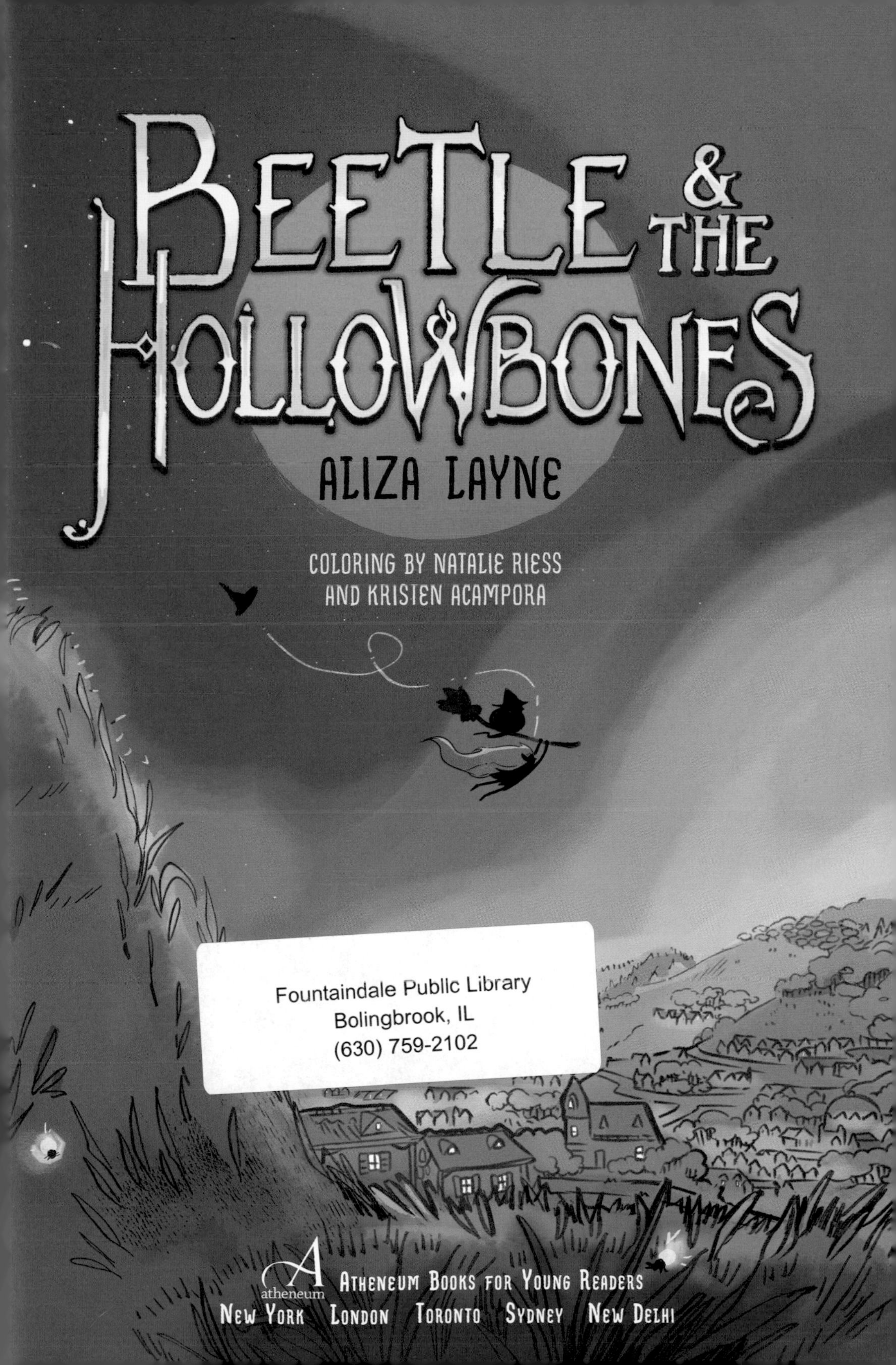

Beetle & the Hollowbones

Aliza Layne

Coloring by Natalie Riess
and Kristen Acampora

atheneum
Atheneum Books for Young Readers
New York London Toronto Sydney New Delhi

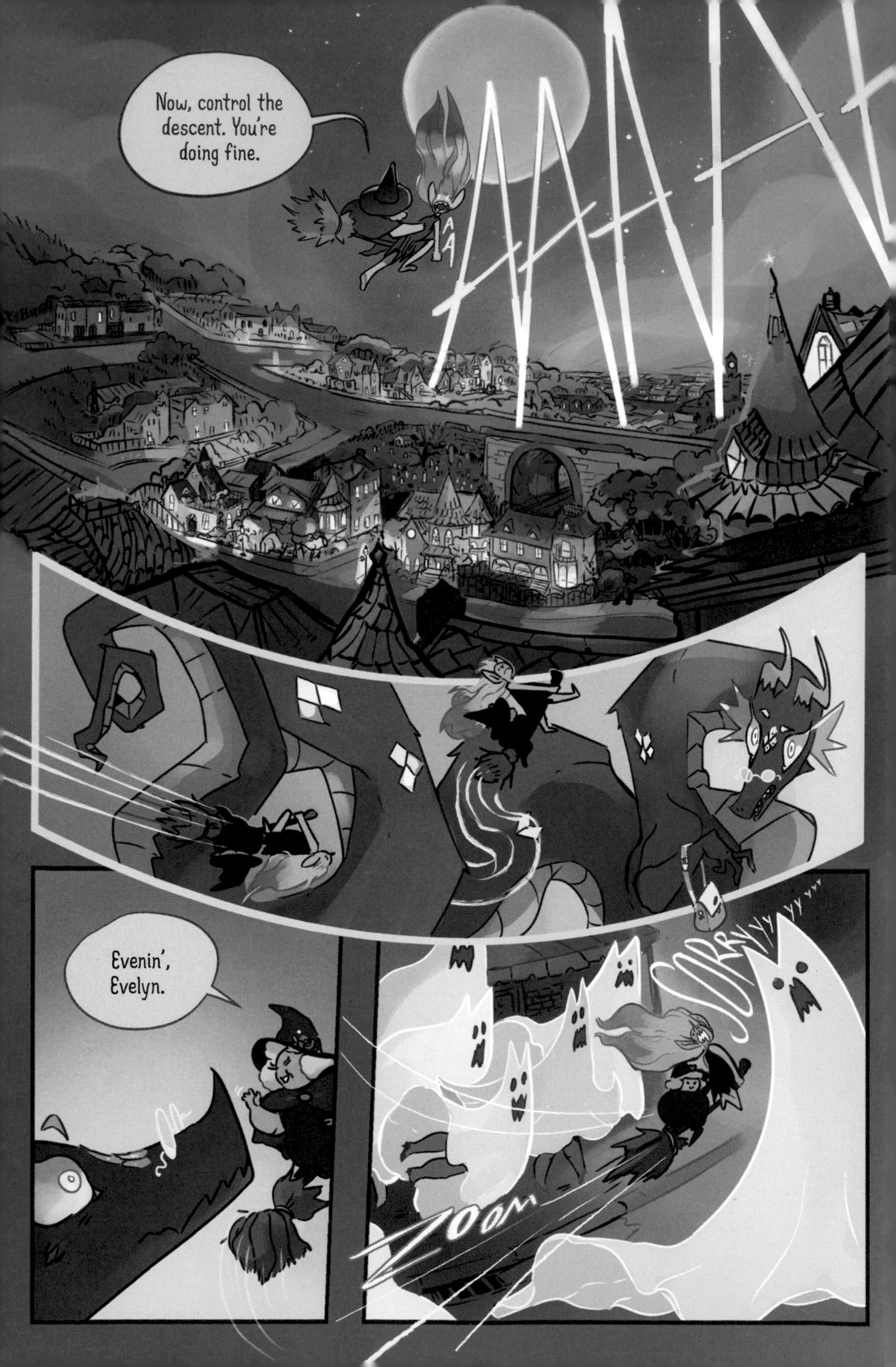

Now, control the descent. You're doing fine.
AA
AAAAA
Evenin', Evelyn.
SORRYYYYYYYYY
ZOOM

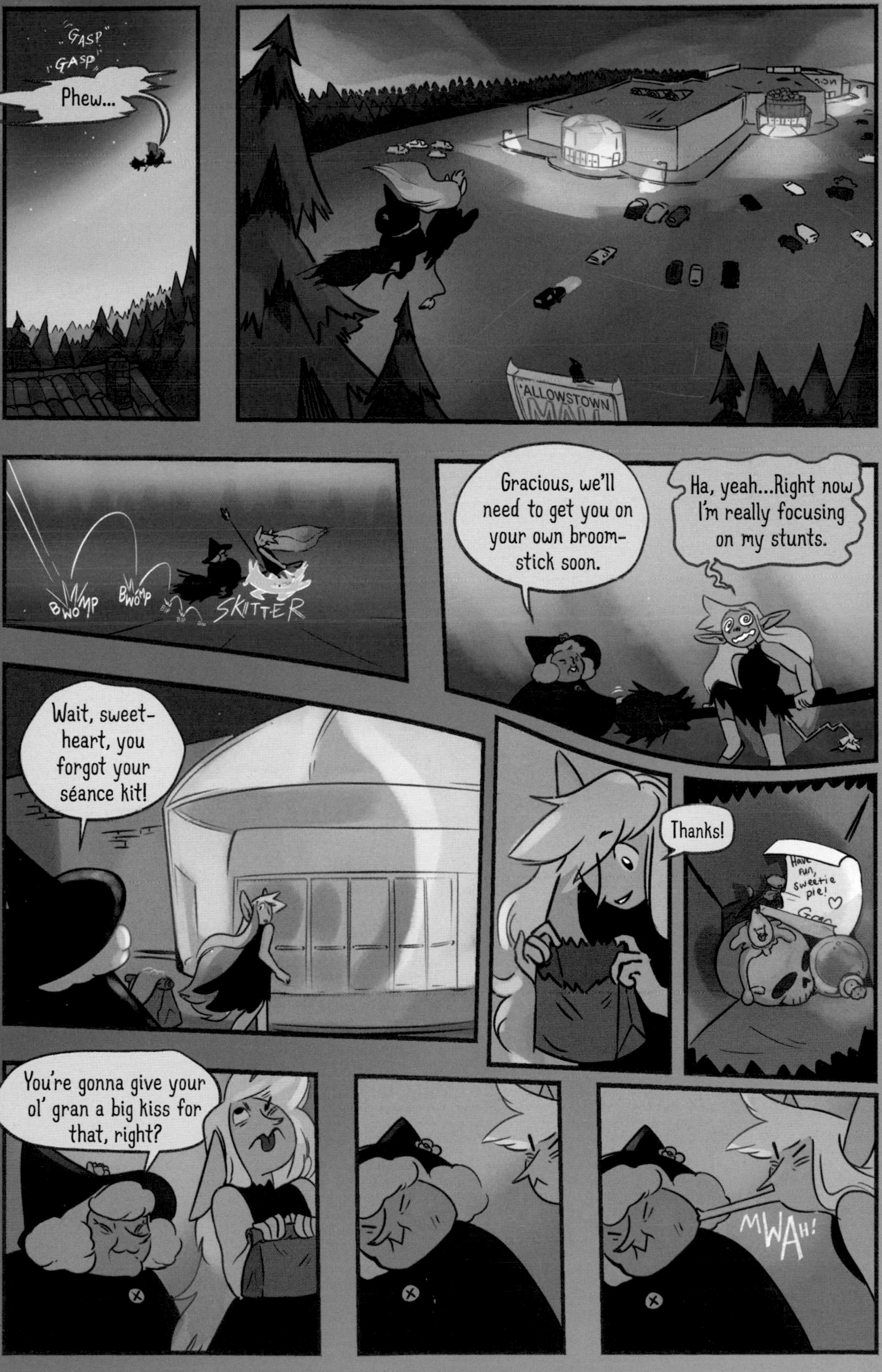

"GASP"
"GASP"
Phew...
ALLOWSTOWN
BWOMP
BWOMP
SKITTER
Gracious, we'll need to get you on your own broom-stick soon.
Ha, yeah...Right now I'm really focusing on my stunts.
Wait, sweet-heart, you forgot your séance kit!
Thanks!
Have fun, sweetie pie! ♥
You're gonna give your ol' gran a big kiss for that, right?
MWAH!

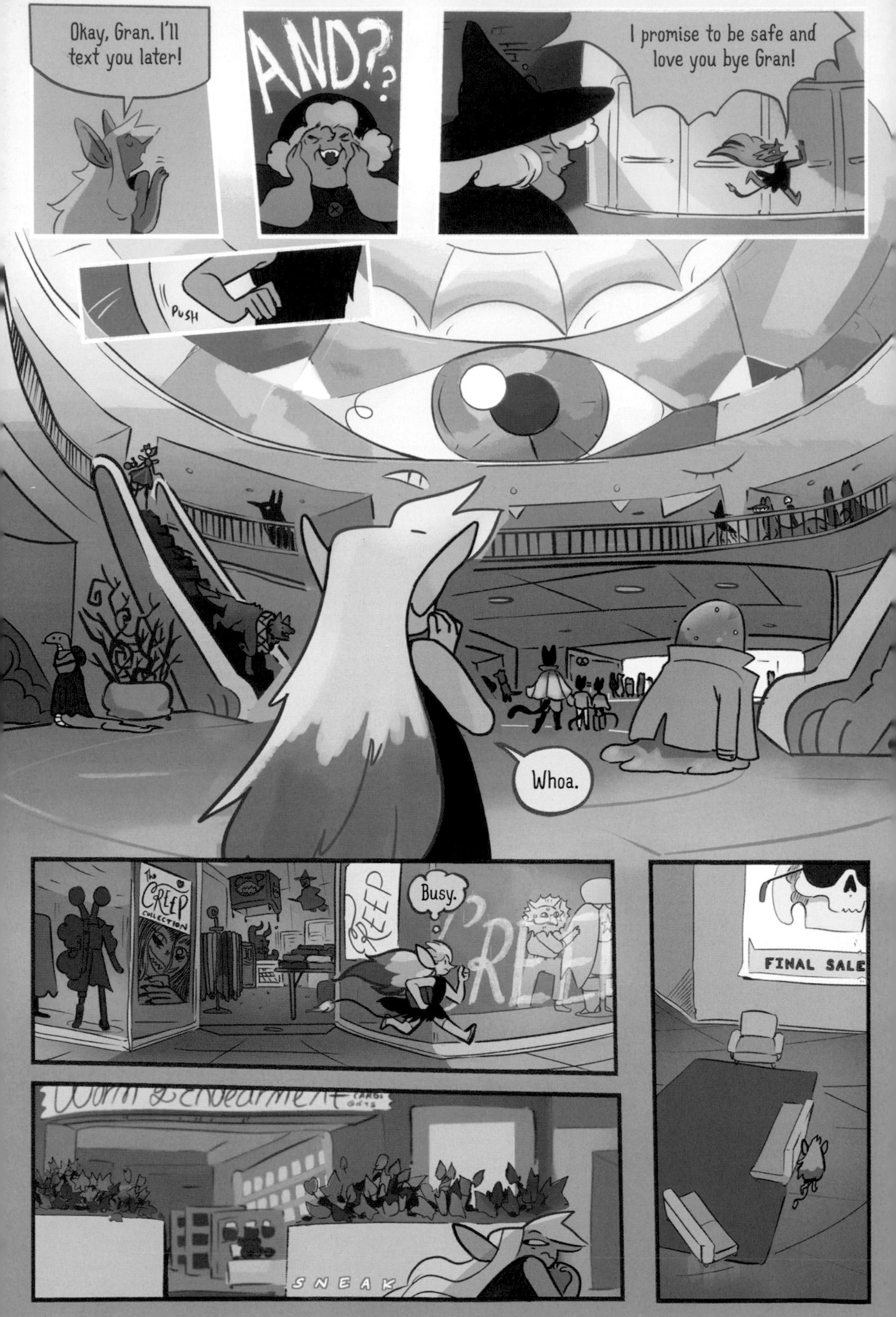
Okay, Gran. I'll text you later!
AND??
I promise to be safe and love you bye Gran!
PUSH
Whoa.
The CREEP COLLECTION
Busy.
FINAL SALE
SNEAK

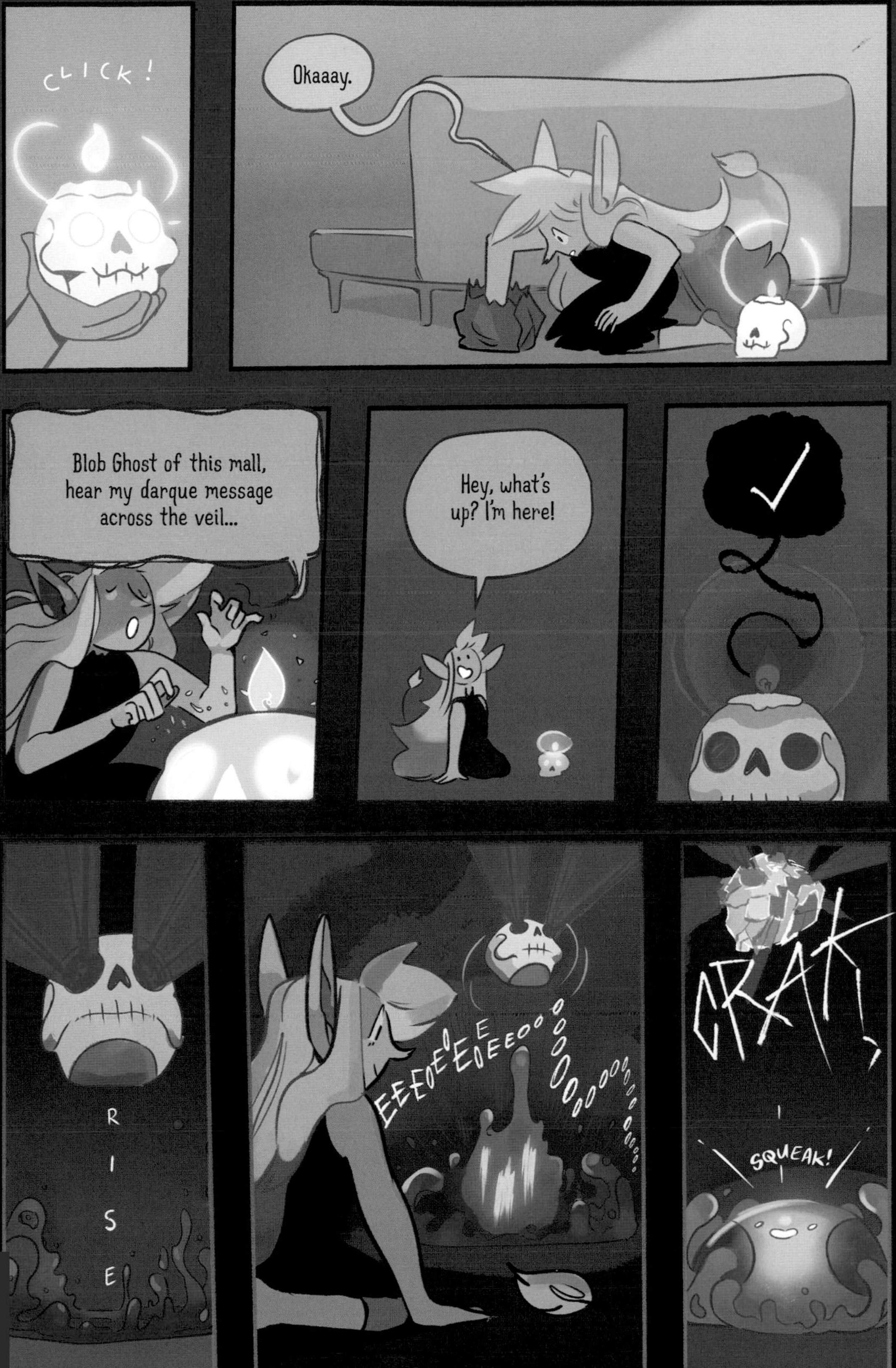
CLICK!
Okaaay.
Blob Ghost of this mall, hear my darque message across the veil...
Hey, what's up? I'm here!
R I S E
EEEEEEEEEEEOOOOOOOOOOOOOO
CRAK!
SQUEAK!

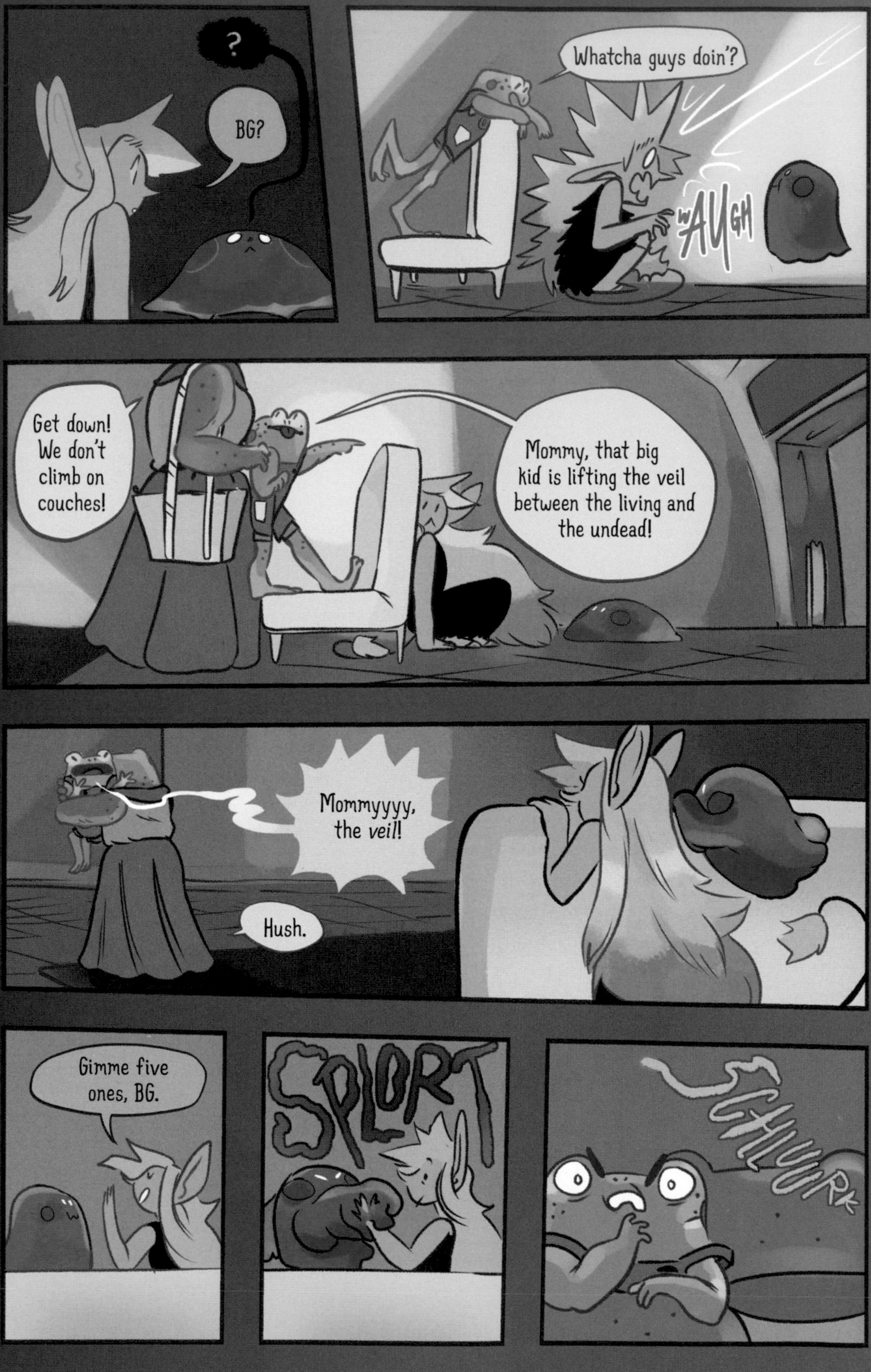
?
BG?
Whatcha guys doin'?
wAYGH
Get down! We don't climb on couches!
Mommy, that big kid is lifting the veil between the living and the undead!
Mommyyyy, the *veil*!
Hush.
Gimme five ones, BG.
SPLORT
SCHLUURK

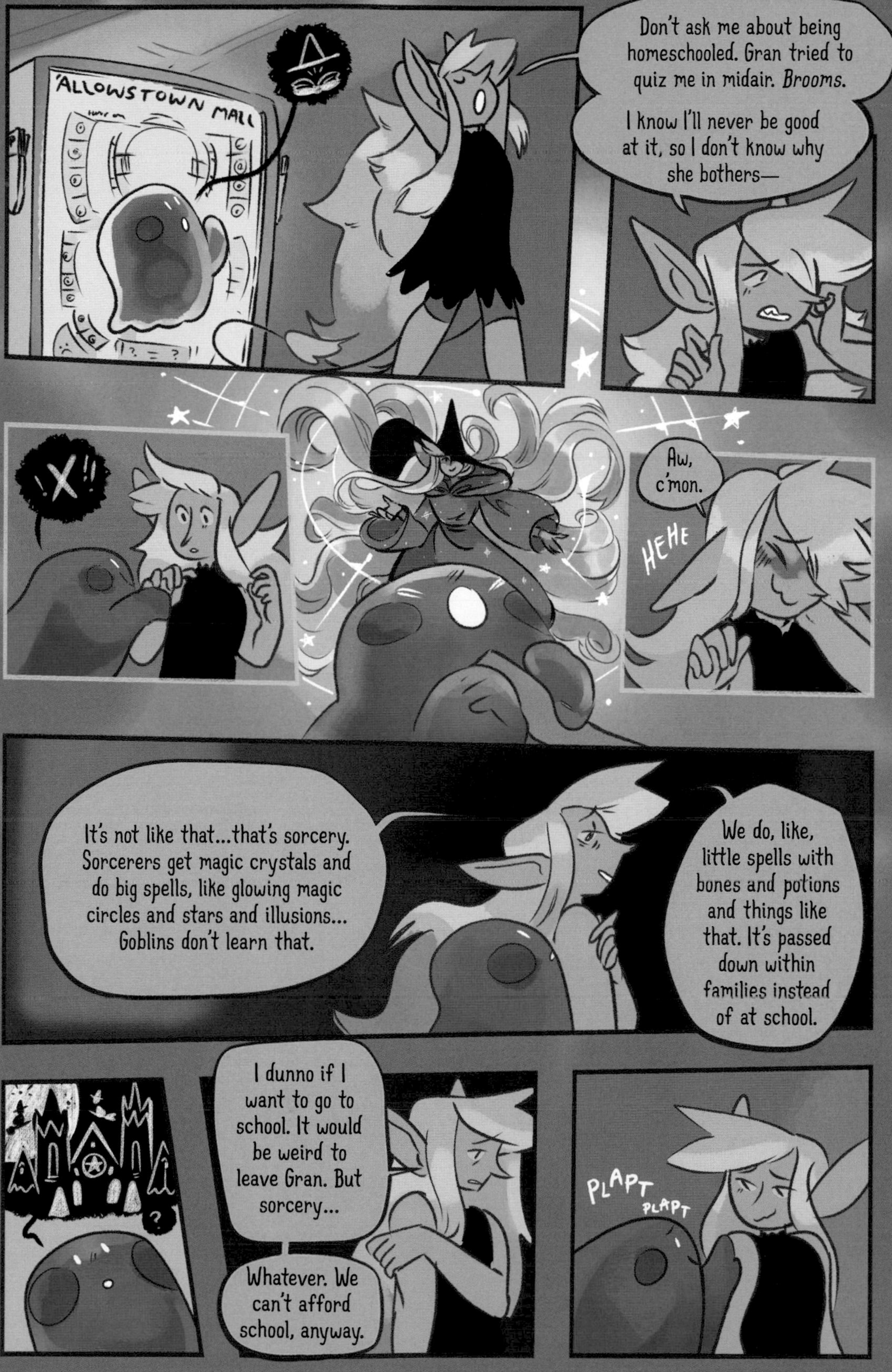
ALLOWSTOWN MALL
Don't ask me about being homeschooled. Gran tried to quiz me in midair. *Brooms.*
I know I'll never be good at it, so I don't know why she bothers—
Aw, c'mon.
HEHE
It's not like that...that's sorcery. Sorcerers get magic crystals and do big spells, like glowing magic circles and stars and illusions... Goblins don't learn that.
We do, like, little spells with bones and potions and things like that. It's passed down within families instead of at school.
I dunno if I want to go to school. It would be weird to leave Gran. But sorcery...
Whatever. We can't afford school, anyway.
PLAPT PLAPT

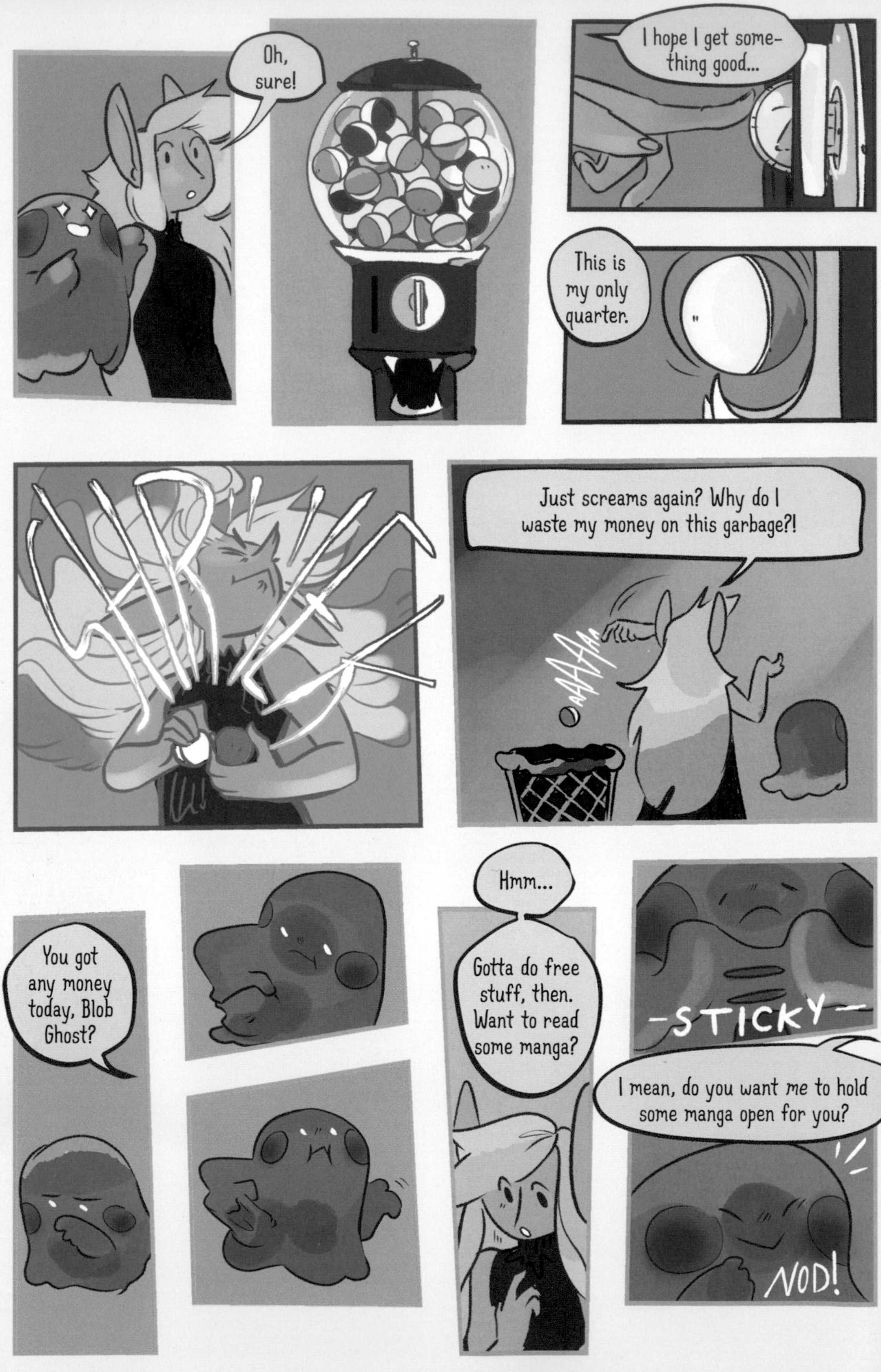
Oh, sure!
I hope I get some-thing good...
This is my only quarter.
Just screams again? Why do I waste my money on this garbage?!
AAAAAA...
You got any money today, Blob Ghost?
Hmm...
Gotta do free stuff, then. Want to read some manga?
-STICKY-
I mean, do you want *me* to hold some manga open for you?
NOD!

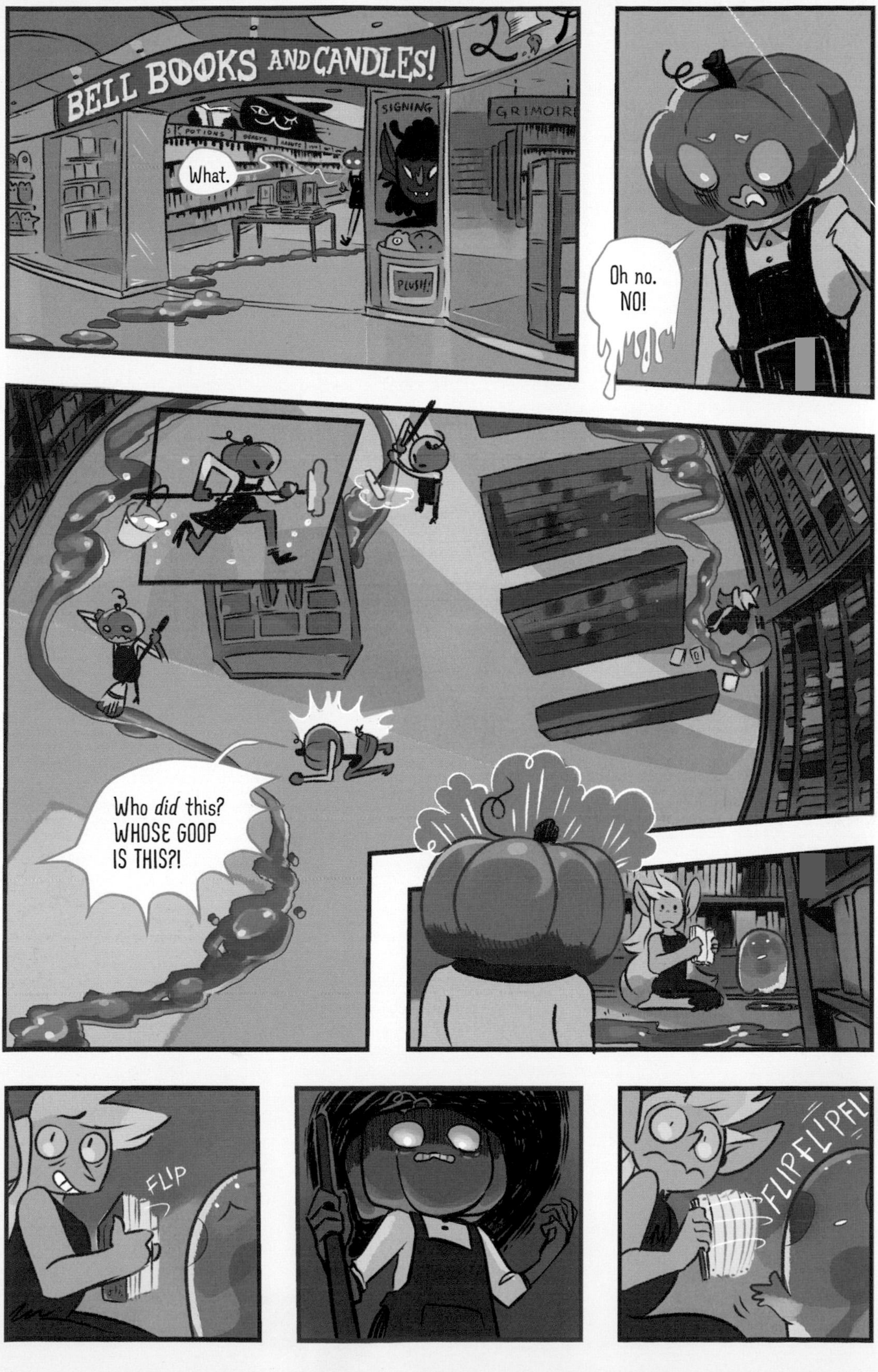
BELL BOOKS AND CANDLES!
SIGNING
GRIMOIRE
POTIONS
PLUSH!
What.
Oh no.
NO!
Who did this?
WHOSE GOOP
IS THIS?!
FLIP
FLIPFLIPFL

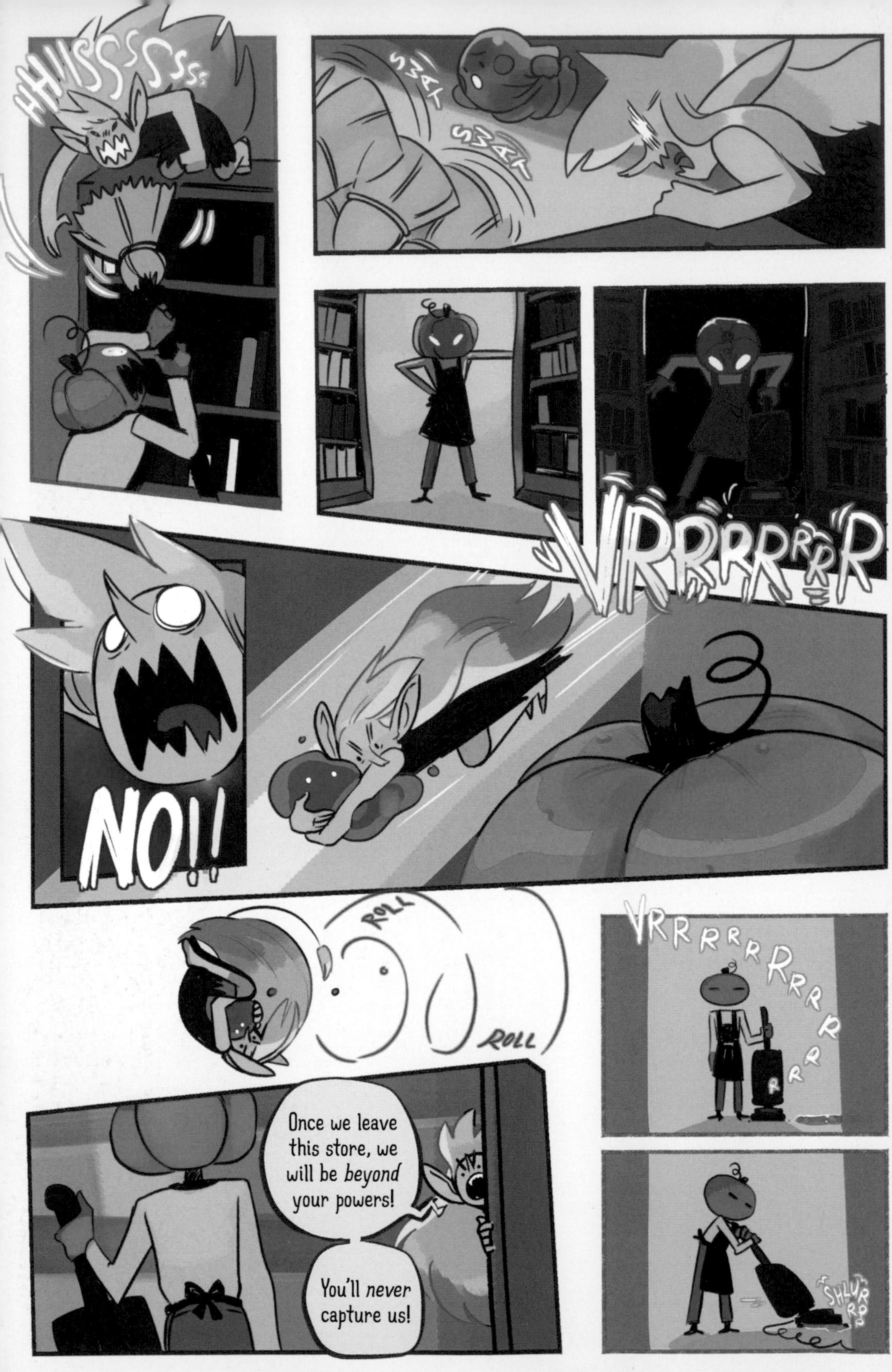
HHISSSSsss
SSZAT
SSZAT
VRRRRRRR
NO!!
ROLL
ROLL
VRRRRRRRRRRRRR
Once we leave this store, we will be *beyond* your powers!
You'll *never* capture us!
SHLURRP

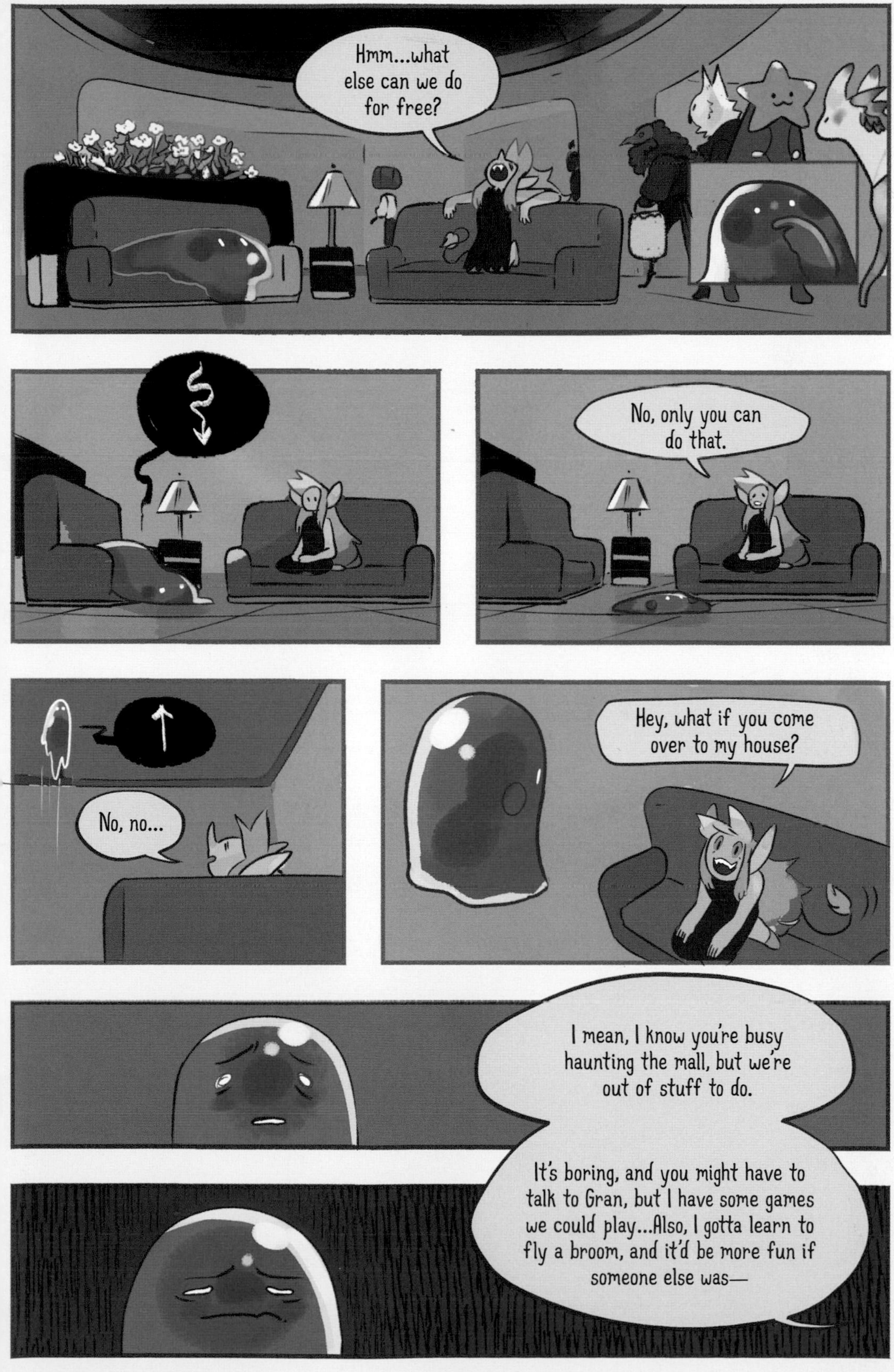
Hmm...what else can we do for free?
No, only you can do that.
No, no...
Hey, what if you come over to my house?
I mean, I know you're busy haunting the mall, but we're out of stuff to do.
It's boring, and you might have to talk to Gran, but I have some games we could play...Also, I gotta learn to fly a broom, and it'd be more fun if someone else was—

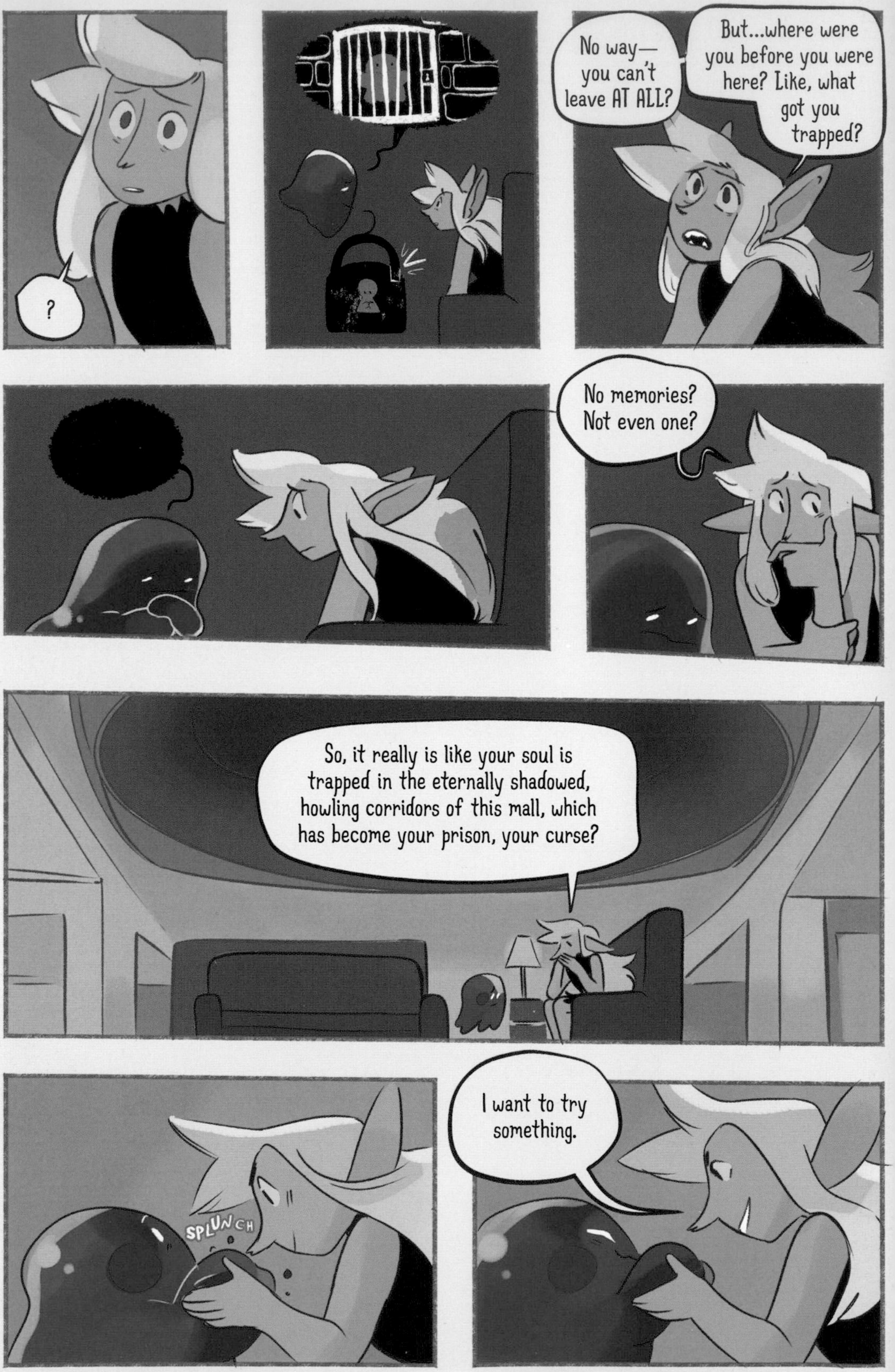
?
No way—you can't leave AT ALL?
But...where were you before you were here? Like, what got you trapped?
No memories? Not even one?
So, it really is like your soul is trapped in the eternally shadowed, howling corridors of this mall, which has become your prison, your curse?
SPLUNCH
I want to try something.

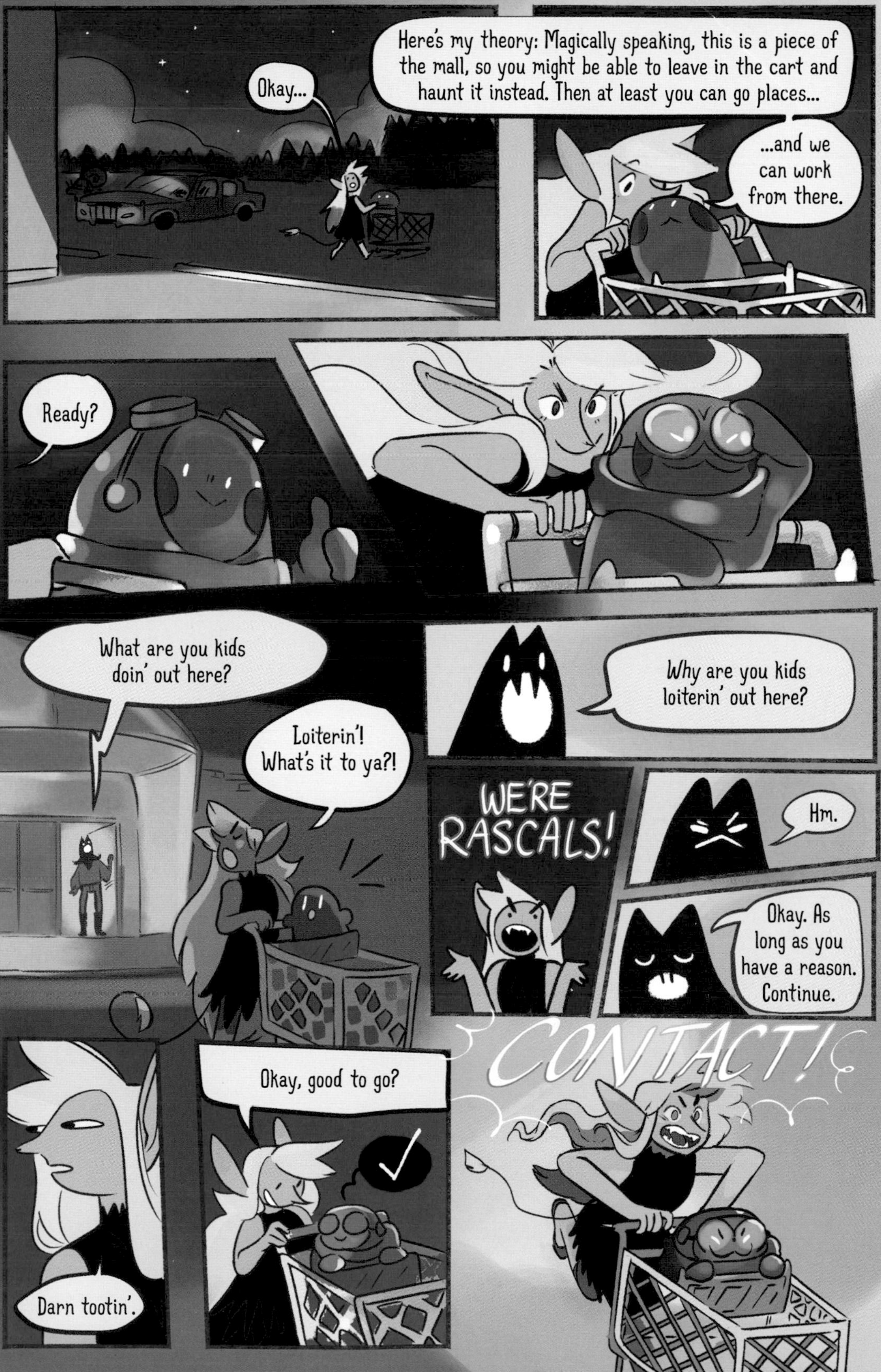
Okay...
Here's my theory: Magically speaking, this is a piece of the mall, so you might be able to leave in the cart and haunt it instead. Then at least you can go places...
...and we can work from there.
Ready?
What are you kids doin' out here?
Loiterin'! What's it to ya?!
Why are you kids loiterin' out here?
WE'RE RASCALS!
Hm.
Okay. As long as you have a reason. Continue.
Darn tootin'.
Okay, good to go?
CONTACT!

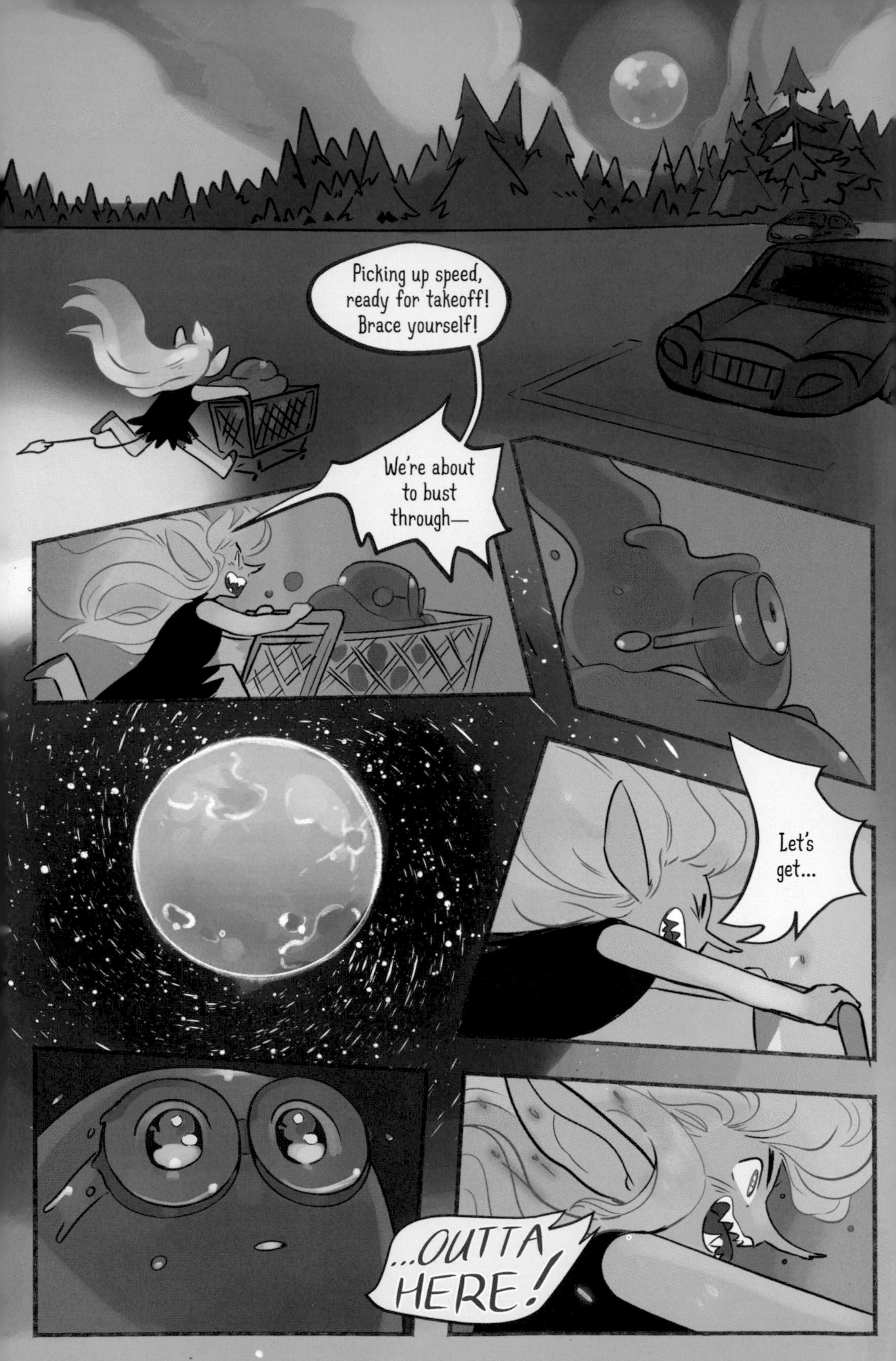
Picking up speed, ready for takeoff! Brace yourself!
We're about to bust through—
Let's get...
...OUTTA HERE!

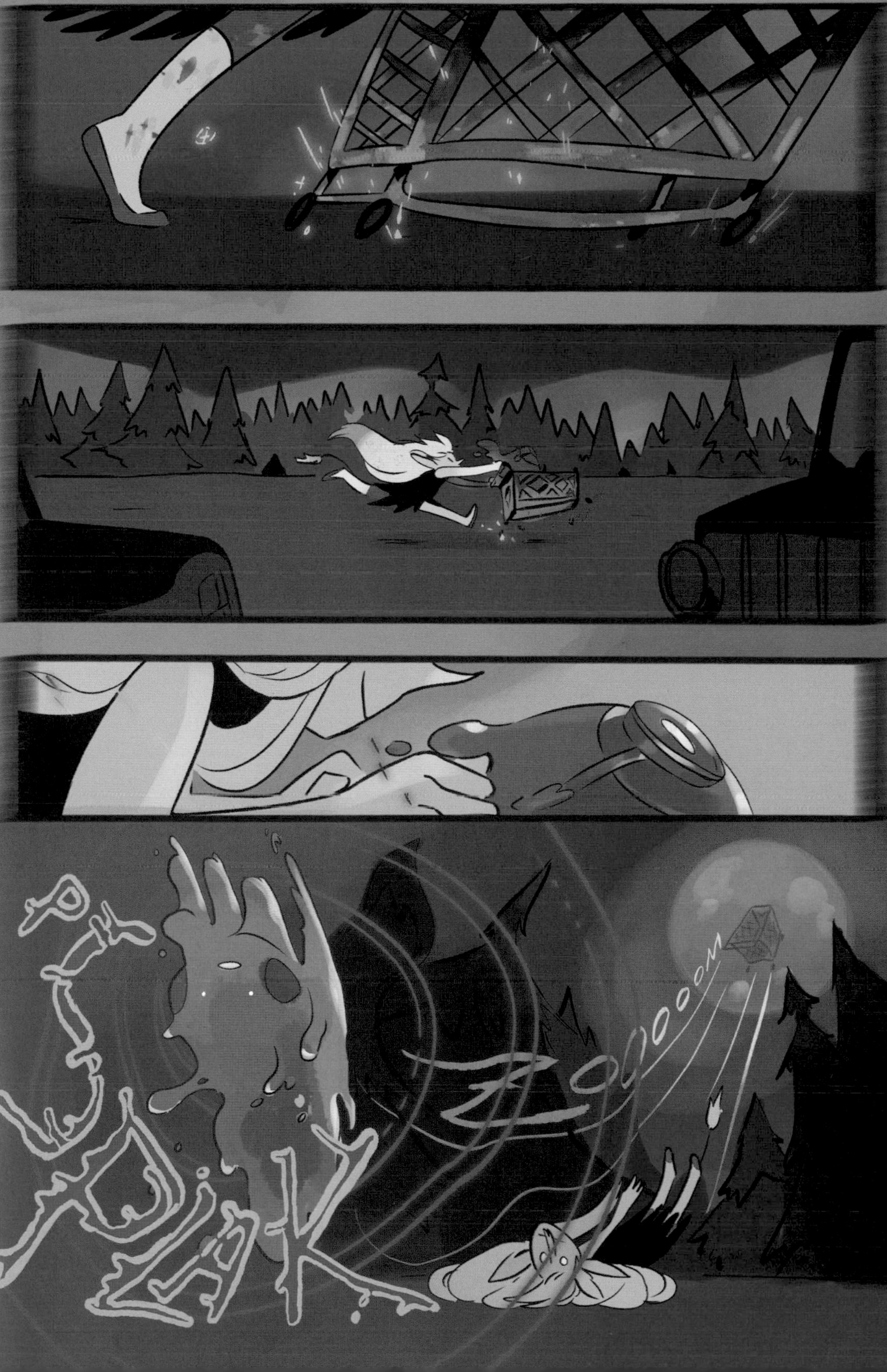
ZOOOOOOM

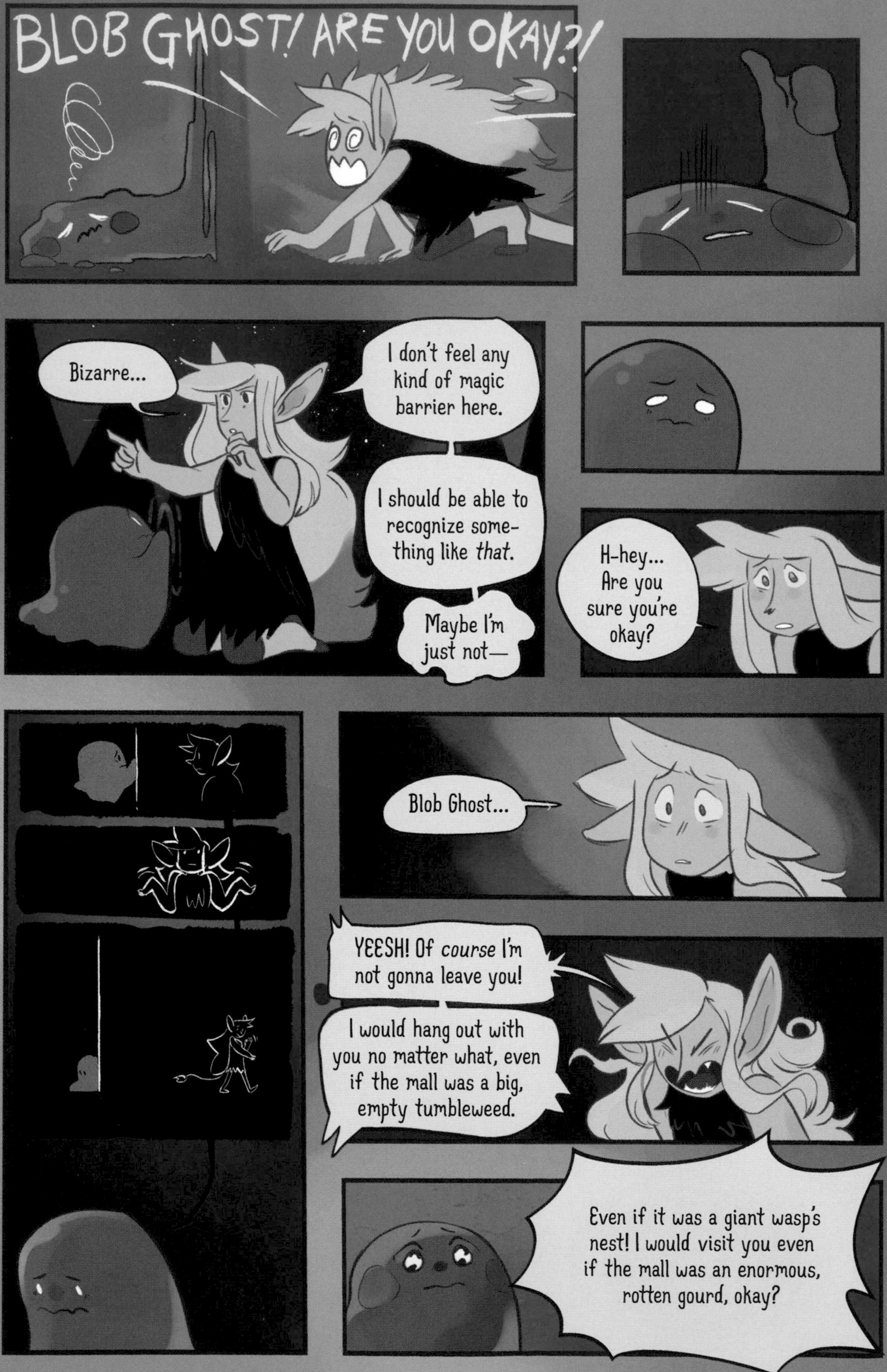
BLOB GHOST! ARE YOU OKAY?!
Bizarre...
I don't feel any kind of magic barrier here.
I should be able to recognize some-thing like *that*.
Maybe I'm just not—
H-hey... Are you sure you're okay?
Blob Ghost...
YEESH! Of *course* I'm not gonna leave you!
I would hang out with you no matter what, even if the mall was a big, empty tumbleweed.
Even if it was a giant wasp's nest! I would visit you even if the mall was an enormous, rotten gourd, okay?

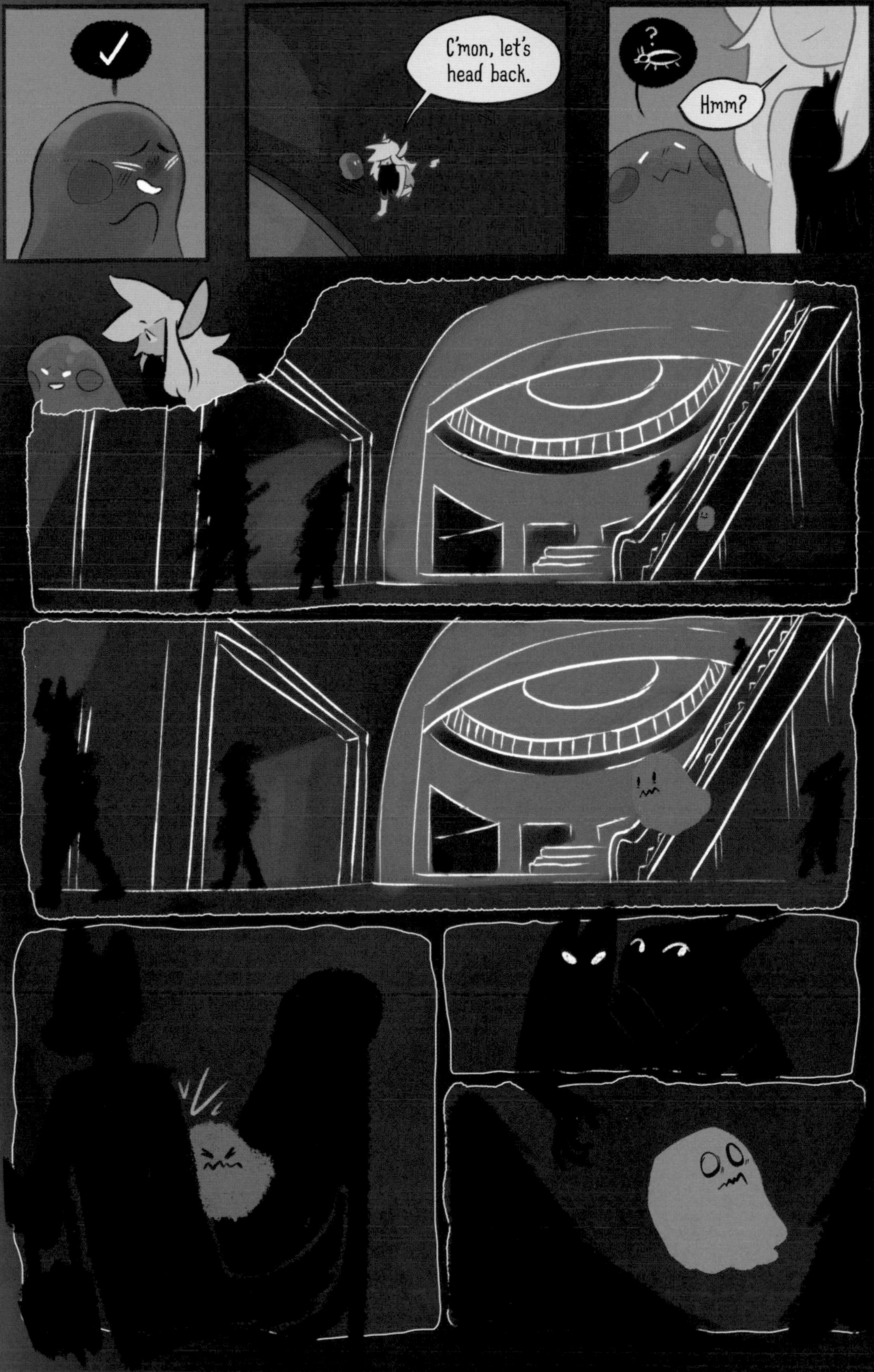
C'mon, let's head back.
Hmm?

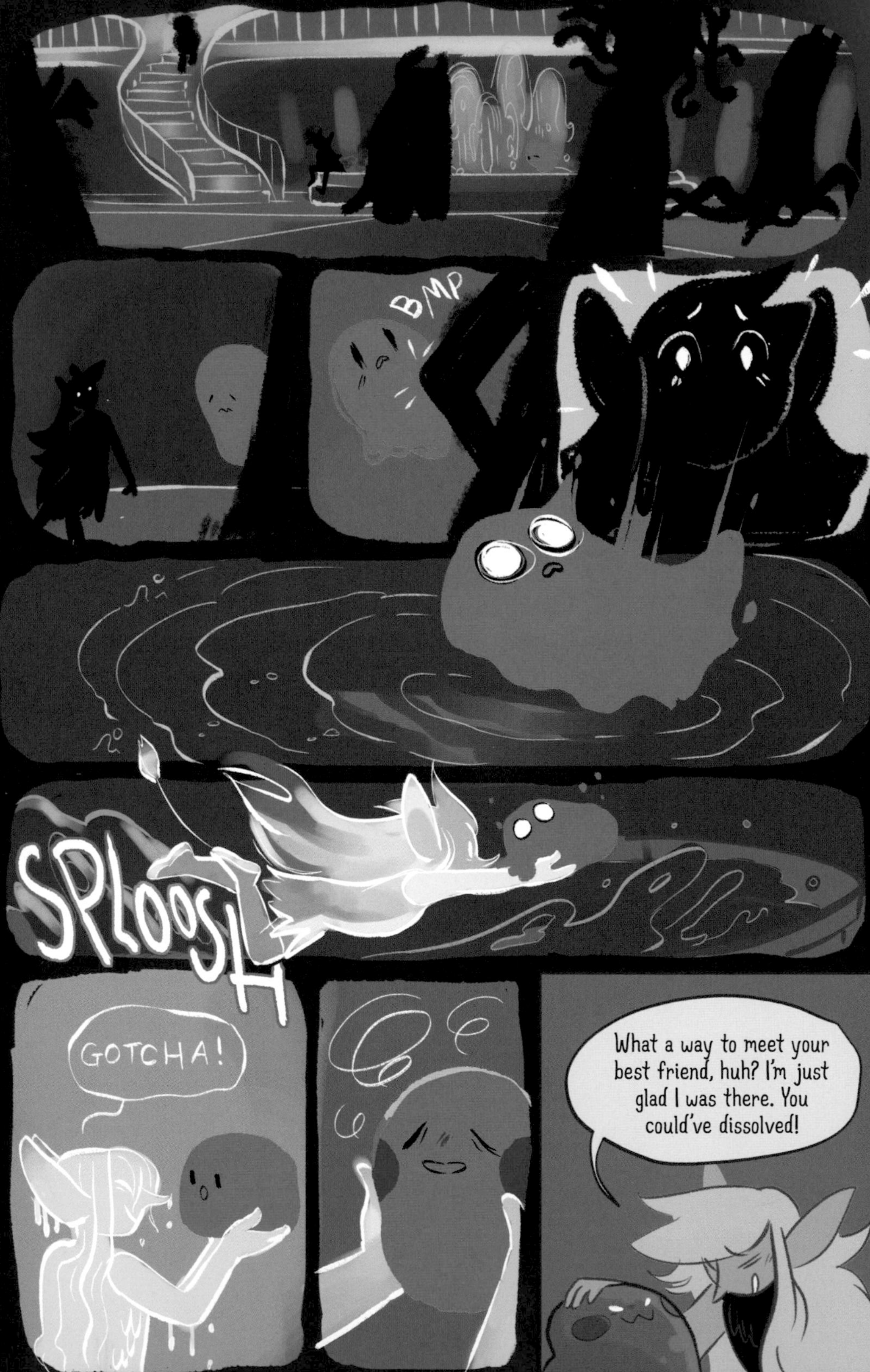
BMP
SPLOOSH
GOTCHA!
What a way to meet your best friend, huh? I'm just glad I was there. You could've dissolved!

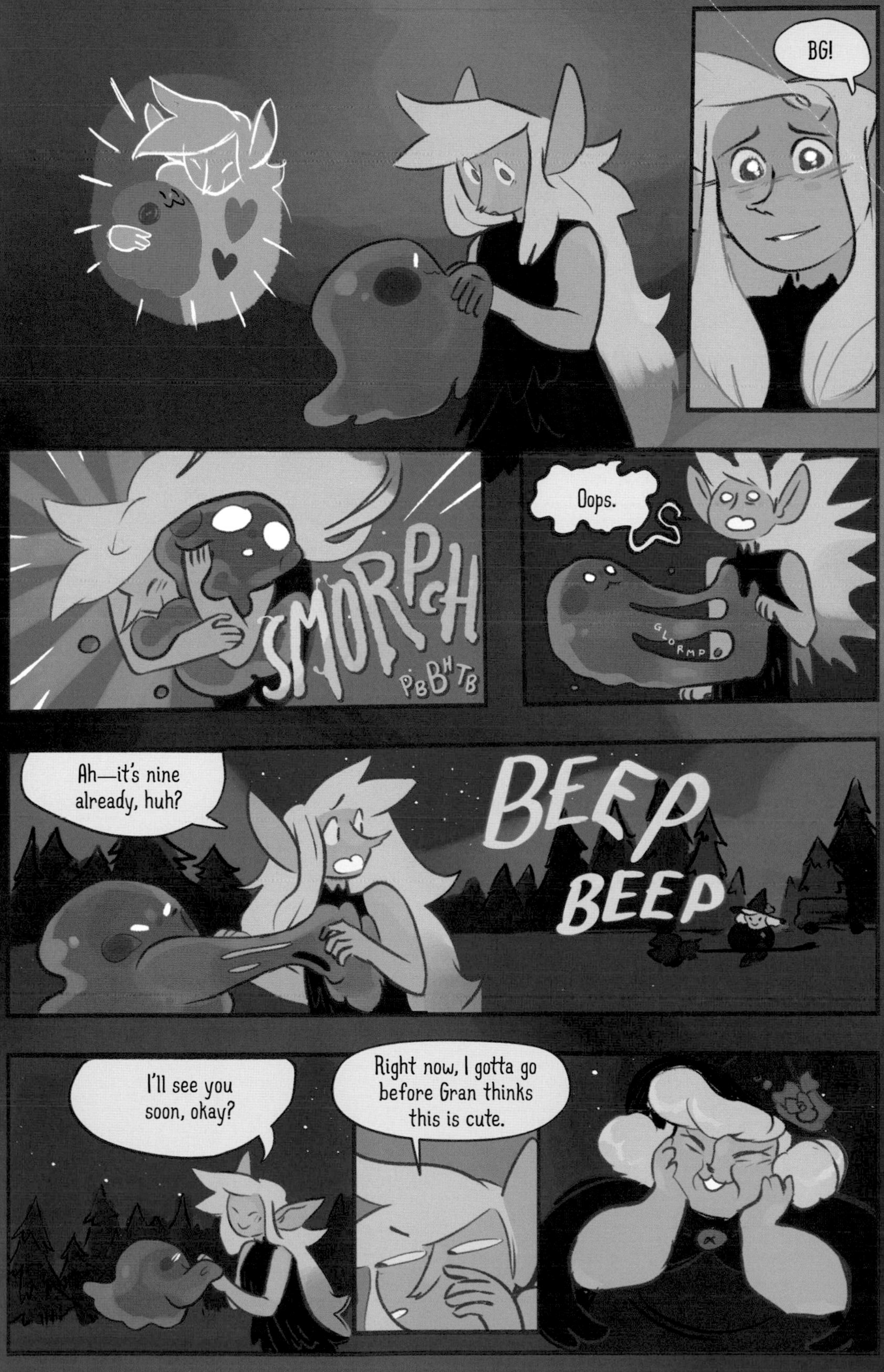
BG!
SMORPCH
PBBHTB
Oops.
GLORMP
Ah—it's nine already, huh?
BEEP
BEEP
I'll see you soon, okay?
Right now, I gotta go before Gran thinks this is cute.

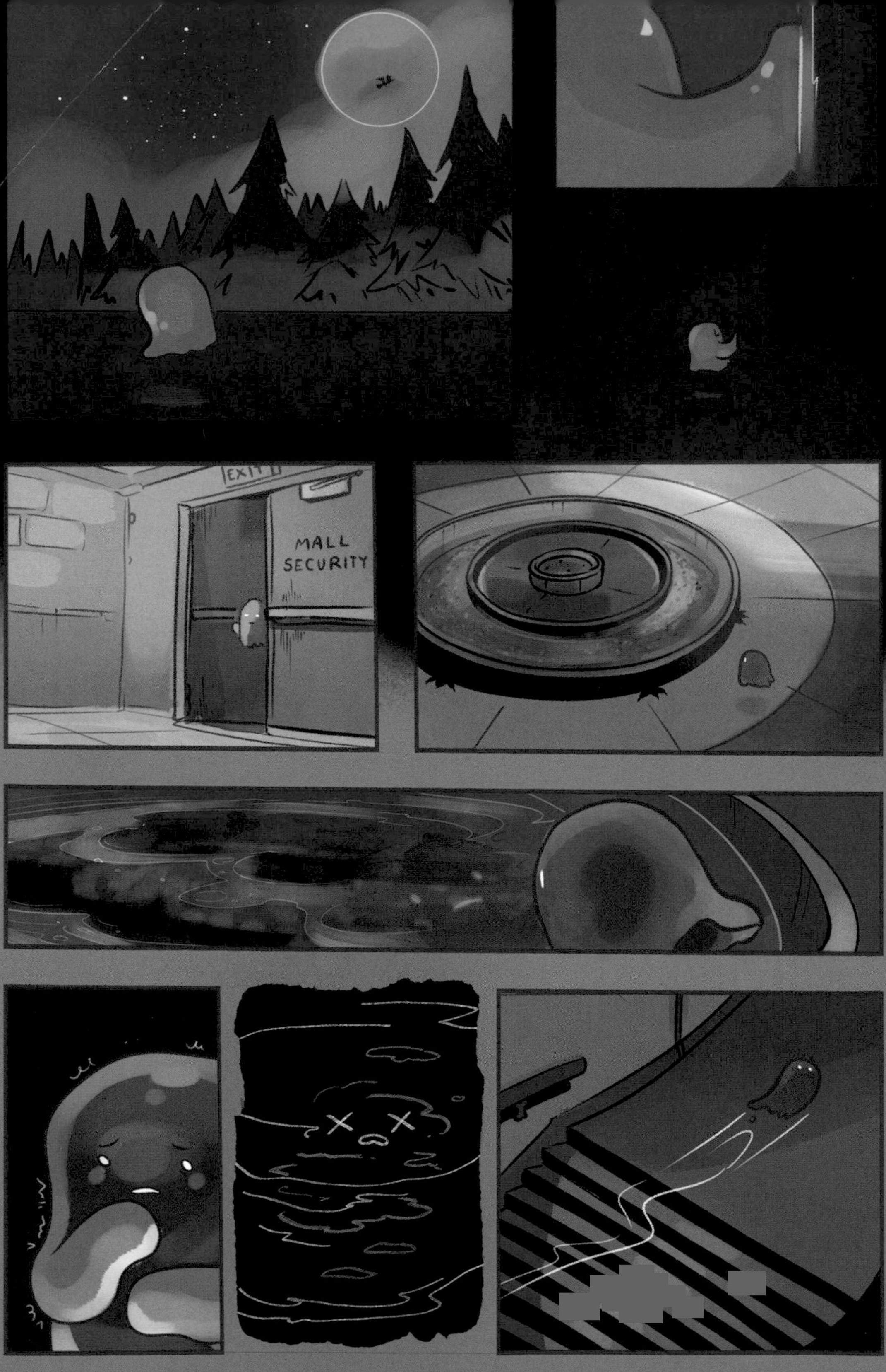
EXIT
MALL
SECURITY

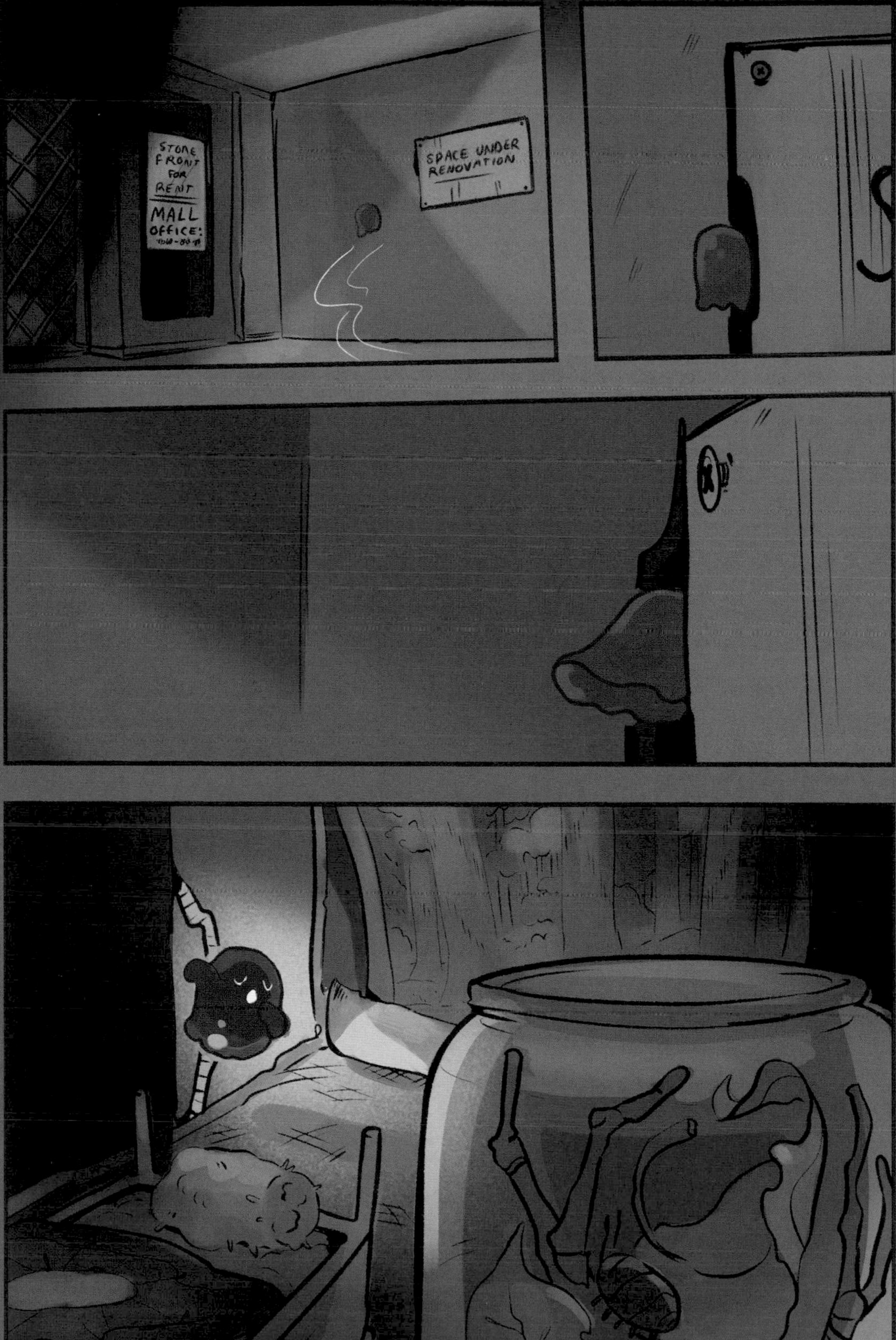
STORE FRONT FOR RENT
MALL OFFICE:
SPACE UNDER RENOVATION

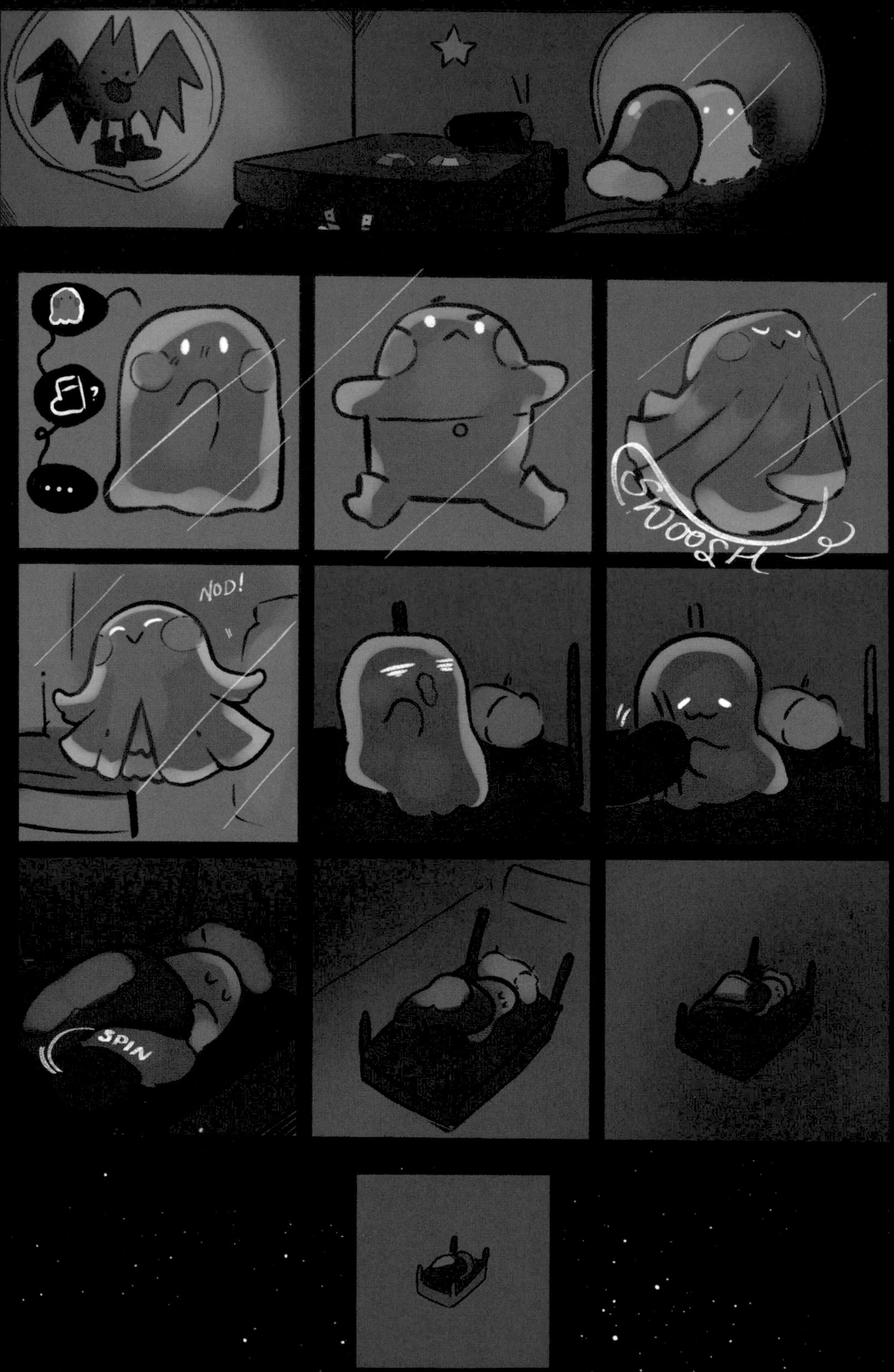

...
SWOOSH
NOD!
SPIN

Posts Past

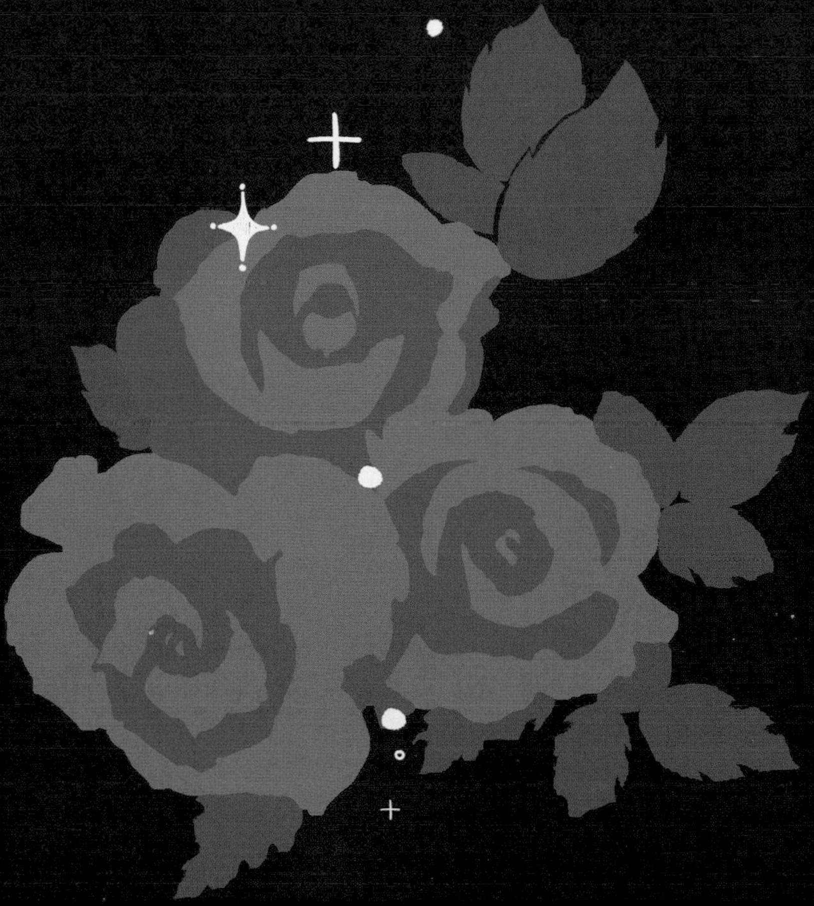

I love you. That's why I refused to fight.

But I...I'm a girl! How could you love *me*?

I may be a giant mantis, but I'm a girl, too. You've shown me that I don't have to hide my heart.

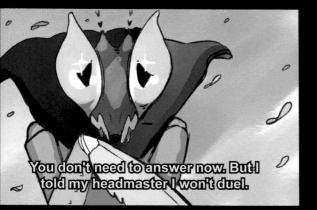

You don't need to answer now. But I told my headmaster I won't duel.

Oh, Argemone.

I'll tell you what's in my heart.

But first, tonight at moonrise...

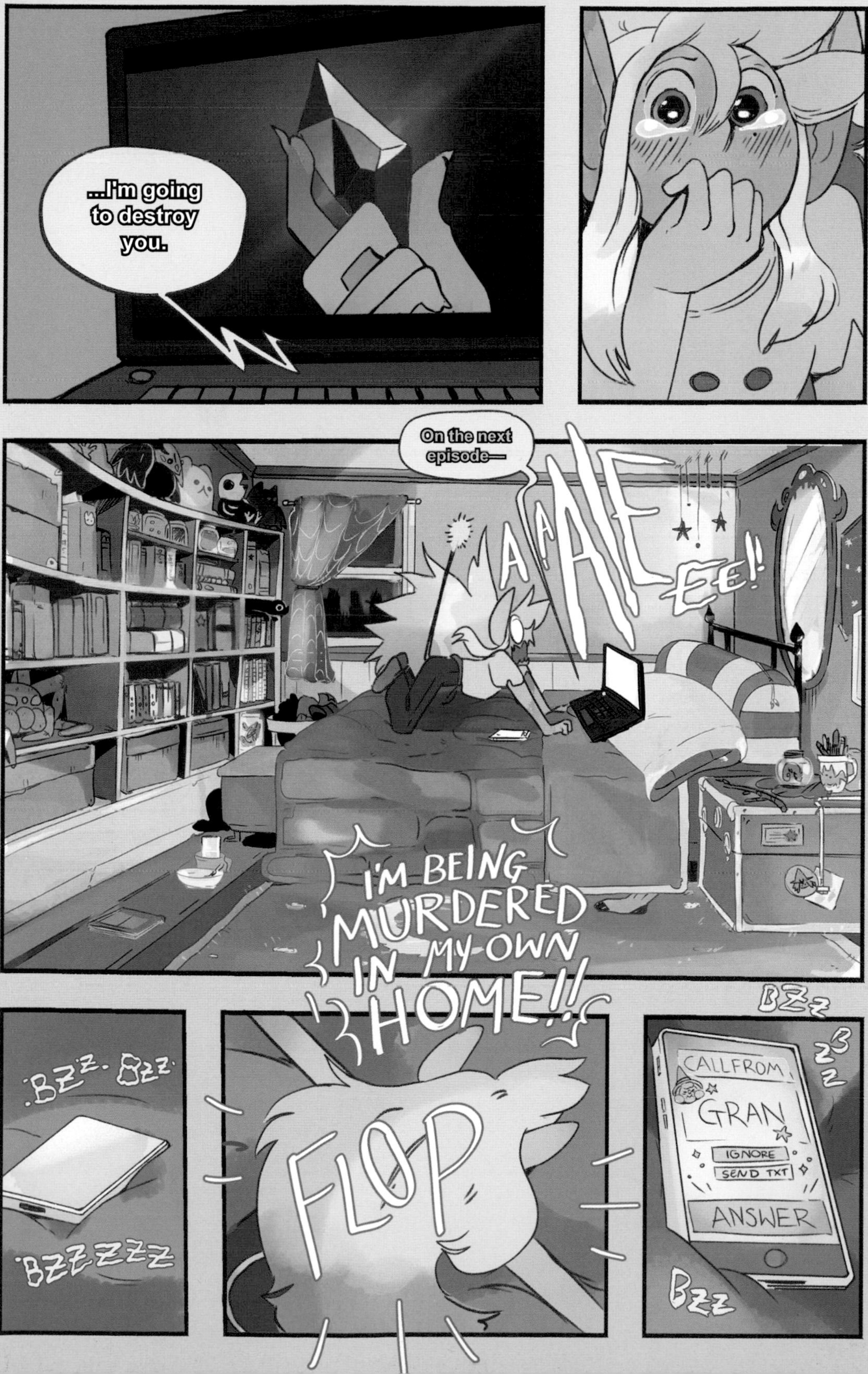

...I'm going to destroy you.
On the next episode—
AAAAEEE!!
I'M BEING MURDERED IN MY OWN HOME!!
BZZ BZZ
BZZZZZZ
FLOP
BZZ
ZZZ
CALL FROM
GRAN
IGNORE
SEND TXT
ANSWER
BZZ

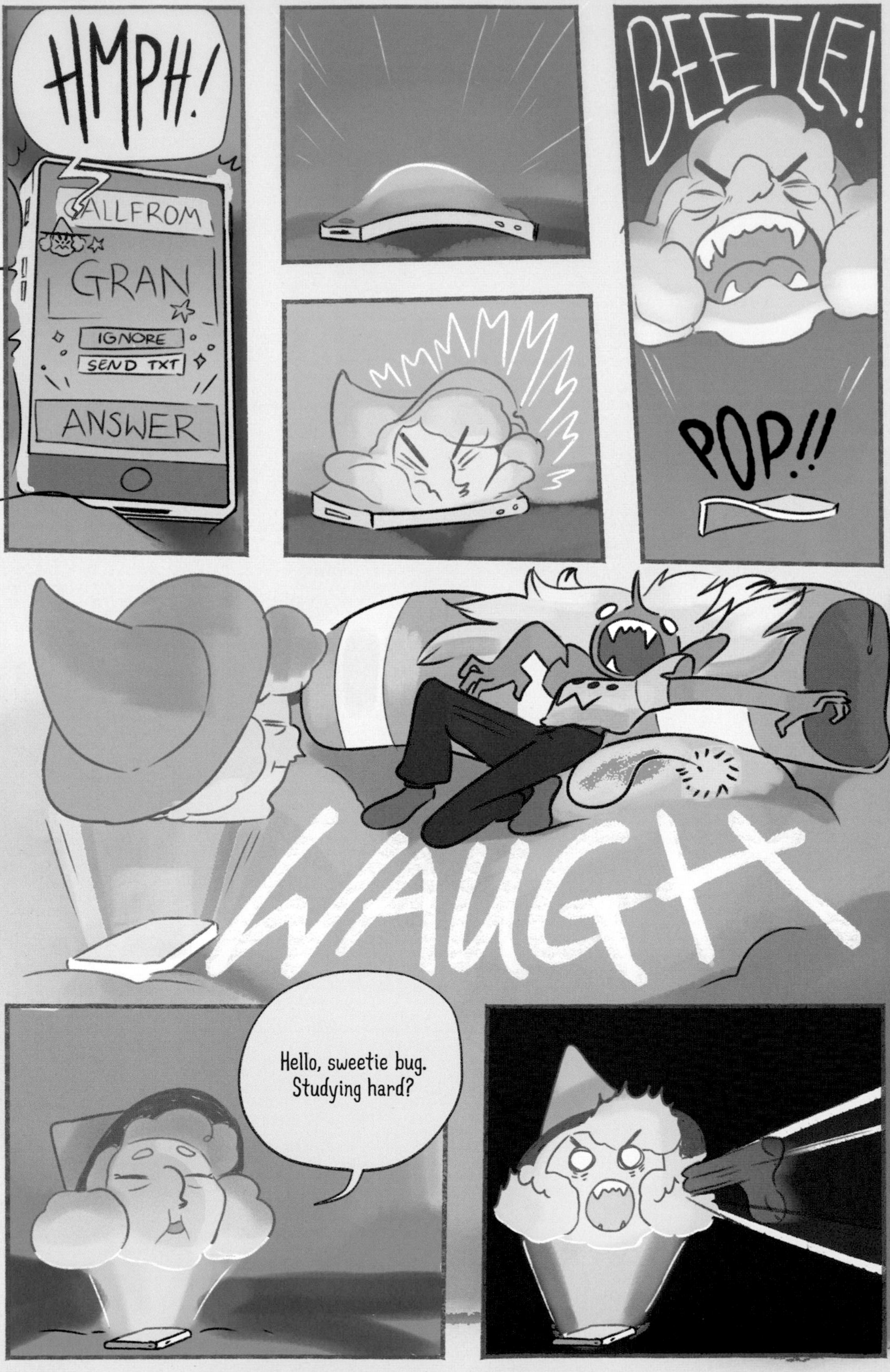
HMPH!
CALLFROM
GRAN
IGNORE
SEND TXT
ANSWER
MMMMMM
BEETLE!
POP!!
WAUGH
Hello, sweetie bug. Studying hard?

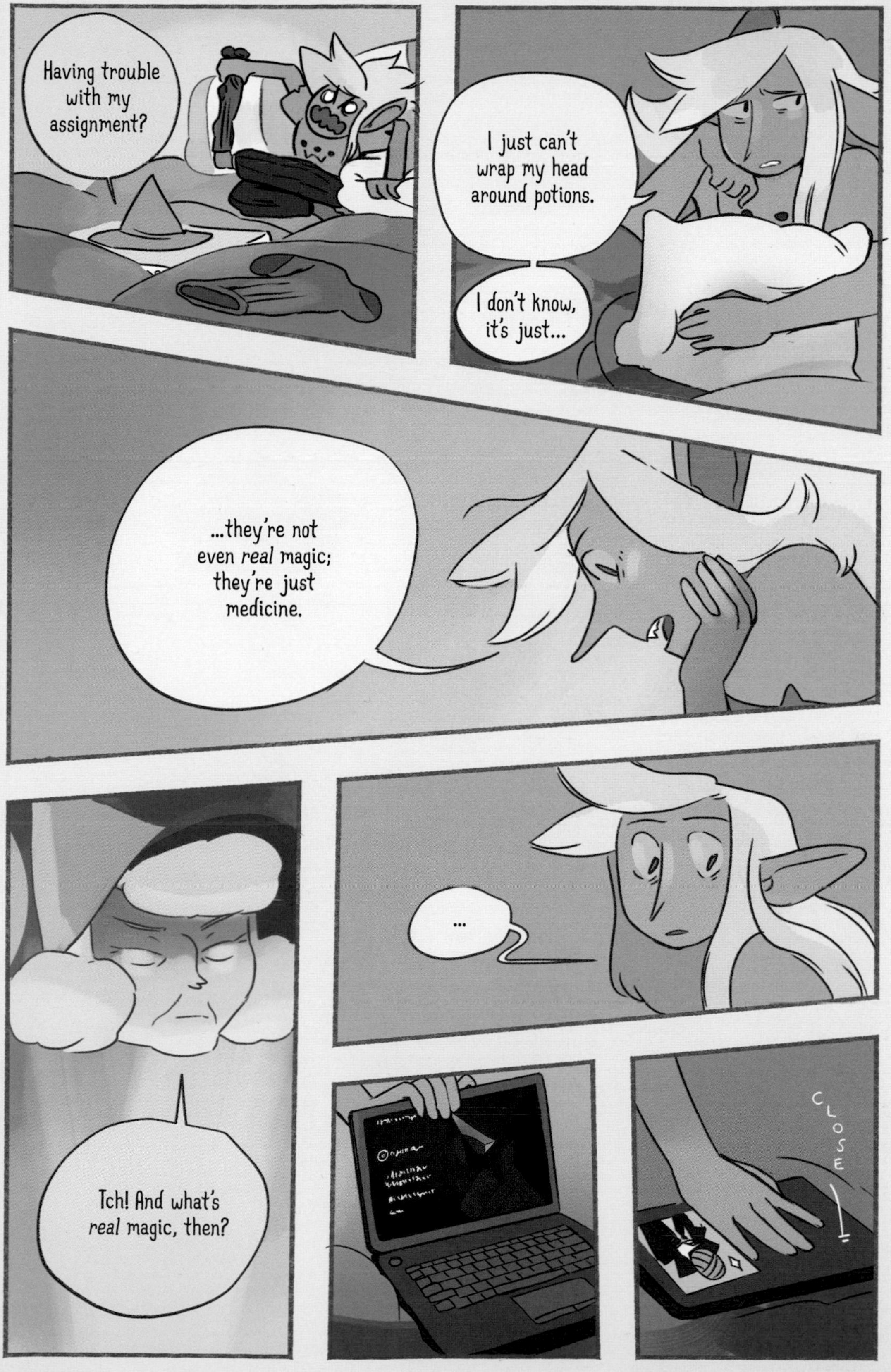
Having trouble with my assignment?
I just can't wrap my head around potions.
I don't know, it's just...
...they're not even *real* magic; they're just medicine.
...
Tch! And what's *real* magic, then?
CLOSE

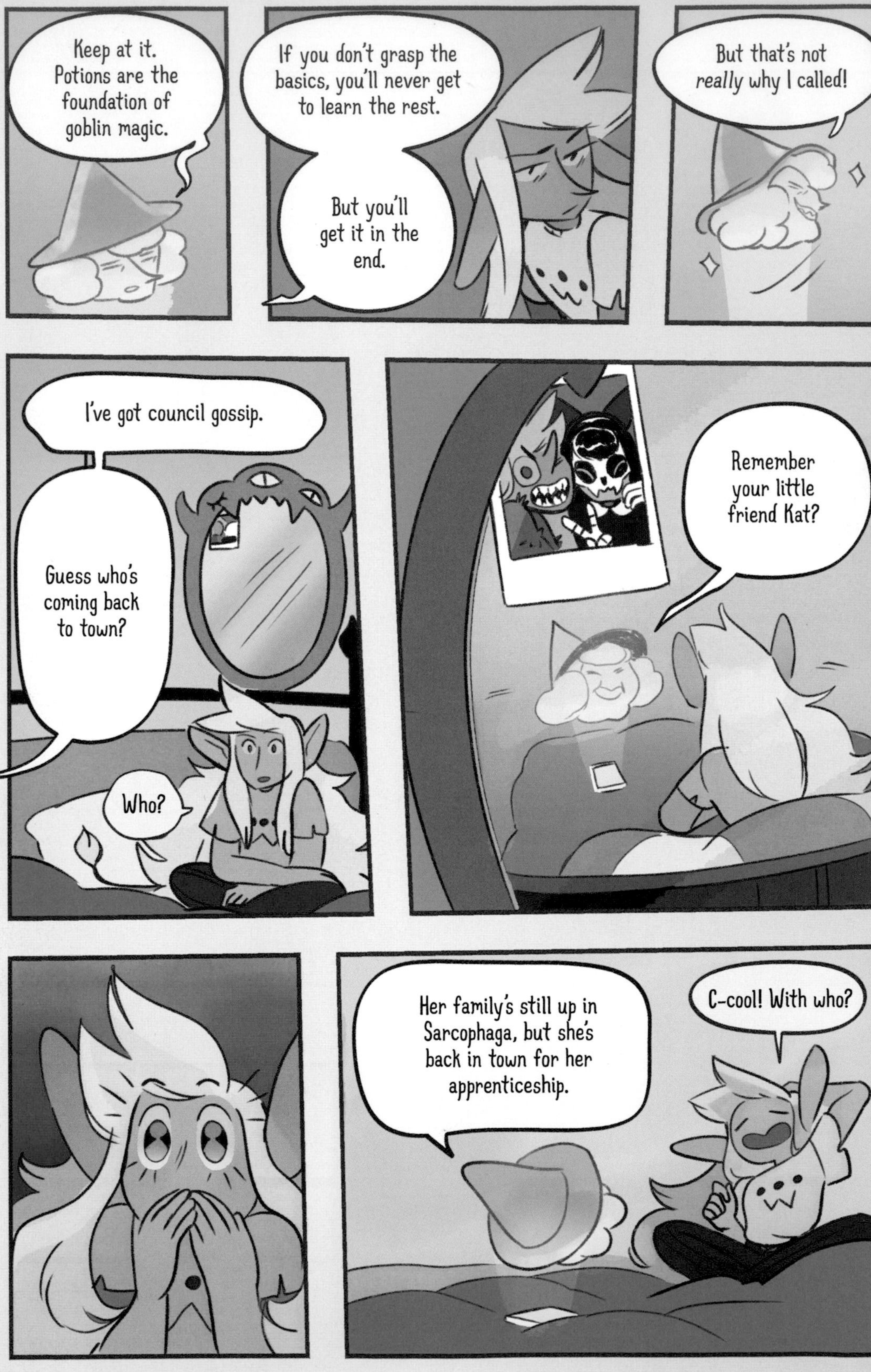
Keep at it. Potions are the foundation of goblin magic.
If you don't grasp the basics, you'll never get to learn the rest.
But you'll get it in the end.
But that's not *really* why I called!
I've got council gossip.
Guess who's coming back to town?
Who?
Remember your little friend Kat?
Her family's still up in Sarcophaga, but she's back in town for her apprenticeship.
C-cool! With who?

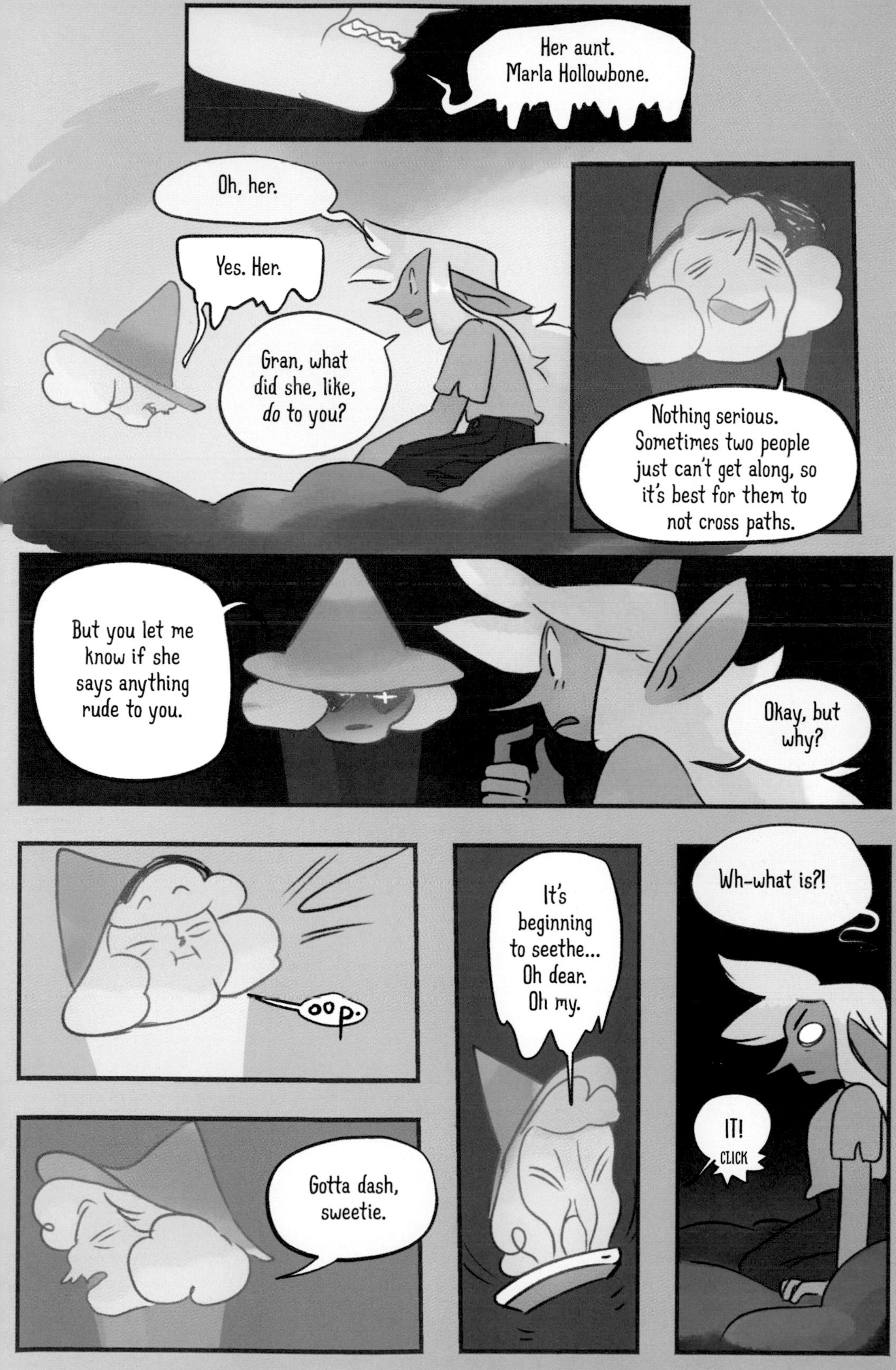
Her aunt. Marla Hollowbone.
Oh, her.
Yes. Her.
Gran, what did she, like, *do* to you?
Nothing serious. Sometimes two people just can't get along, so it's best for them to not cross paths.
But you let me know if she says anything rude to you.
Okay, but why?
oop.
Gotta dash, sweetie.
It's beginning to seethe... Oh dear. Oh my.
Wh-what is?!
IT!
CLICK

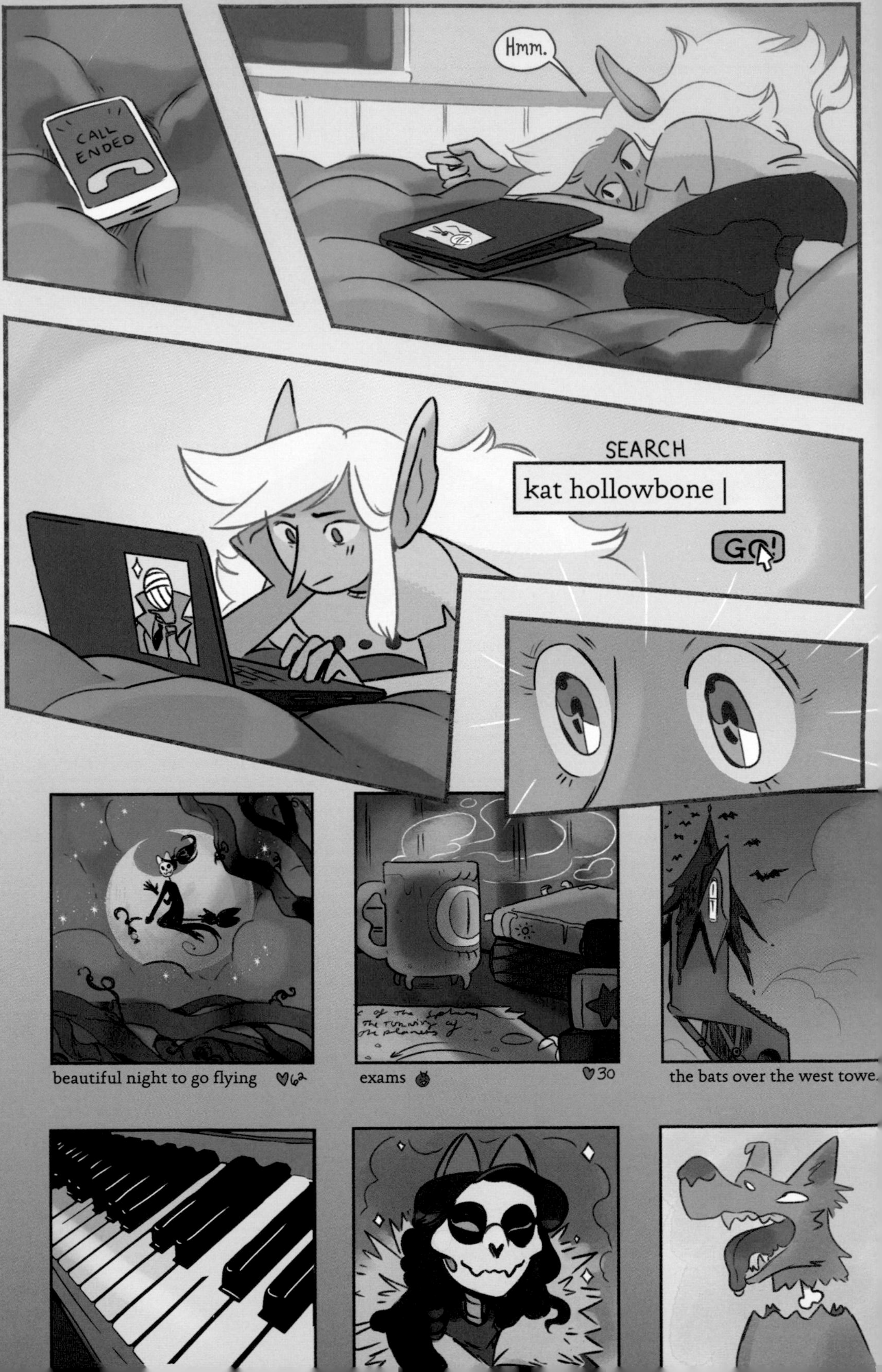
CALL ENDED
Hmm.
SEARCH
kat hollowbone |
GO!
beautiful night to go flying
62
exams
30
the bats over the west towe

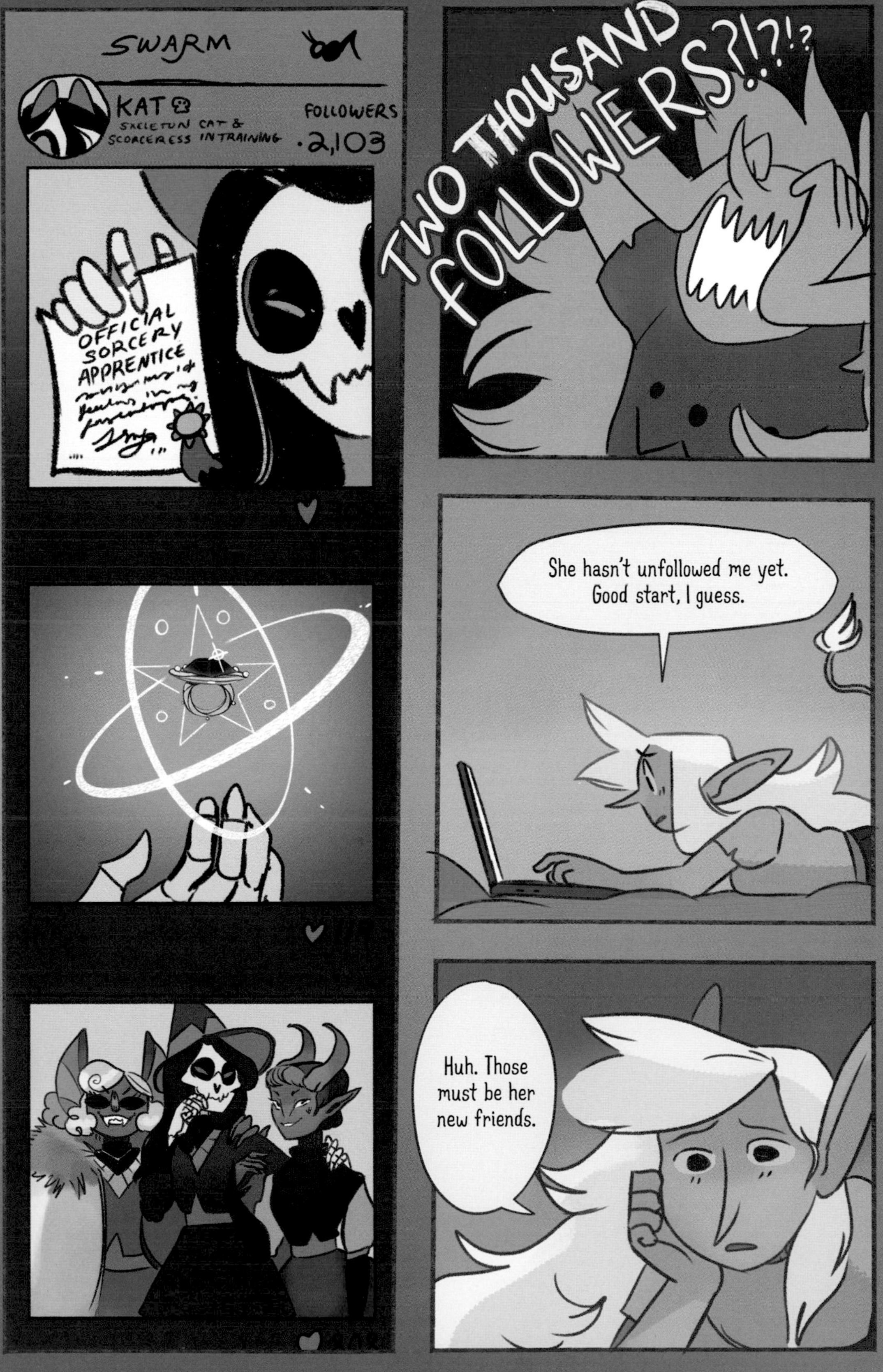
SWARM
KAT
SKELETON CAT &
SCORCERESS IN TRAINING
FOLLOWERS
·2,103
OFFICIAL SORCERY APPRENTICE
TWO THOUSAND FOLLOWERS?!?!?
She hasn't unfollowed me yet. Good start, I guess.
Huh. Those must be her new friends.

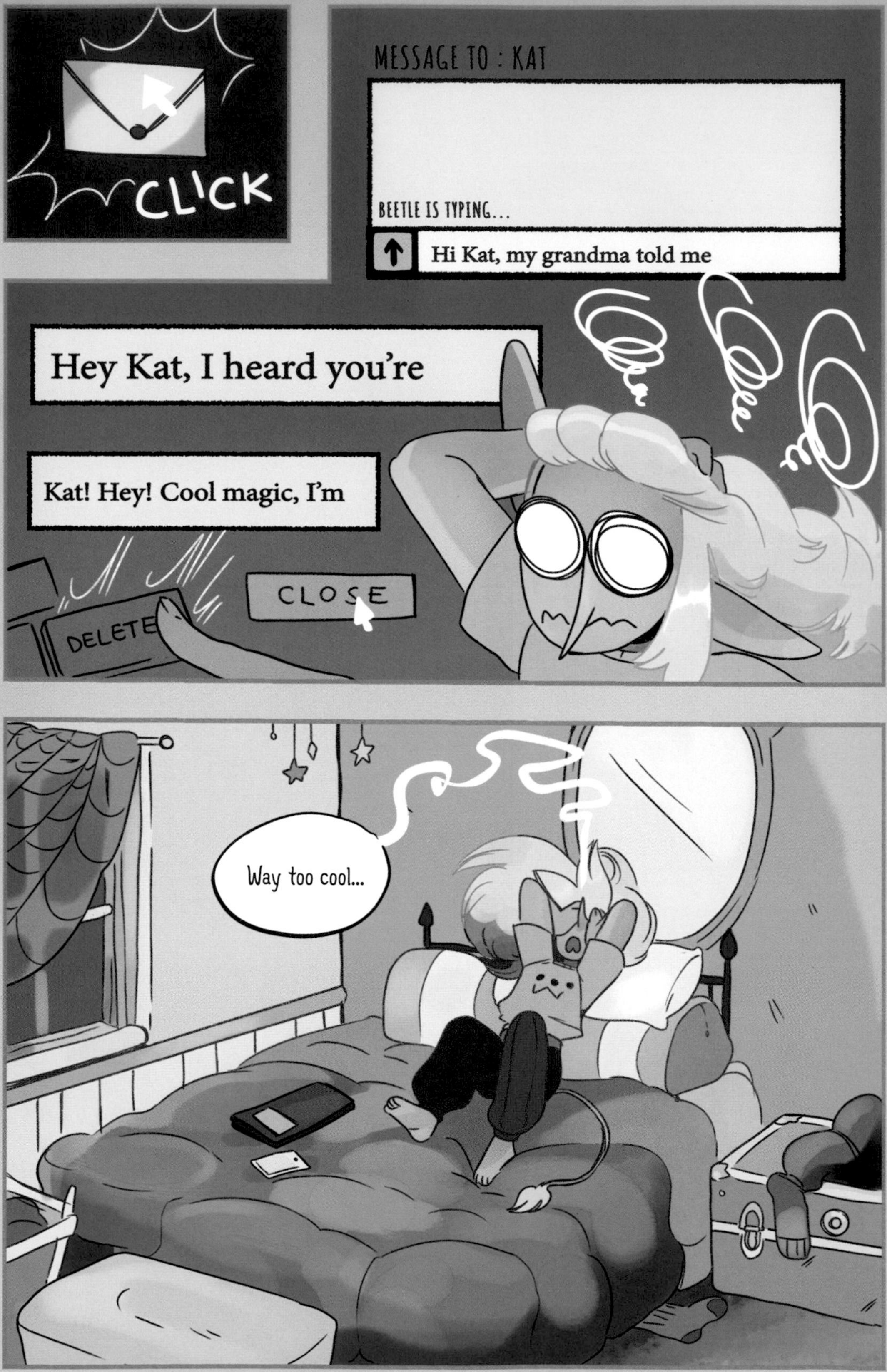
CLICK
MESSAGE TO : KAT
BEETLE IS TYPING...
Hi Kat, my grandma told me
Hey Kat, I heard you're
Kat! Hey! Cool magic, I'm
DELETE
CLOSE
Way too cool...

Kat Hollowbone

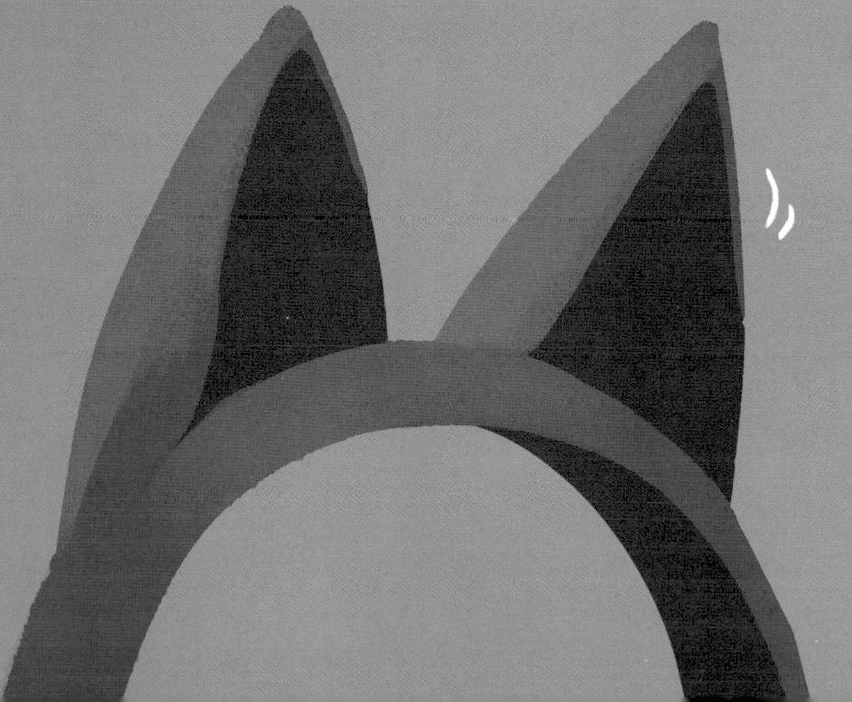

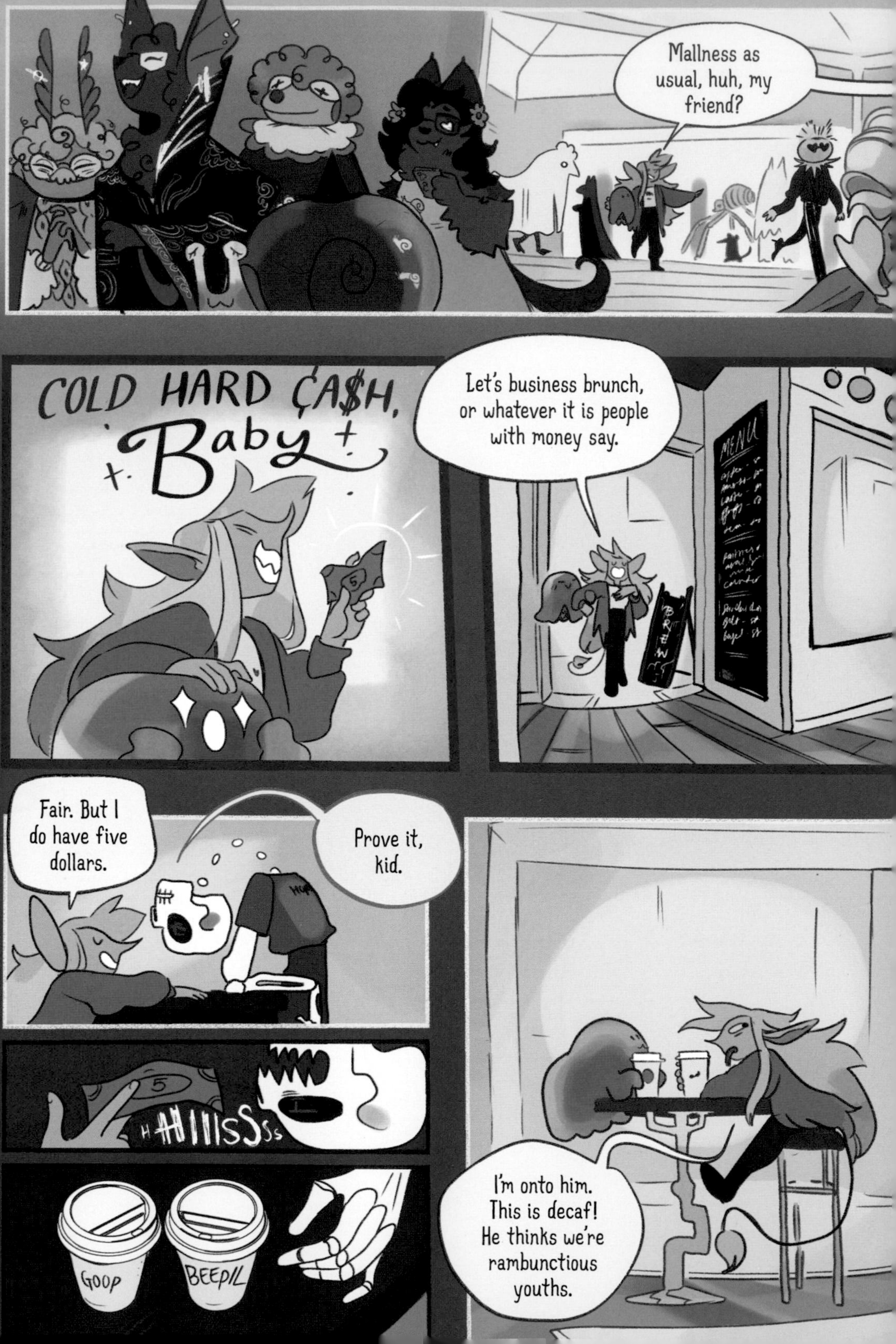
Mallness as usual, huh, my friend?
COLD HARD ÇA$H, Baby!
Let's business brunch, or whatever it is people with money say.
MENU
BREW
Fair. But I do have five dollars.
Prove it, kid.
HHHIIISSSs
GOOP
BEEPIL
I'm onto him. This is decaf! He thinks we're rambunctious youths.

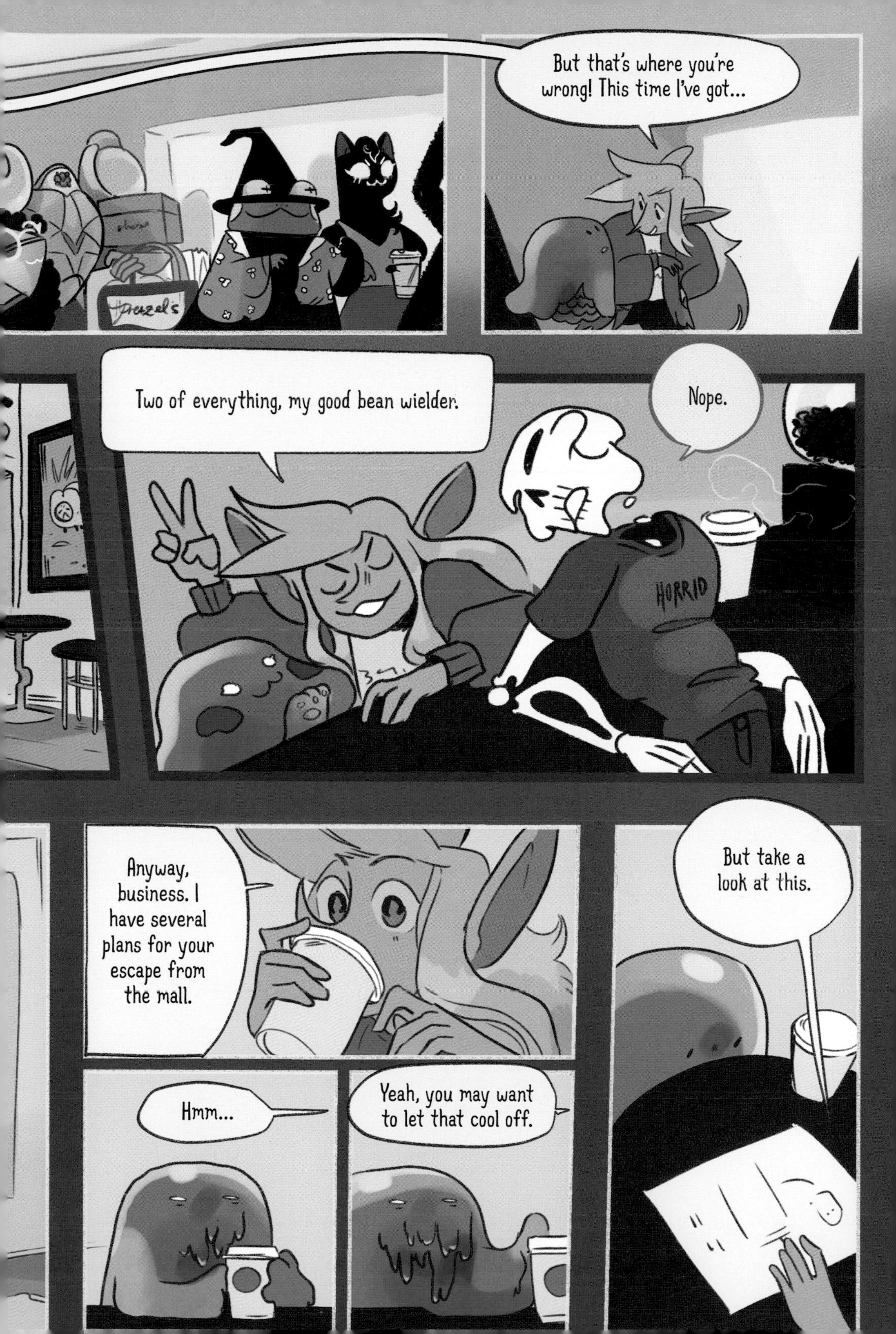
But that's where you're wrong! This time I've got...
Pretzel's
Two of everything, my good bean wielder.
Nope.
HORRID
Anyway, business. I have several plans for your escape from the mall.
But take a look at this.
Hmm...
Yeah, you may want to let that cool off.

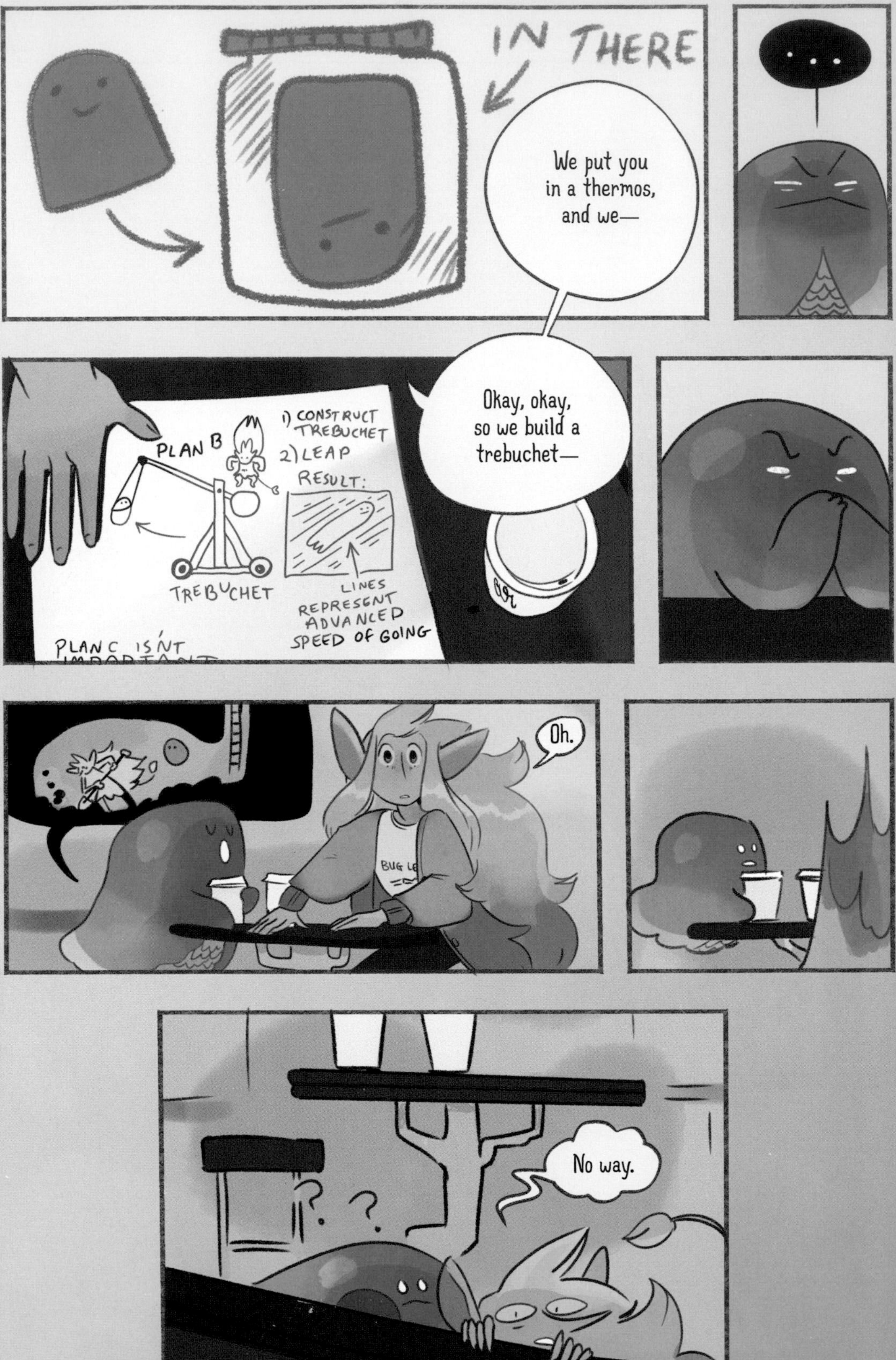
IN THERE
We put you in a thermos, and we—
...
PLAN B
1) CONSTRUCT TREBUCHET
2) LEAP
RESULT:
TREBUCHET
LINES REPRESENT ADVANCED SPEED OF GOING
PLAN C ISN'T
Okay, okay, so we build a trebuchet—
BUG LE
Oh.
No way.

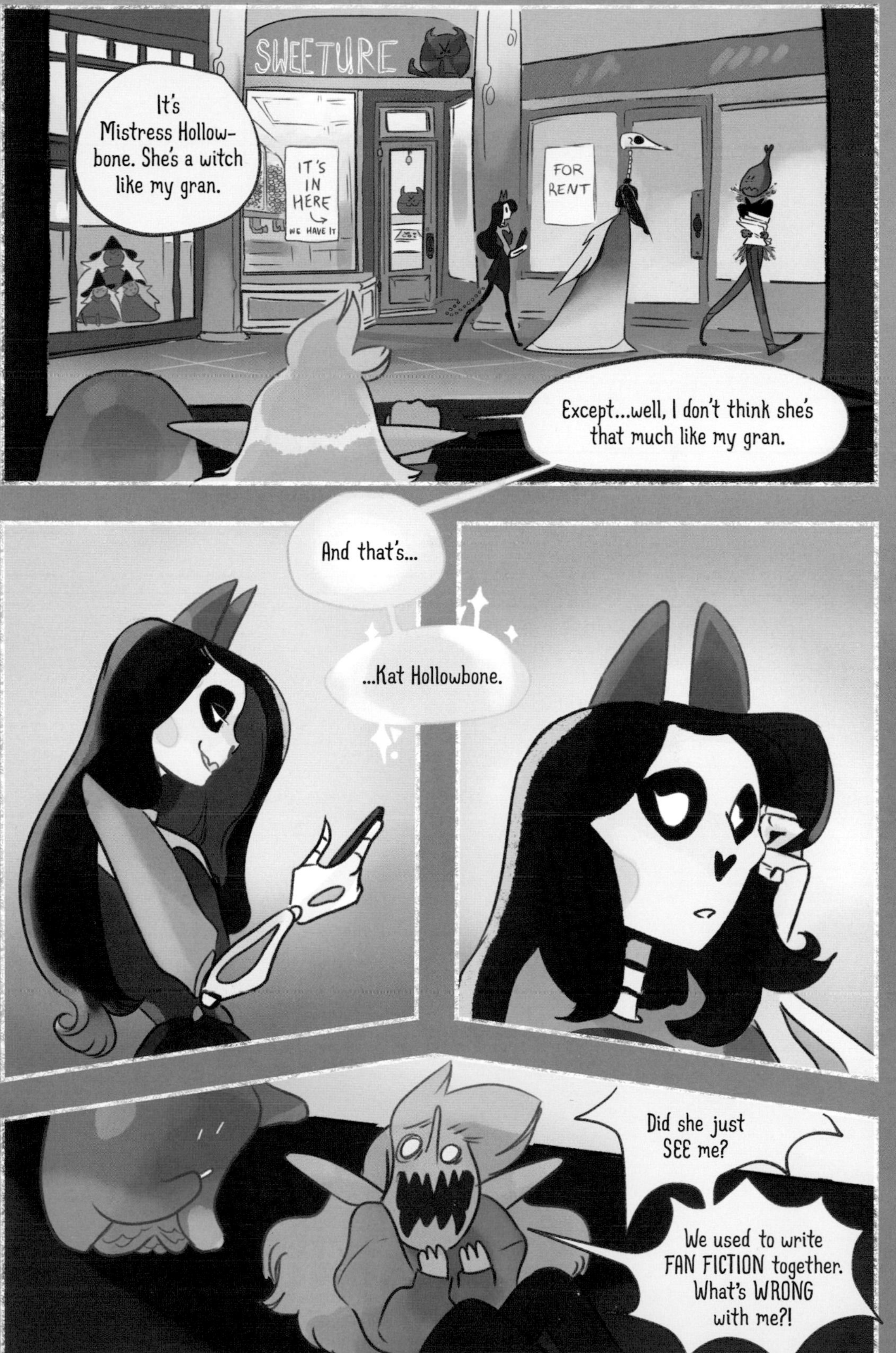
SWEETURE
It's Mistress Hollow-bone. She's a witch like my gran.
IT'S IN HERE WE HAVE IT
FOR RENT
Except...well, I don't think she's that much like my gran.
And that's...
...Kat Hollowbone.
Did she just SEE me?
We used to write FAN FICTION together. What's WRONG with me?!

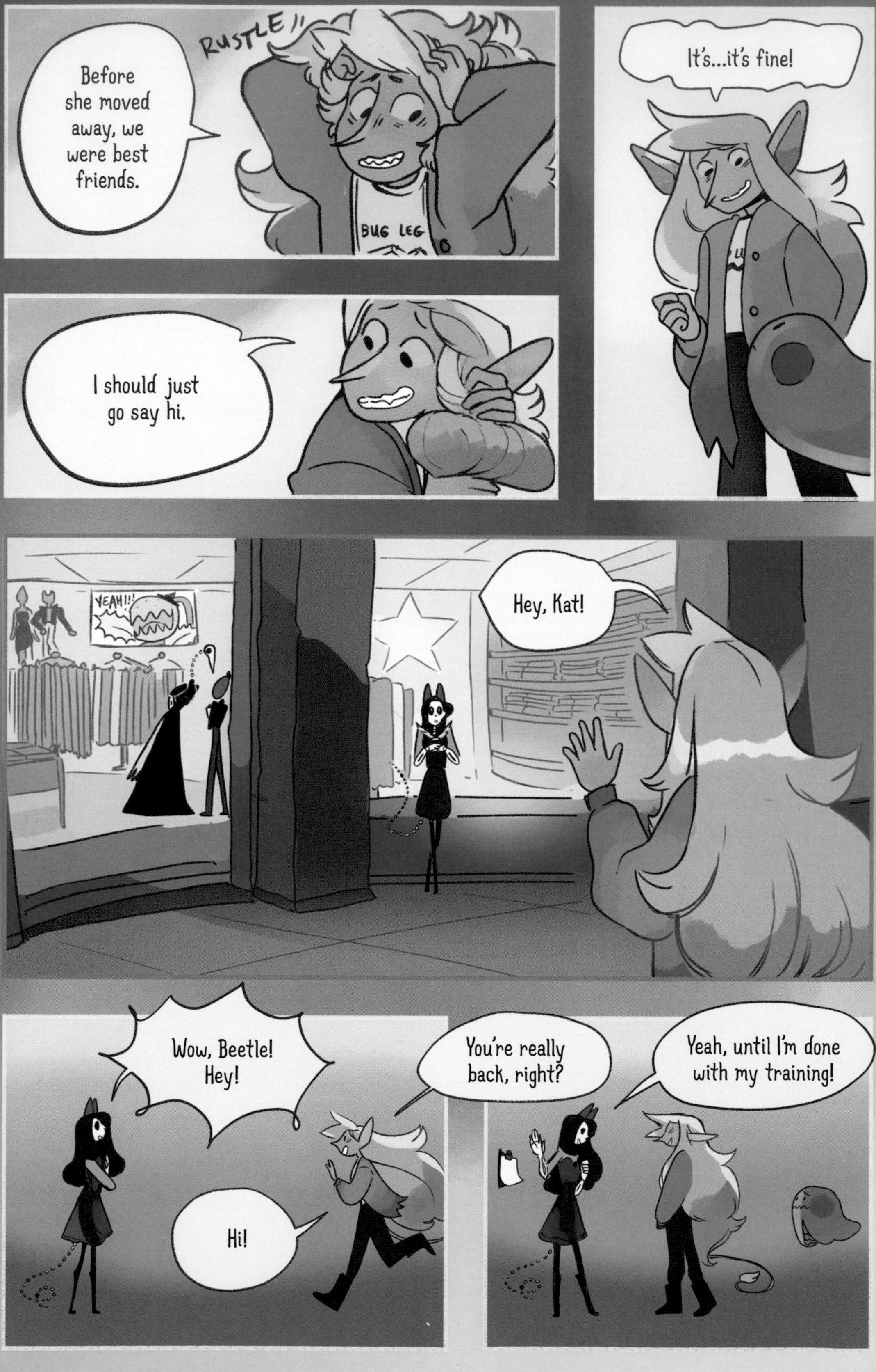

Before she moved away, we were best friends.
RUSTLE
BUG LEG
It's...it's fine!
I should just go say hi.
YEAH!!!
Hey, Kat!
Wow, Beetle! Hey!
Hi!
You're really back, right?
Yeah, until I'm done with my training!

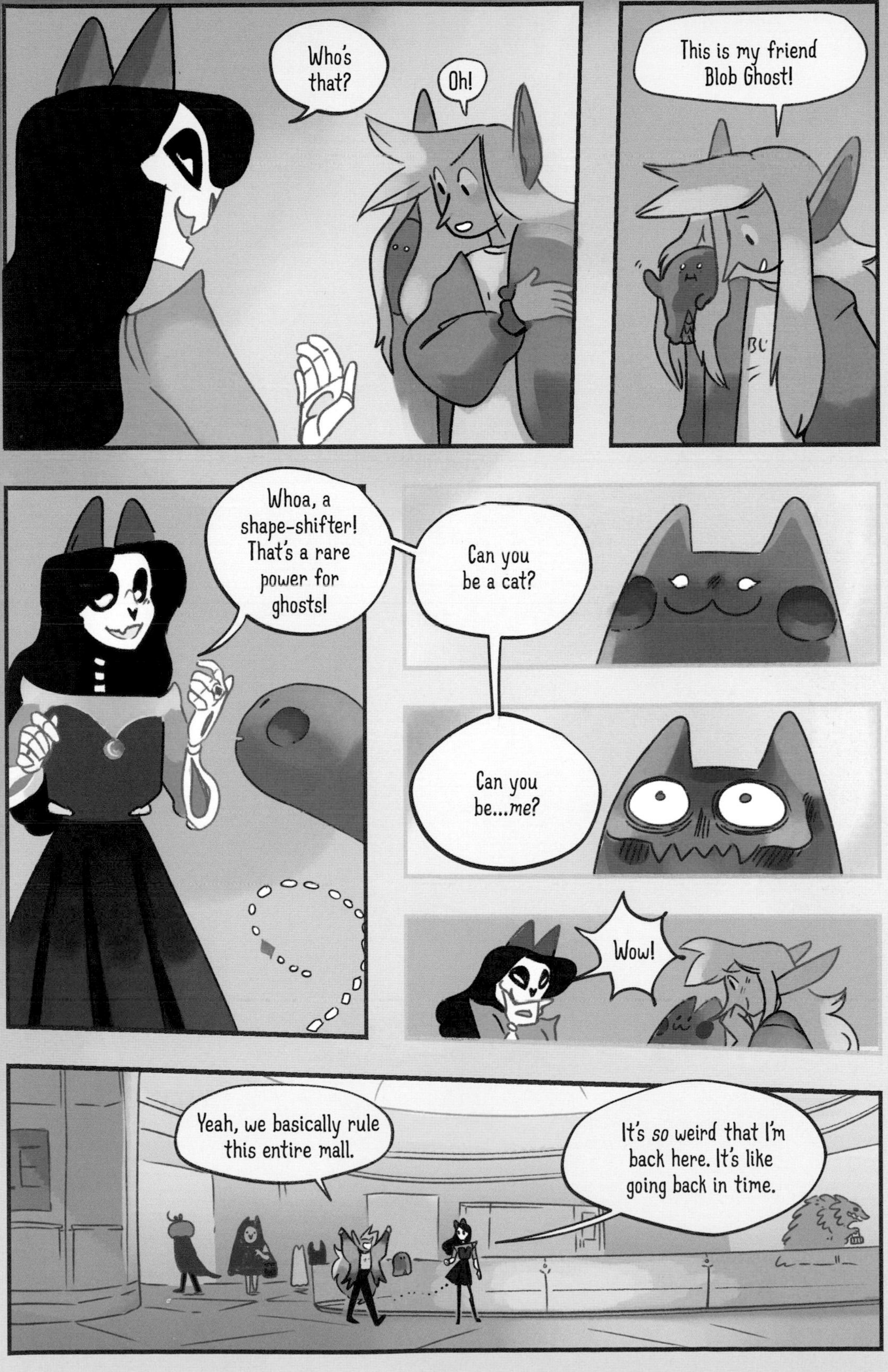

Who's that?
Oh!
This is my friend Blob Ghost!
BL
Whoa, a shape-shifter! That's a rare power for ghosts!
Can you be a cat?
Can you be...*me*?
Wow!
Yeah, we basically rule this entire mall.
It's *so* weird that I'm back here. It's like going back in time.

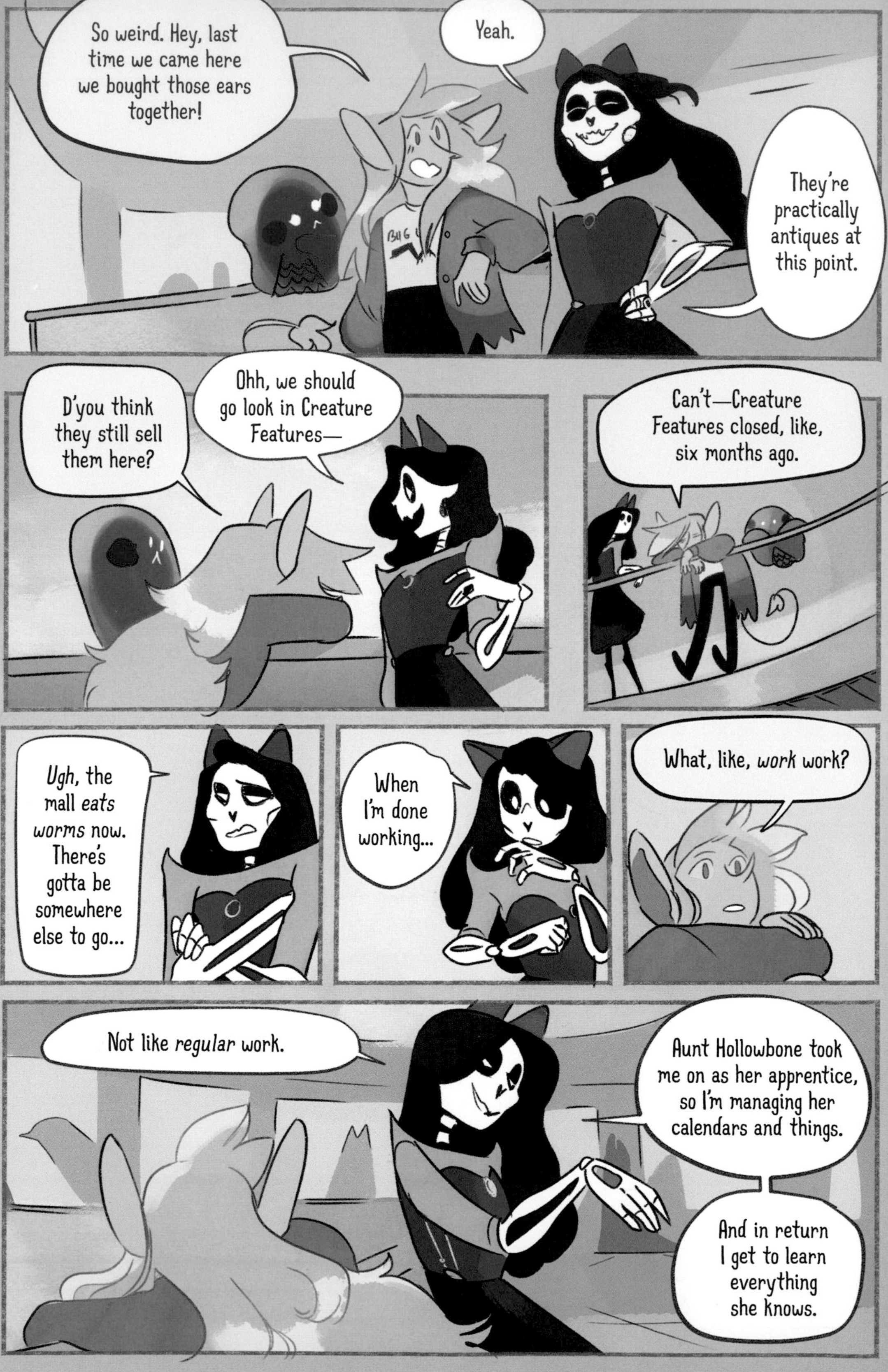
So weird. Hey, last time we came here we bought those ears together!
Yeah.
They're practically antiques at this point.
BUG
D'you think they still sell them here?
Ohh, we should go look in Creature Features—
Can't—Creature Features closed, like, six months ago.
Ugh, the mall *eats worms* now. There's gotta be somewhere else to go...
When I'm done working...
What, like, *work* work?
Not like *regular* work.
Aunt Hollowbone took me on as her apprentice, so I'm managing her calendars and things.
And in return I get to learn everything she knows.

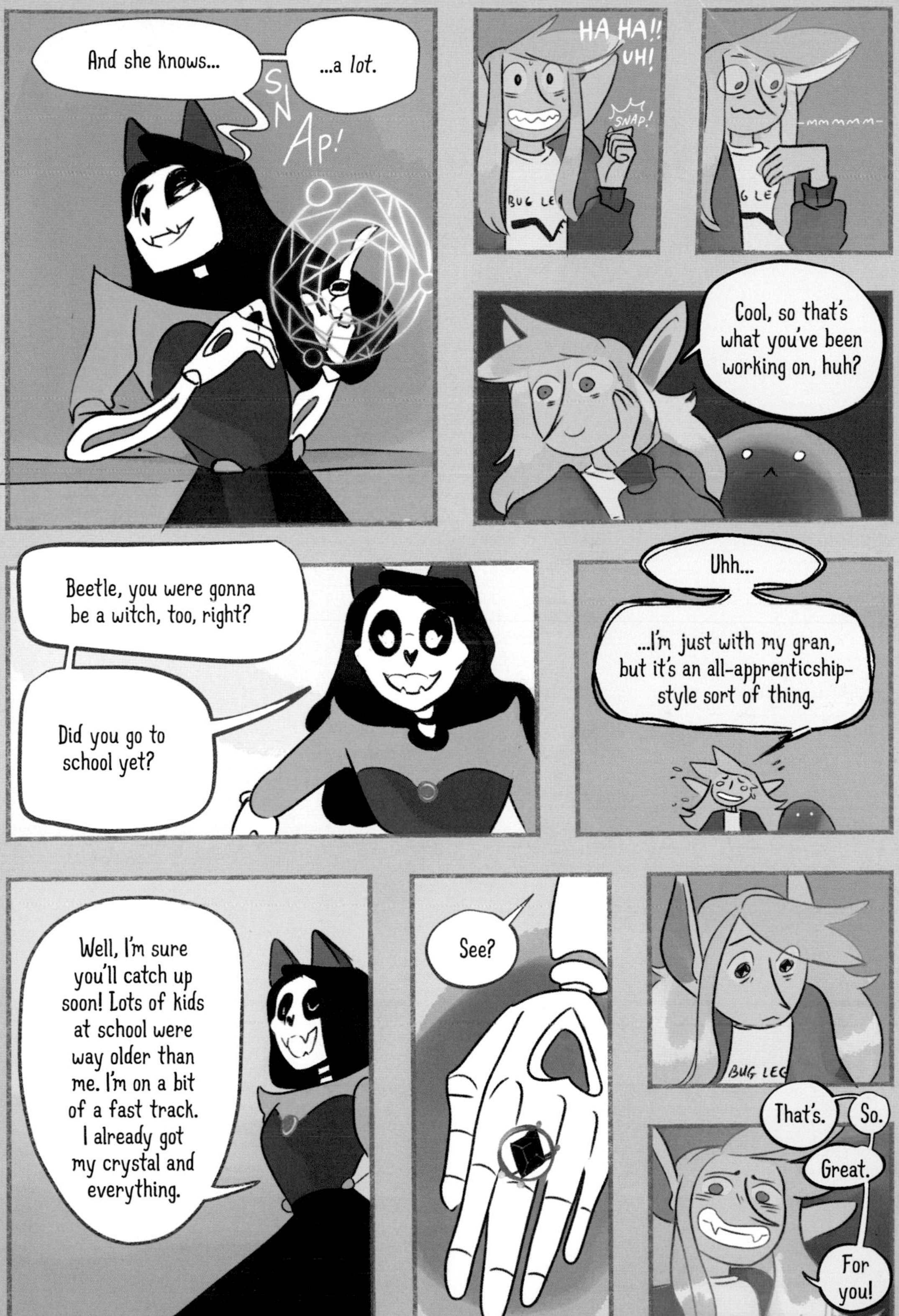
And she knows...
...a lot.
SNAP!
HA HA!! UH!
SNAP!
BUG LEG
-mmmmm-
Cool, so that's what you've been working on, huh?
Beetle, you were gonna be a witch, too, right?
Did you go to school yet?
Uhh...
...I'm just with my gran, but it's an all-apprenticship-style sort of thing.
Well, I'm sure you'll catch up soon! Lots of kids at school were way older than me. I'm on a bit of a fast track. I already got my crystal and everything.
See?
BUG LEG
That's.
So.
Great.
For you!

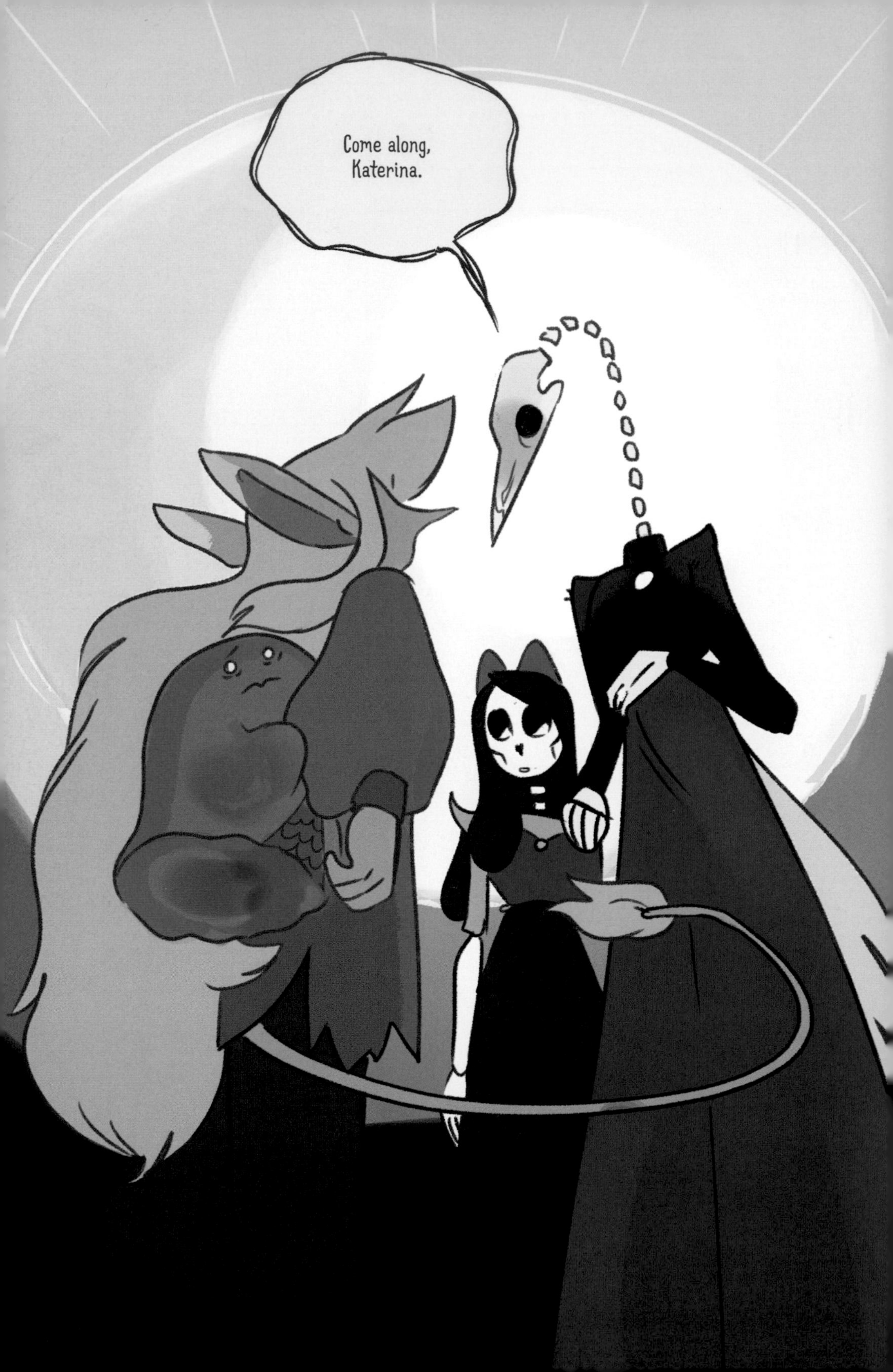
Come along, Katerina.

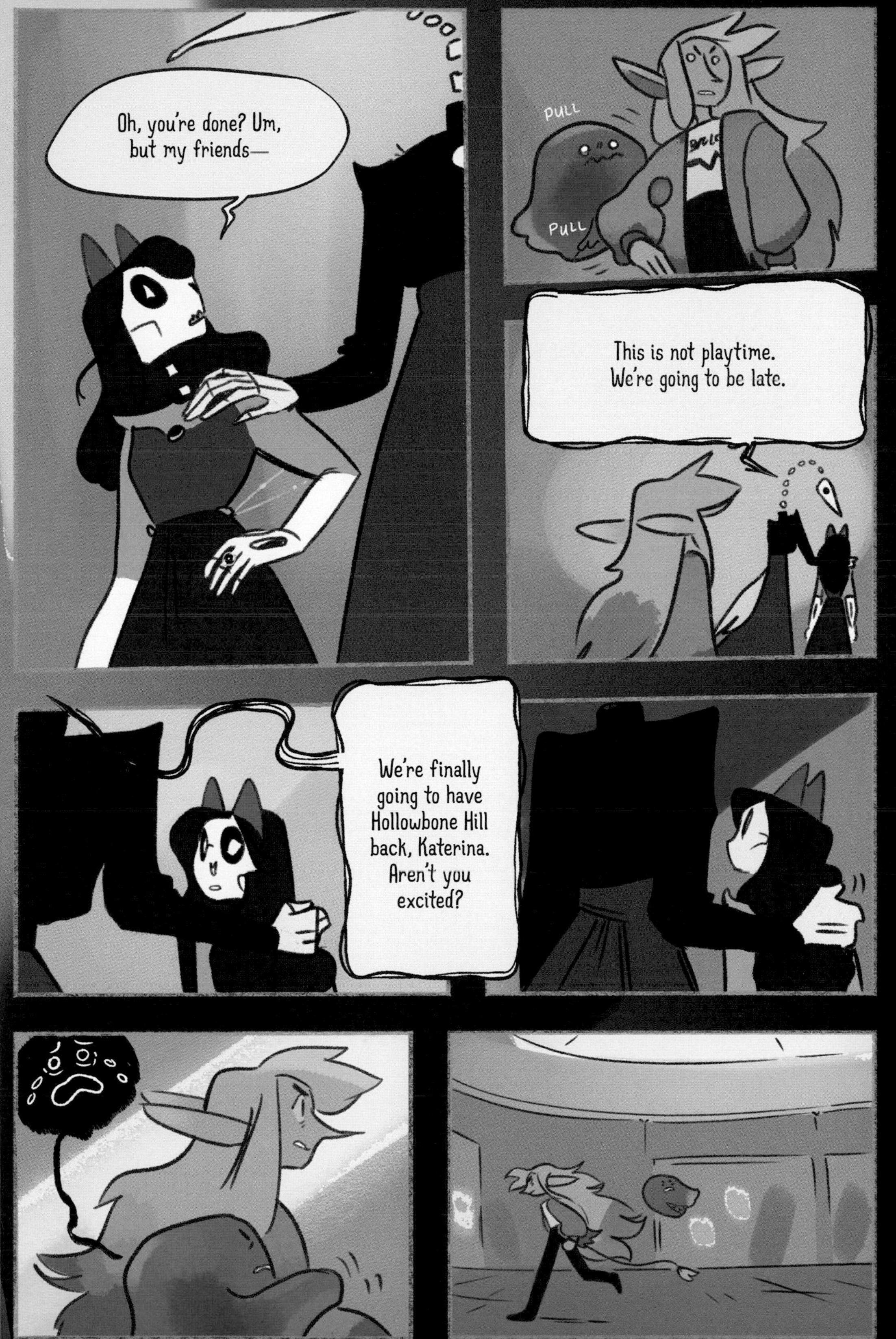
Oh, you're done? Um, but my friends—
PULL
PULL
This is not playtime. We're going to be late.
We're finally going to have Hollowbone Hill back, Katerina. Aren't you excited?

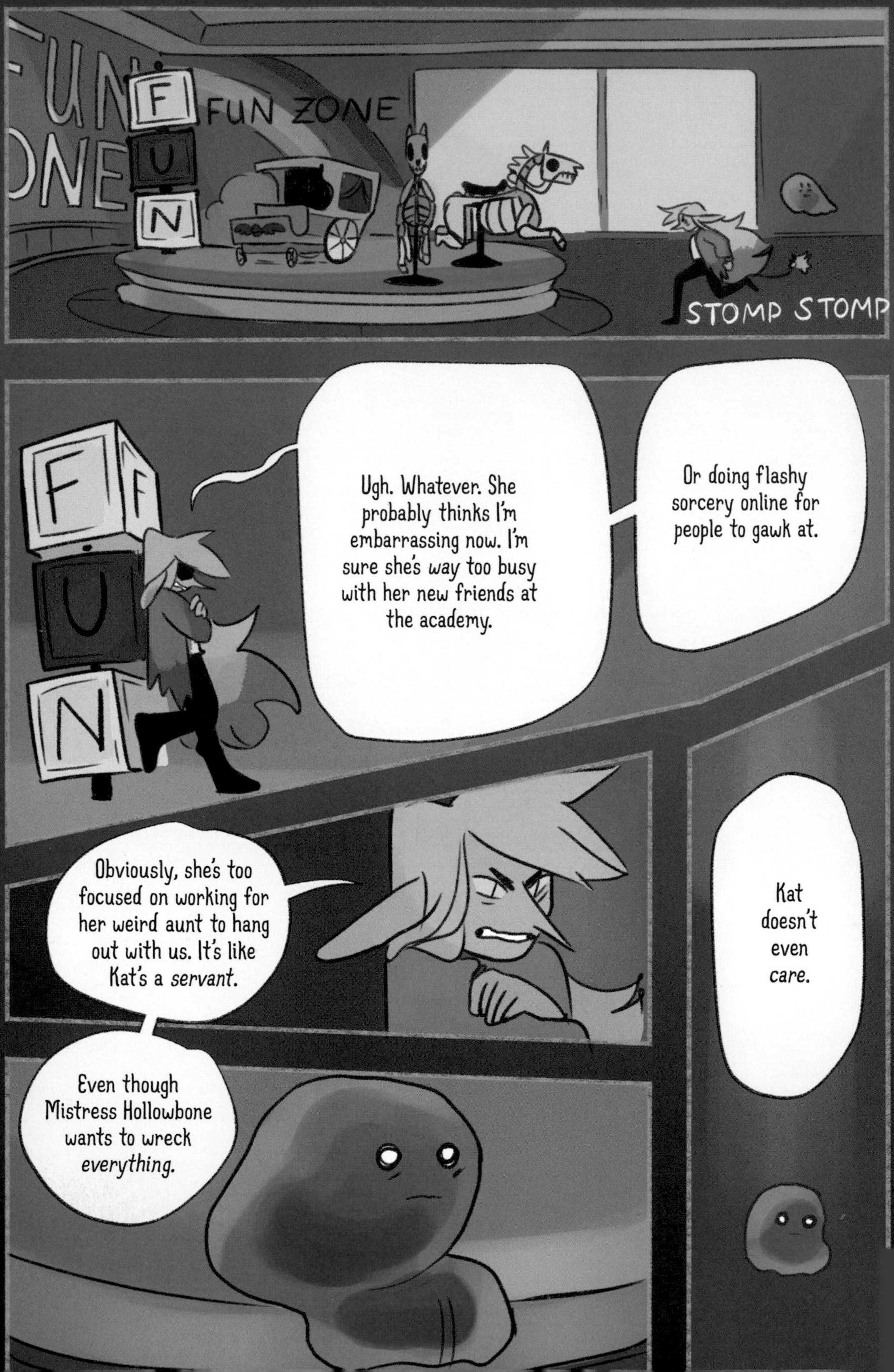
FUN ZONE
FUN
FUN ZONE
STOMP STOMP
FUN
Ugh. Whatever. She probably thinks I'm embarrassing now. I'm sure she's *way* too busy with her new friends at the academy.
Or doing flashy sorcery online for people to gawk at.
Obviously, she's too focused on working for her weird aunt to hang out with us. It's like Kat's a *servant*.
Even though Mistress Hollowbone wants to wreck *everything*.
Kat doesn't even *care*.

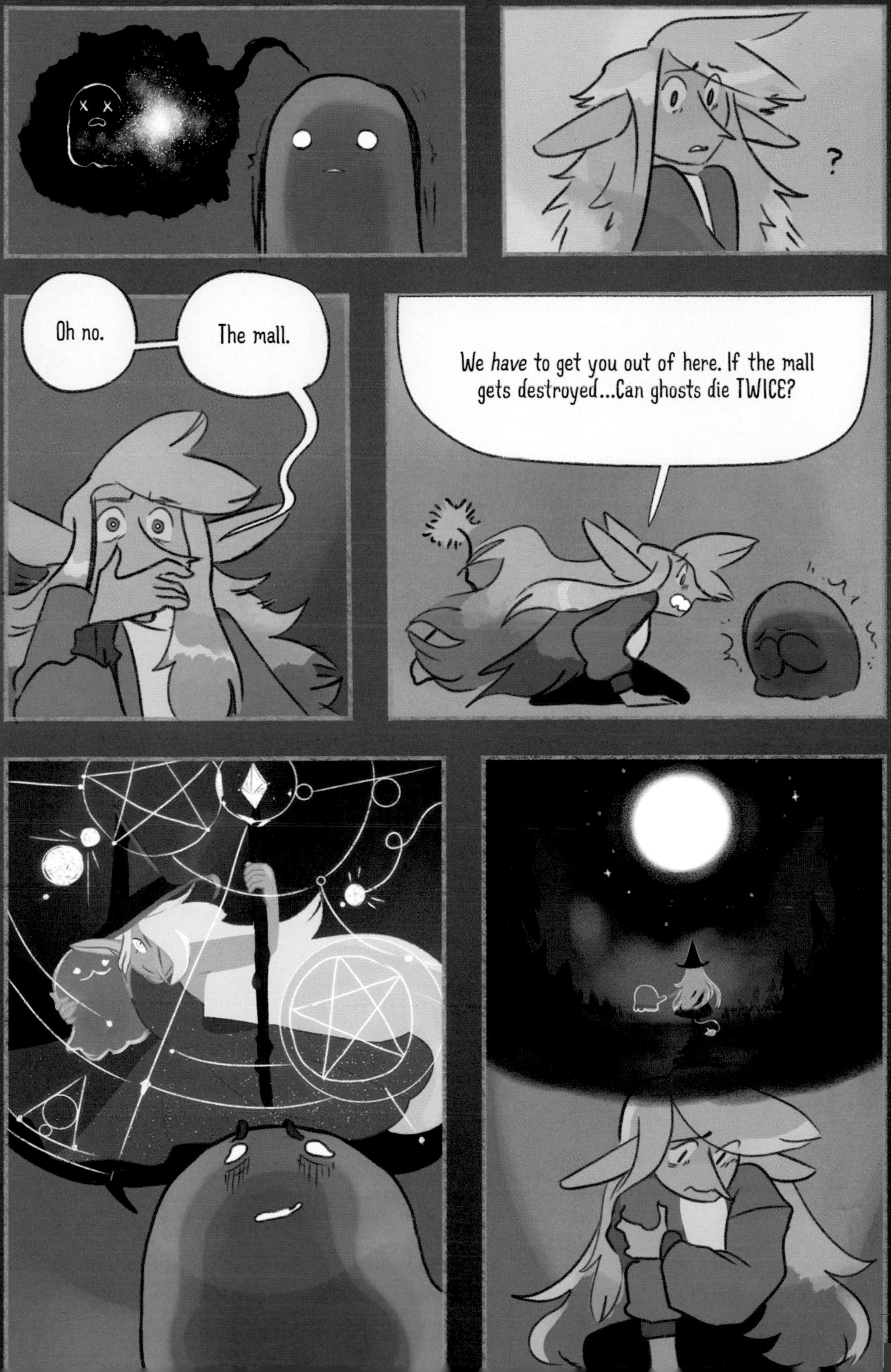
?
Oh no.
The mall.
We *have* to get you out of here. If the mall gets destroyed...Can ghosts die TWICE?

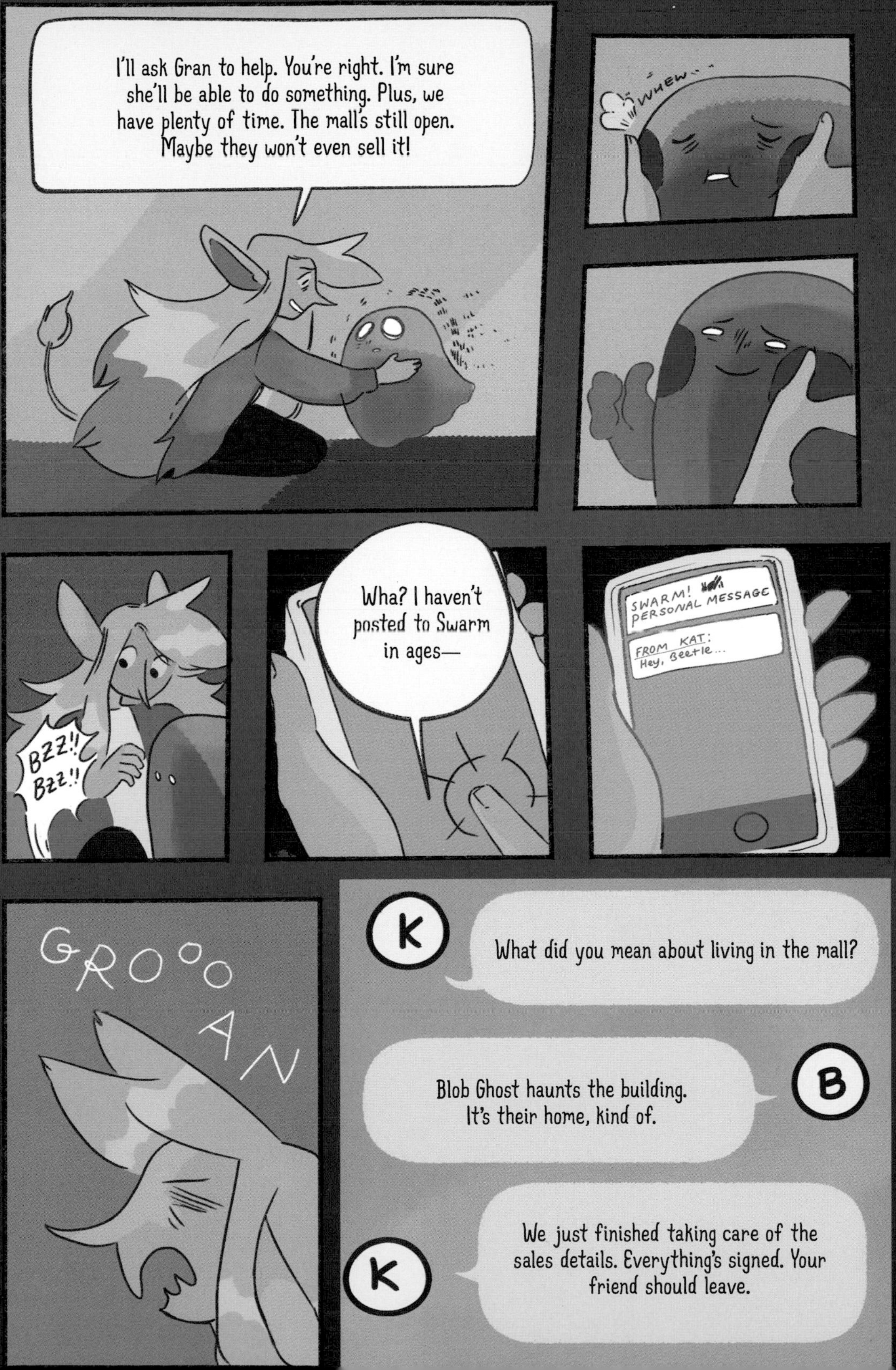
I'll ask Gran to help. You're right. I'm sure she'll be able to do something. Plus, we have plenty of time. The mall's still open. Maybe they won't even sell it!
WHEW
BZZ!! Bzz!!
Wha? I haven't posted to Swarm in ages—
SWARM! PERSONAL MESSAGE
FROM KAT: Hey, Beetle...
GROOOAN
K
What did you mean about living in the mall?
B
Blob Ghost haunts the building. It's their home, kind of.
K
We just finished taking care of the sales details. Everything's signed. Your friend should leave.

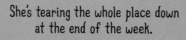

She's tearing the whole place down
at the end of the week.

Worm Threat

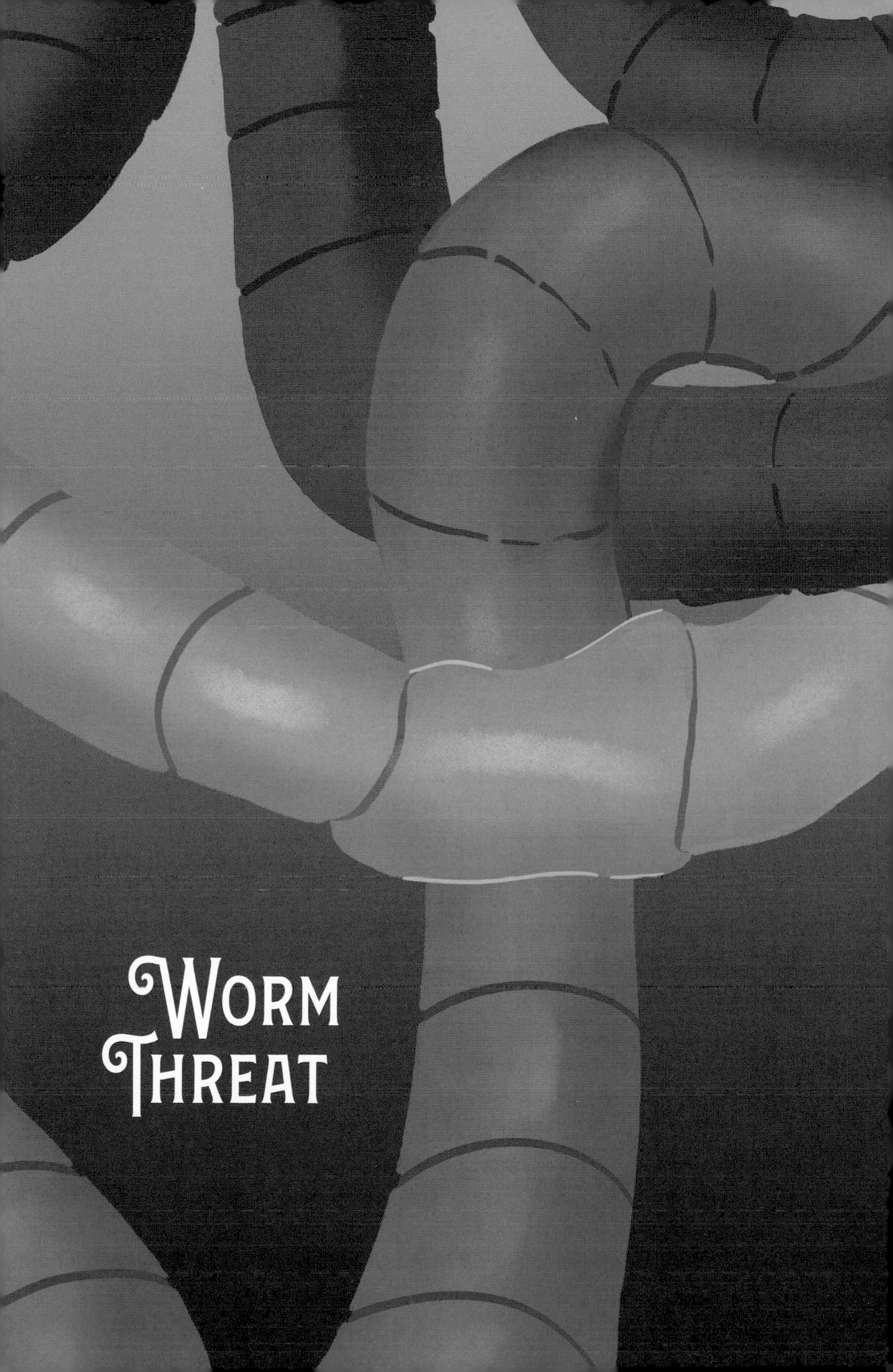

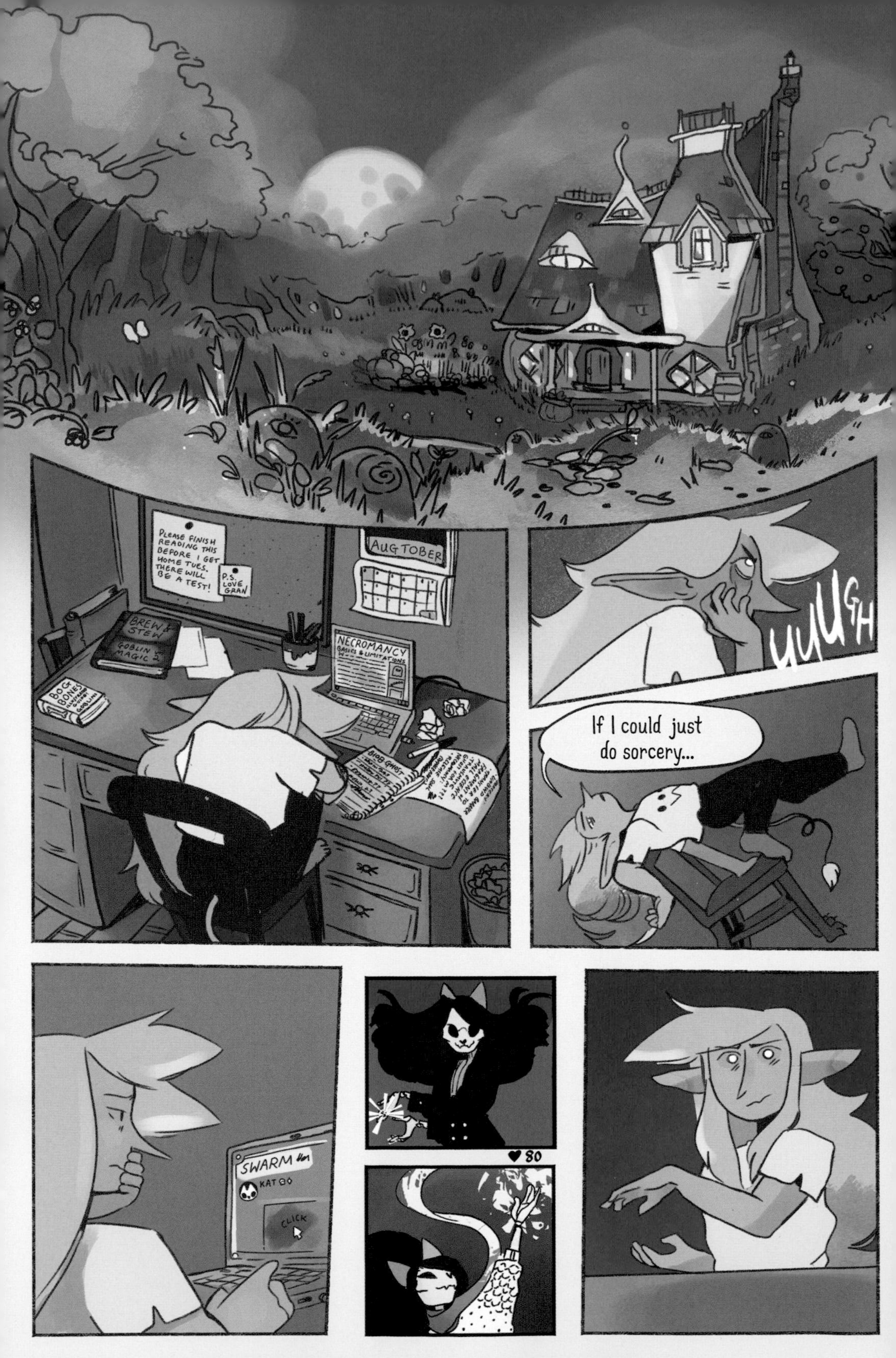

PLEASE FINISH READING THIS BEFORE I GET HOME TUES. THERE WILL BE A TEST!
P.S. LOVE GRAN
AUGTOBER
BREW & STEW
GOBLIN MAGIC 2
BOG BONES
NECROMANCY
BASICS & LIMITATIONS
BLOB GHOST
UUUGH
If I could just do sorcery...
SWARM
KAT
CLICK
80

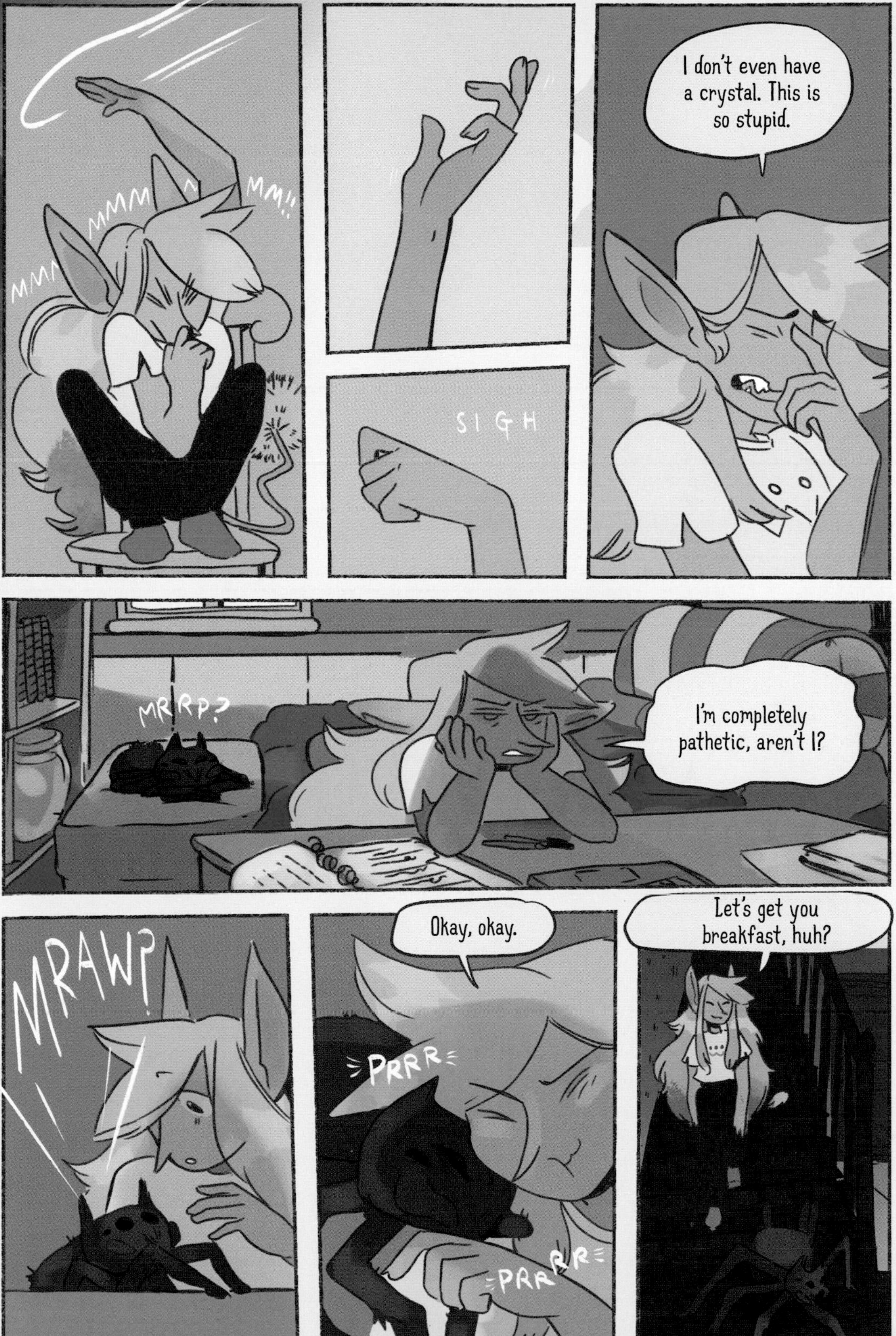
MMMMMMMM!!
I don't even have a crystal. This is so stupid.
SIGH
MRRP?
I'm completely pathetic, aren't I?
MRAW?
Okay, okay.
PRRR
PRRRR
Let's get you breakfast, huh?

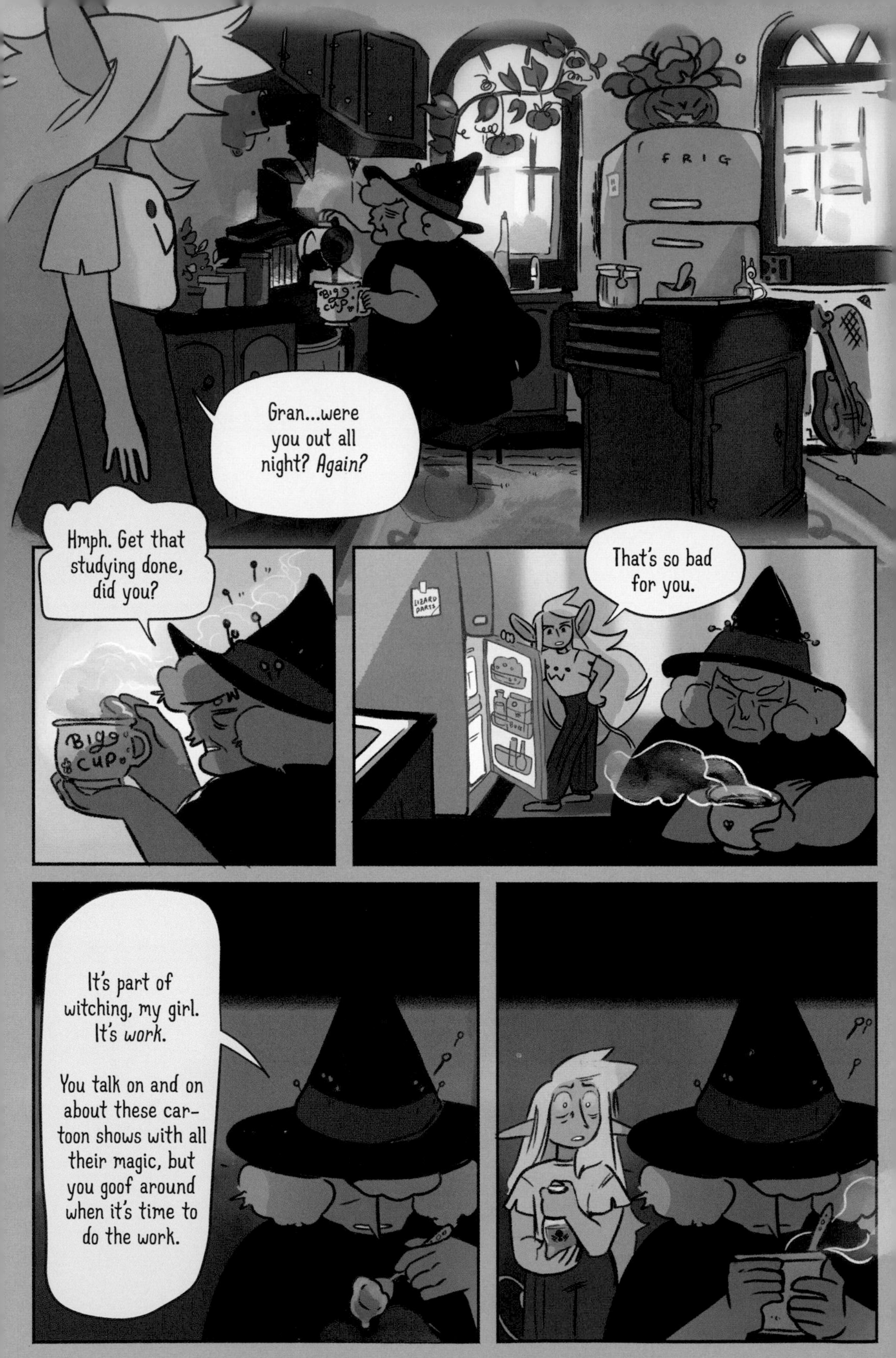
FRIG
Gran...were you out all night? Again?
Hmph. Get that studying done, did you?
BIGG CUP
LIZARD PARTS
That's so bad for you.
It's part of witching, my girl. It's *work*.
You talk on and on about these car-toon shows with all their magic, but you goof around when it's time to do the work.

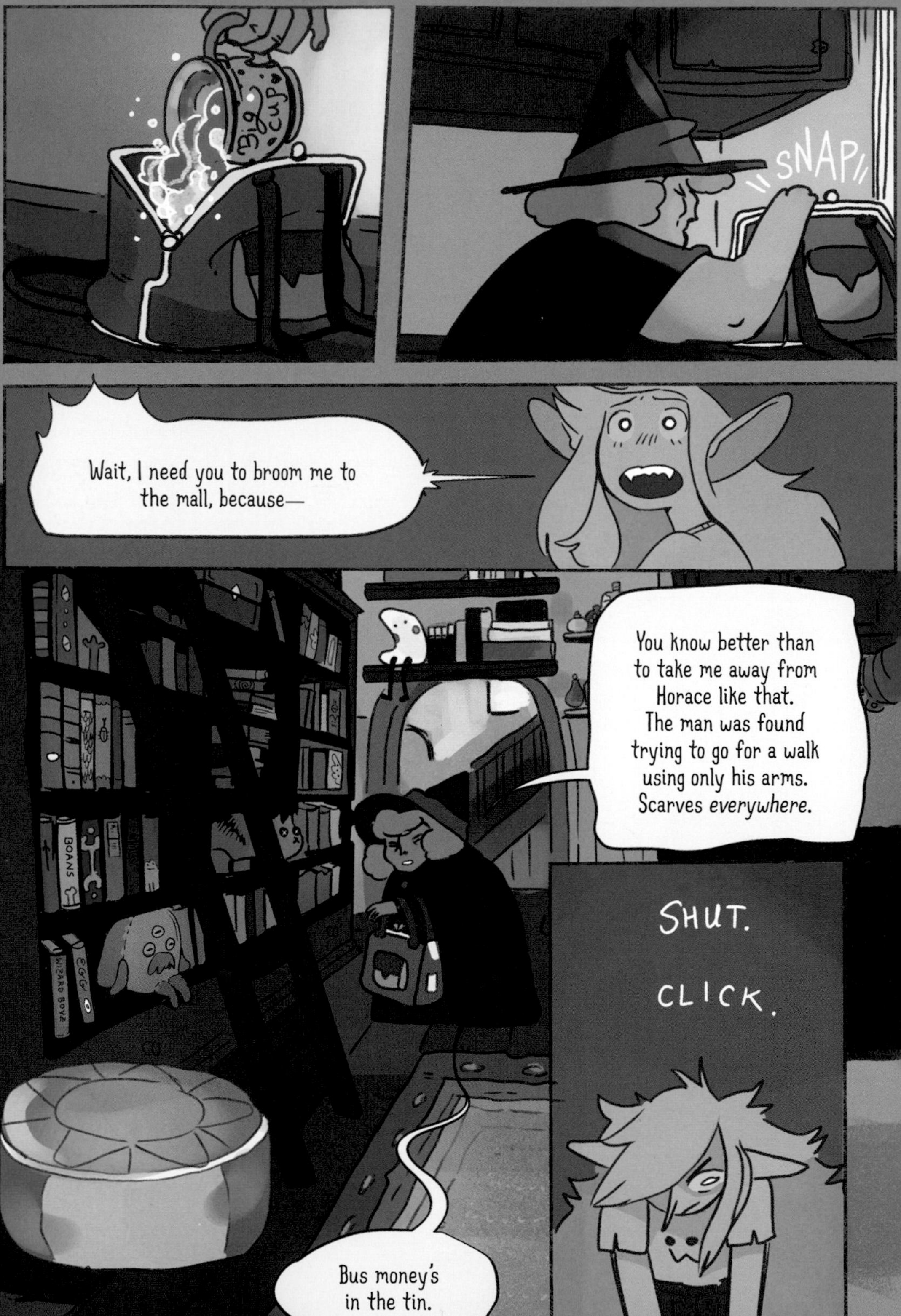
Big cup
SNAP
Wait, I need you to broom me to the mall, because—
You know better than to take me away from Horace like that. The man was found trying to go for a walk using only his arms. Scarves *everywhere*.
BOANS
WIZARD BOYZ
SHUT.
CLICK.
Bus money's in the tin.

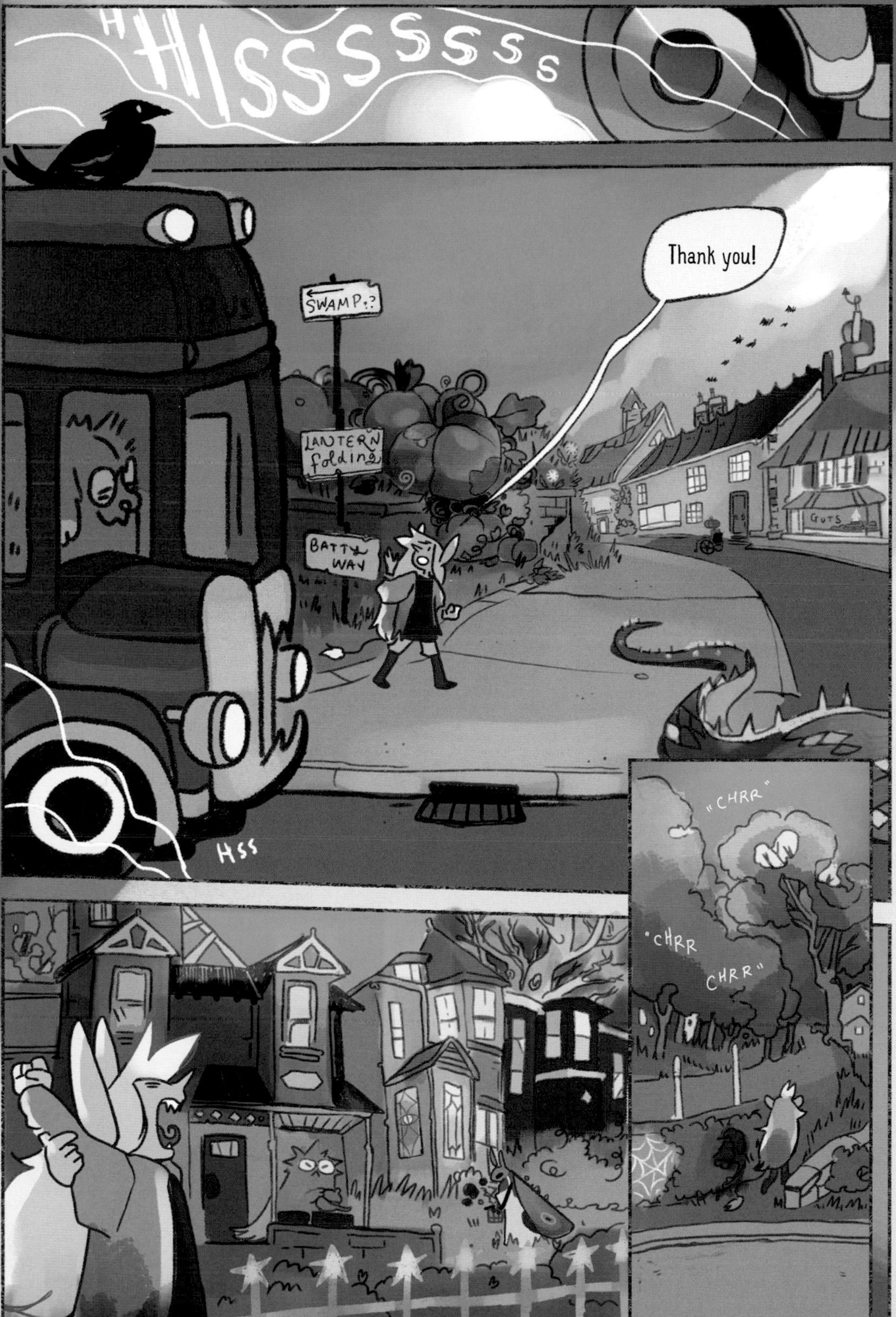
HHISSSSSSs
SWAMP?
LANTERN folding
BATTY WAY
Thank you!
GUTS
HSS
"CHRR"
"CHRR
CHRR"

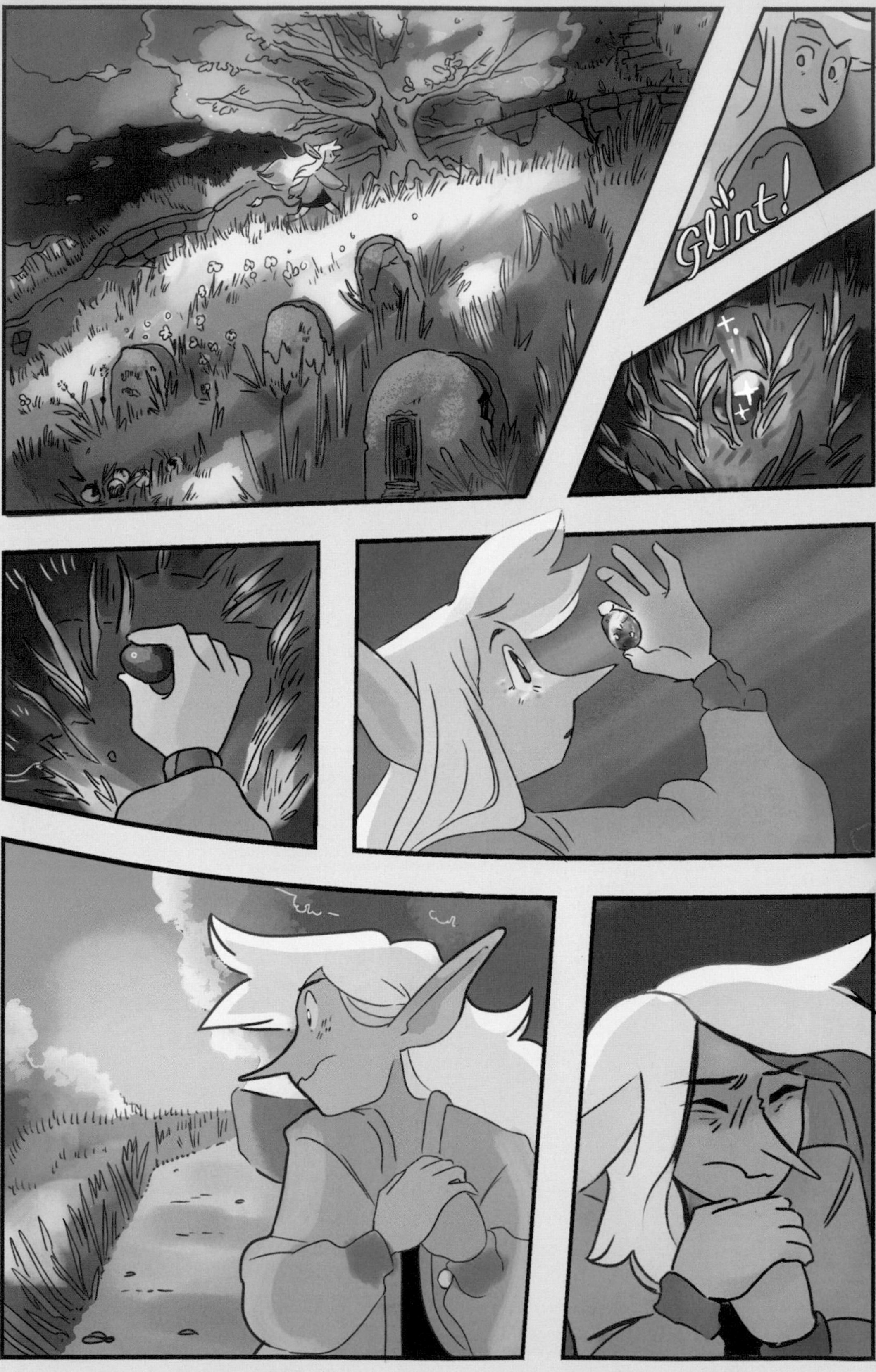
Glint!

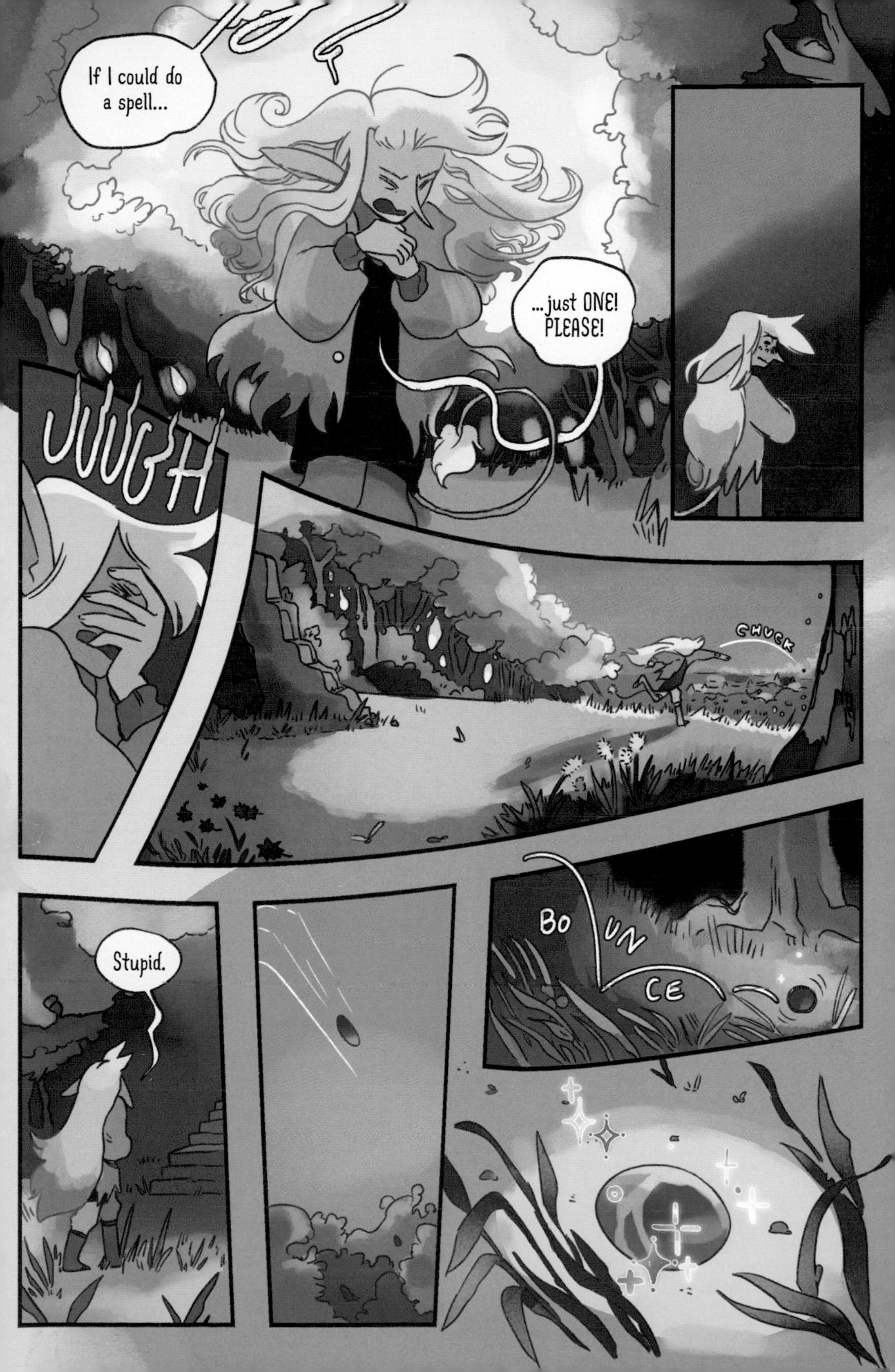
If I could do a spell...
...just ONE! PLEASE!
UUUGH
CHUCK
Stupid.
BOUNCE

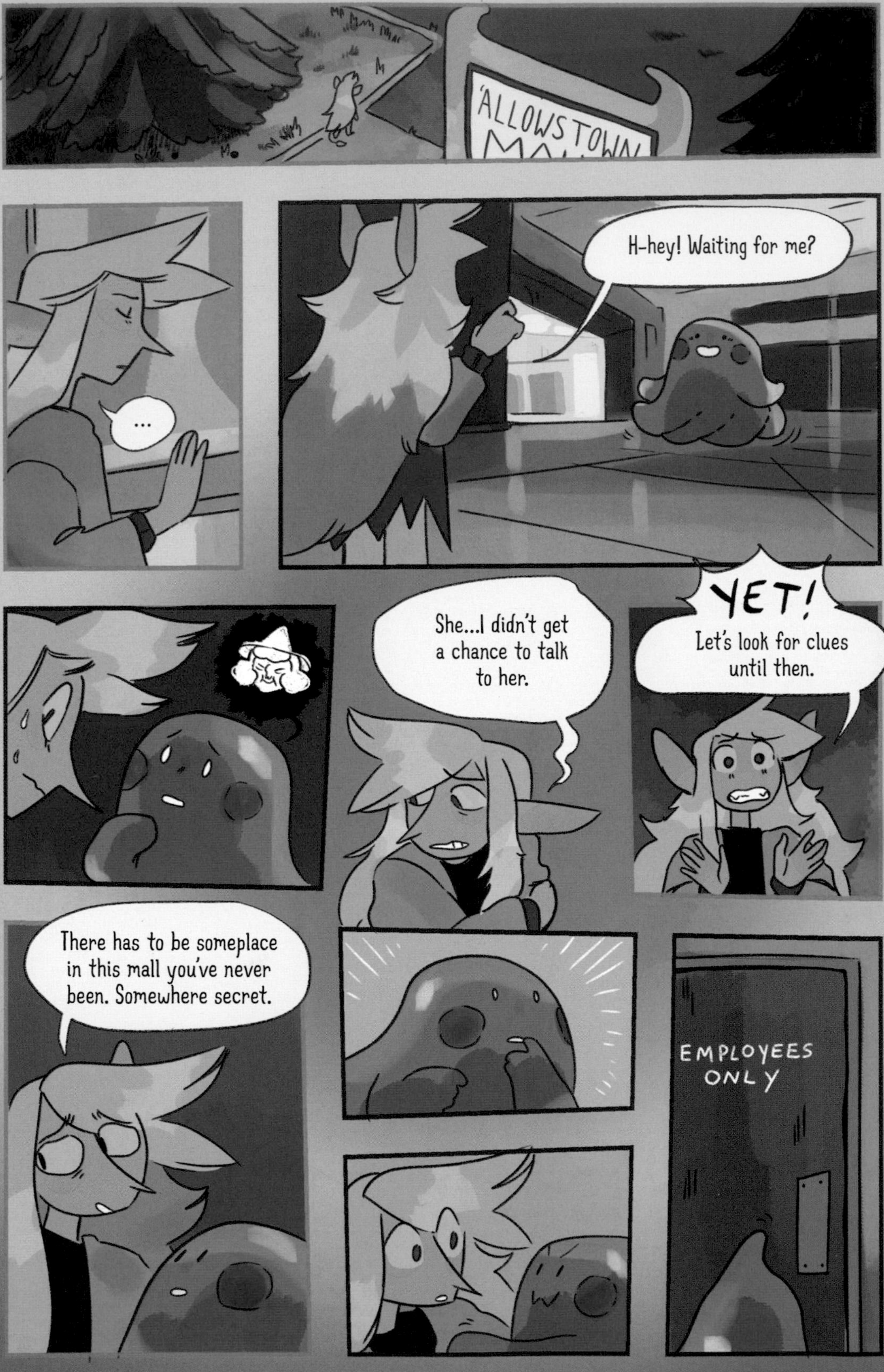
'ALLOWSTOWN MA
...
H-hey! Waiting for me?
She...I didn't get a chance to talk to her.
YET!
Let's look for clues until then.
There has to be someplace in this mall you've never been. Somewhere secret.
EMPLOYEES ONLY

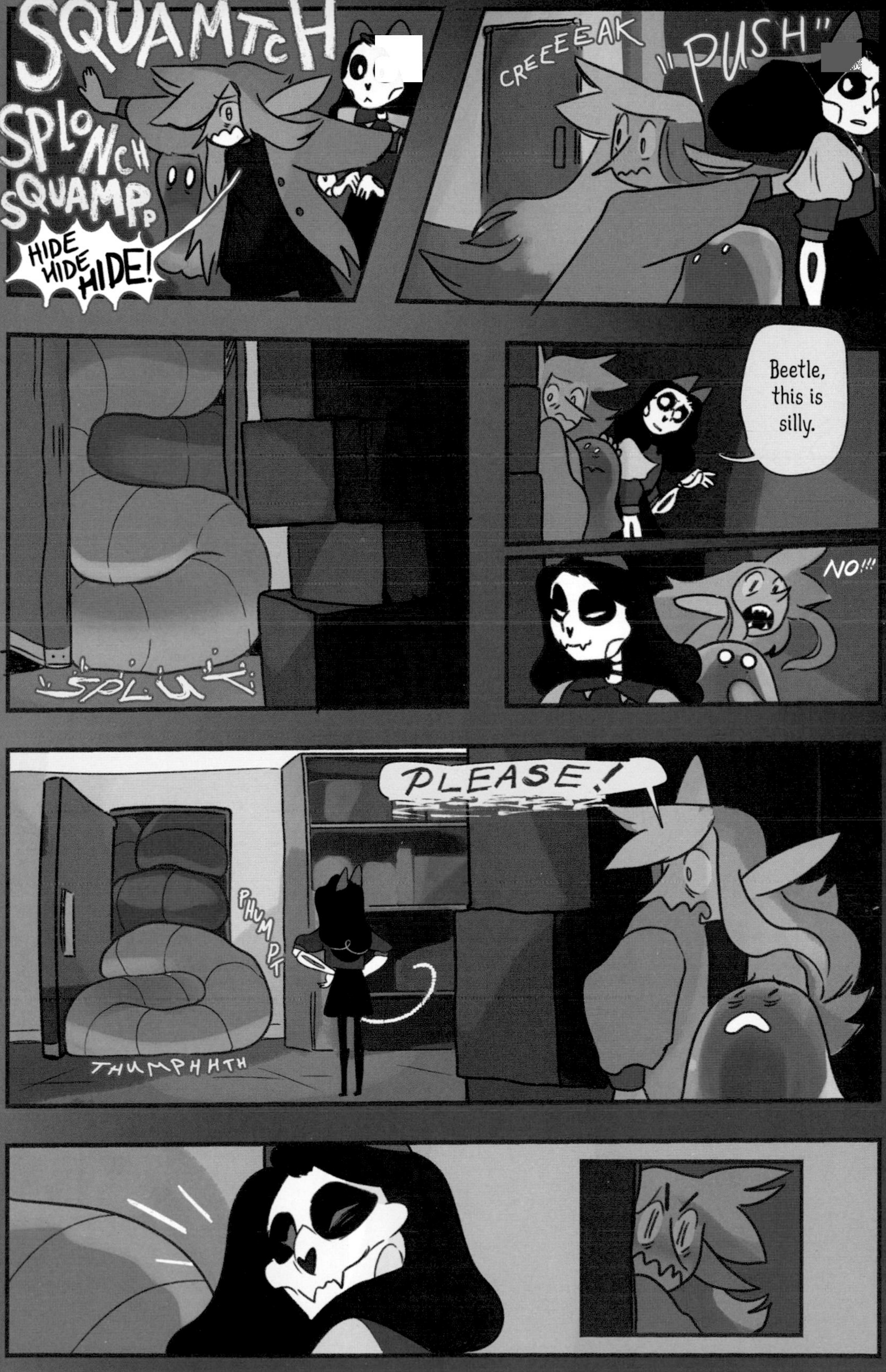
SQUAMTCH
SPLONCH
SQUAMPP
HIDE HIDE HIDE!
CREEEEAK
"PUSH"
SPLUT
Beetle, this is silly.
NO!!!
PLEASE!
PHUMPK
THUMPHHTH

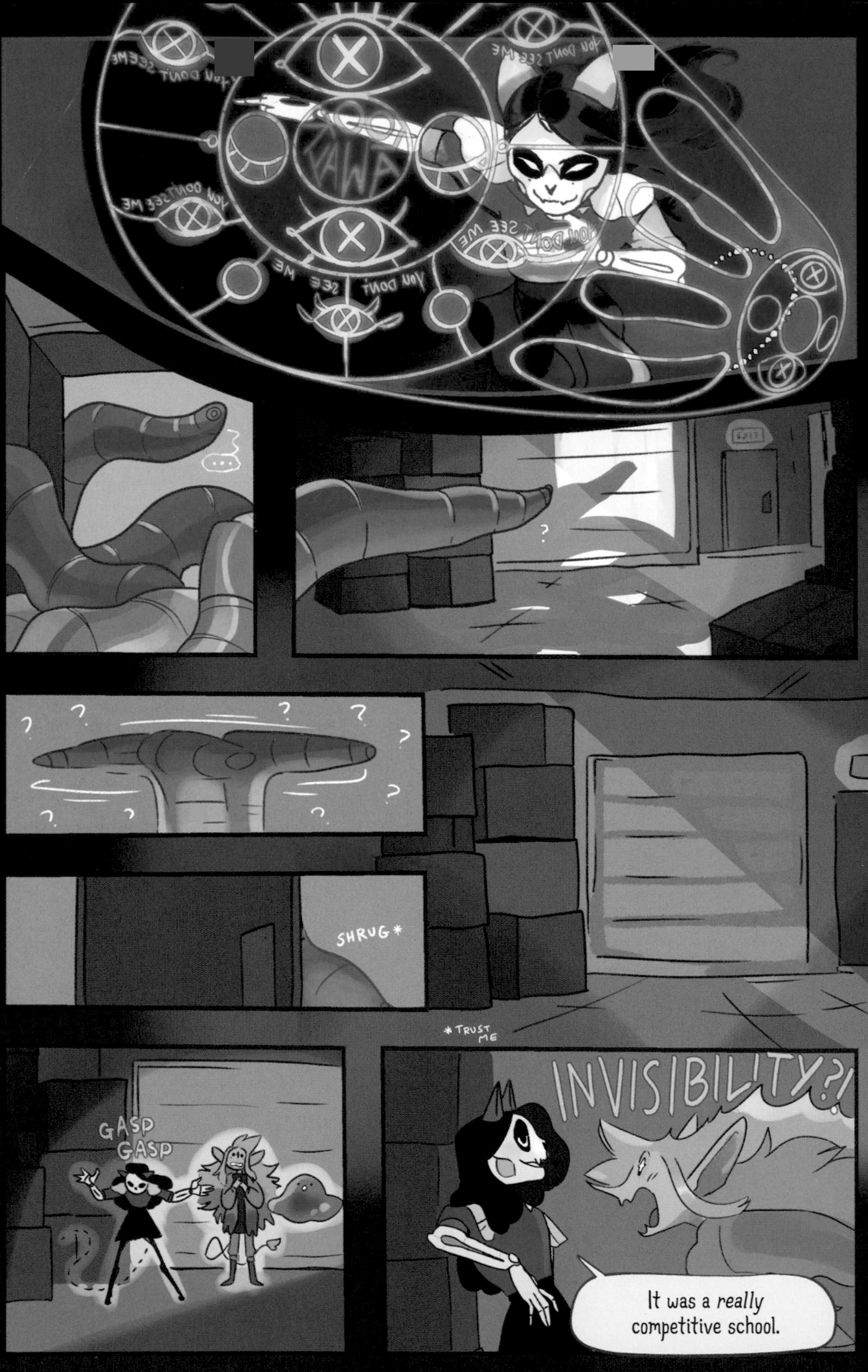
YOU DONT SEE ME
YOU DONT SEE ME
YOU DONT SEE ME
YOU DONT SEE ME
YOU DONT SEE ME
...
?
SHRUG*
*TRUST ME
GASP GASP
INVISIBILITY?!
It was a *really* competitive school.

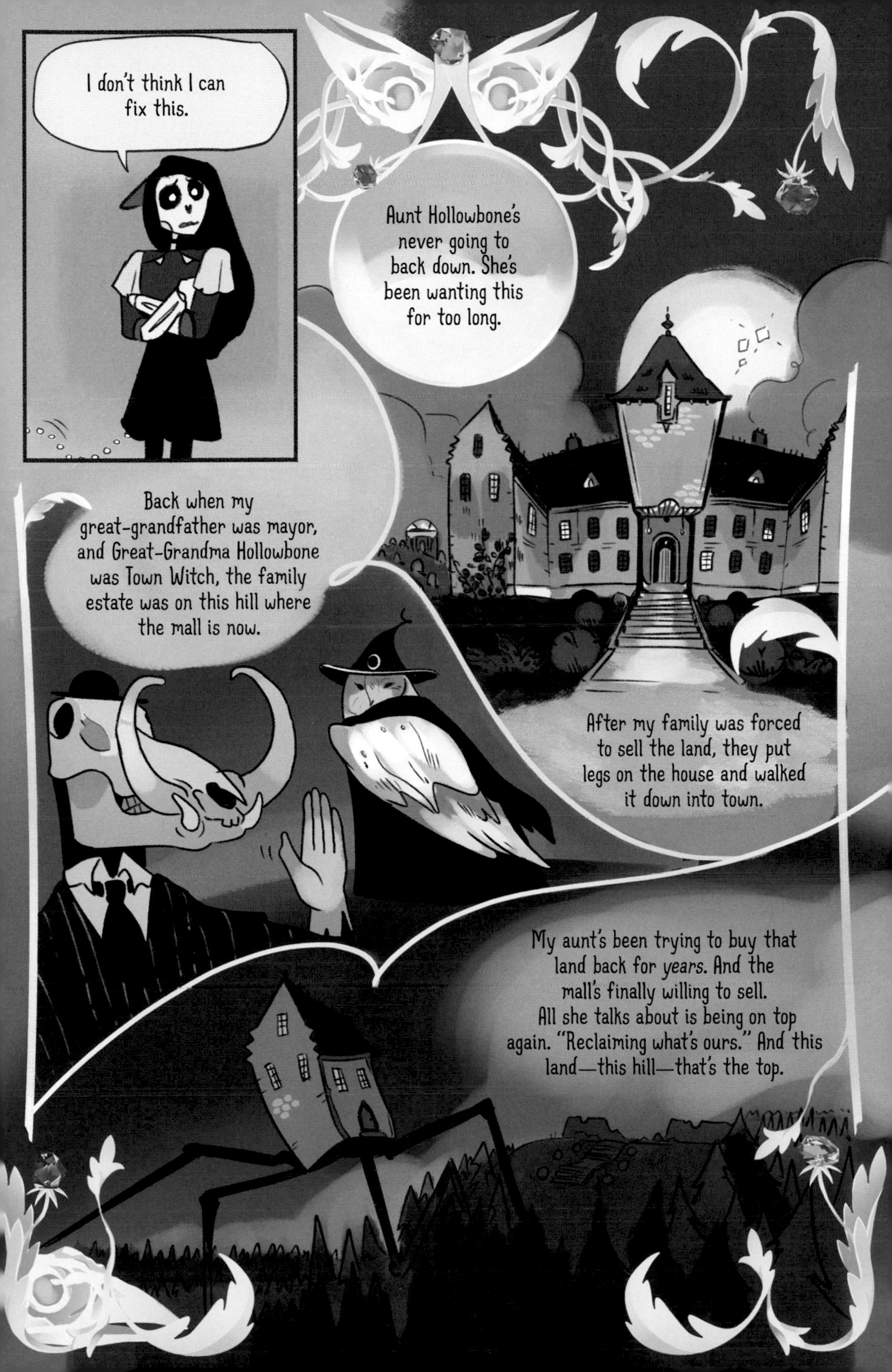
I don't think I can fix this.
Aunt Hollowbone's never going to back down. She's been wanting this for too long.
Back when my great-grandfather was mayor, and Great-Grandma Hollowbone was Town Witch, the family estate was on this hill where the mall is now.
After my family was forced to sell the land, they put legs on the house and walked it down into town.
My aunt's been trying to buy that land back for *years*. And the mall's finally willing to sell. All she talks about is being on top again. "Reclaiming what's ours." And this land—this hill—that's the top.

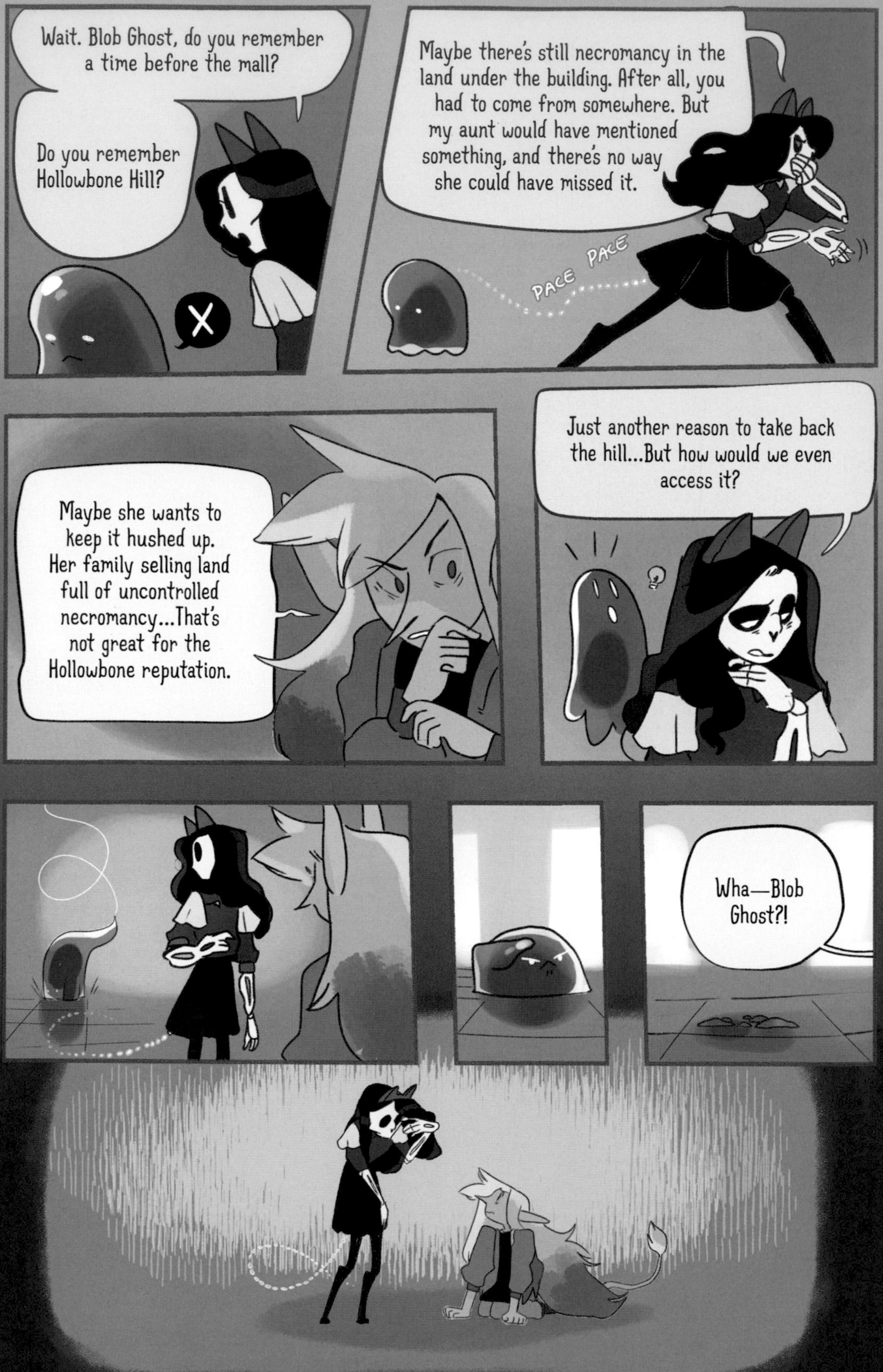
Wait. Blob Ghost, do you remember a time before the mall?
Do you remember Hollowbone Hill?
X
Maybe there's still necromancy in the land under the building. After all, you had to come from somewhere. But my aunt would have mentioned something, and there's no way she could have missed it.
PACE PACE
Maybe she wants to keep it hushed up. Her family selling land full of uncontrolled necromancy...That's not great for the Hollowbone reputation.
Just another reason to take back the hill...But how would we even access it?
Wha—Blob Ghost?!

The Undermall

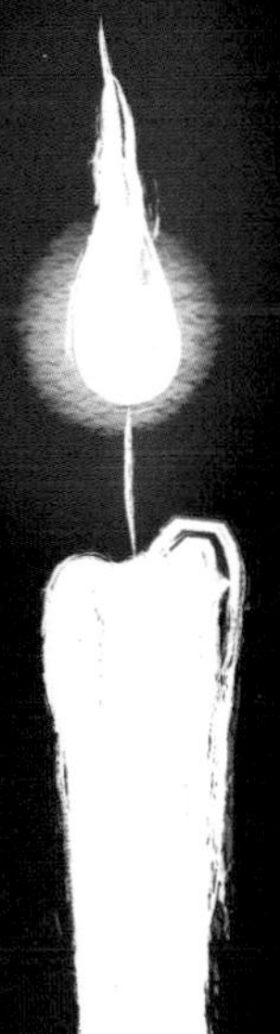

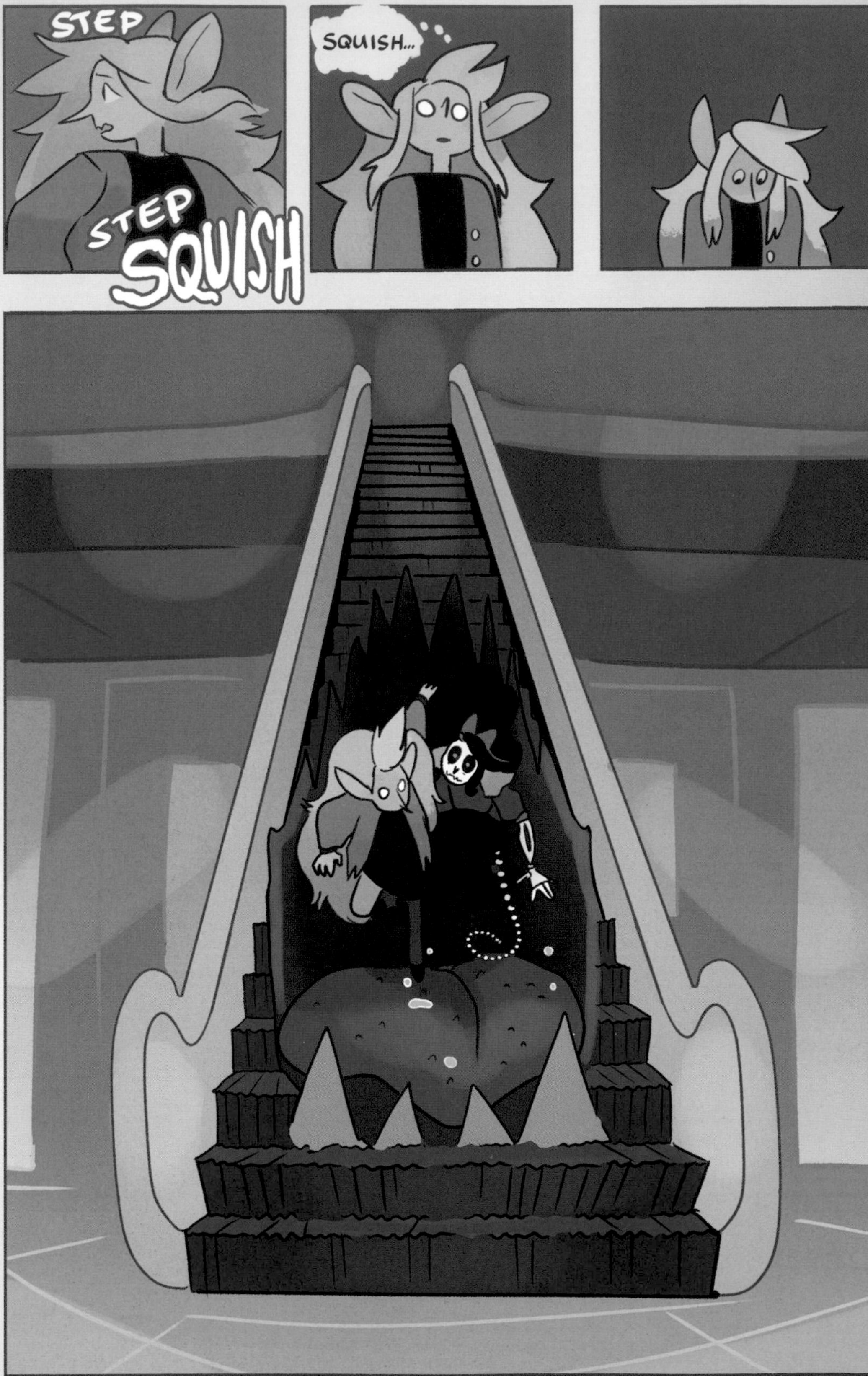
STEP
STEP
SQUISH
SQUISH...

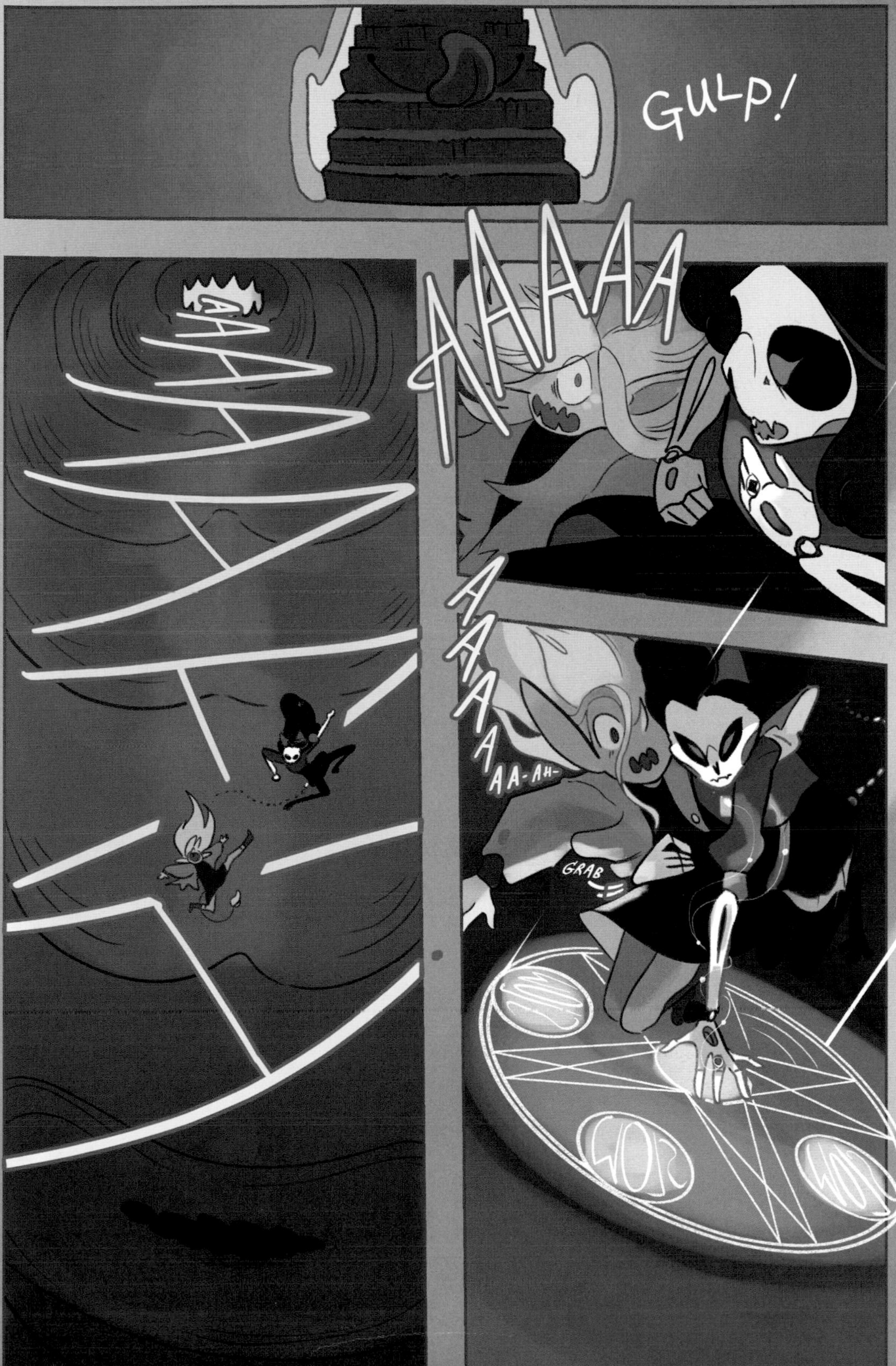
GULP!
AAAAA
AAAAAAA-AH-
GRAB

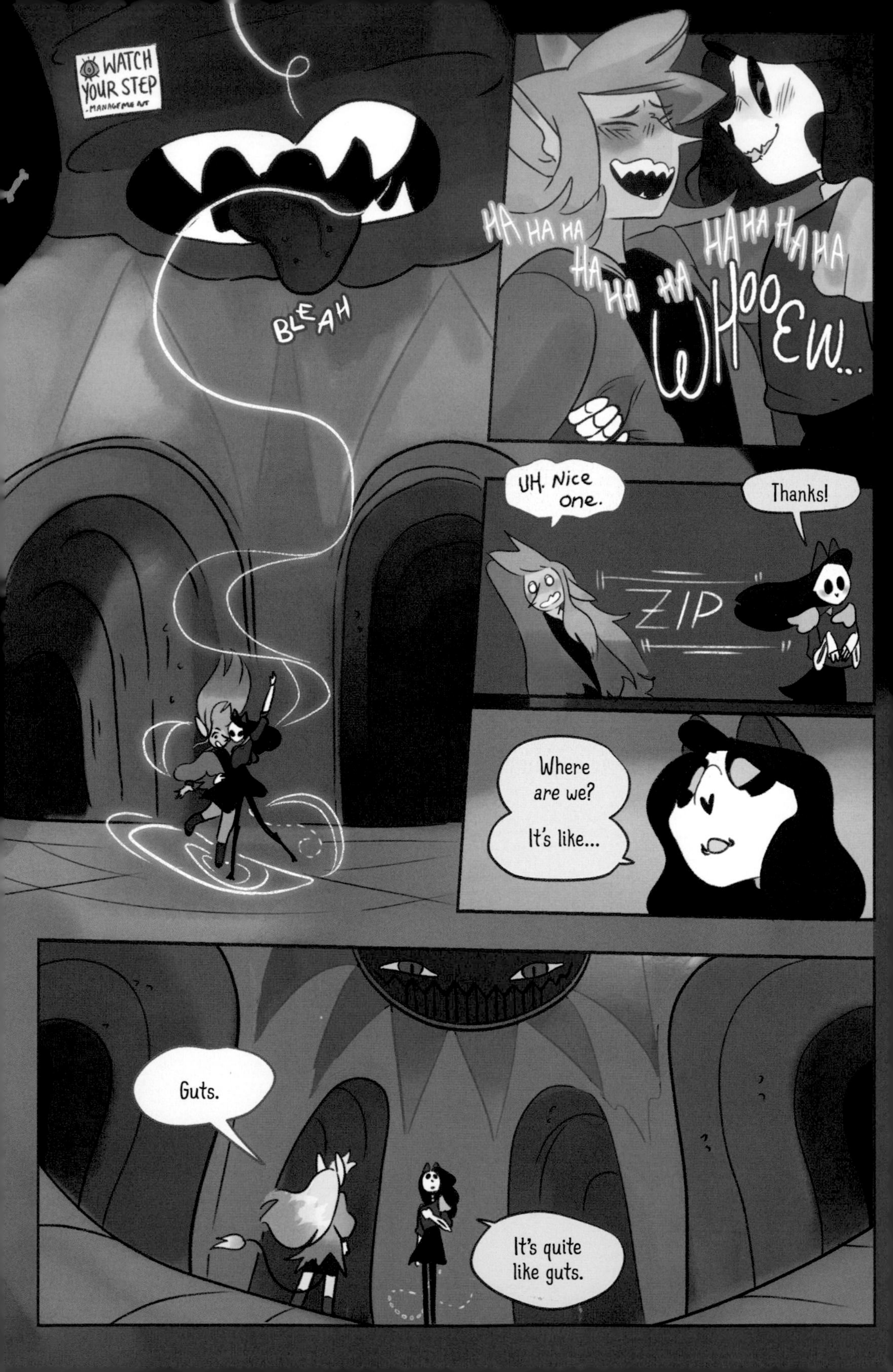

WATCH YOUR STEP
-MANAGEMENT
BLEAH
HA HA HA HA HA HA HA HA HA HA HA HA
WHOOEW...
UH. Nice one.
Thanks!
ZIP
Where are we?
It's like...
Guts.
It's quite like guts.

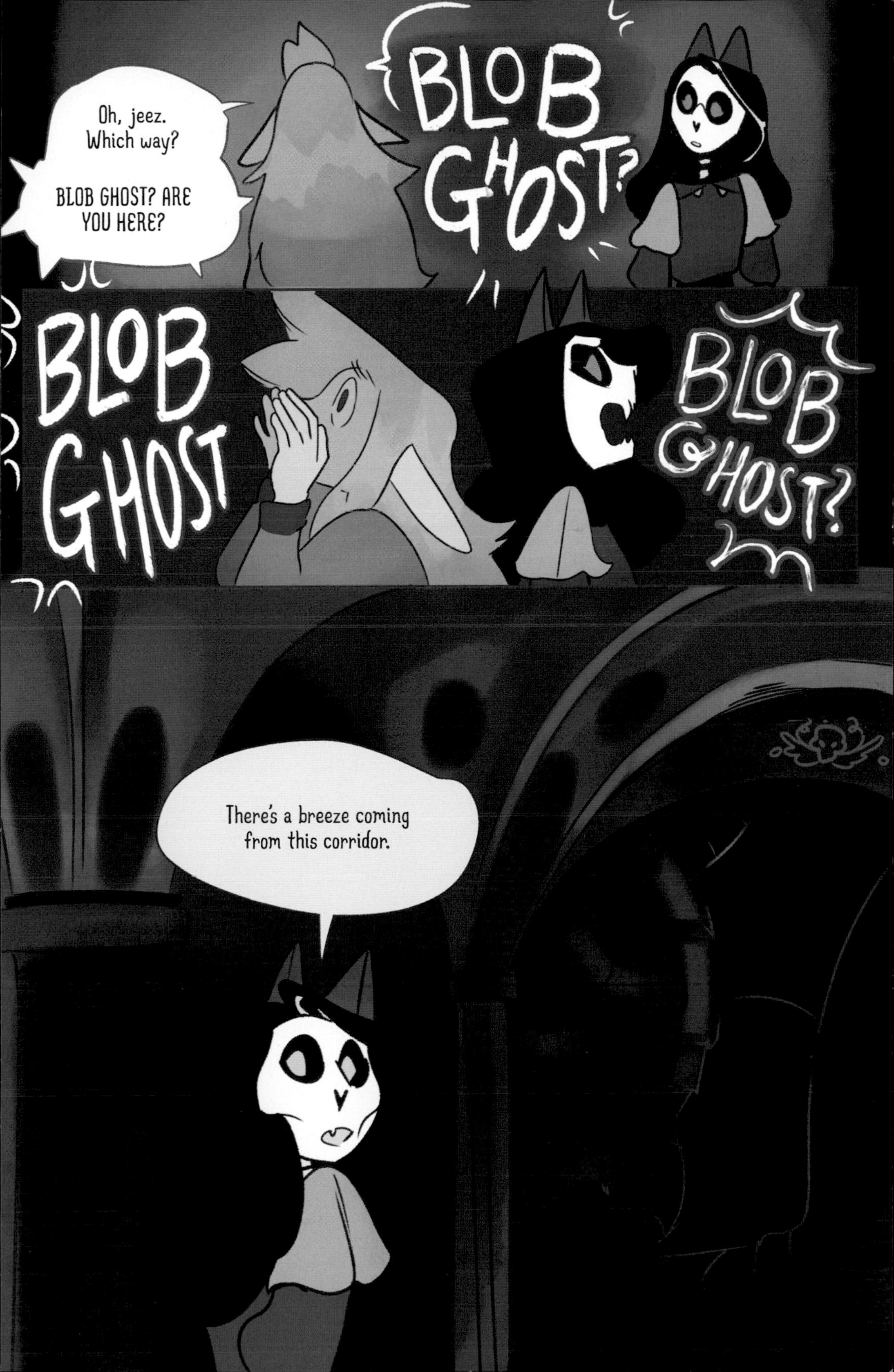
Oh, jeez.
Which way?
BLOB GHOST? ARE YOU HERE?
BLOB GHOST?
BLOB GHOST
BLOB GHOST?
There's a breeze coming from this corridor.

It's like a dungeon.

I don't know. It looks...

I meant like a light spell.

Um, I don't have a crystal, remember?

Oh.

Oh, um, it's my heart.

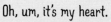

Oh, I didn't bring a flashlight.

Hey, I could use some light.

Okay—I can do it. I'm just not supposed to use too much magic, is all.

What's that?

All undead creatures have their souls bound to an object: our hearts.

That's why undead kids grow into adults. And if you're an undead witch, it's your magical core.

The necromancy inside my locket keeps me alive.

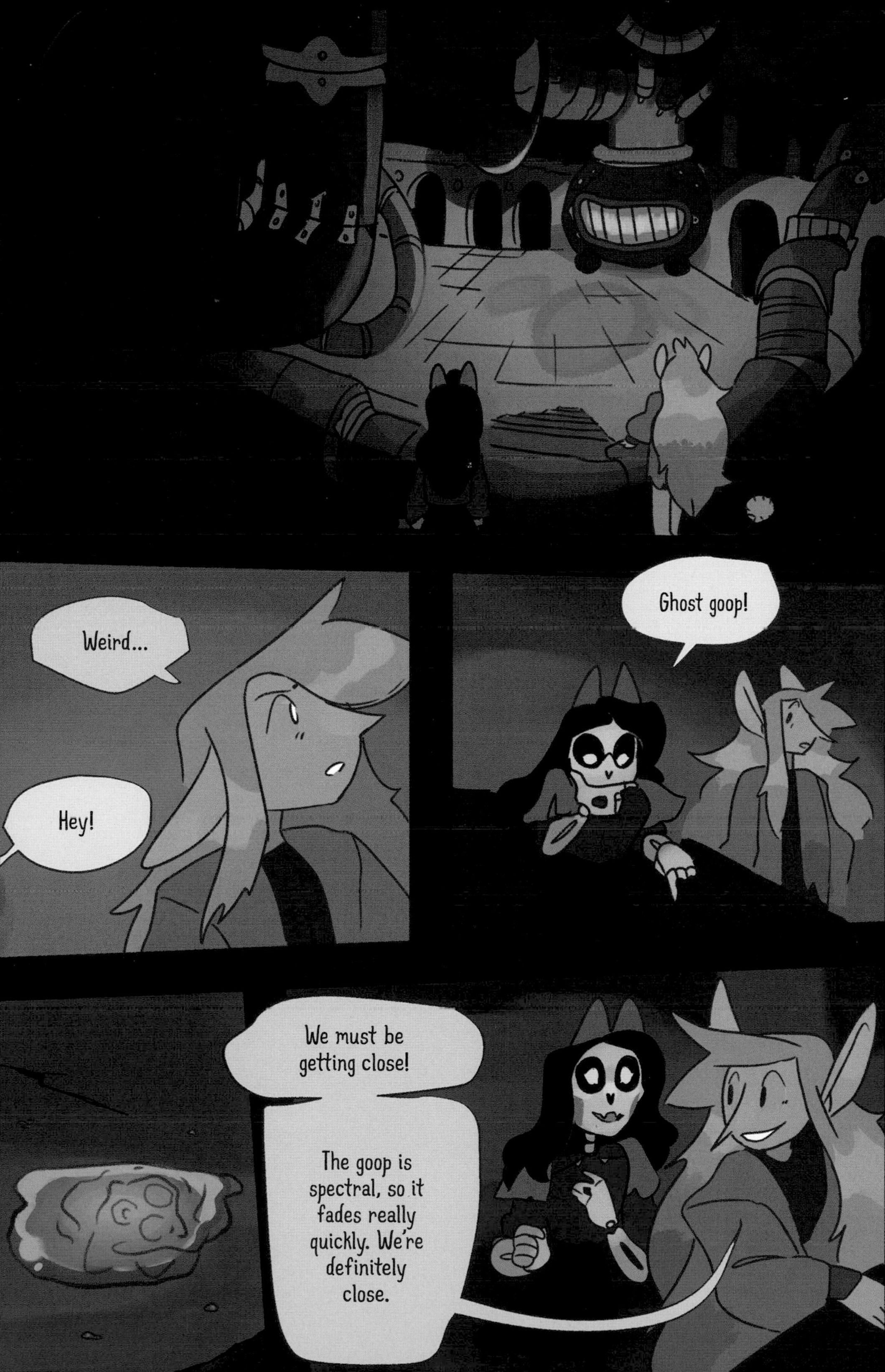
Weird...
Hey!
Ghost goop!
We must be getting close!
The goop is spectral, so it fades really quickly. We're definitely close.

BLOB GHOST?

BLOB GHOST!

Why can't they hear us? They should be really close.

We'll keep going until we find them.

Okay.

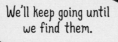

...

Hey.

I'm sorry that I didn't text you very much while I was gone. I was really busy at Sarcophaga.

It's fine.

I bet everyone was really cool.

Hmm
Hmm...
HM?
THUD
THUD THUD SKITTER SKITTER
HSS
PUSH
HESTER
CUSTODIAN
Now, what are you kids doin' down *here*?

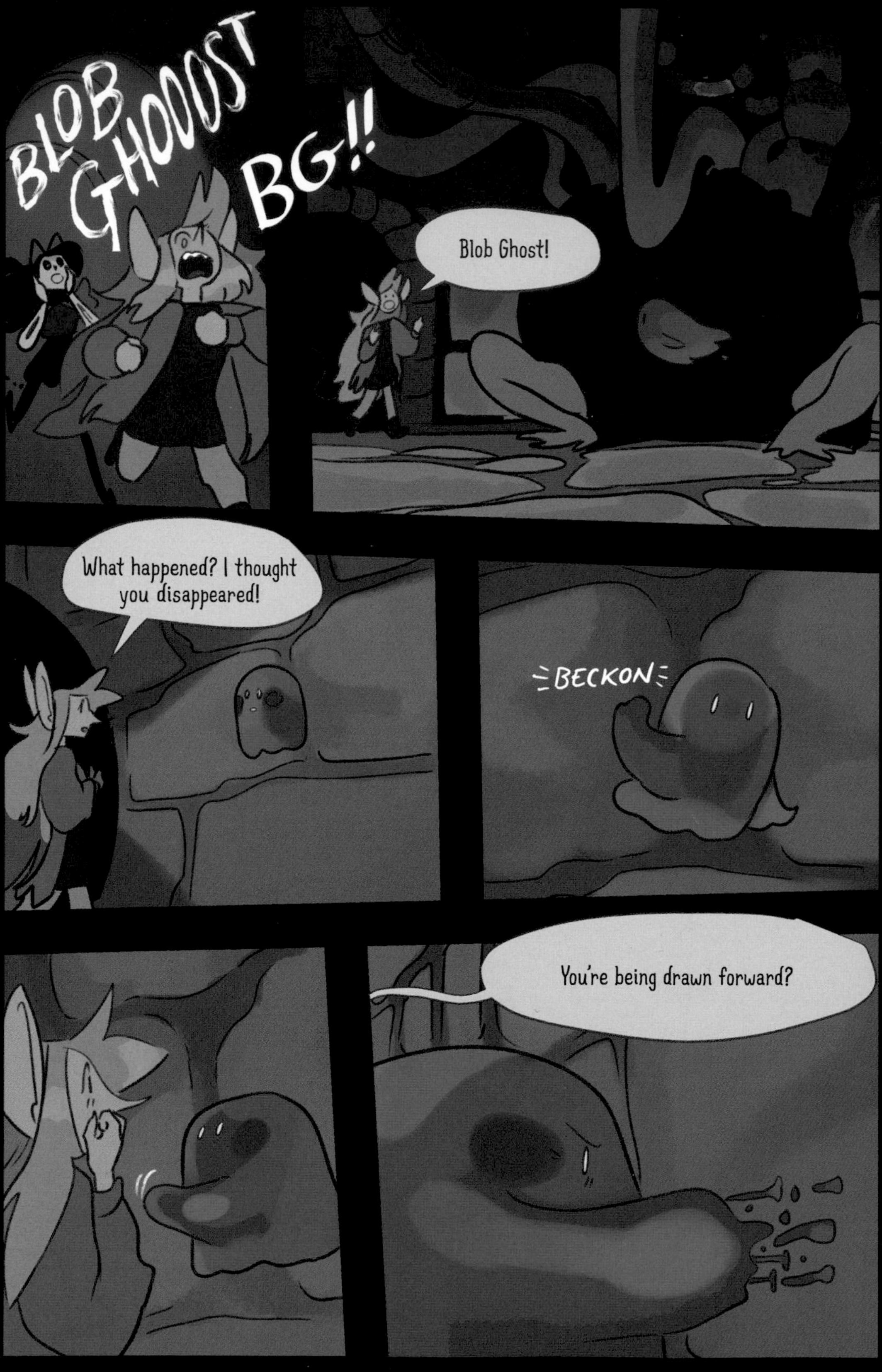

BLOB GHOOOST
BG!!
Blob Ghost!
What happened? I thought you disappeared!
BECKON
You're being drawn forward?

It's something behind this wall. Why don't you just go through?

Water. This must be the plumbing system for something in the mall. Why would you be pulled toward *that?* Can you even go in water?

WHOOSH

Nobody's going to make you go in there, okay? You're not gonna dissolve.

It feels like necromancy, but...I'm not sensing anything out of the ordinary. It just feels like the magic that holds any undead person together, although I could be getting a false positive off of Blob Ghost.

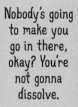

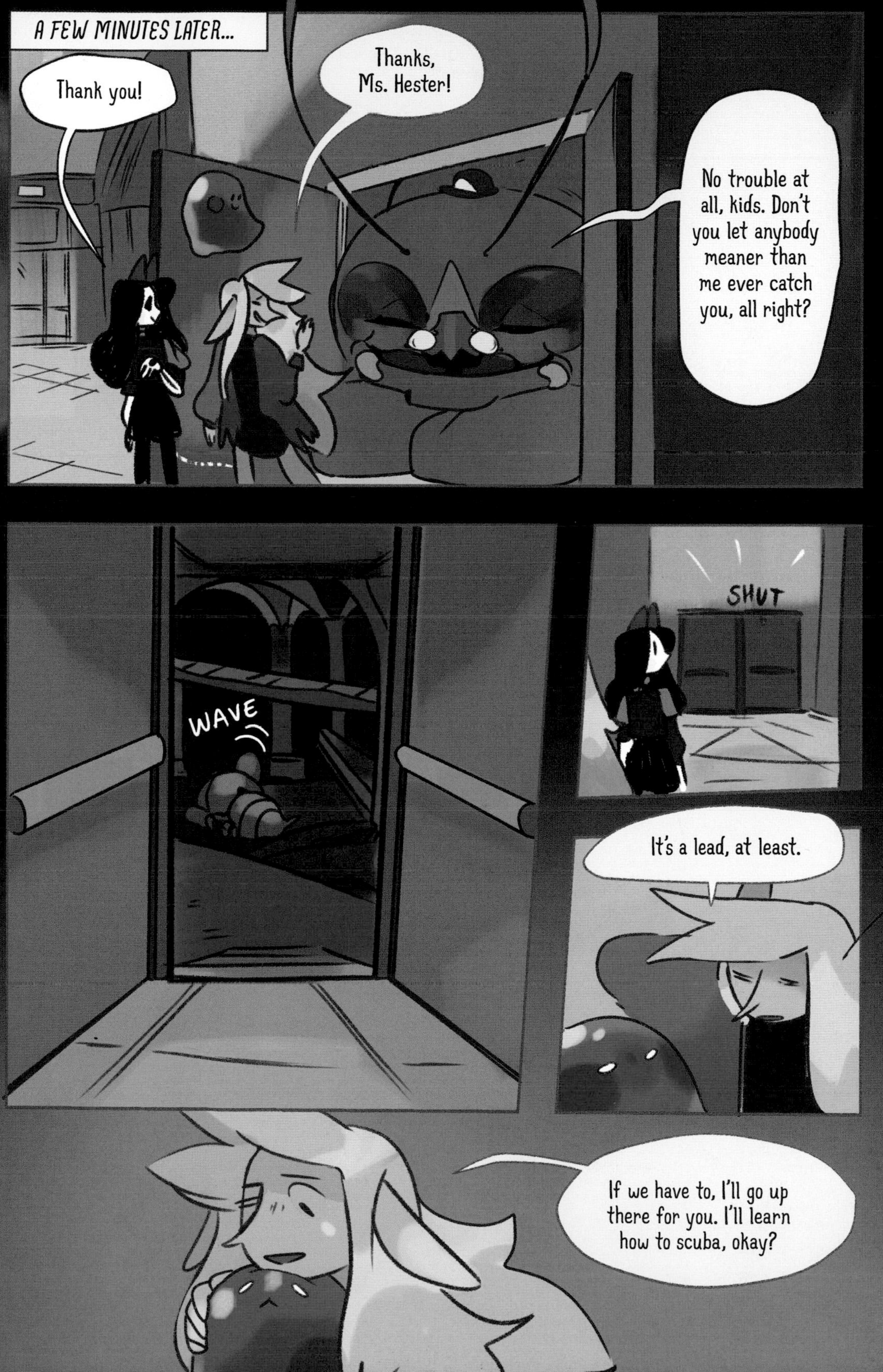

A FEW MINUTES LATER...
Thank you!
Thanks, Ms. Hester!
No trouble at all, kids. Don't you let anybody meaner than me ever catch you, all right?
WAVE
SHUT
It's a lead, at least.
If we have to, I'll go up there for you. I'll learn how to scuba, okay?

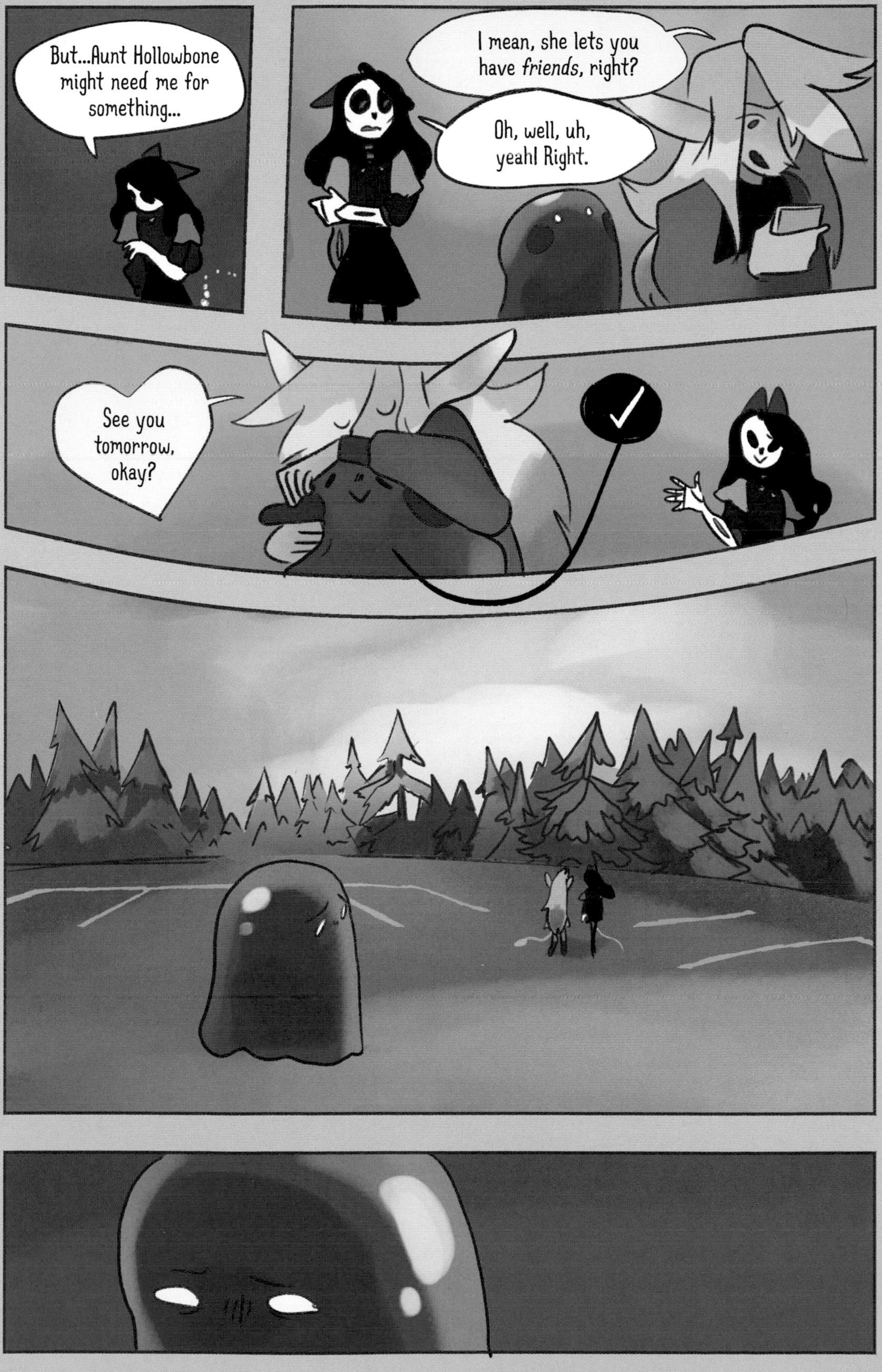
But...Aunt Hollowbone might need me for something...
I mean, she lets you have *friends*, right?
Oh, well, uh, yeah! Right.
See you tomorrow, okay?

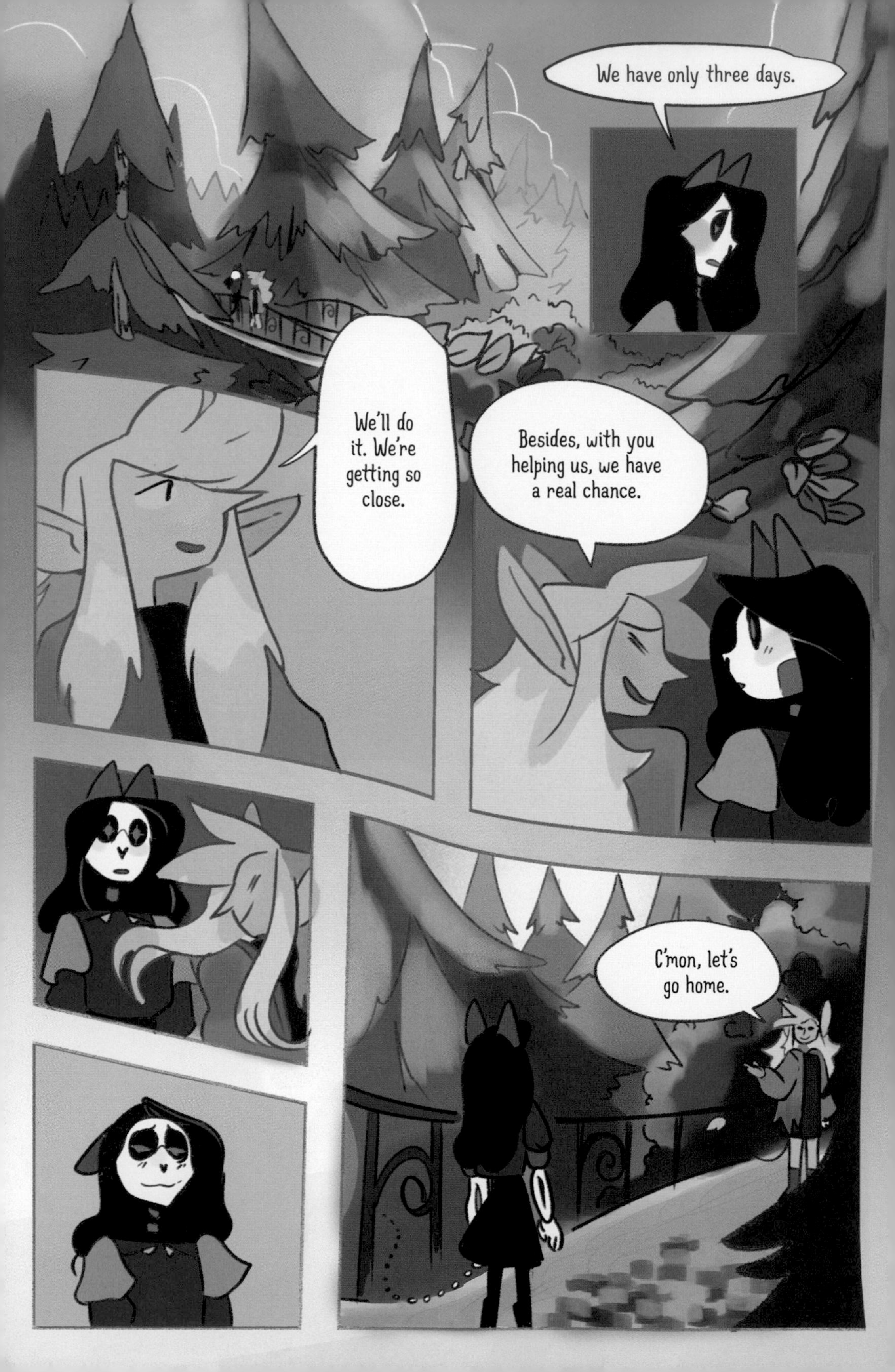
We have only three days.
We'll do it. We're getting so close.
Besides, with you helping us, we have a real chance.
C'mon, let's go home.

WHAT WE WROTE

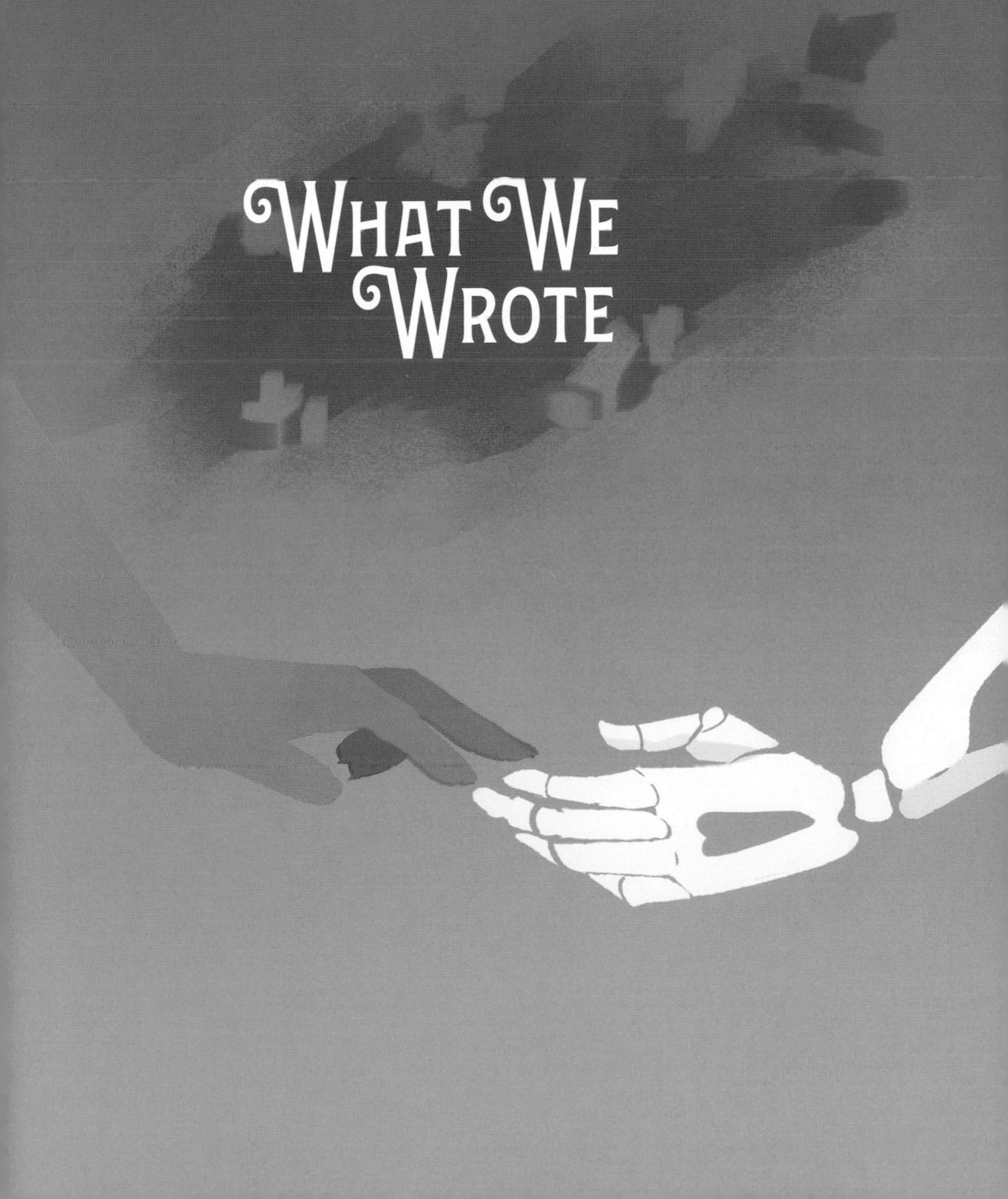

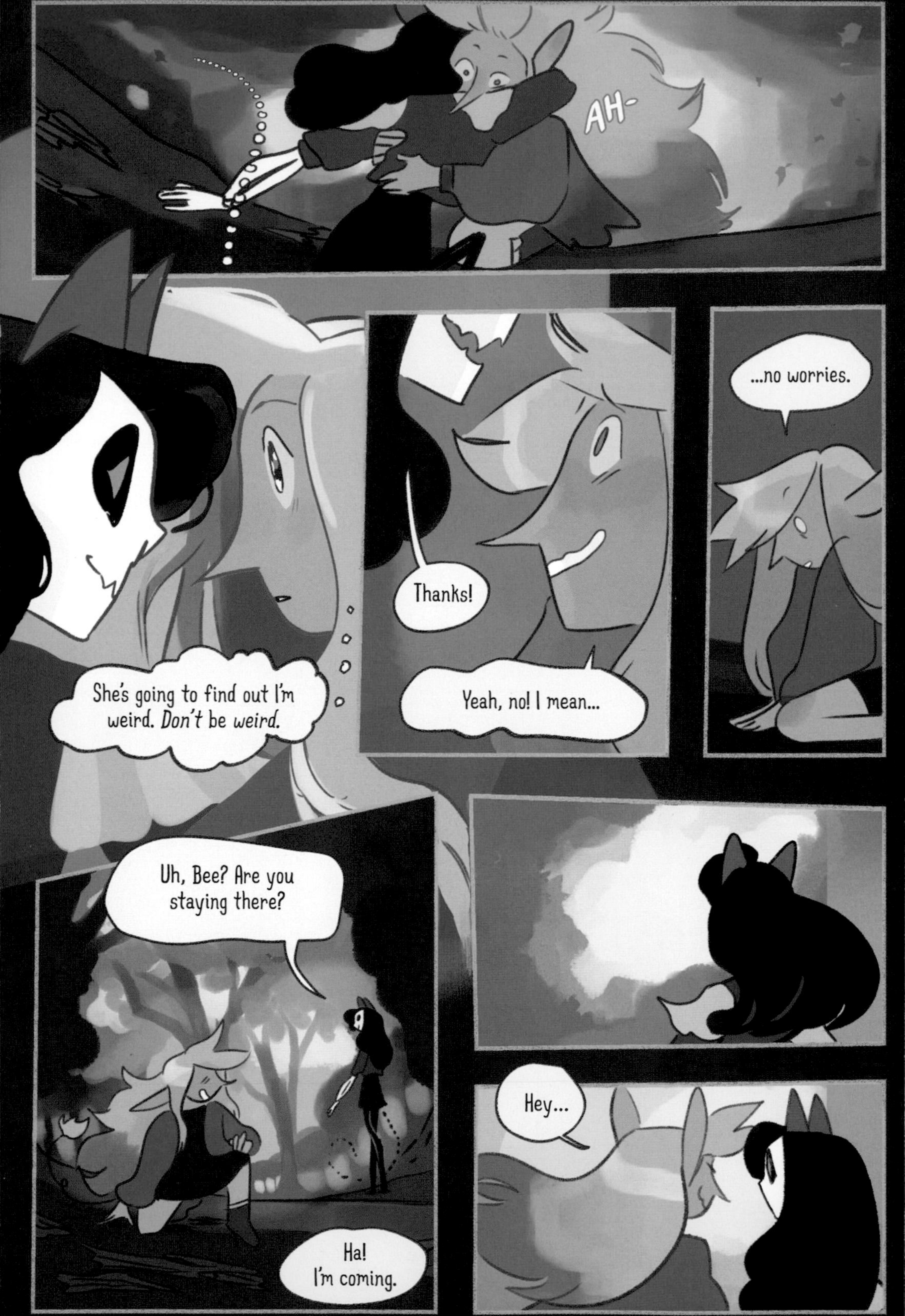
AH-
She's going to find out I'm weird. *Don't be weird.*
Thanks!
Yeah, no! I mean...
...no worries.
Uh, Bee? Are you staying there?
Ha! I'm coming.
Hey...

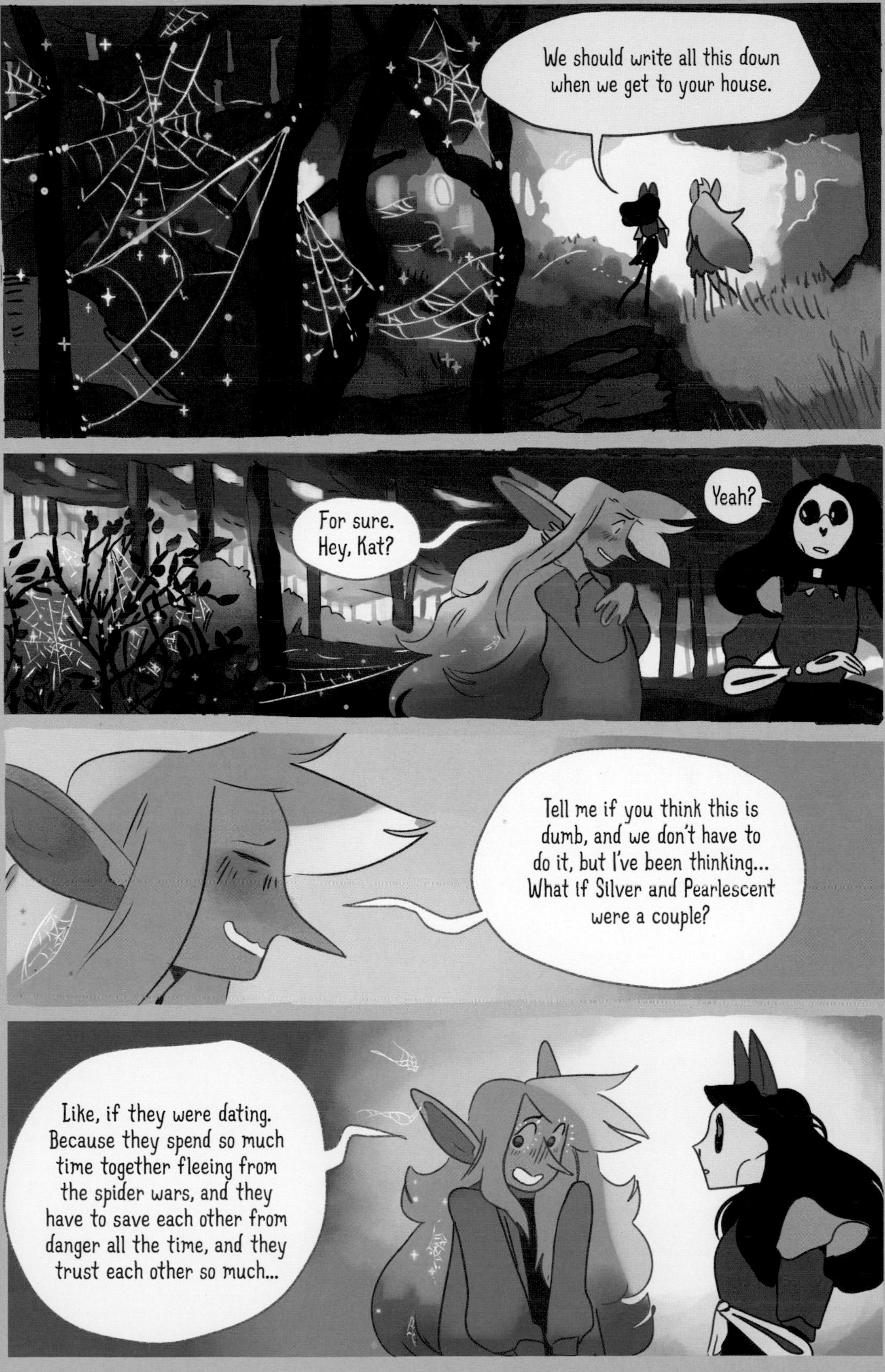
We should write all this down when we get to your house.
For sure. Hey, Kat?
Yeah?
Tell me if you think this is dumb, and we don't have to do it, but I've been thinking... What if Silver and Pearlescent were a couple?
Like, if they were dating. Because they spend so much time together fleeing from the spider wars, and they have to save each other from danger all the time, and they trust each other so much...

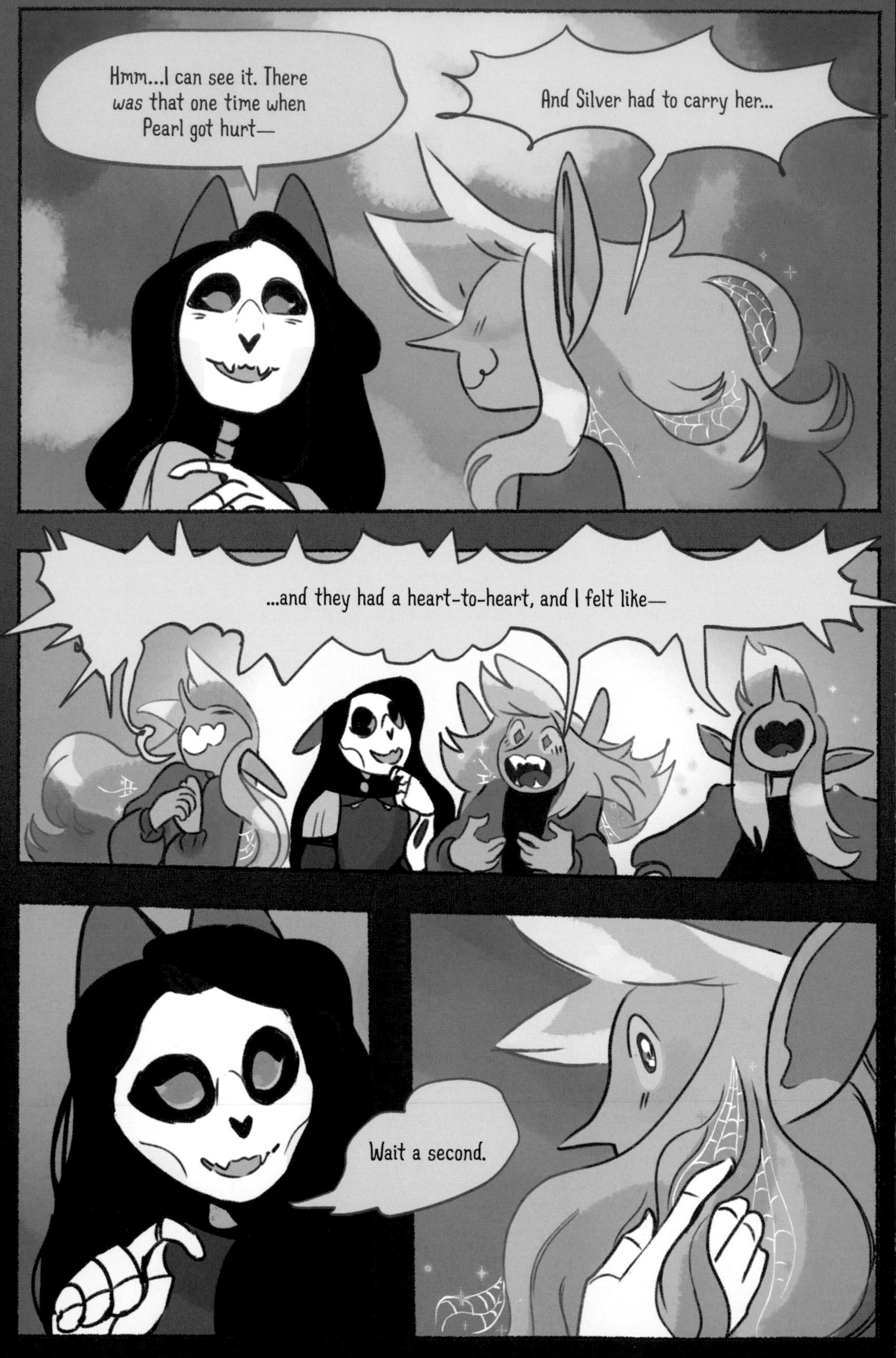
Hmm...I can see it. There *was* that one time when Pearl got hurt—
And Silver had to carry her...
...and they had a heart-to-heart, and I felt like—
Wait a second.

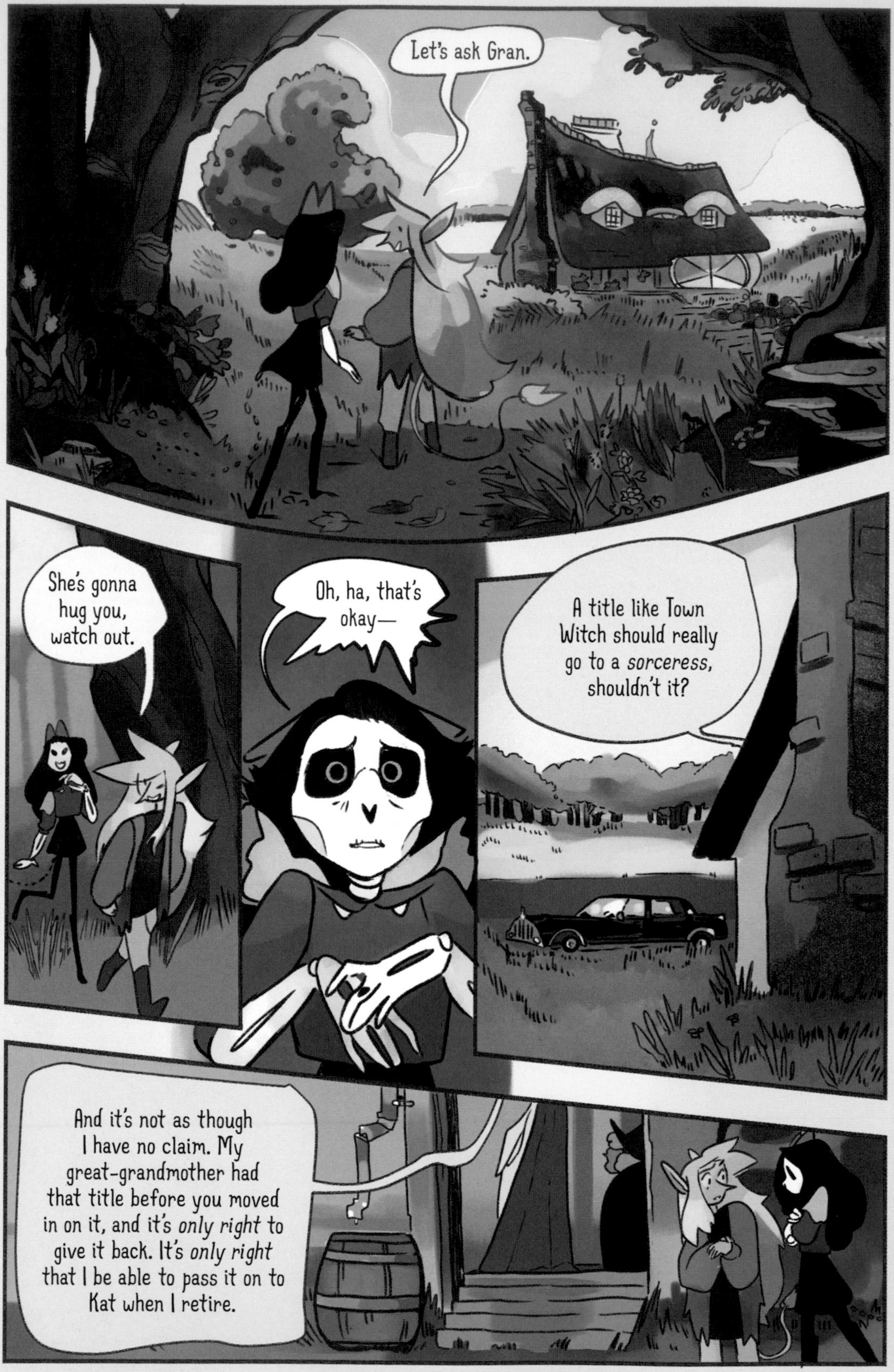
Let's ask Gran.
She's gonna hug you, watch out.
Oh, ha, that's okay—
A title like Town Witch should really go to a *sorceress*, shouldn't it?
And it's not as though I have no claim. My great-grandmother had that title before you moved in on it, and it's *only right* to give it back. It's *only right* that I be able to pass it on to Kat when I retire.

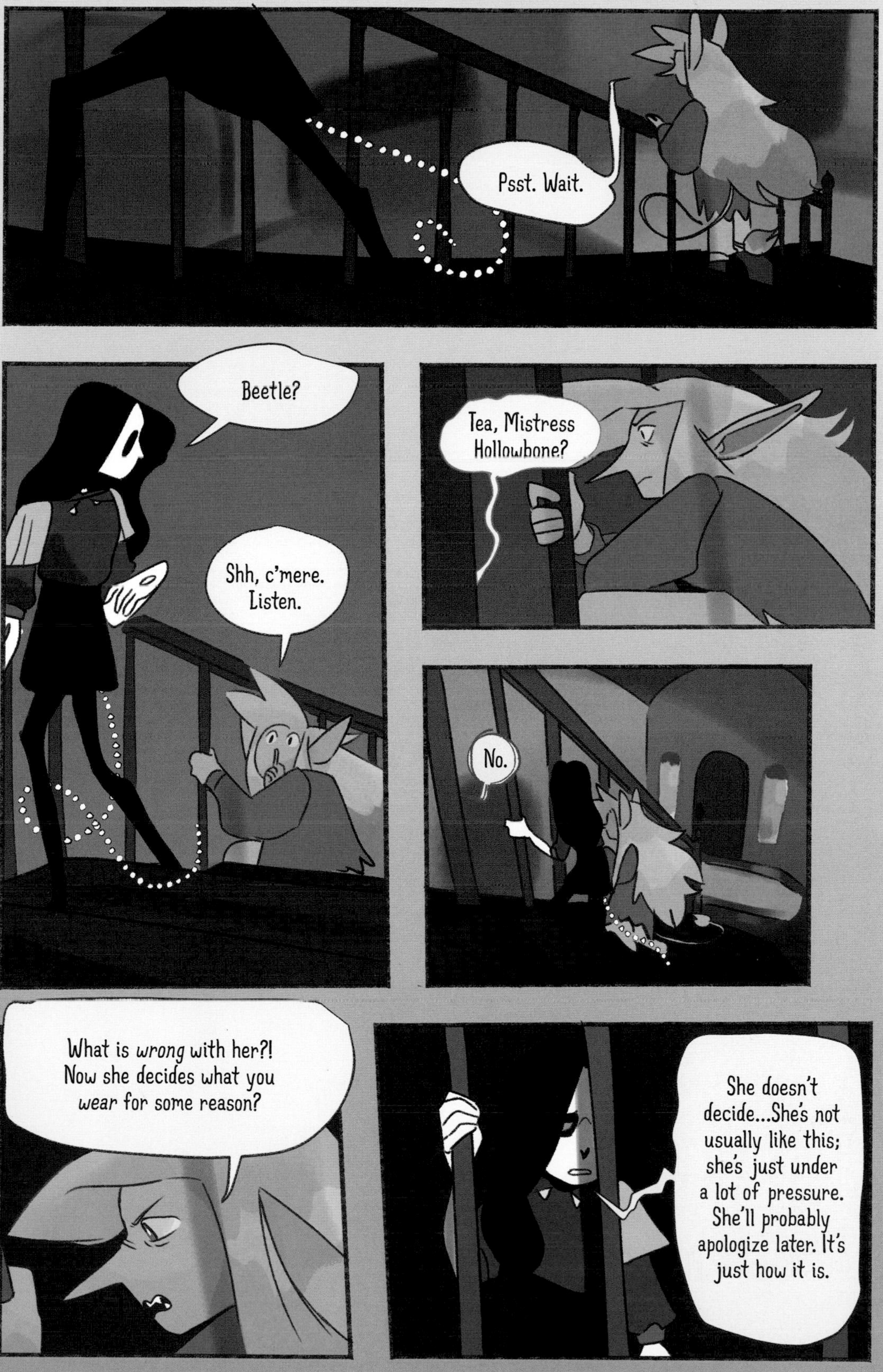
Psst. Wait.
Beetle?
Shh, c'mere. Listen.
Tea, Mistress Hollowbone?
No.
What is *wrong* with her?! Now she decides what you *wear* for some reason?
She doesn't decide...She's not usually like this; she's just under a lot of pressure. She'll probably apologize later. It's just how it is.

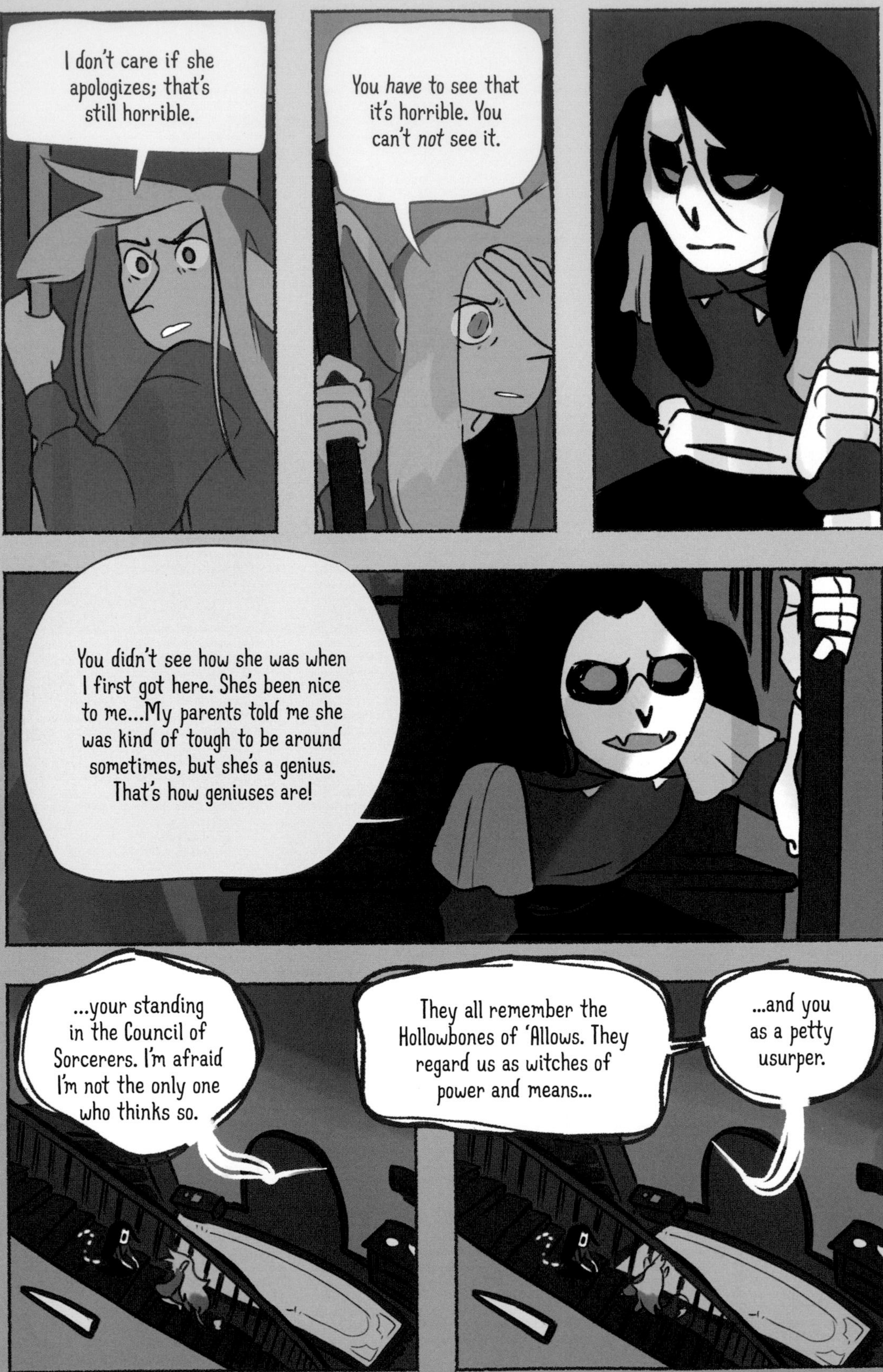
I don't care if she apologizes; that's still horrible.
You *have* to see that it's horrible. You can't *not* see it.
You didn't see how she was when I first got here. She's been nice to me...My parents told me she was kind of tough to be around sometimes, but she's a genius. That's how geniuses are!
...your standing in the Council of Sorcerers. I'm afraid I'm not the only one who thinks so.
They all remember the Hollowbones of 'Allows. They regard us as witches of power and means...
...and you as a petty usurper.

It's a surprise, I must say. I hardly thought the council would take notice, much less form opinons, of a little goblin like me.

Exactly. You'd be happier out in a swamp somewhere, I'm sure.

WHO DOES SHE THINK SHE IS!

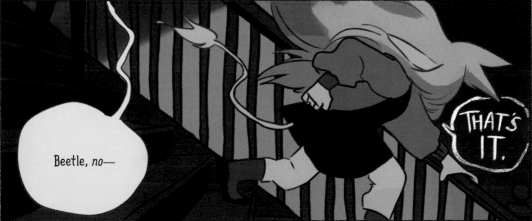

Beetle, no—

THAT'S IT.

That's the kind of witch you want to be? And it's worth being treated like you're *nothing*?
Maybe to *you* it wouldn't be worth it.
Your family doesn't *expect* anything of you. Mine expects me to be perfect.
And to...
...NEVER...
...lose.
So don't lecture me about what a witch is like *you'd* know.

You don't need her. My gran would treat you like you MATTER, and she's way more powerful than your aunt. Just because your stupid parents might not like it—
Ha.
I'm sure I can take *your* word for it.
Your grandmother is *powerful*? Okay. Sure. She's not sending you to school. You have no real witches to compare her to, but sure. So, what's she teaching you?
Can you actually *do* any magic? Because I can, and here's *my* advice: this pretend playing is *ridiculous*.
I don't know *what* you think you're doing, but you're certainly not a *witch*.

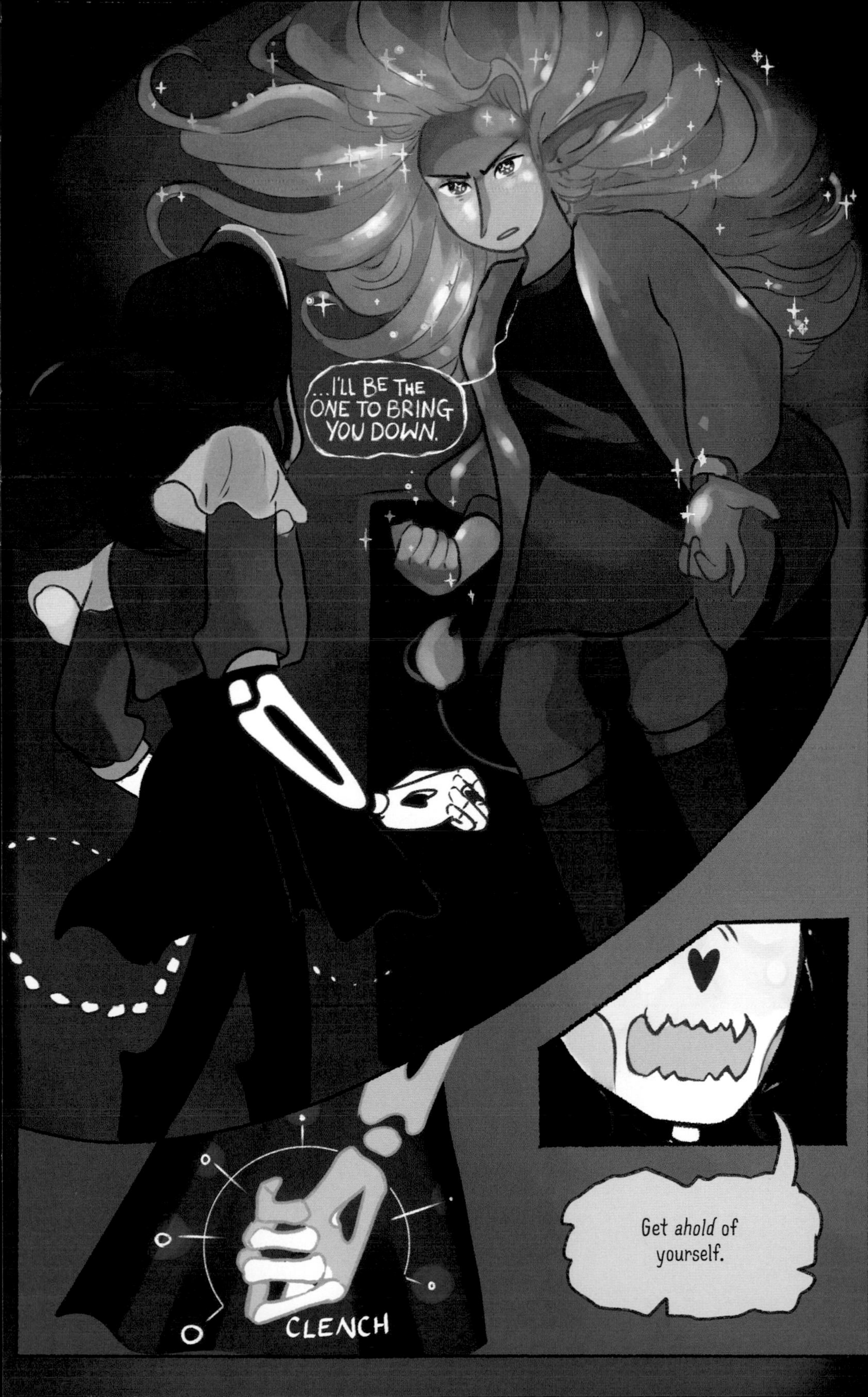
...I'LL BE THE ONE TO BRING YOU DOWN.
Get ahold of yourself.
CLENCH

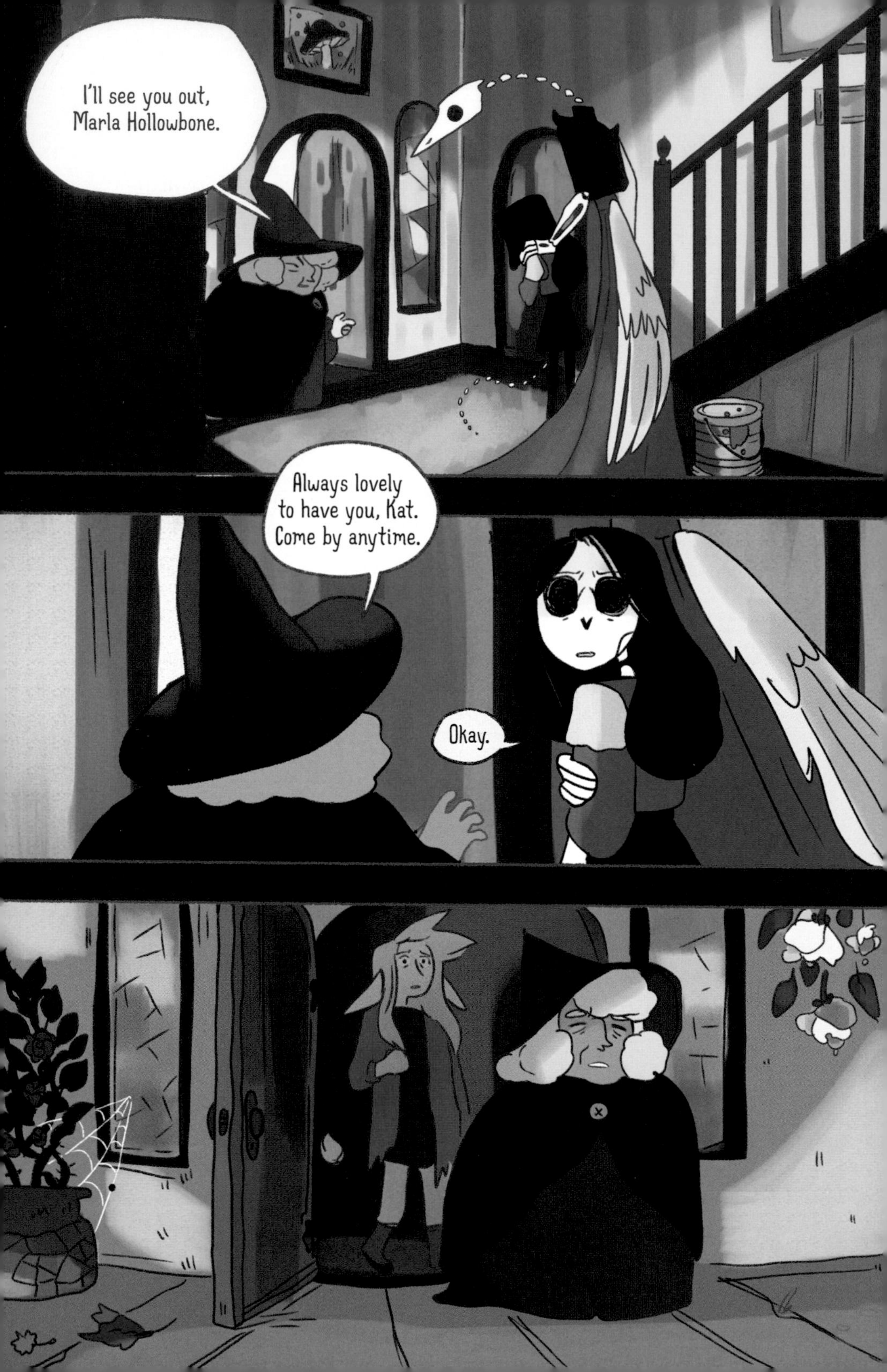
I'll see you out, Marla Hollowbone.
Always lovely to have you, Kat. Come by anytime.
Okay.

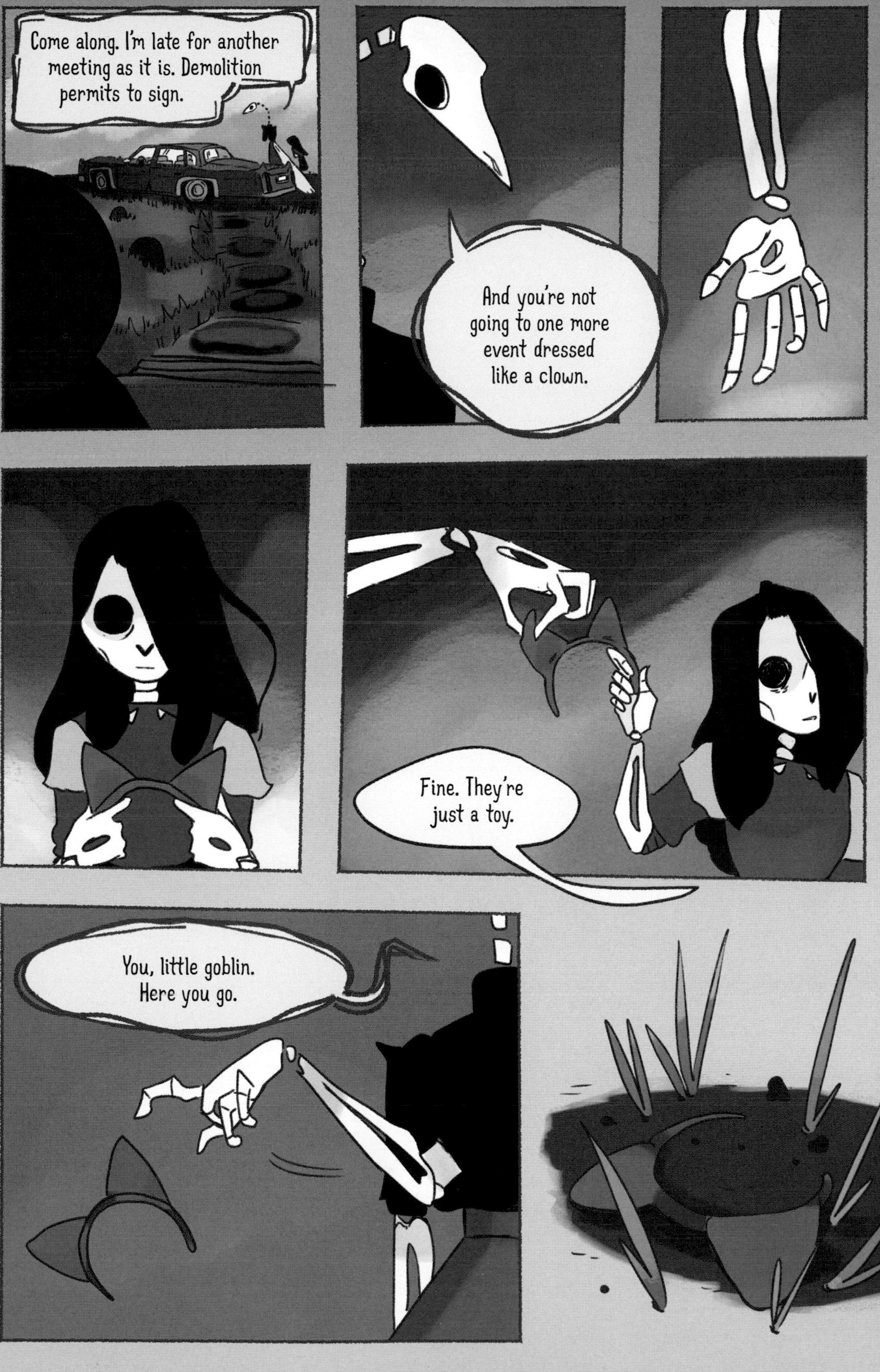
Come along. I'm late for another meeting as it is. Demolition permits to sign.
And you're not going to one more event dressed like a clown.
Fine. They're just a toy.
You, little goblin. Here you go.

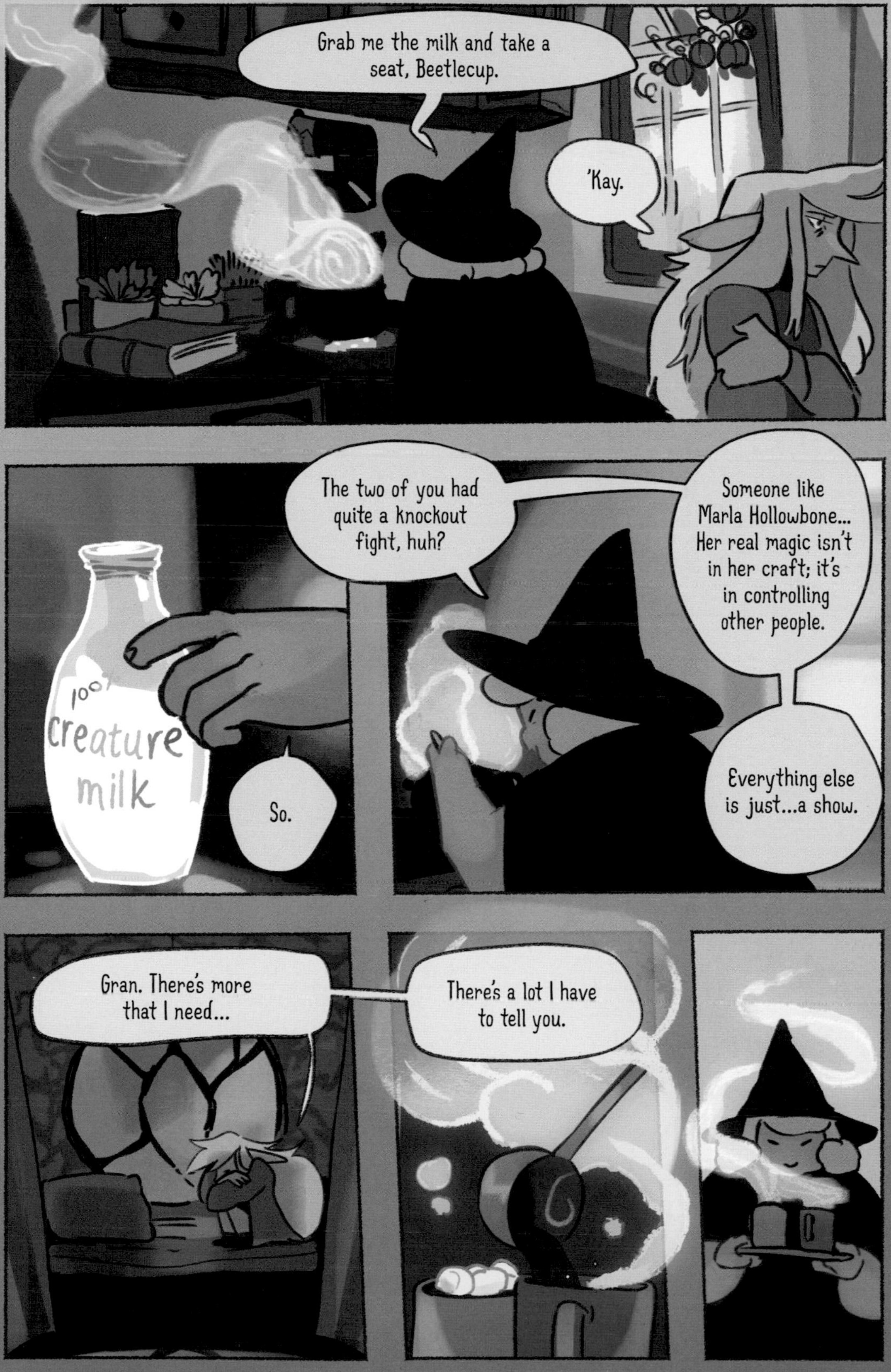
Grab me the milk and take a seat, Beetlecup.
'Kay.
The two of you had quite a knockout fight, huh?
100% creature milk
So.
Someone like Marla Hollowbone... Her real magic isn't in her craft; it's in controlling other people.
Everything else is just...a show.
Gran. There's more that I need...
There's a lot I have to tell you.

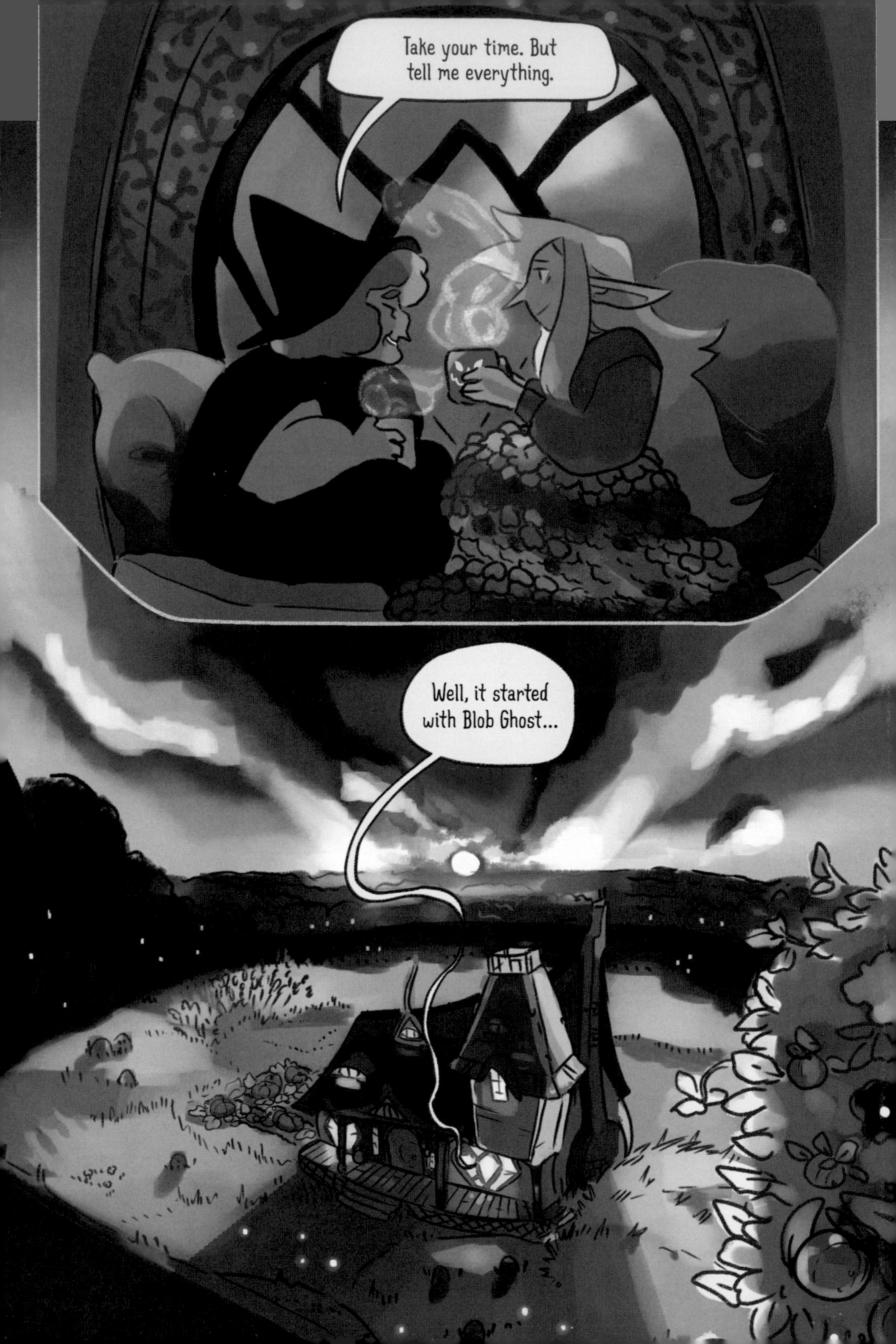
Take your time. But tell me everything.
Well, it started with Blob Ghost...

THE JAR

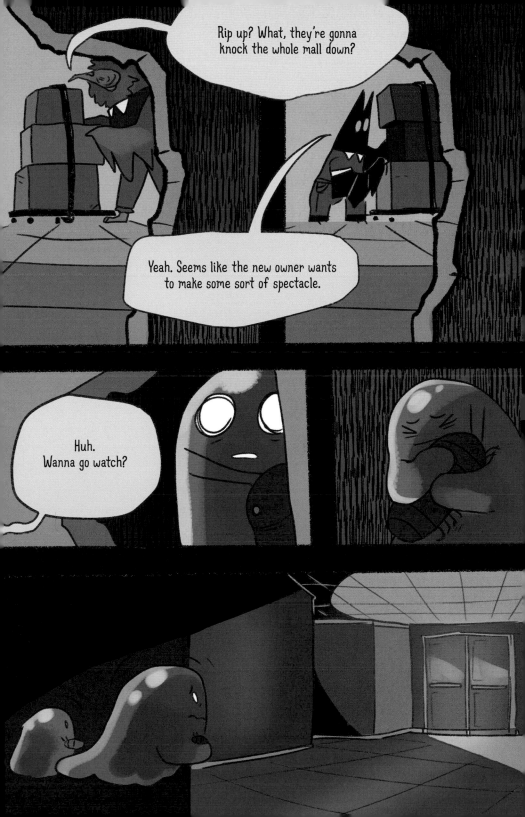

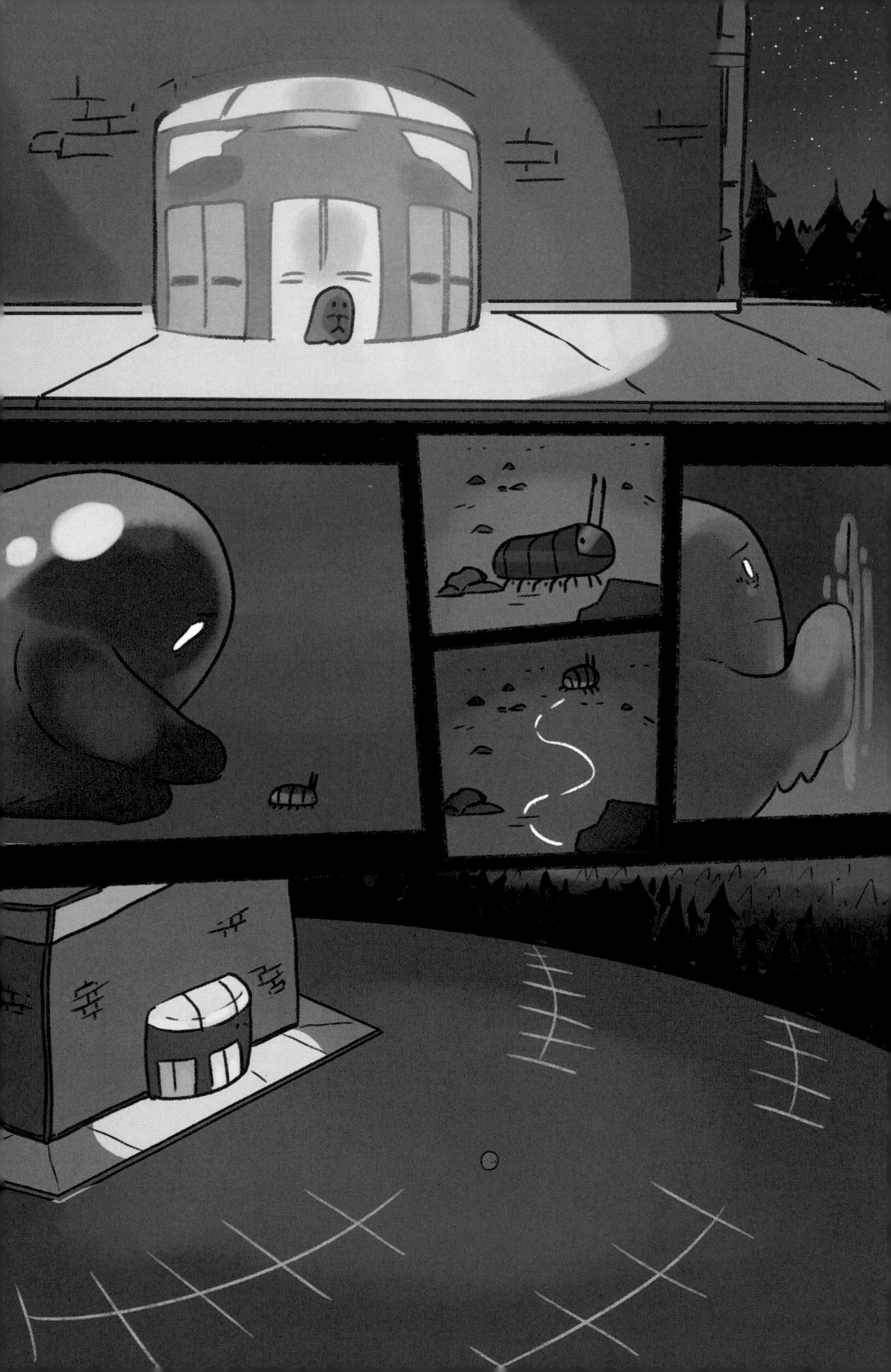

SORCERY

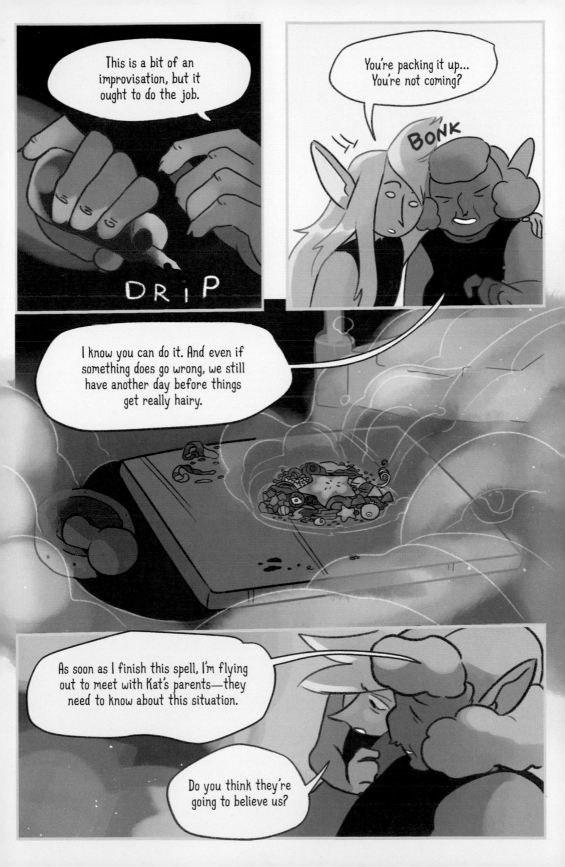

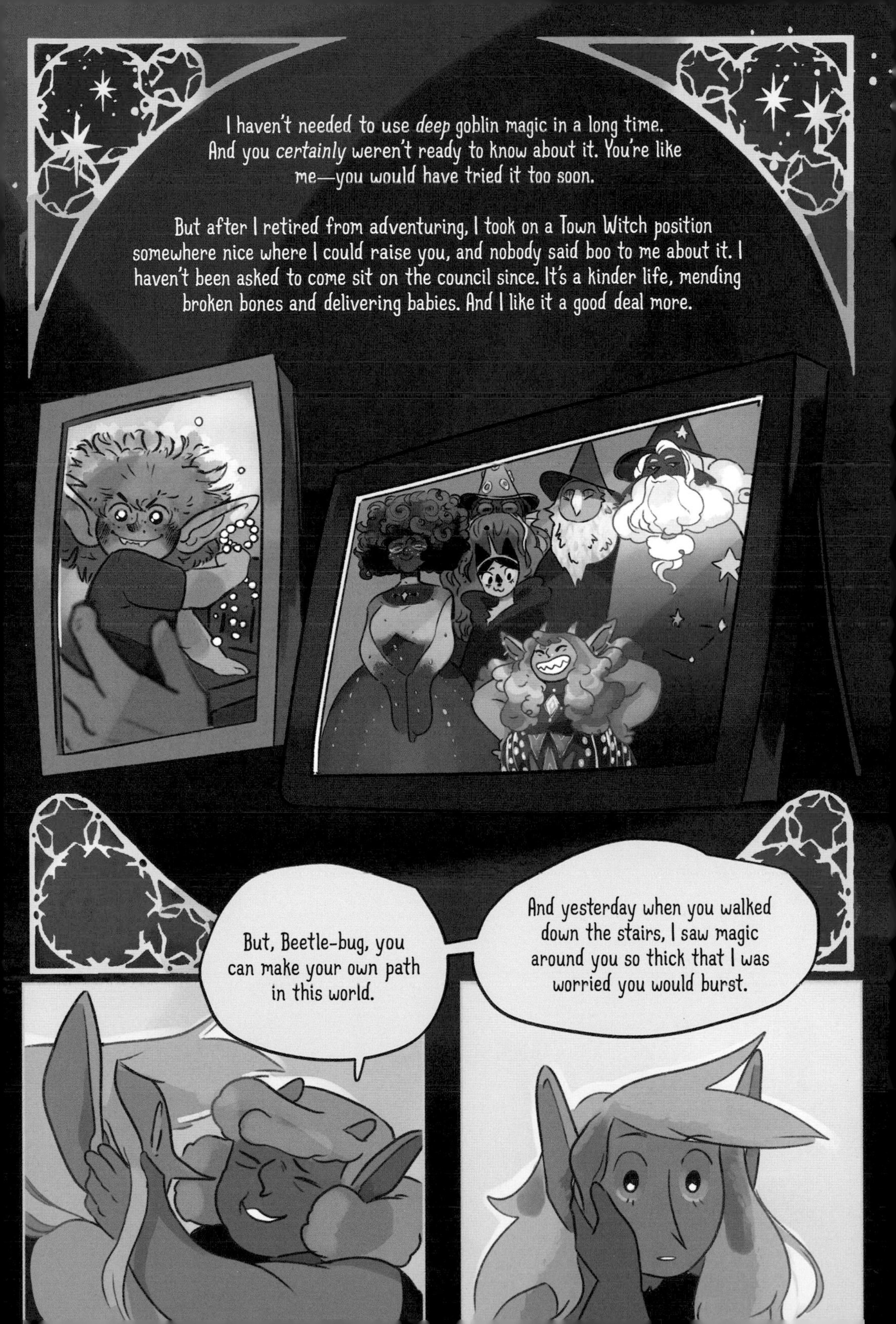
I haven't needed to use *deep* goblin magic in a long time. And you *certainly* weren't ready to know about it. You're like me—you would have tried it too soon.
But after I retired from adventuring, I took on a Town Witch position somewhere nice where I could raise you, and nobody said boo to me about it. I haven't been asked to come sit on the council since. It's a kinder life, mending broken bones and delivering babies. And I like it a good deal more.
But, Beetle-bug, you can make your own path in this world.
And yesterday when you walked down the stairs, I saw magic around you so thick that I was worried you would burst.

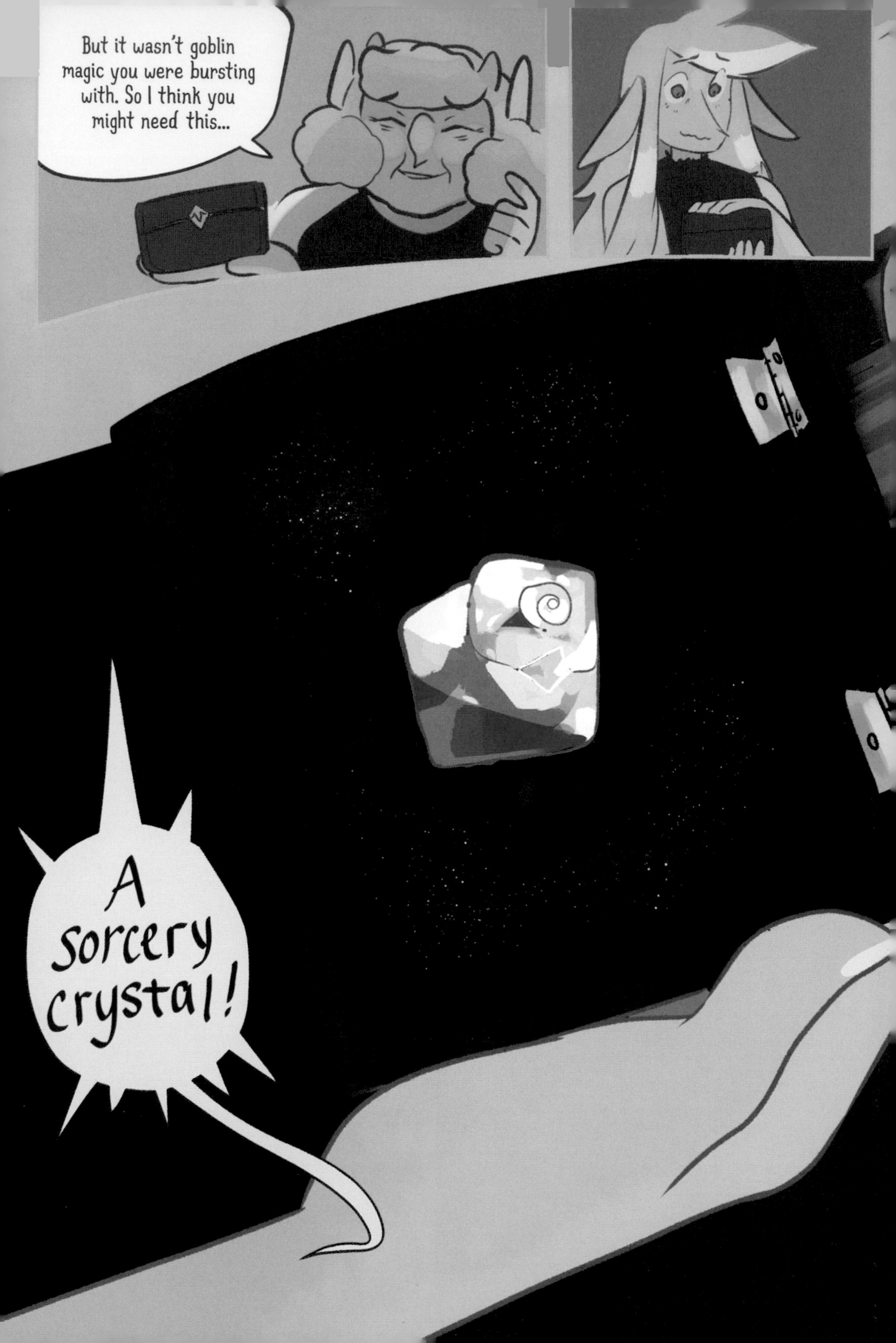
But it wasn't goblin magic you were bursting with. So I think you might need this...
A sorcery crystal!

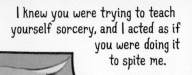

I knew you were trying to teach yourself sorcery, and I acted as if you were doing it to spite me.

Presented to our esteemed councilor
Opal Auguratricis

I know that it never had anything to do with me. I'm sorry, luvvie.

It's okay, Gran.

Okay.

PAT PAT

When you're ready.

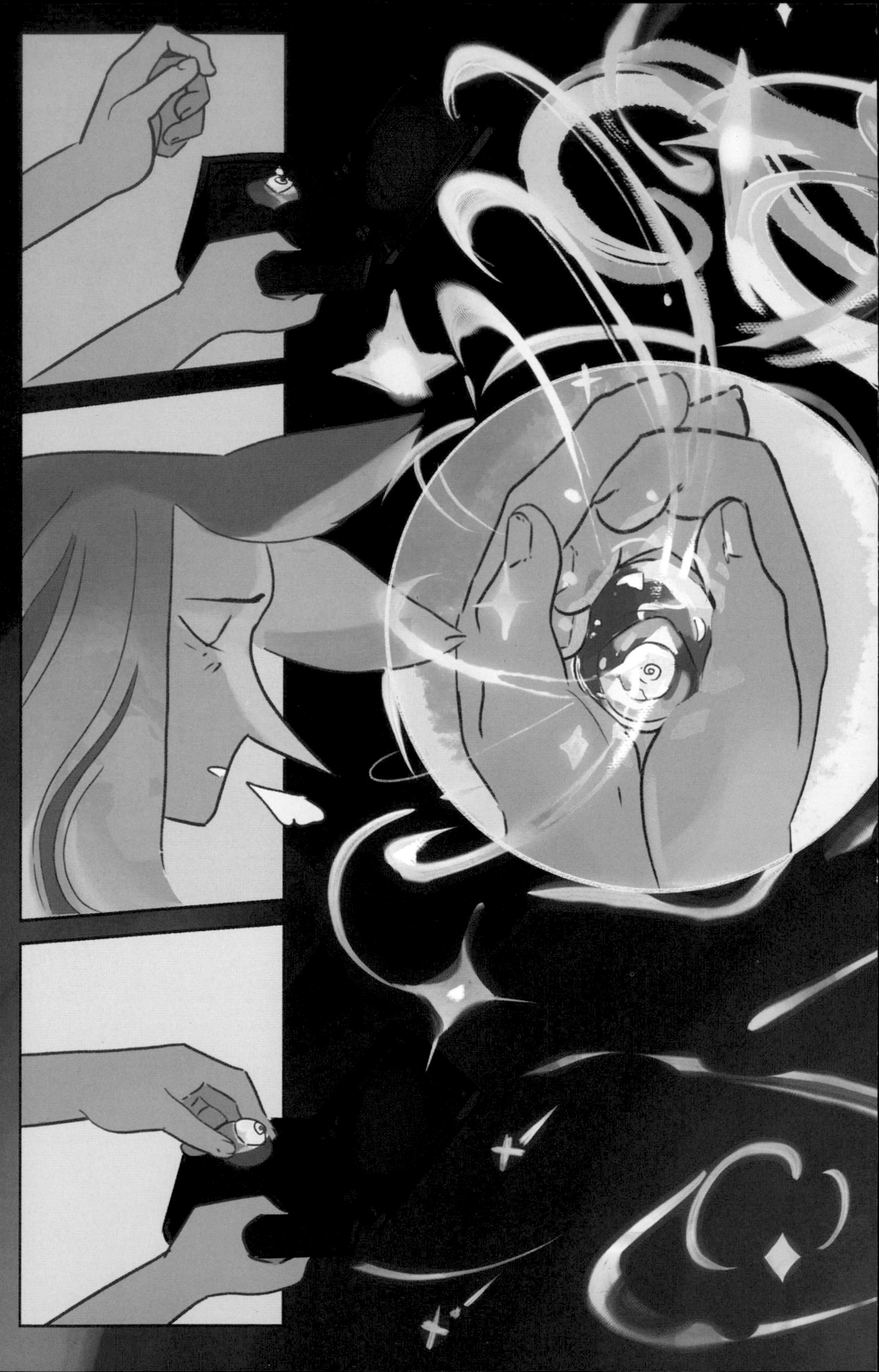

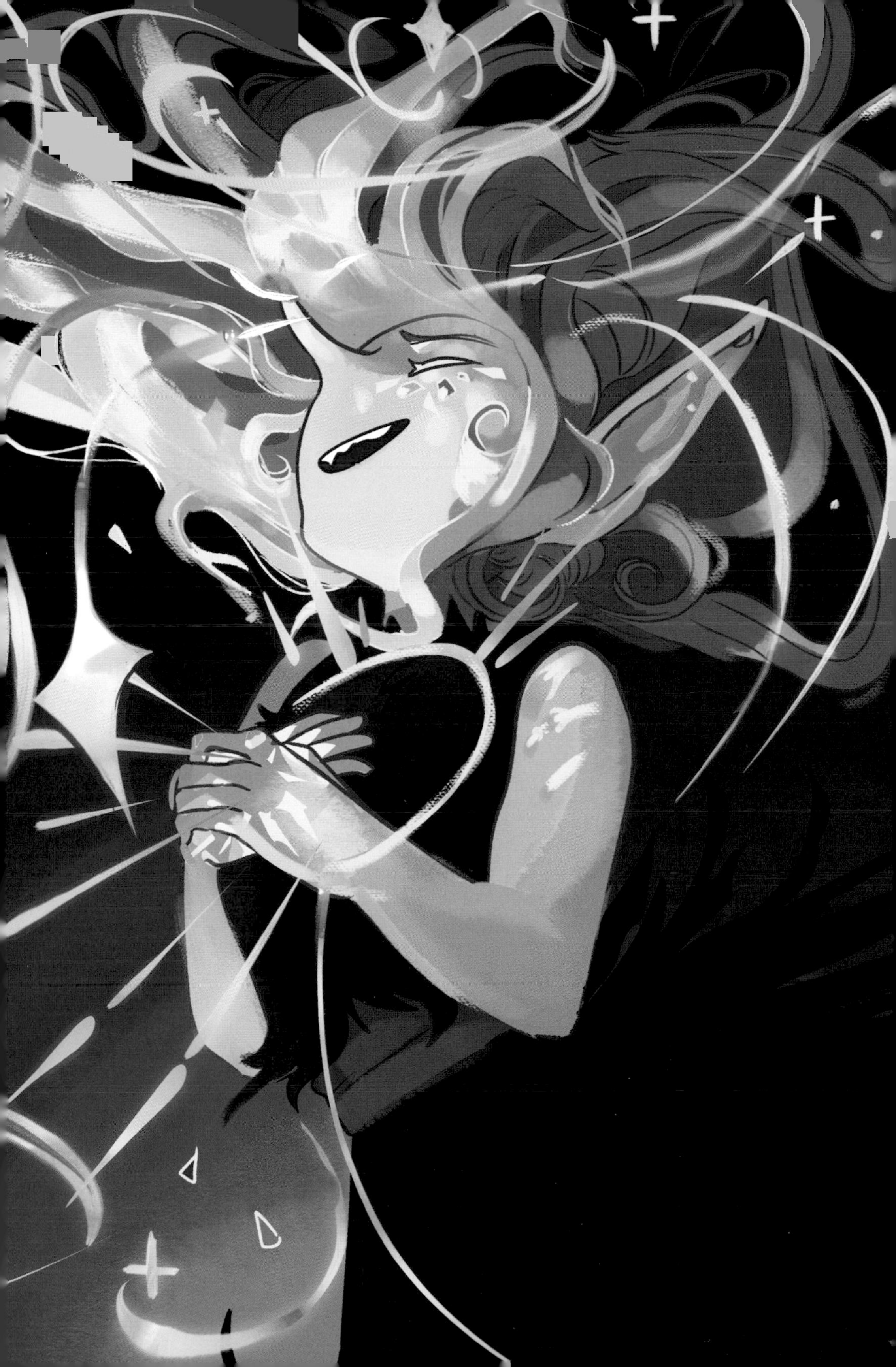

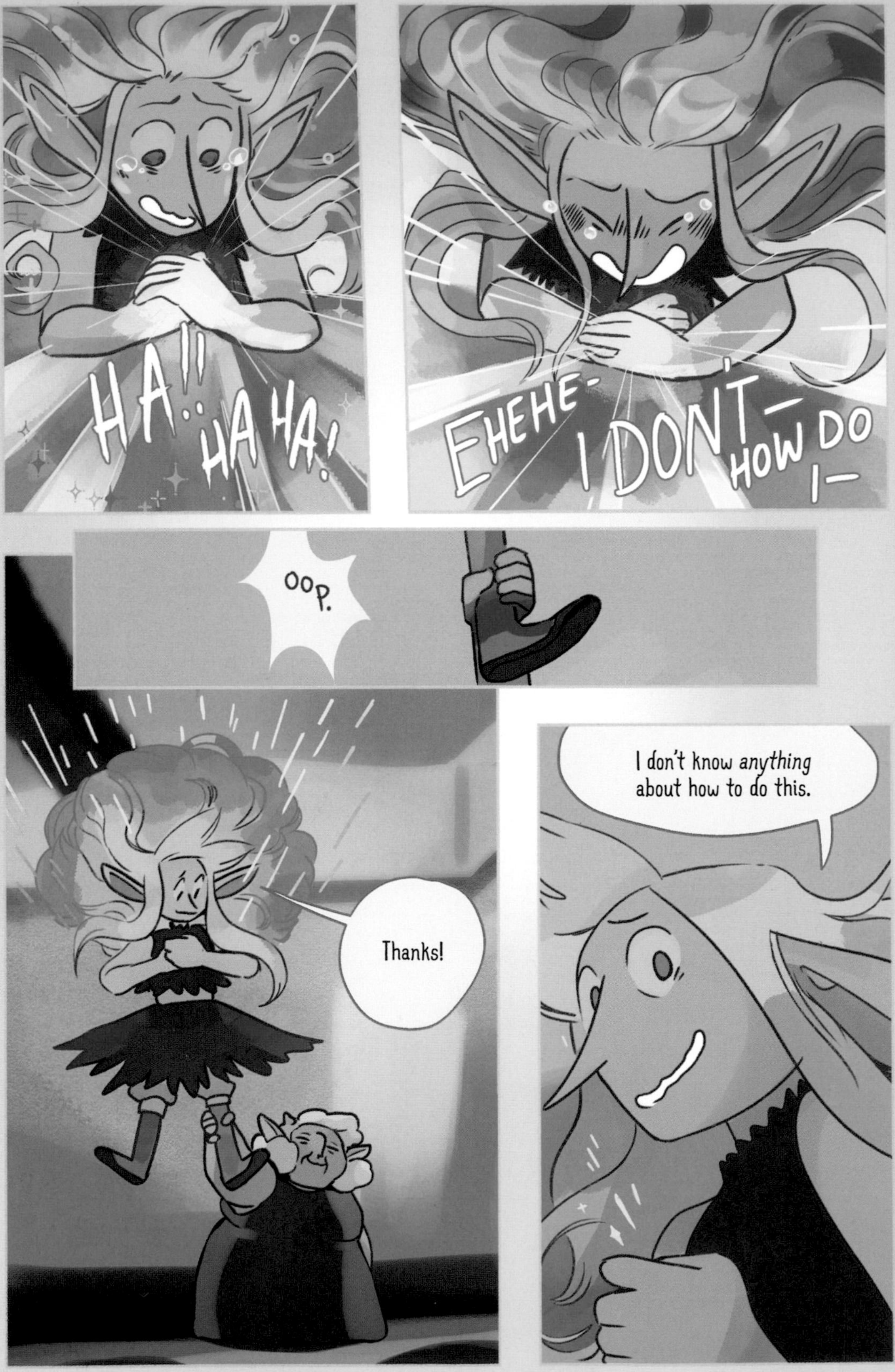
HA!! .. HA HA!
EHEHE-
I DON'T—
HOW DO I—
OOP.
Thanks!
I don't know *anything* about how to do this.

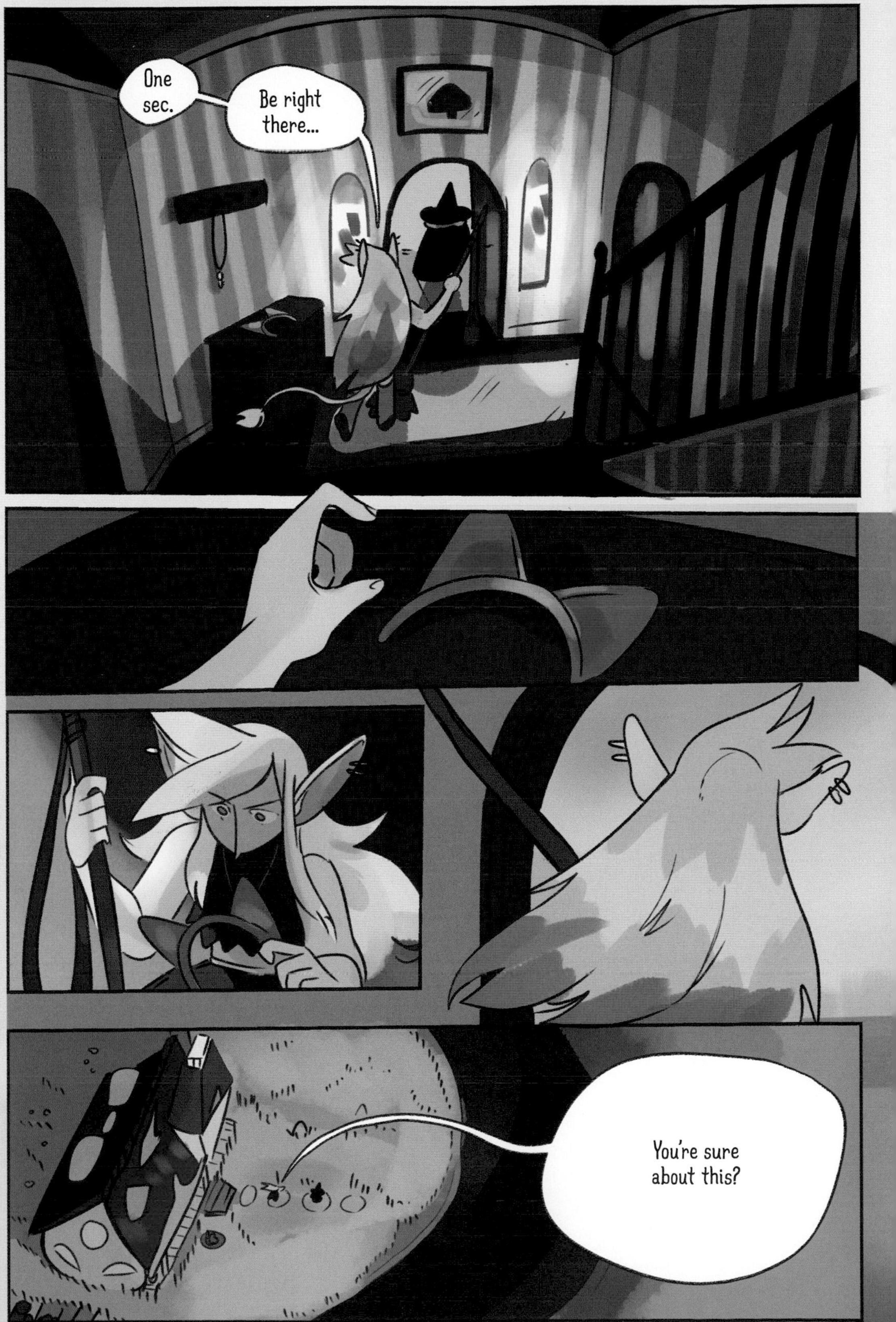
One sec.
Be right there...
You're sure about this?

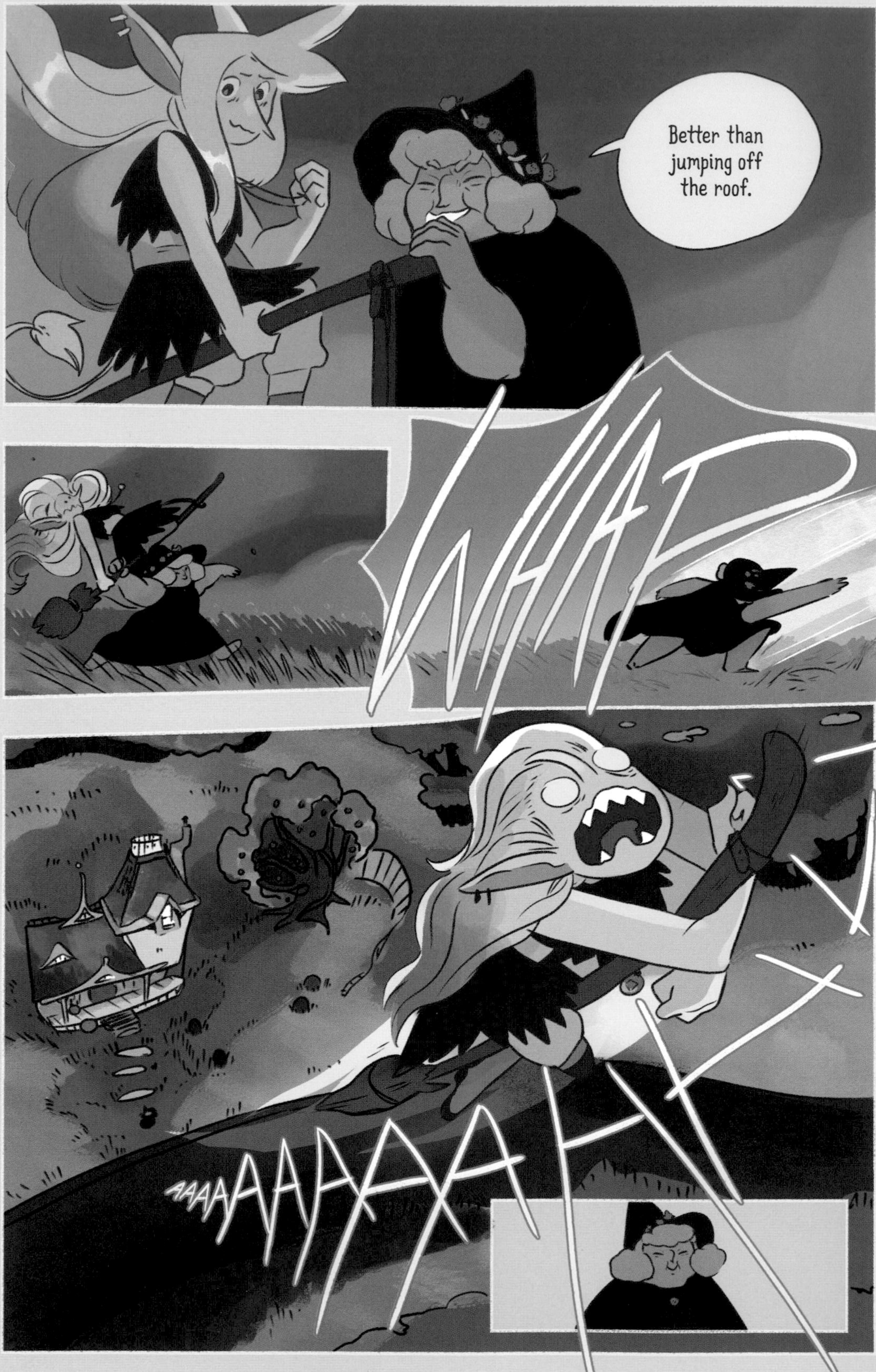
Better than jumping off the roof.
WHAT?
AAAAAAAAAAH

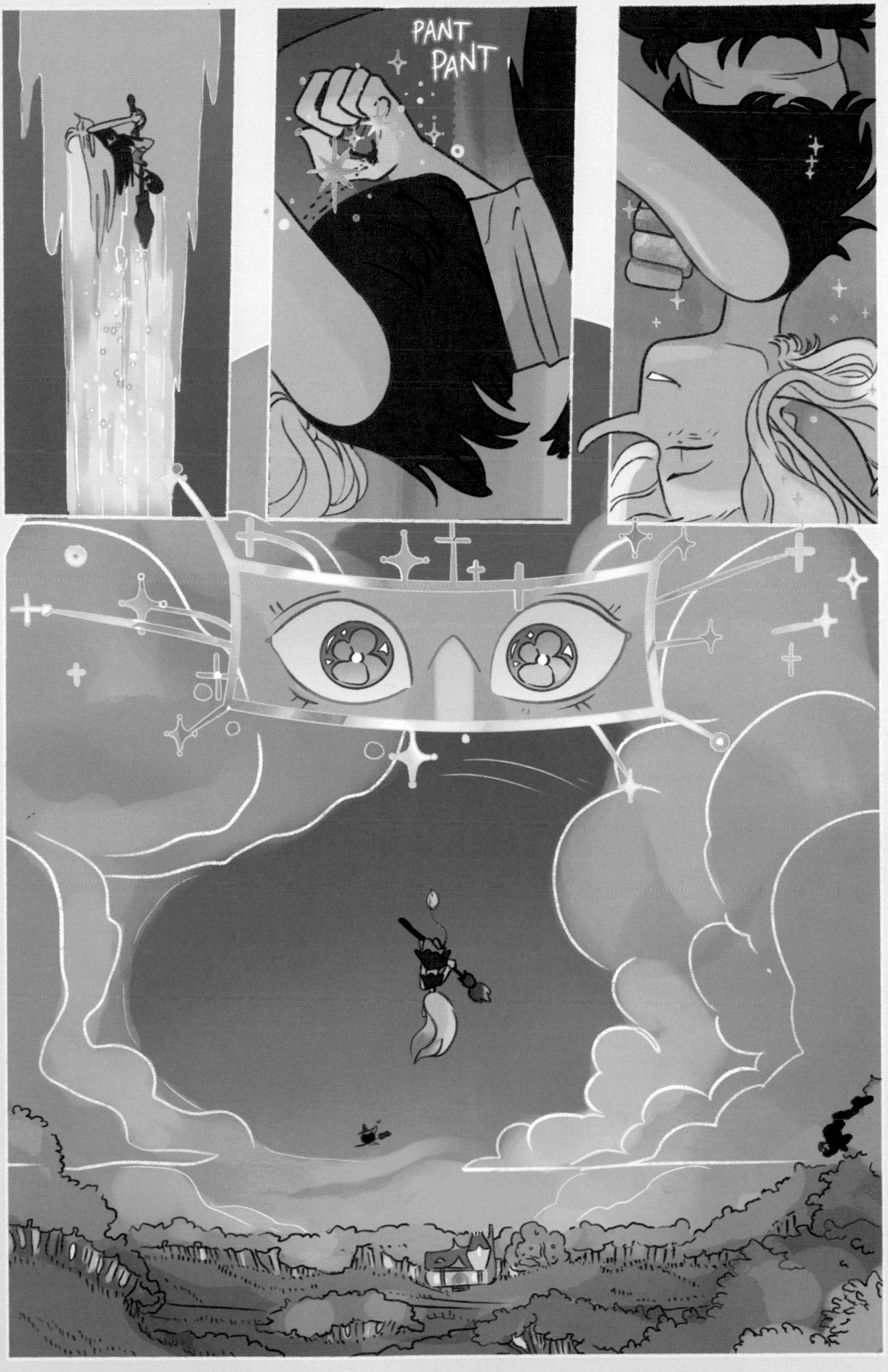
PANT
PANT

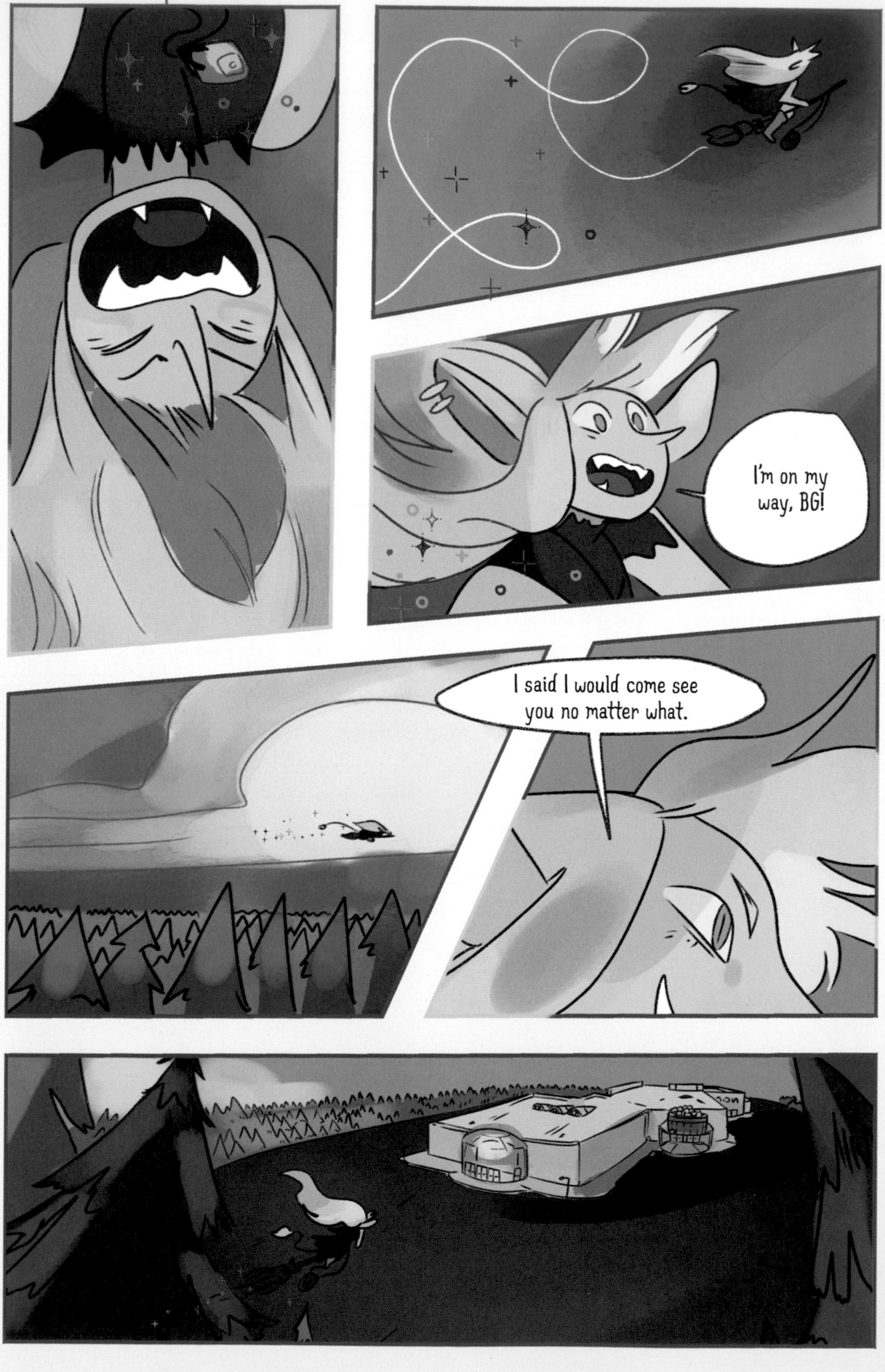
I'm on my way, BG!
I said I would come see you no matter what.

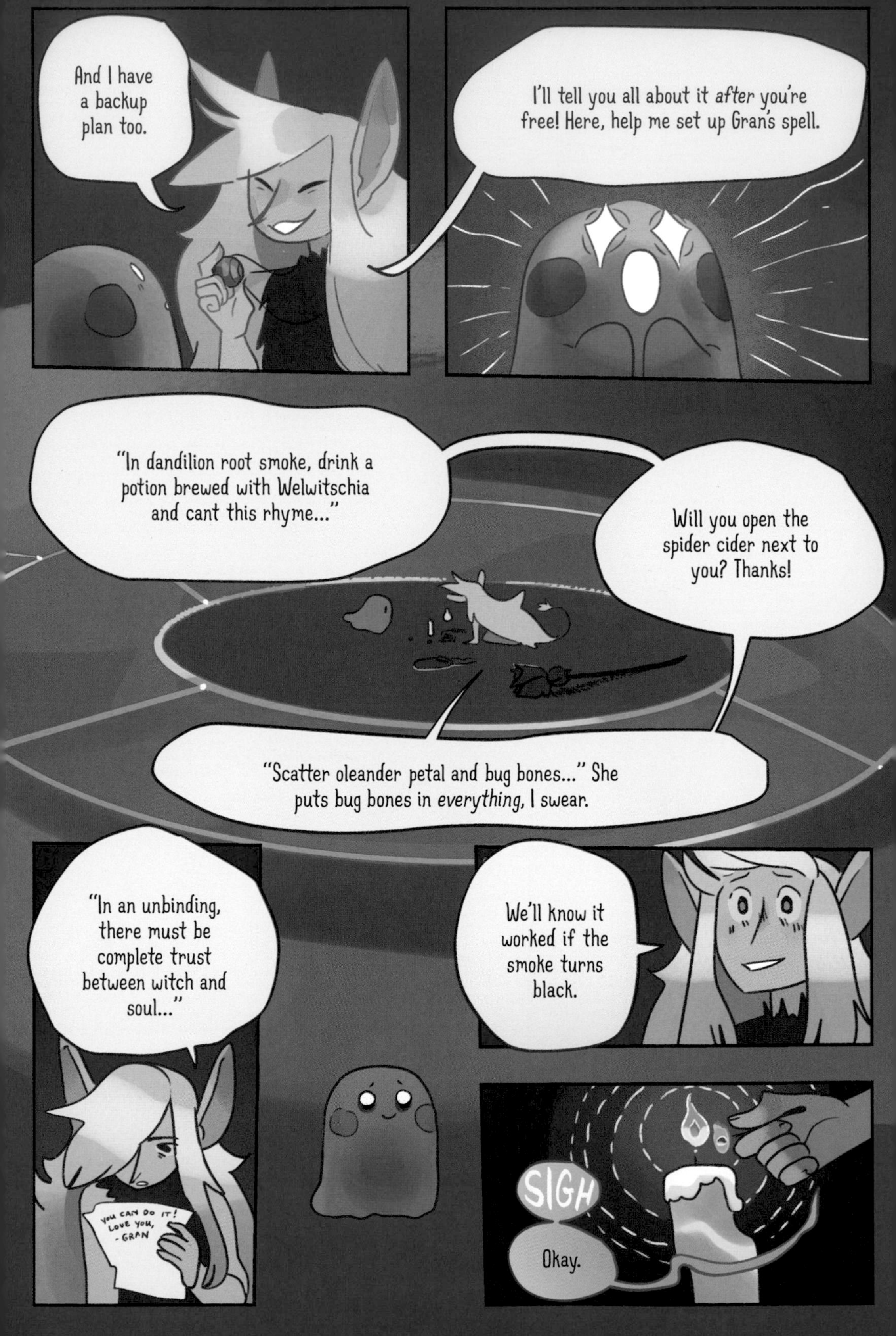
And I have a backup plan too.
I'll tell you all about it *after* you're free! Here, help me set up Gran's spell.
"In dandilion root smoke, drink a potion brewed with Welwitschia and cant this rhyme..."
Will you open the spider cider next to you? Thanks!
"Scatter oleander petal and bug bones..." She puts bug bones in *everything*, I swear.
"In an unbinding, there must be complete trust between witch and soul..."
YOU CAN DO IT! LOVE YOU, - GRAN
We'll know it worked if the smoke turns black.
SIGH
Okay.

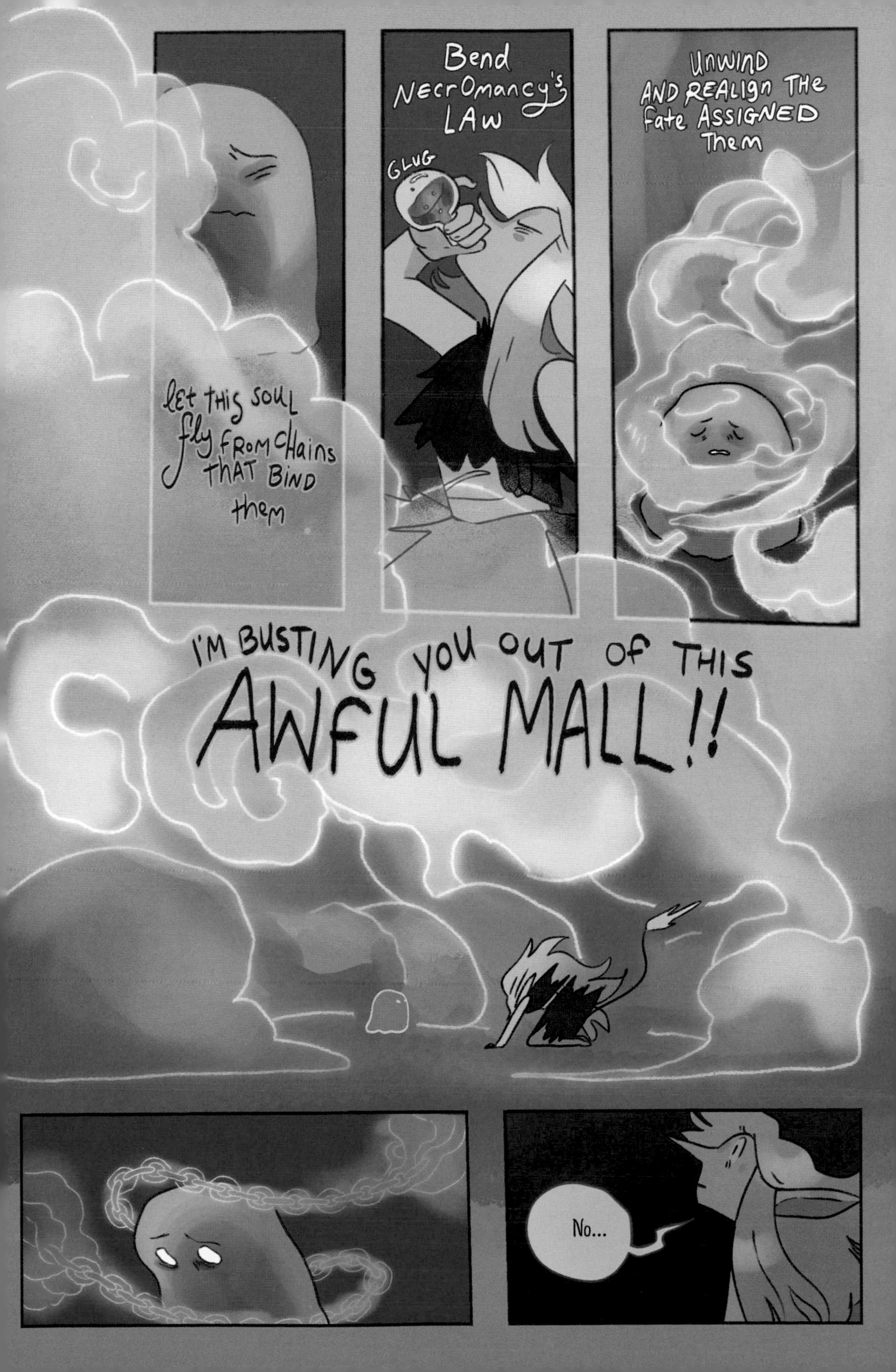
let this soul fly from chains that bind them
GLUG
Bend Necromancy's LAW
Unwind and realign the fate assigned them
I'M BUSTING YOU OUT OF THIS AWFUL MALL!!
No...

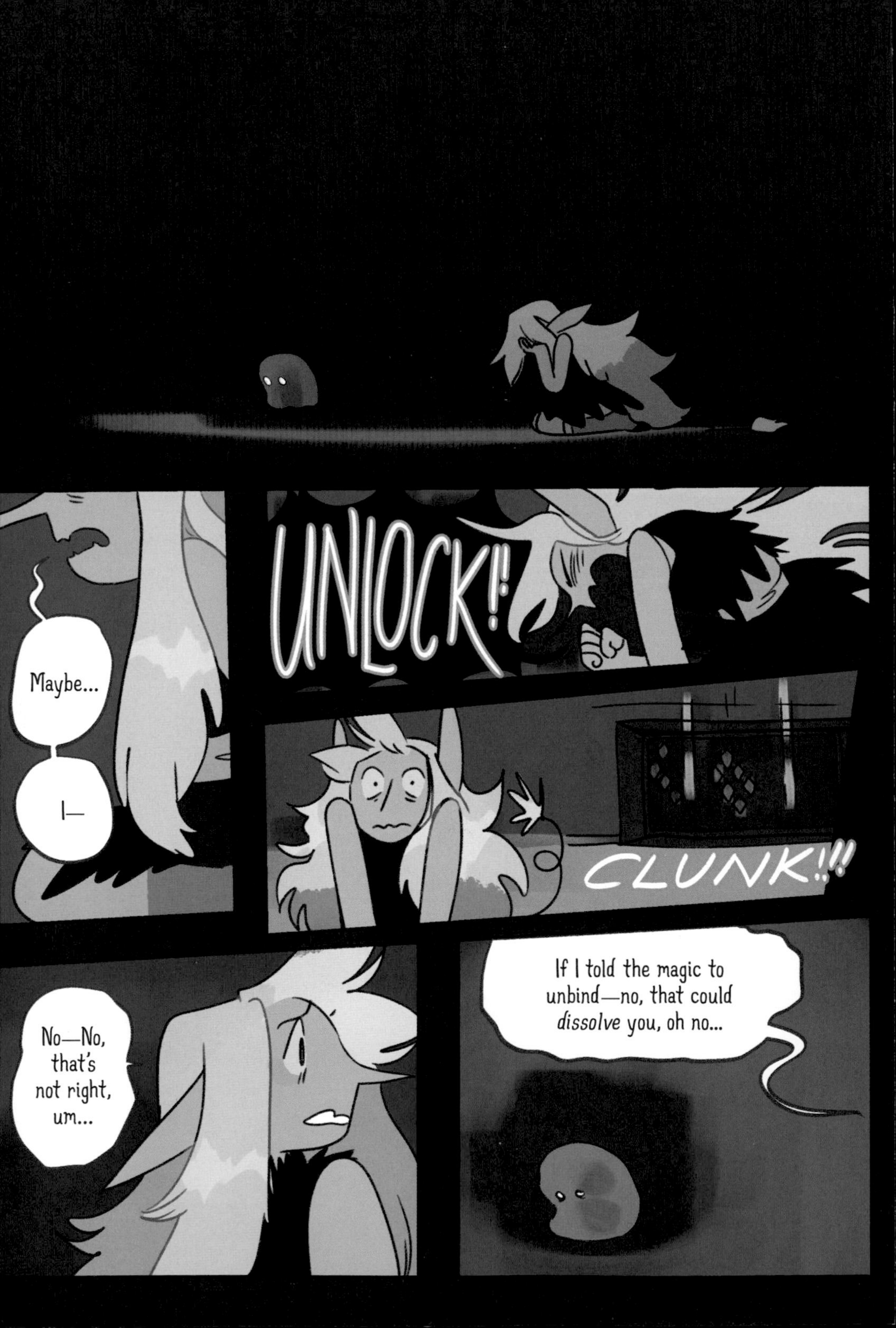

Maybe...
I—
UNLOCK!!
CLUNK!!!
No—No, that's not right, um...
If I told the magic to unbind—no, that could *dissolve* you, oh no...

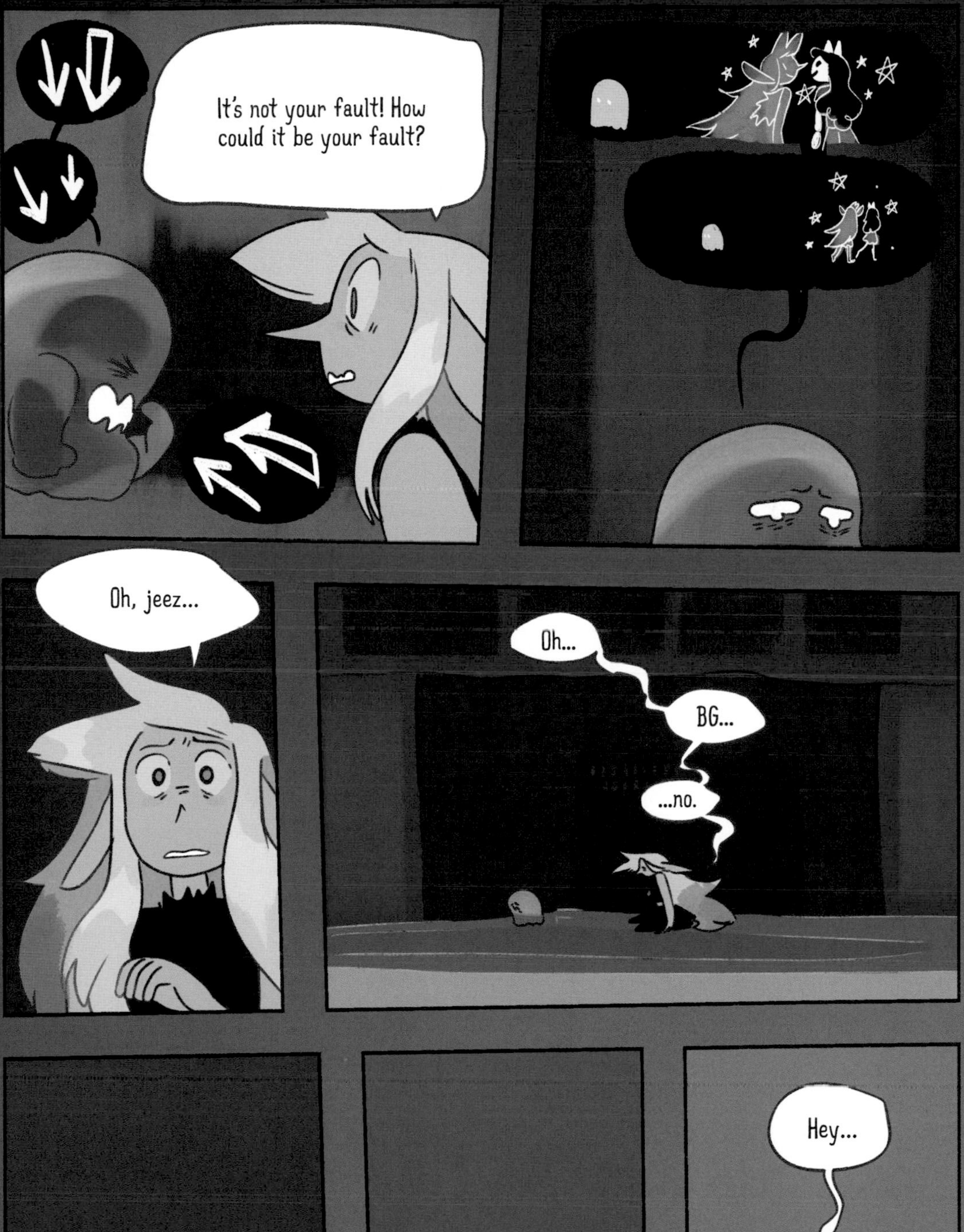
It's not your fault! How could it be your fault?
Oh, jeez...
Oh...
BG...
...no.
Hey...

I hope this isn't weird to ask, but...I was hoping that when you're free, you'd want to come live at my house.
Then I won't have to come find you when I want to watch back-to-back episodes of *Toad Behold*. And when one of us is upset, the other one will be right there.
And it's okay if you find out all the baby names Gran calls me, because it's worth it to have you around.
I get how it seemed. And why you were worried. But my feelings about you and Kat aren't the same at all.
OOPS
SQUELPH

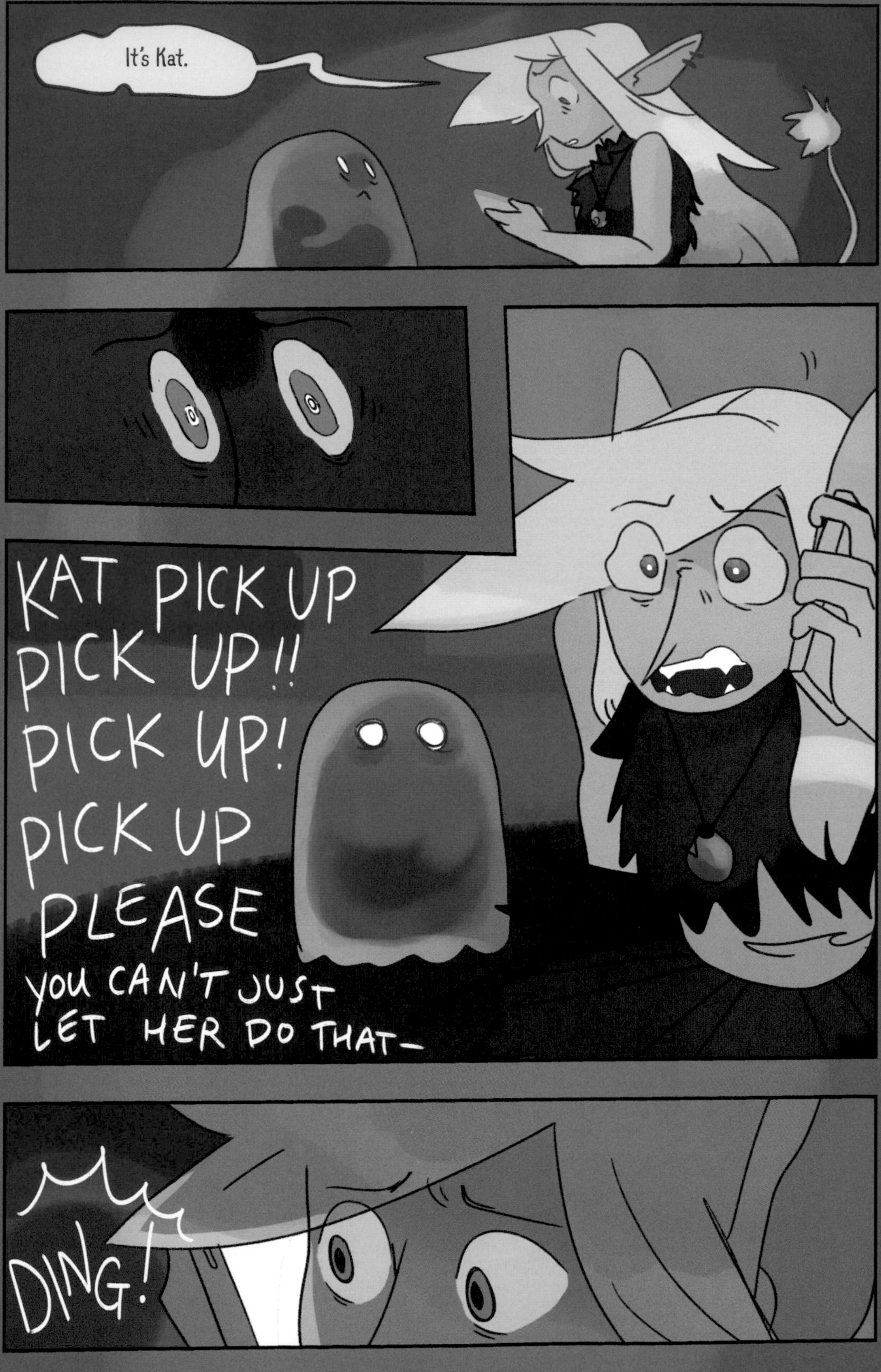
It's Kat.
KAT PICK UP
PICK UP!!
PICK UP!
PICK UP
PLEASE
YOU CAN'T JUST
LET HER DO THAT—
DING!

SWARM!
PERSONAL MESSAGE
FROM KAT:
THIS IS FOR BLOB GHOST'S SAKE, AND I KNOW THEY DON'T HAVE A PHONE. GET OUT OF THE MALL OR GET UNDERGROUND. SHE'S DEMOLISHING IT EARLY, AND WE'RE HEADING THERE NOW.
THIS IS M. HOLLOWBONE. DO NOT CONTACT MY NIECE AGAIN.
Gran...Gran, pick up THE PHONE!
PULL
OHhh voicemail—GRAN, they're tearing the mall down TODAY with US INSIDE they're doing it SOON come QUICK answer the PHONE
I'll keep calling her; she's probably flying or something...
BG, what are you doing?

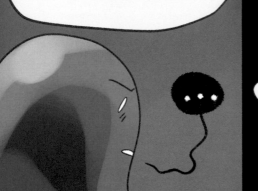

It has to still be here...It has to be something that nobody would take when they gutted everything, since you didn't get pulled out.

It'd have to be someplace weird. A place you can't get to, even if you felt pulled toward it by your heart...

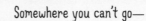

Somewhere you can't go—

Feel anything here, BG?

Of course.

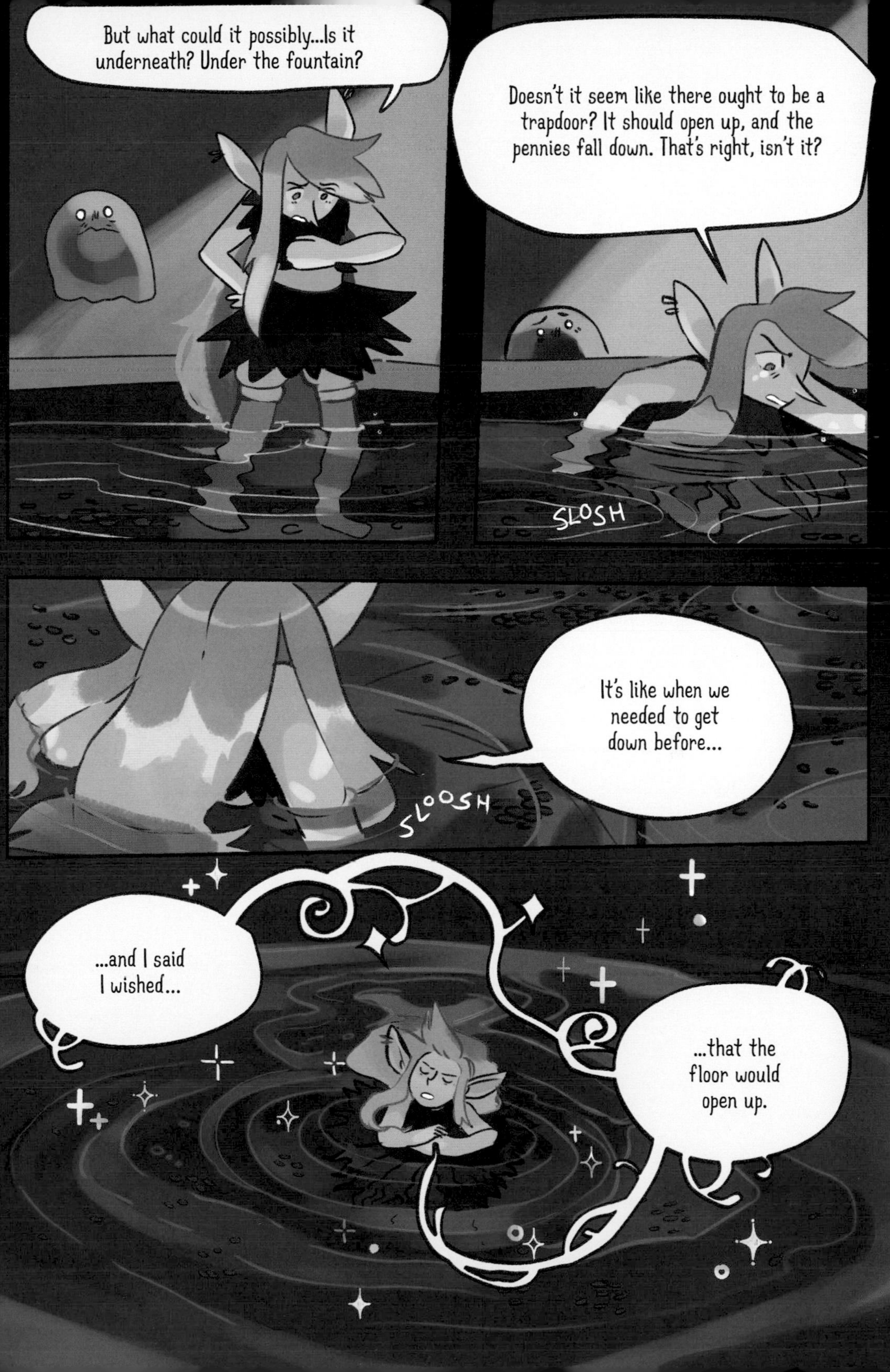
But what could it possibly...Is it underneath? Under the fountain?
Doesn't it seem like there ought to be a trapdoor? It should open up, and the pennies fall down. That's right, isn't it?
SLOSH
It's like when we needed to get down before...
SLOOSH
...and I said I wished...
...that the floor would open up.

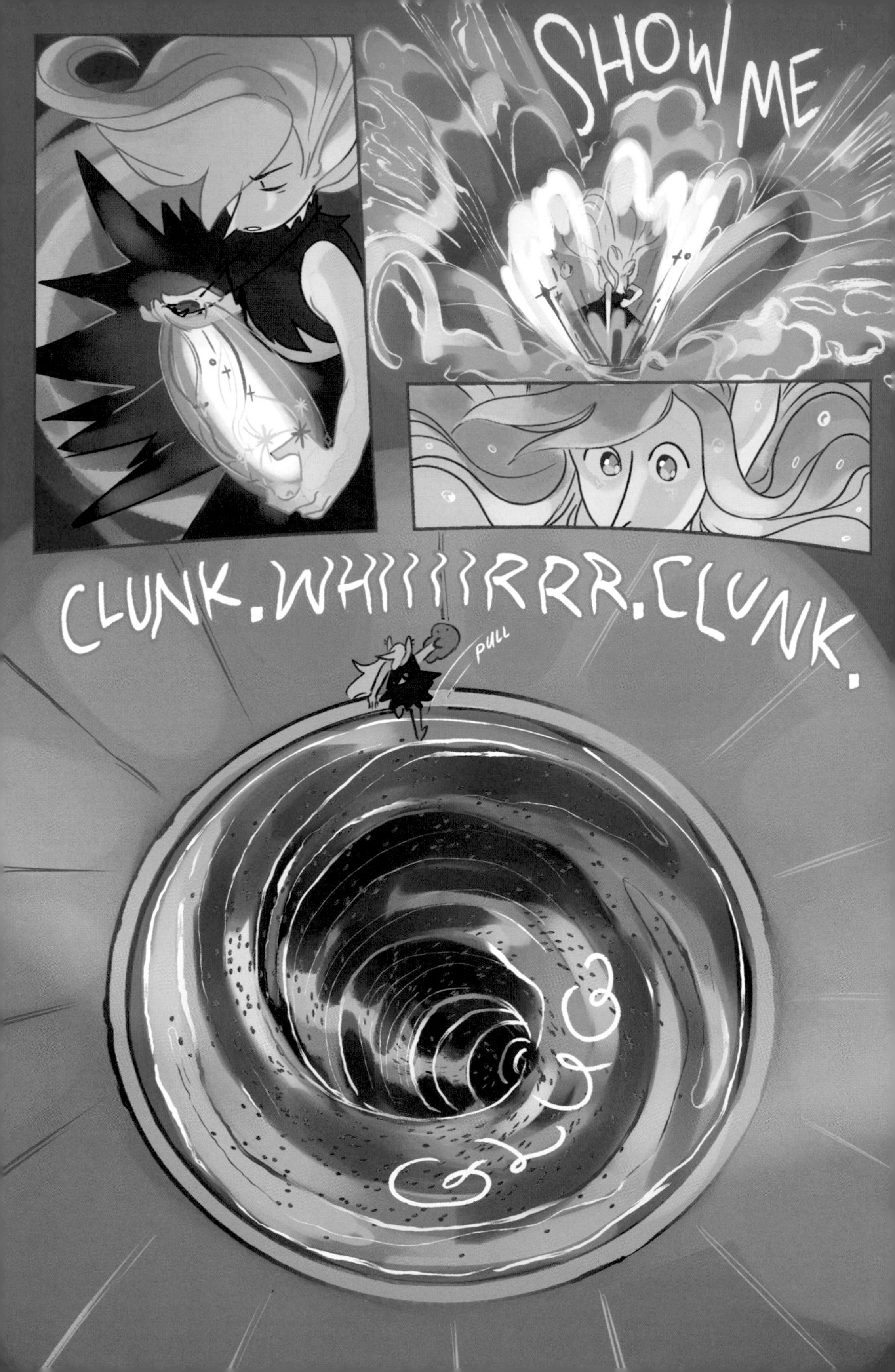
SHOW ME
CLUNK. WHIIIIRRR. CLUNK.
PULL

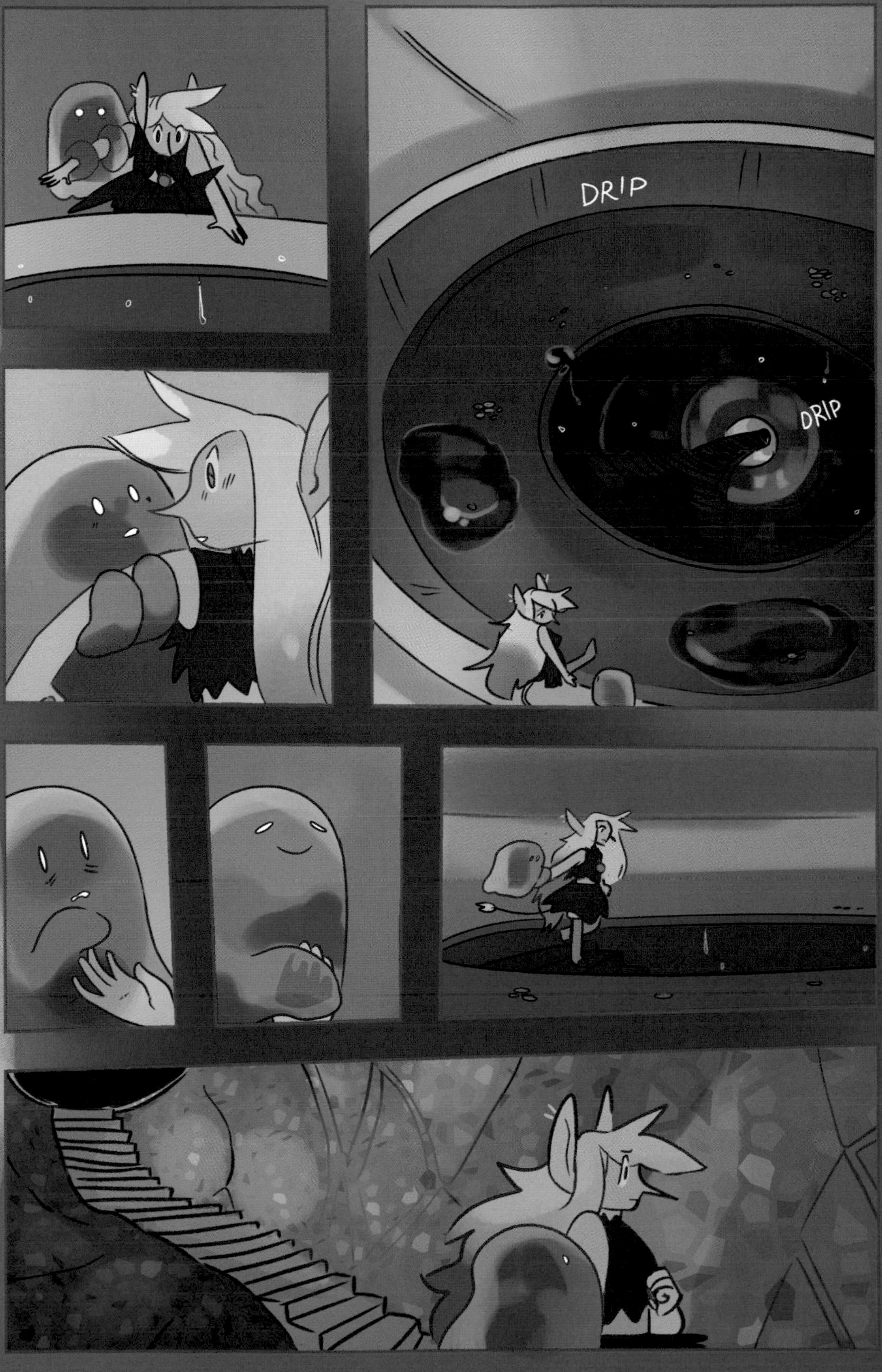
DRIP
DRIP

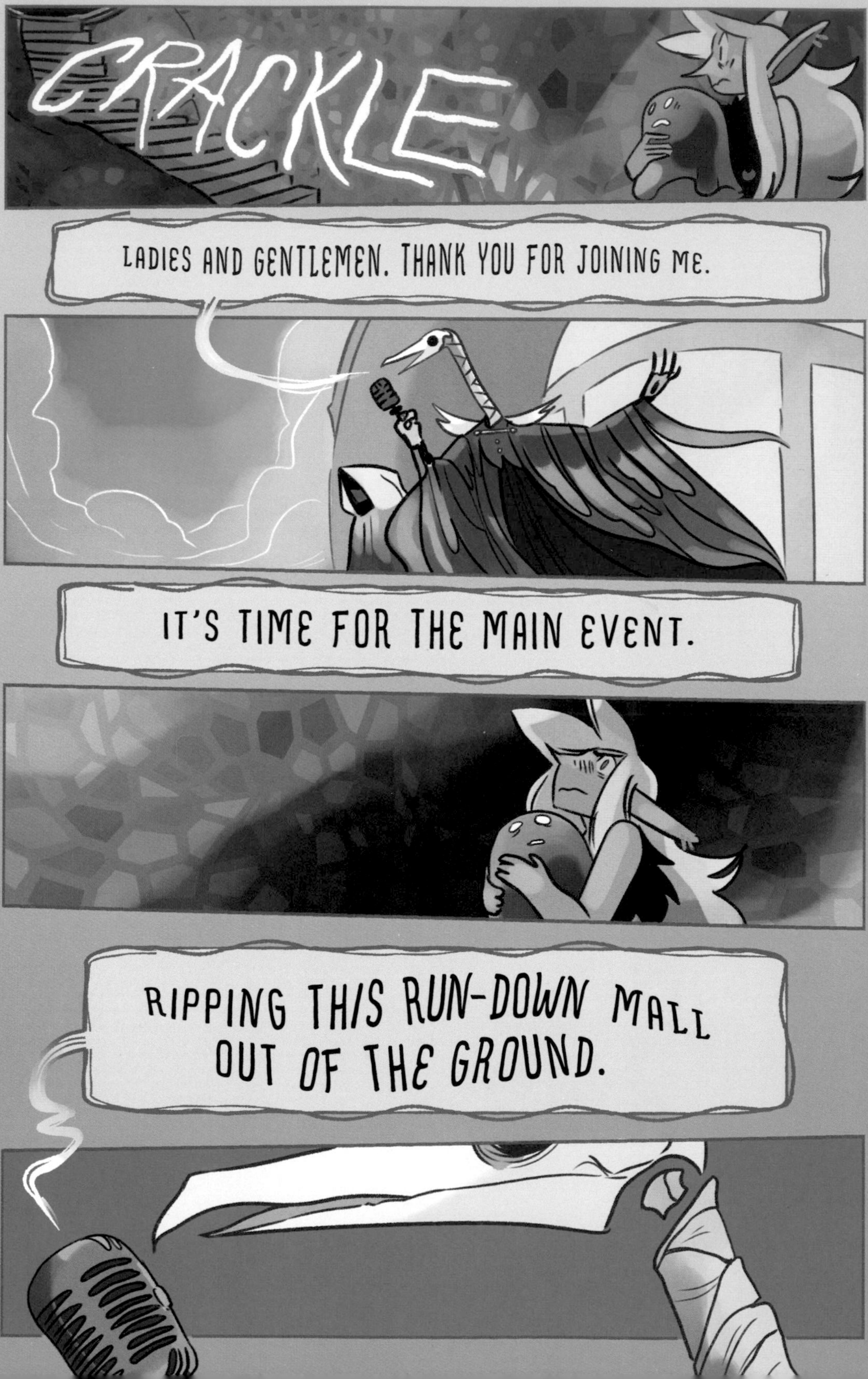
CRACKLE
LADIES AND GENTLEMEN. THANK YOU FOR JOINING ME.
IT'S TIME FOR THE MAIN EVENT.
RIPPING THIS RUN-DOWN MALL OUT OF THE GROUND.

The Haunted Heart

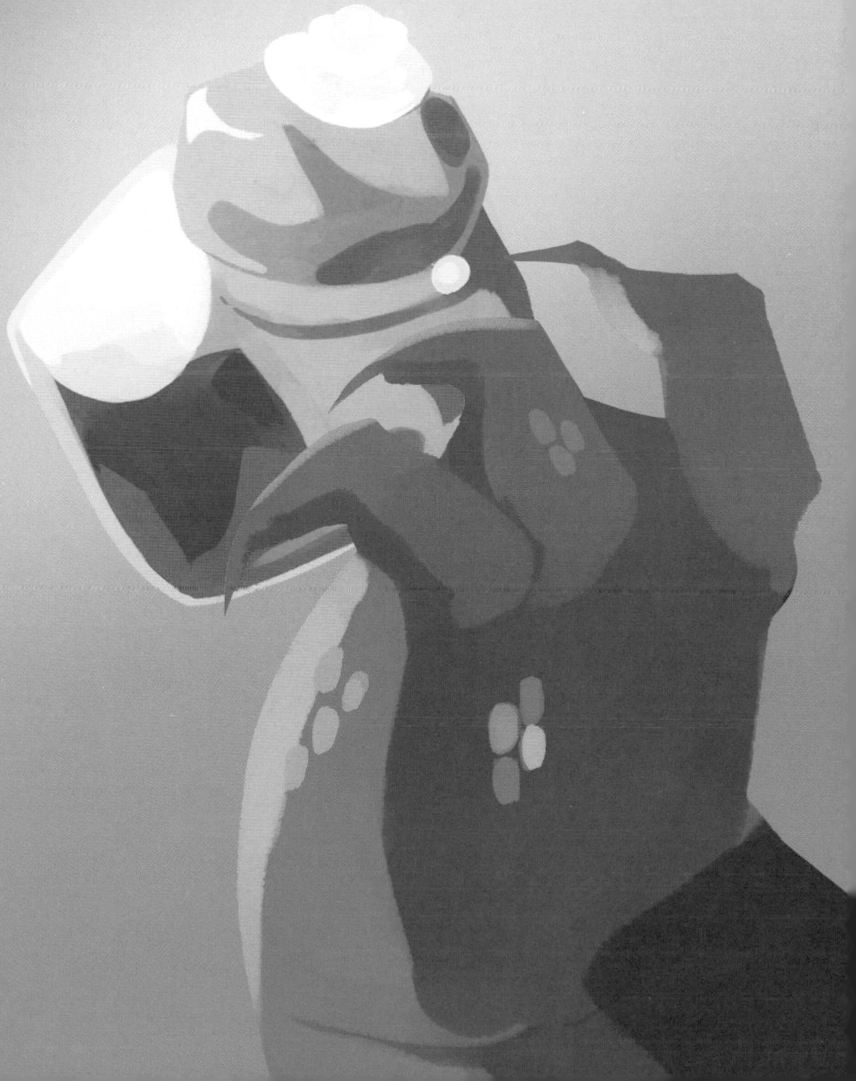

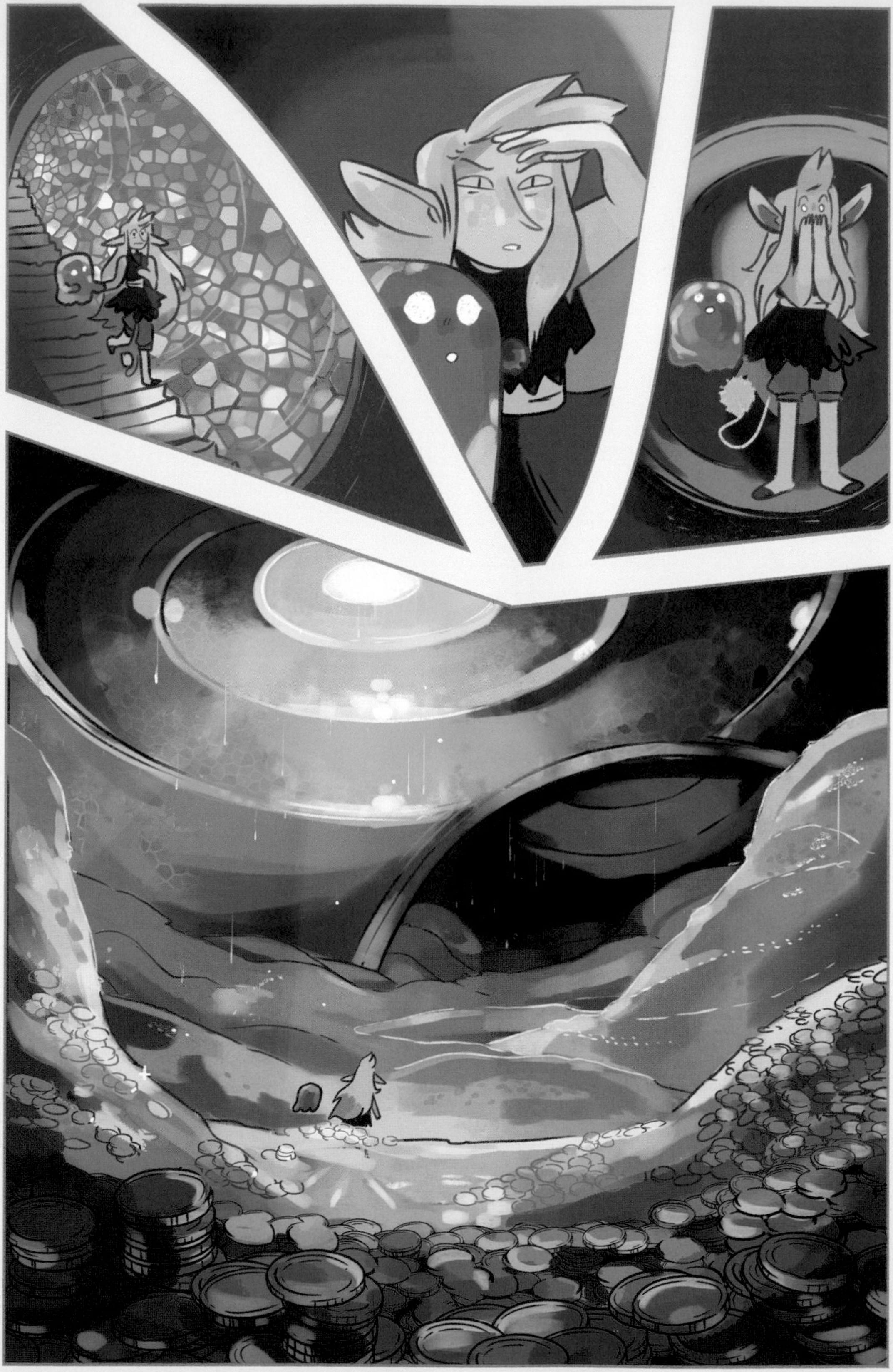

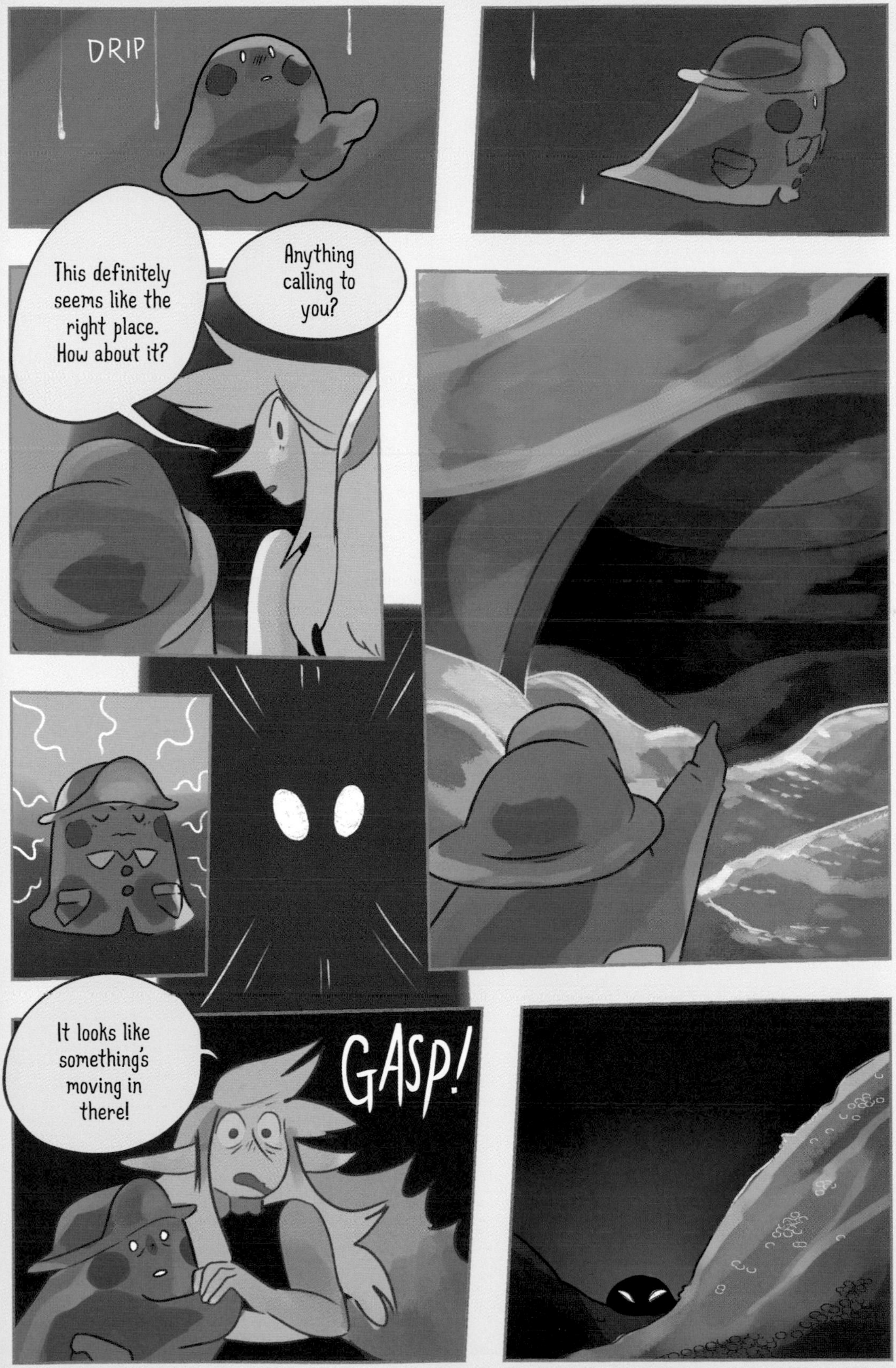
DRIP
This definitely seems like the right place. How about it?
Anything calling to you?
It looks like something's moving in there!
GASP!

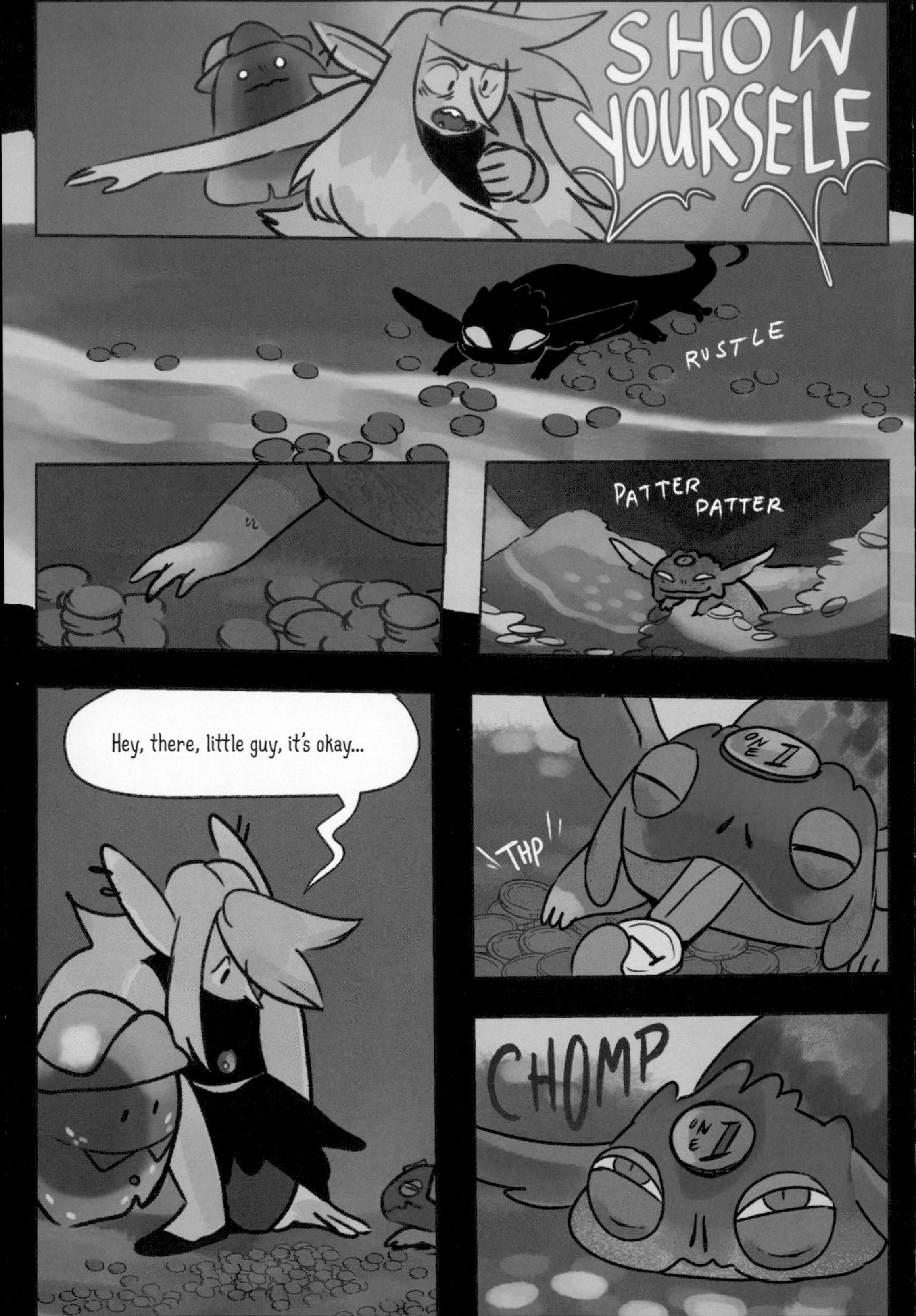
SHOW YOURSELF
RUSTLE
PATTER PATTER
Hey, there, little guy, it's okay...
THP
CHOMP

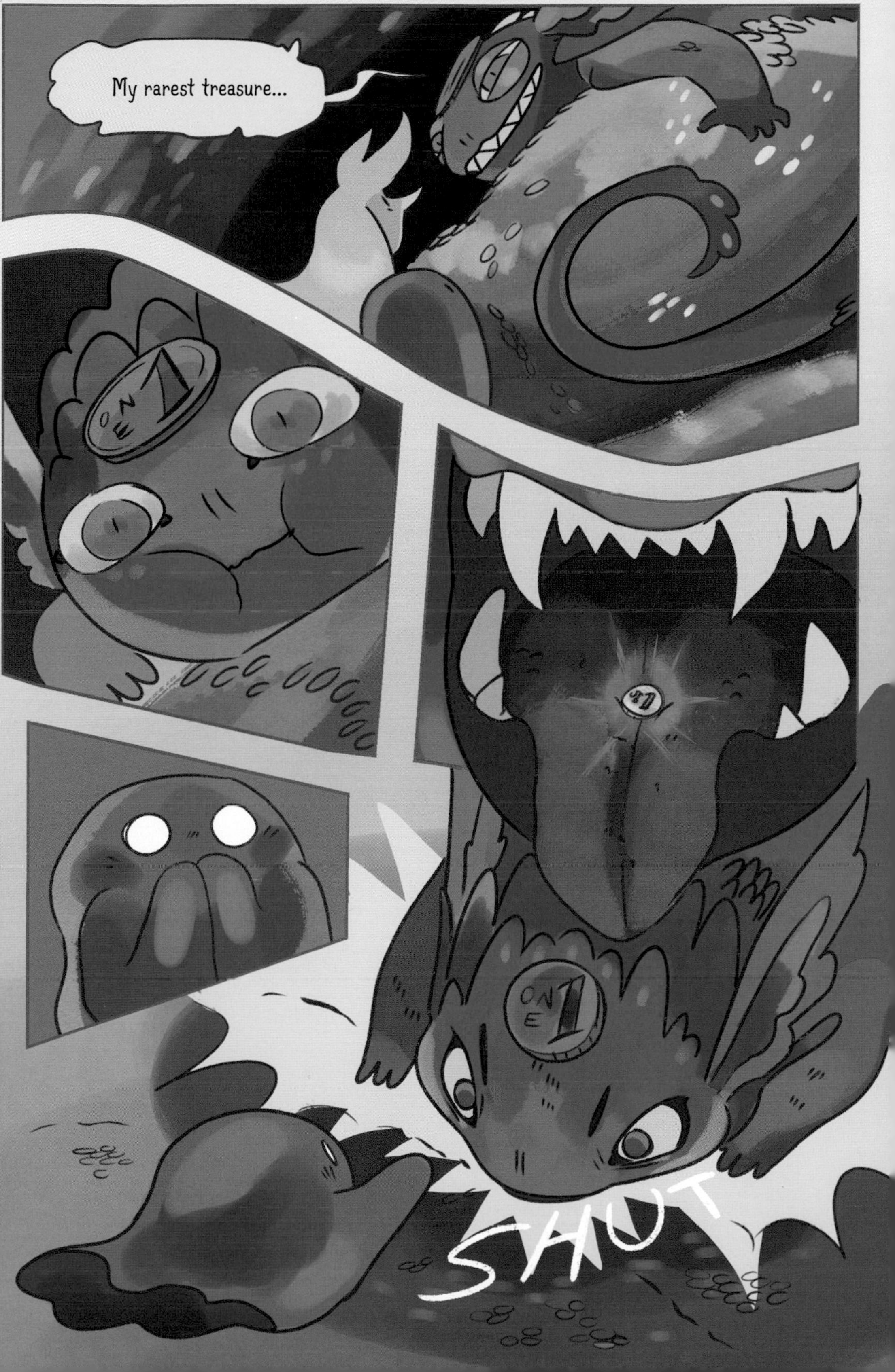
My rarest treasure...
ONE 1
SHUT

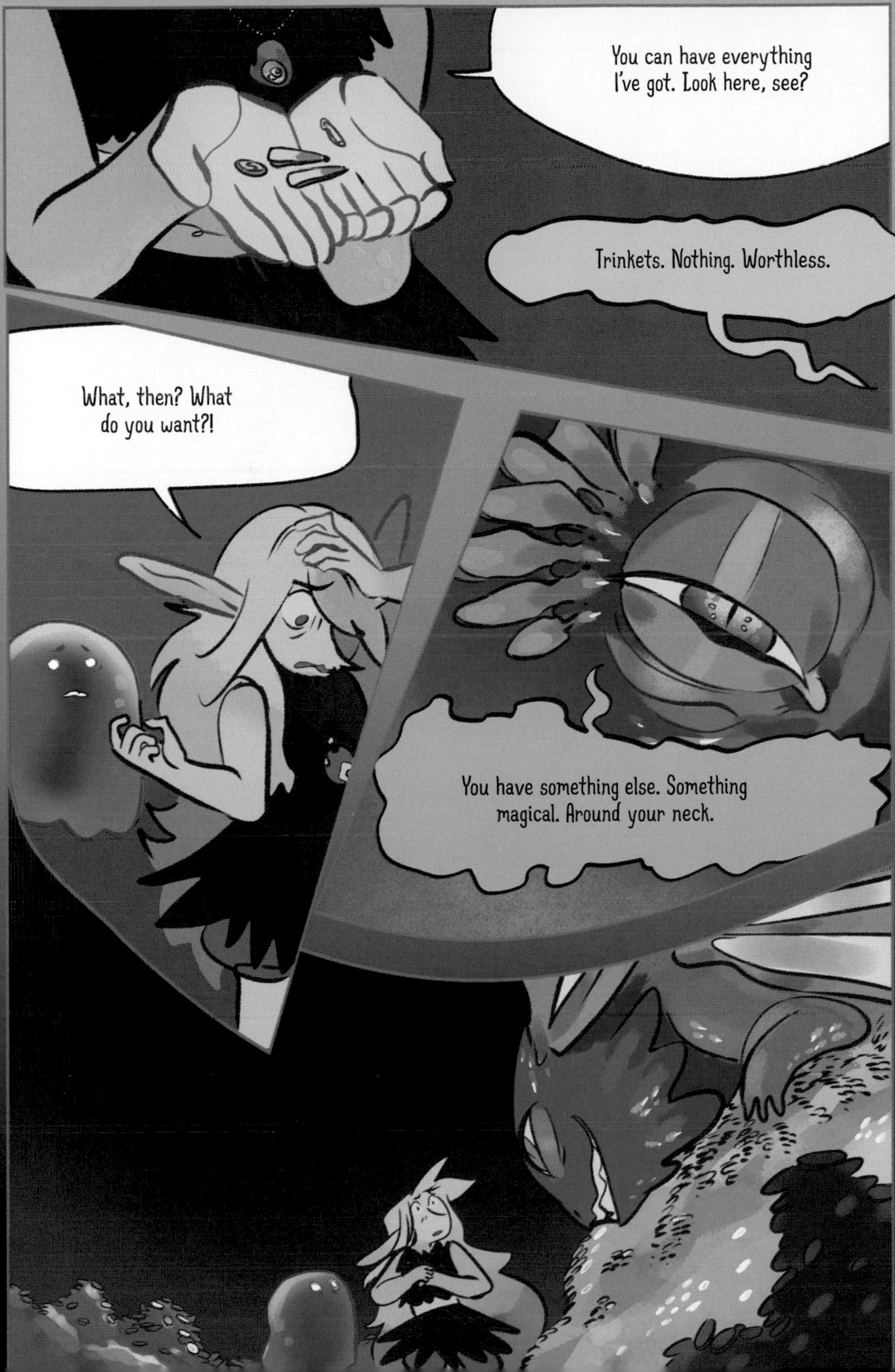
You can have everything I've got. Look here, see?
Trinkets. Nothing. Worthless.
What, then? What do you want?!
You have something else. Something magical. Around your neck.

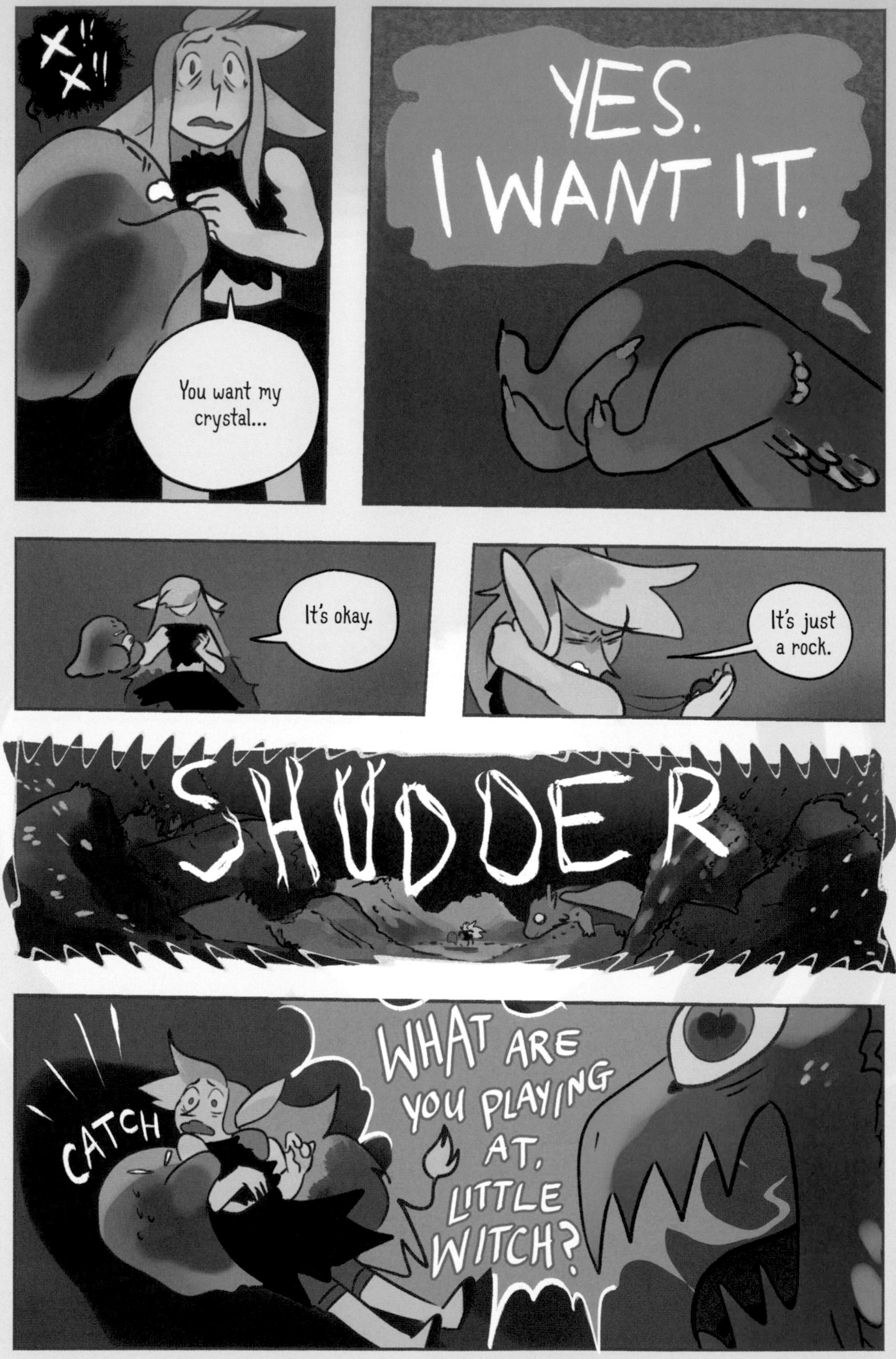

You want my crystal...
YES. I WANT IT.
It's okay.
It's just a rock.
SHUDDER
CATCH
WHAT ARE YOU PLAYING AT, LITTLE WITCH?

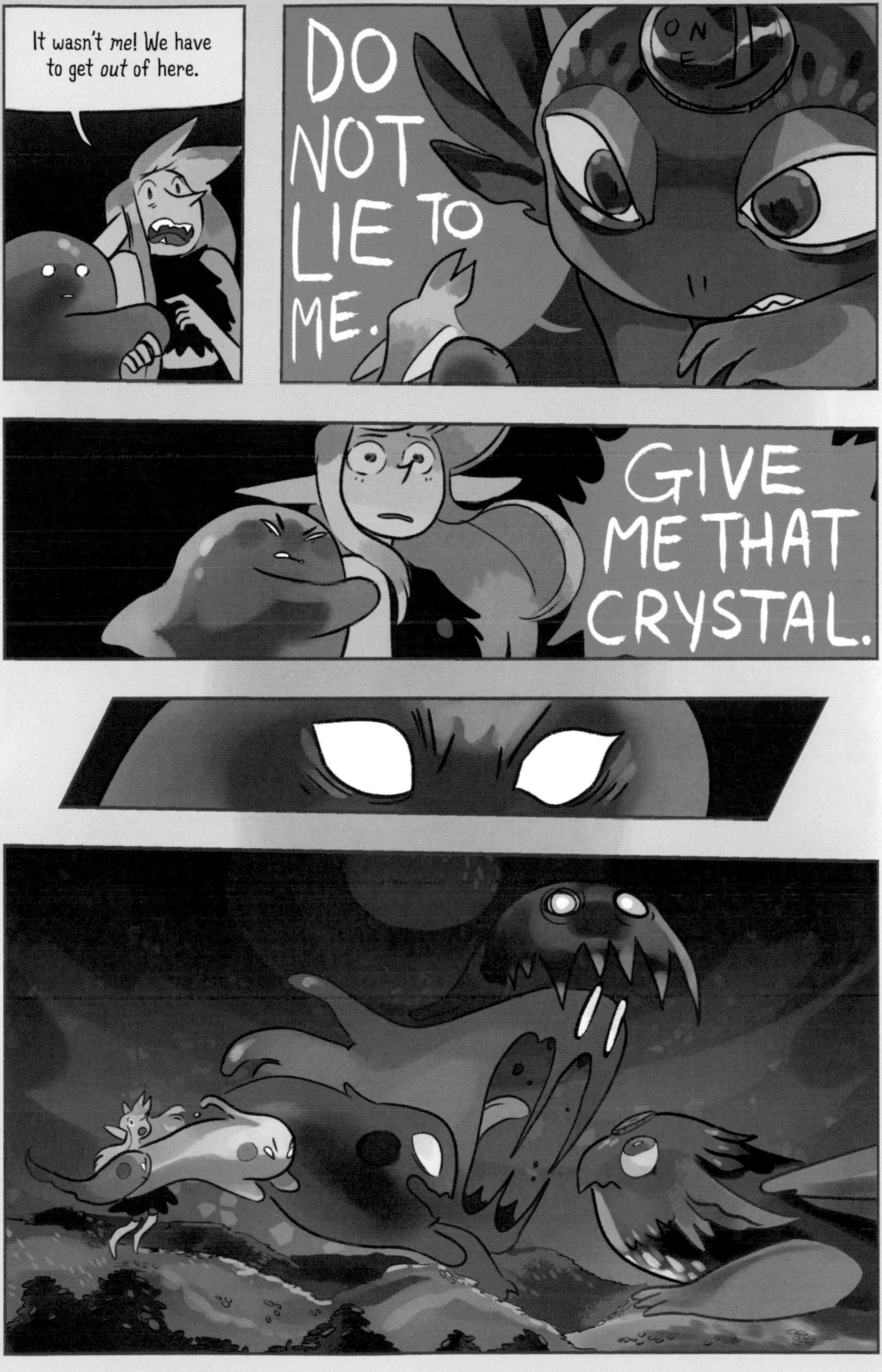
It wasn't *me*! We have to get *out* of here.
DO NOT LIE TO ME.
GIVE ME THAT CRYSTAL.

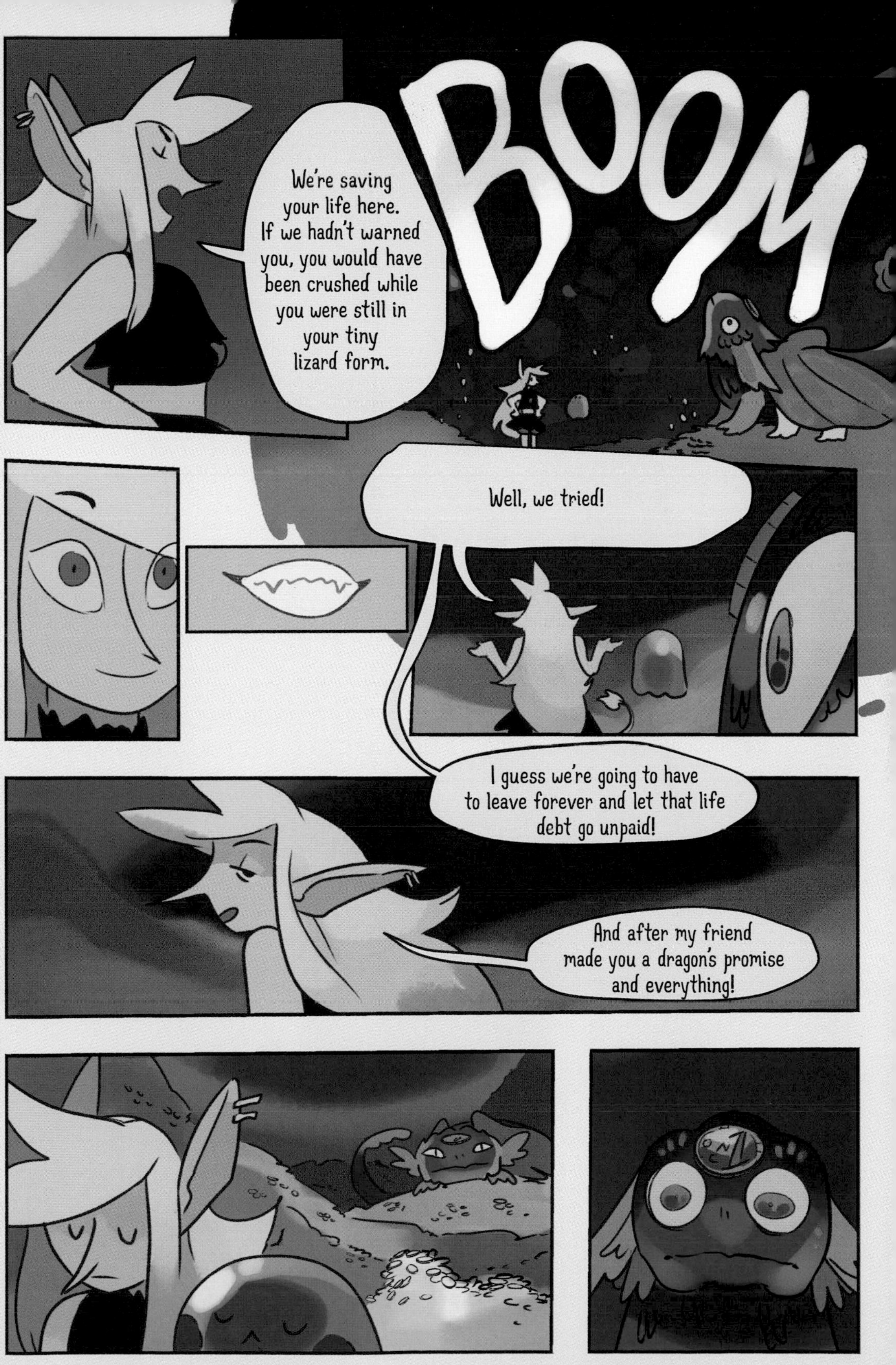
We're saving your life here. If we hadn't warned you, you would have been crushed while you were still in your tiny lizard form.
BOOM
Well, we tried!
I guess we're going to have to leave forever and let that life debt go unpaid!
And after my friend made you a dragon's promise and everything!

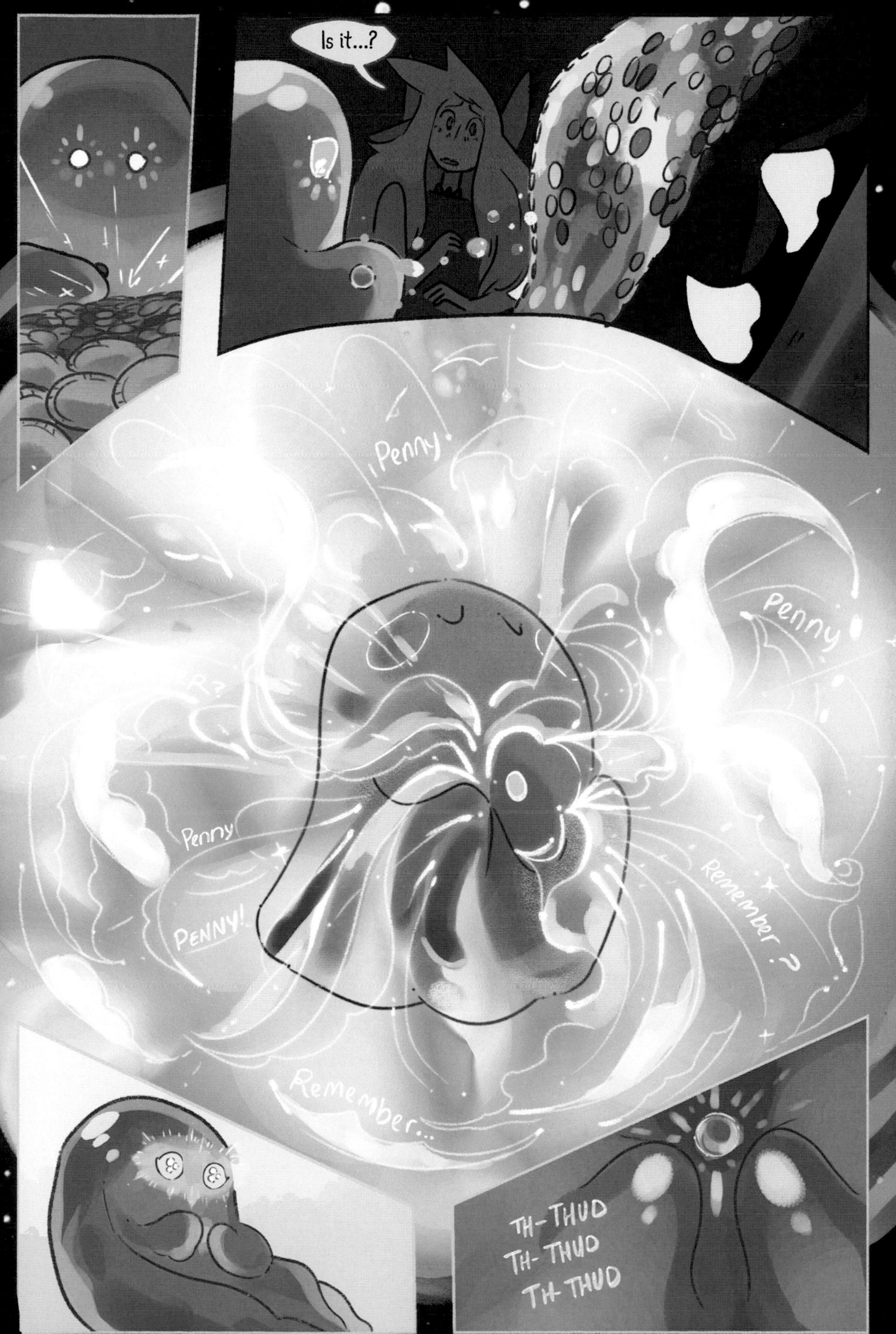

Is it...?
Penny
Penny
R?
Penny
PENNY!
Remember?
Remember...
TH-THUD
TH-THUD
TH-THUD

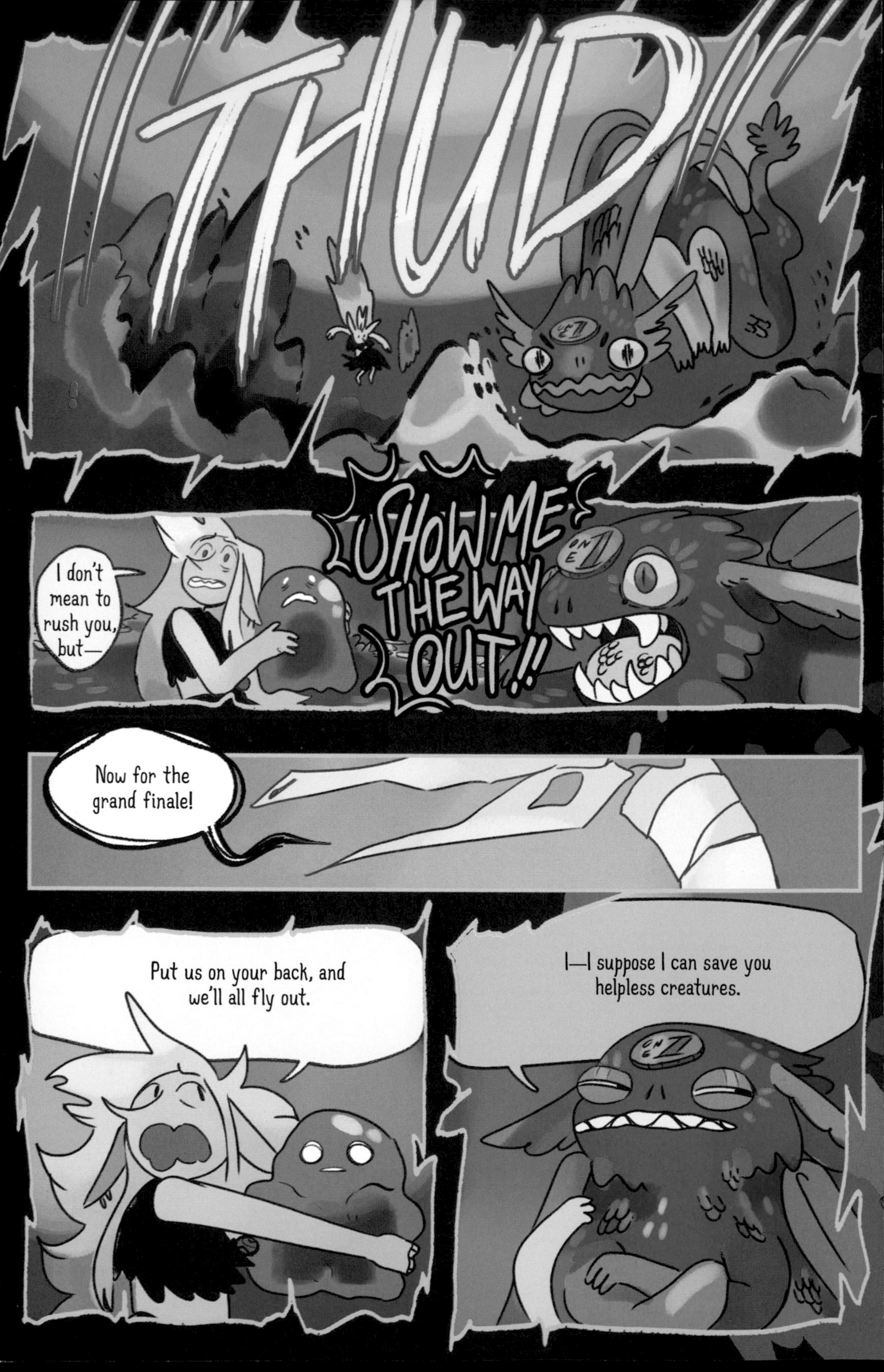
THUD!!
I don't mean to rush you, but—
SHOW ME THE WAY OUT!!
Now for the grand finale!
Put us on your back, and we'll all fly out.
I—I suppose I can save you helpless creatures.

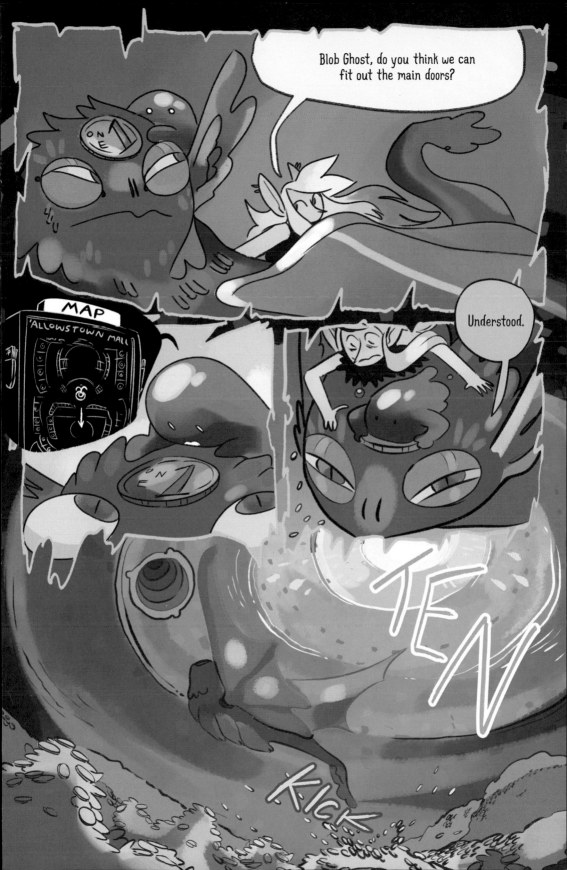

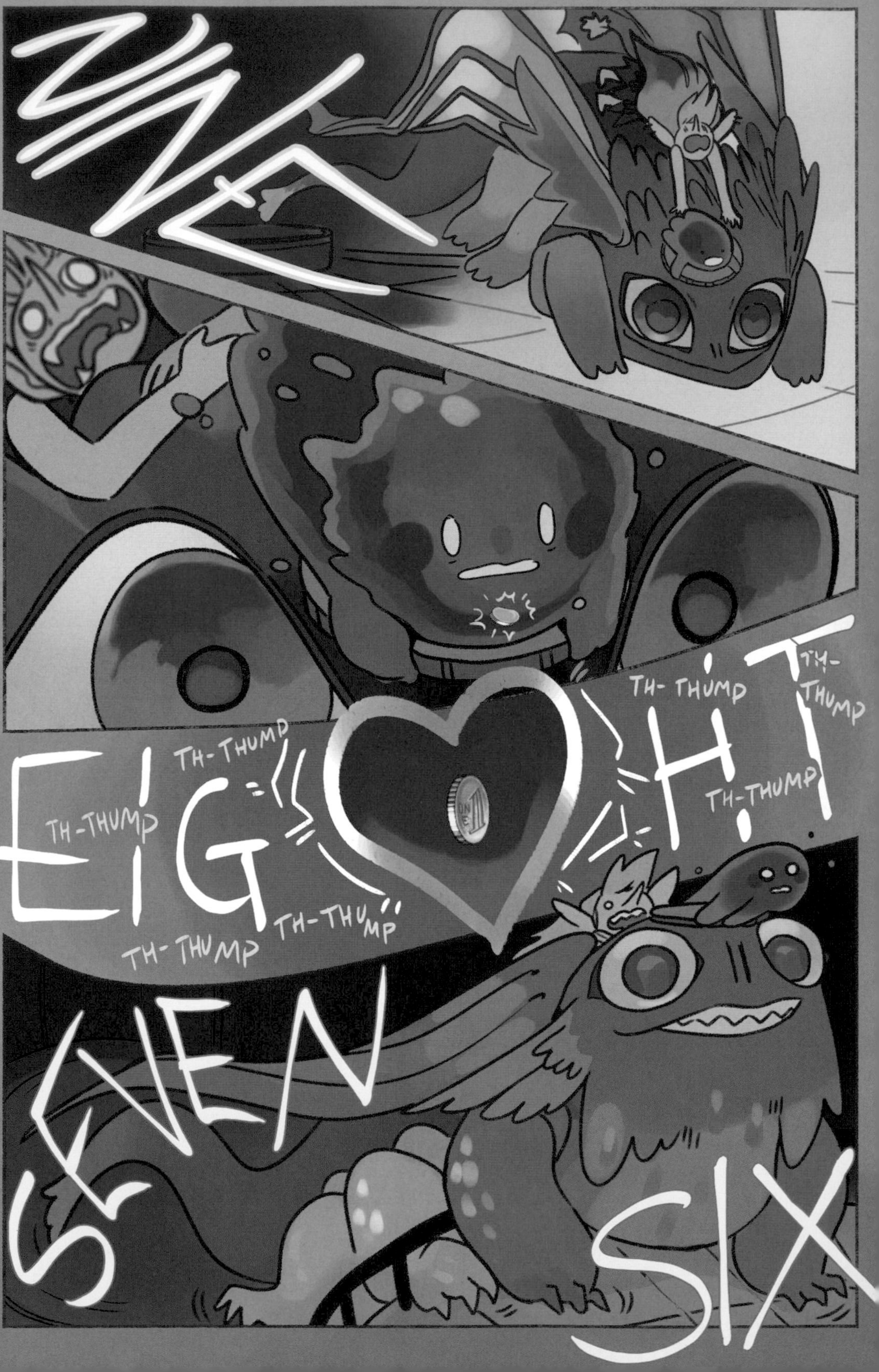
NINE
TH-THUMP
TH-THUMP
EIGHT
TH-THUMP
TH-THUMP
TH-THUMP
TH-THUMP
TH-THUMP
SEVEN
SIX

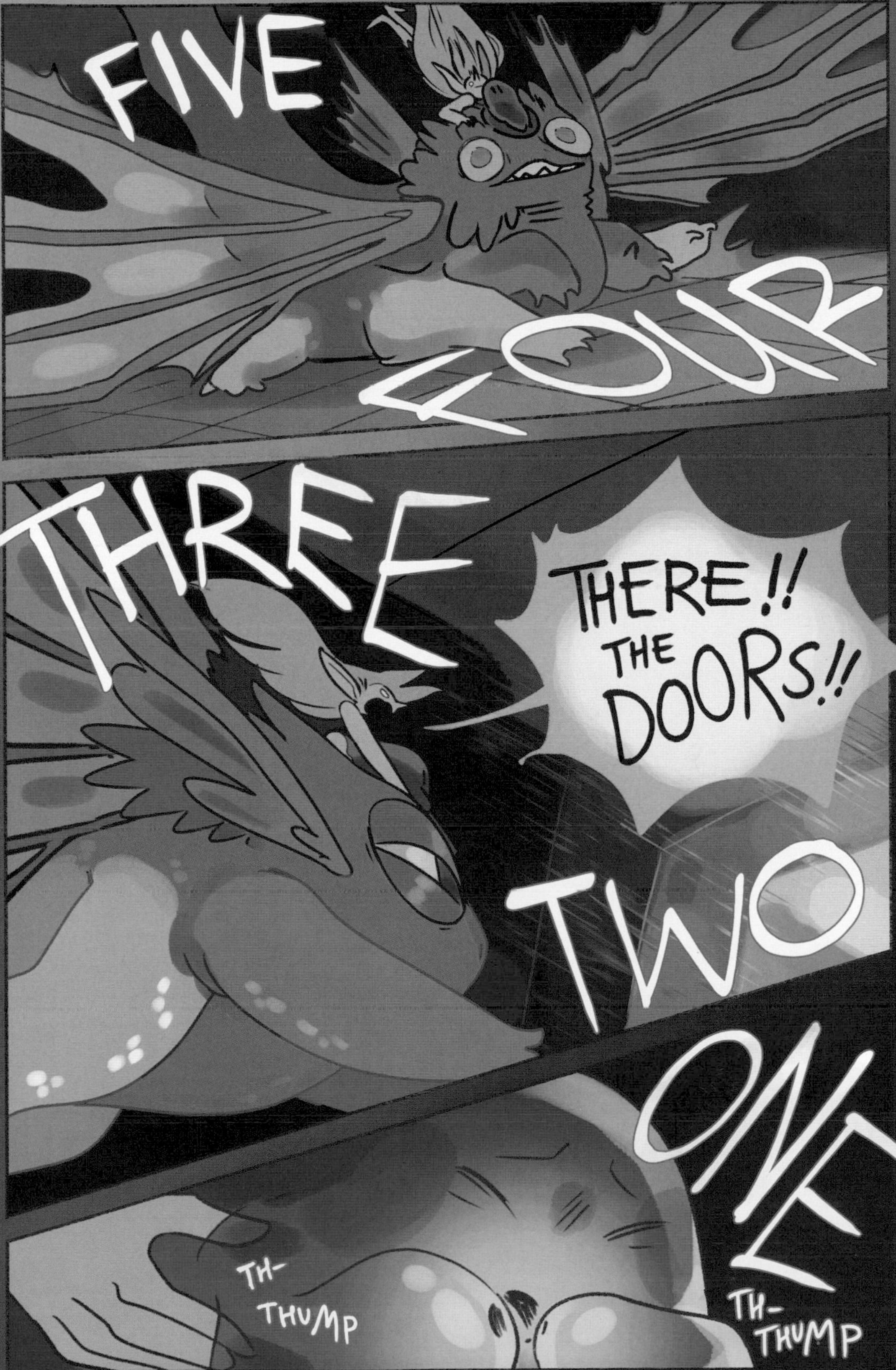
FIVE
FOUR
THREE
THERE!! THE DOORS!!
TWO
ONE
TH-THUMP
TH-THUMP

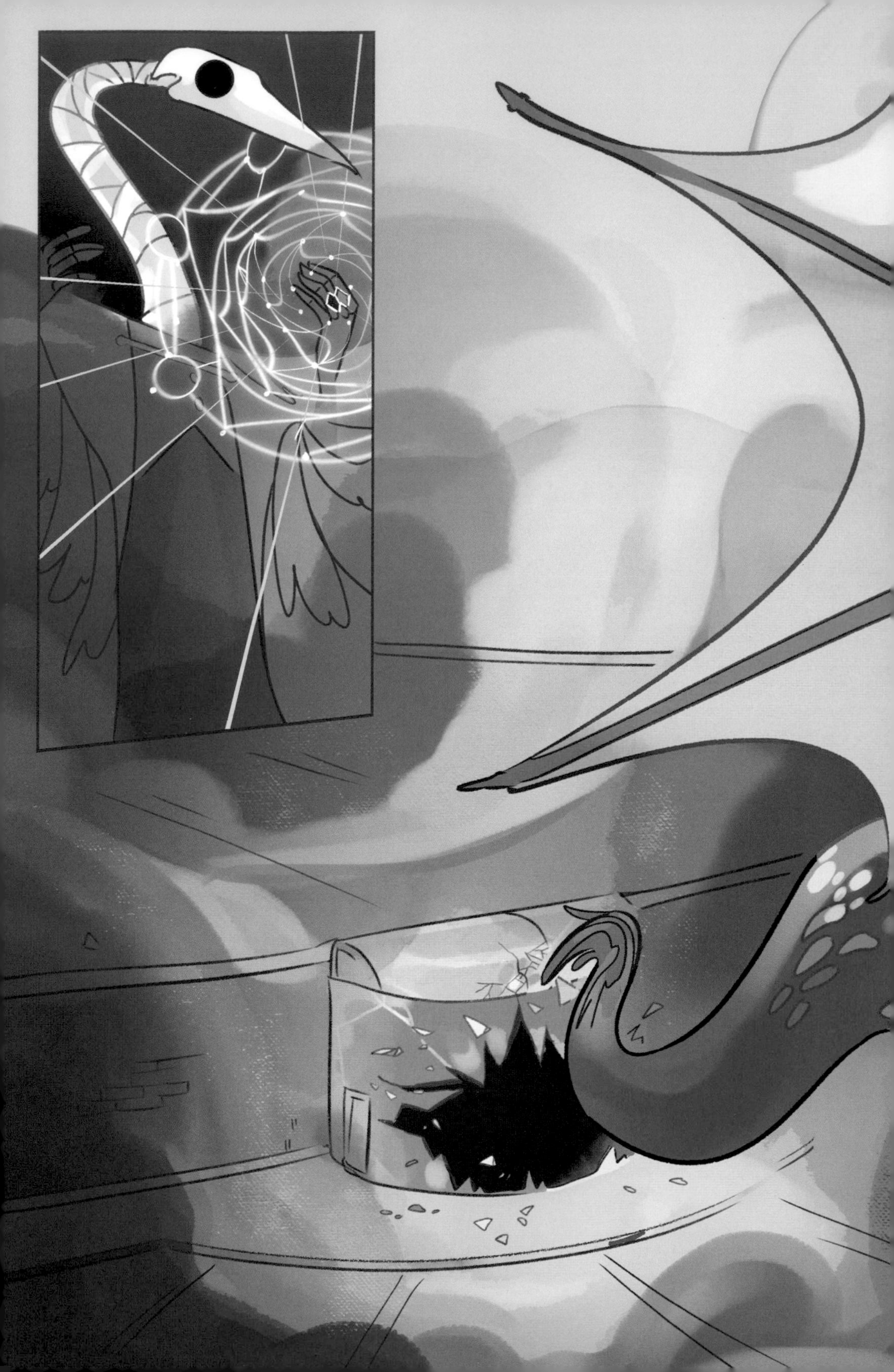

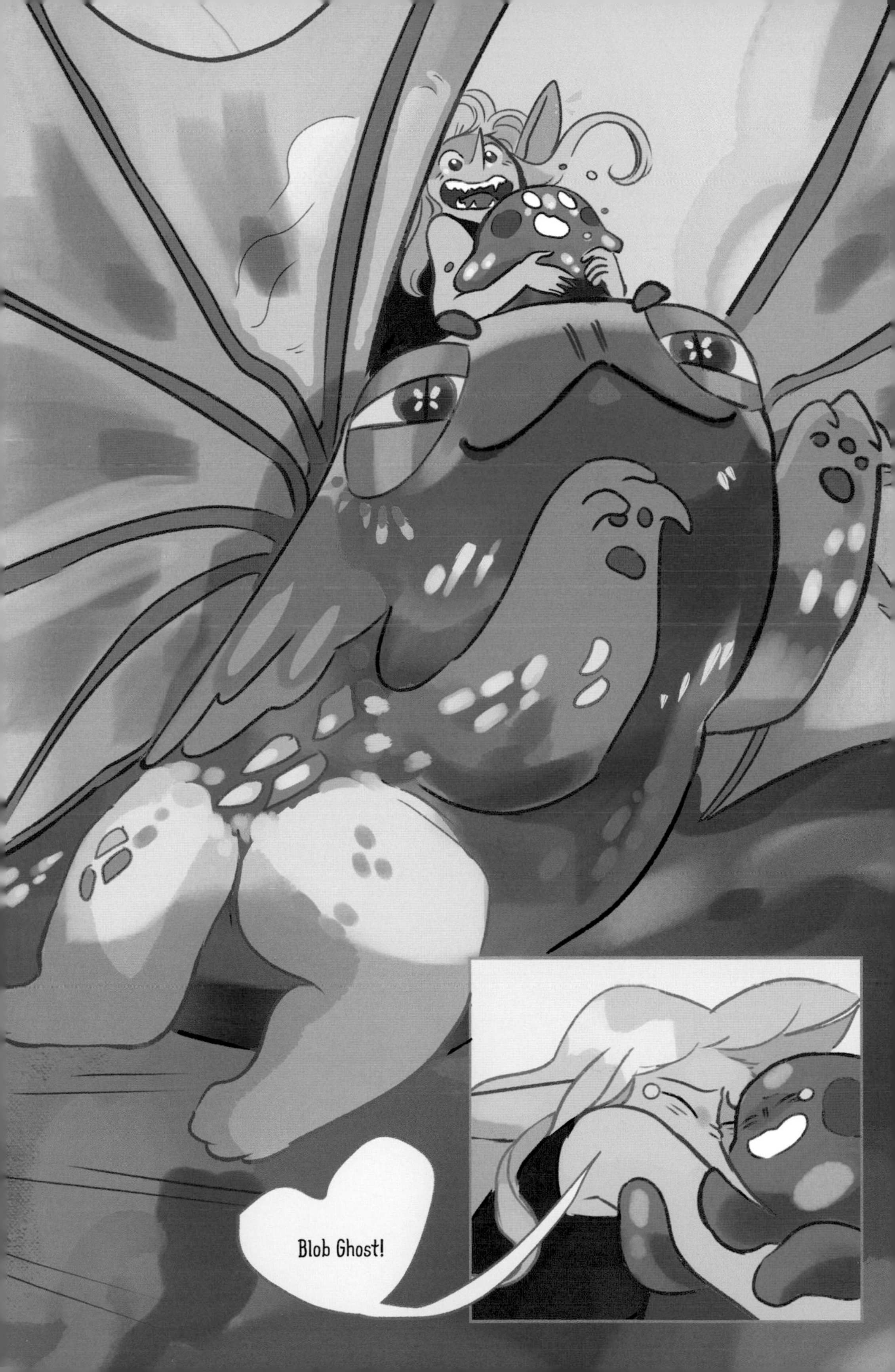
Blob Ghost!

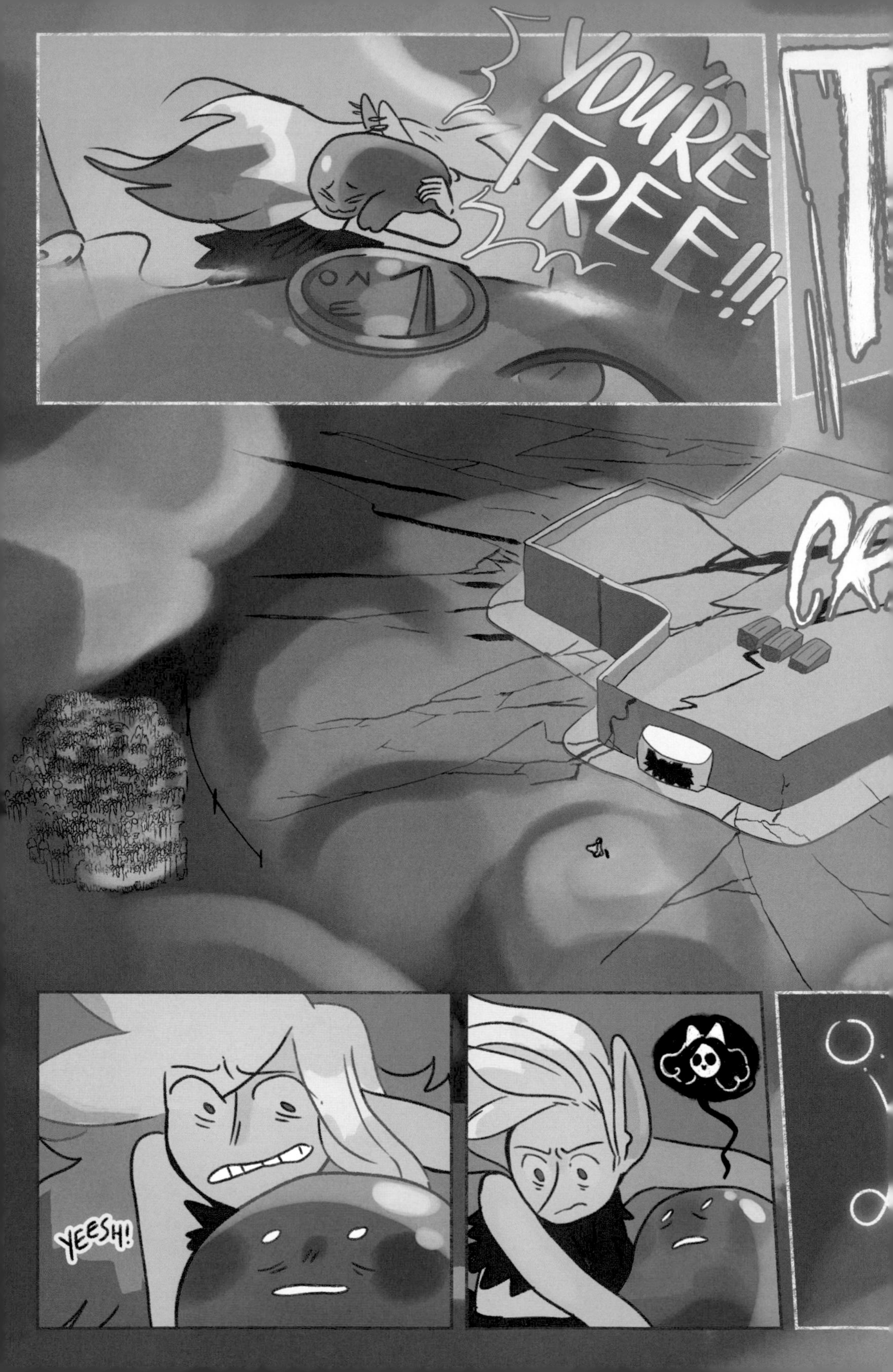

YOU'RE FREE!!!
YEESH!

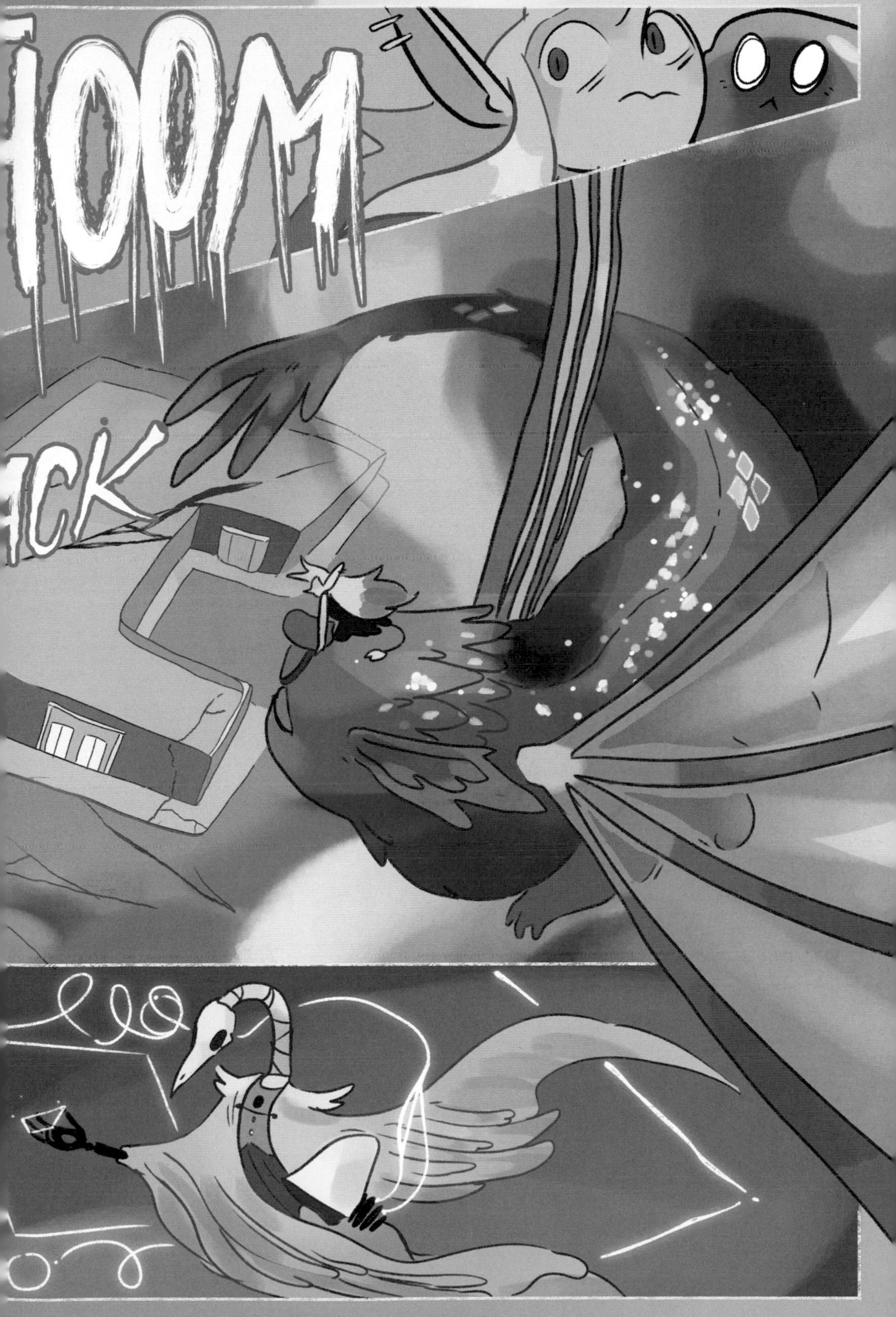
OOM
CK!

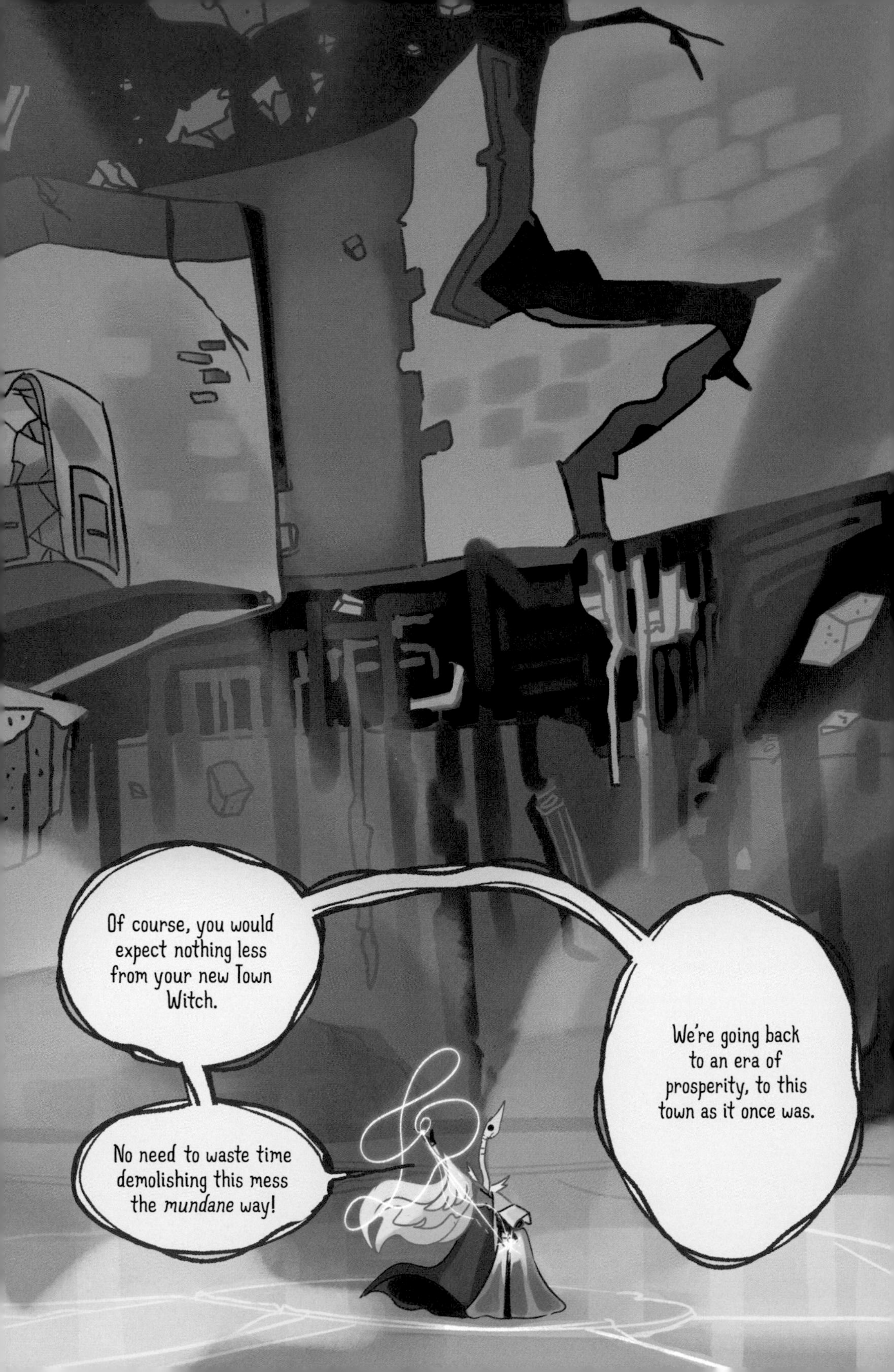
Of course, you would expect nothing less from your new Town Witch.
We're going back to an era of prosperity, to this town as it once was.
No need to waste time demolishing this mess the *mundane* way!

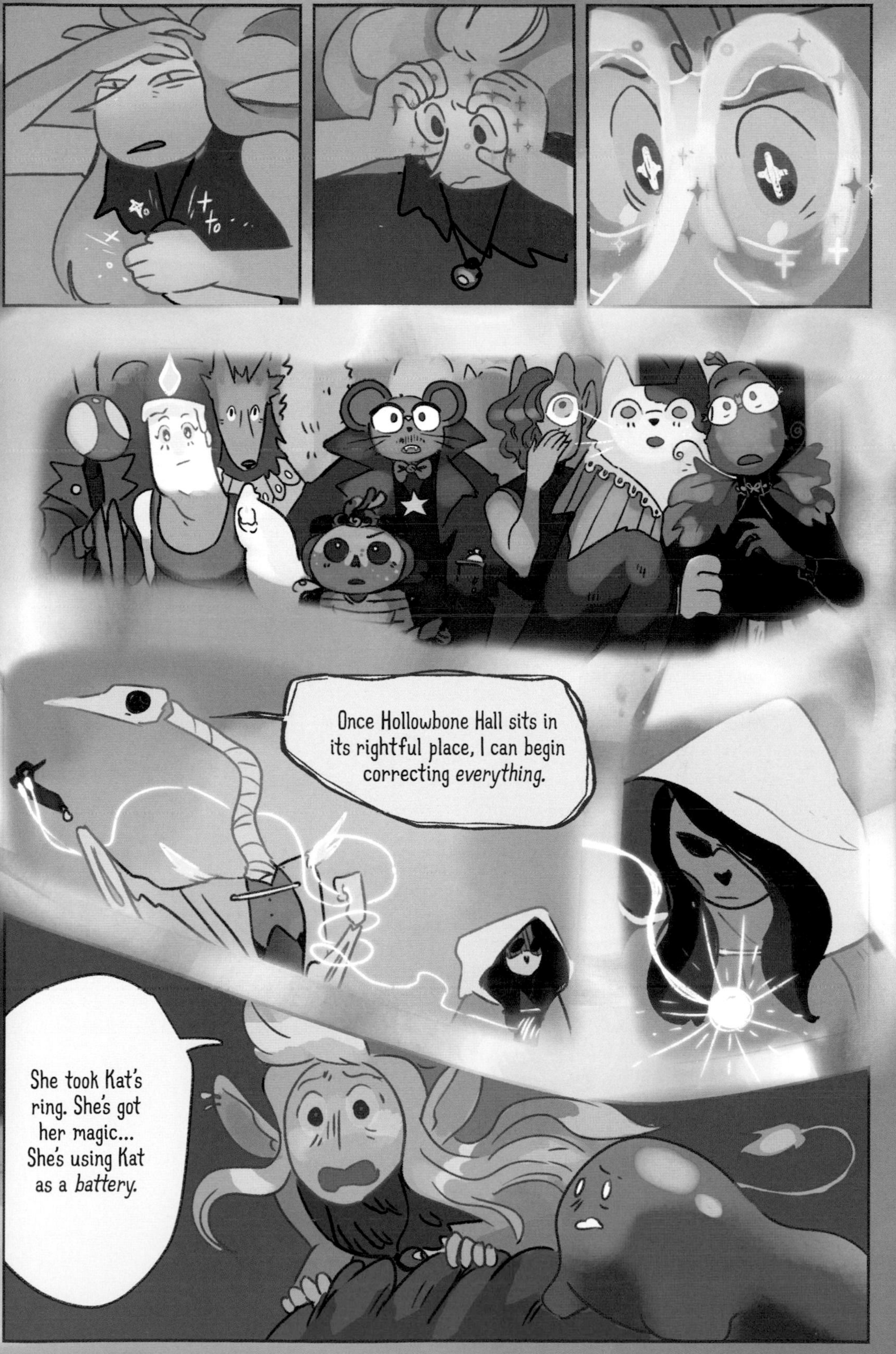
Once Hollowbone Hall sits in its rightful place, I can begin correcting *everything*.
She took Kat's ring. She's got her magic... She's using Kat as a *battery*.

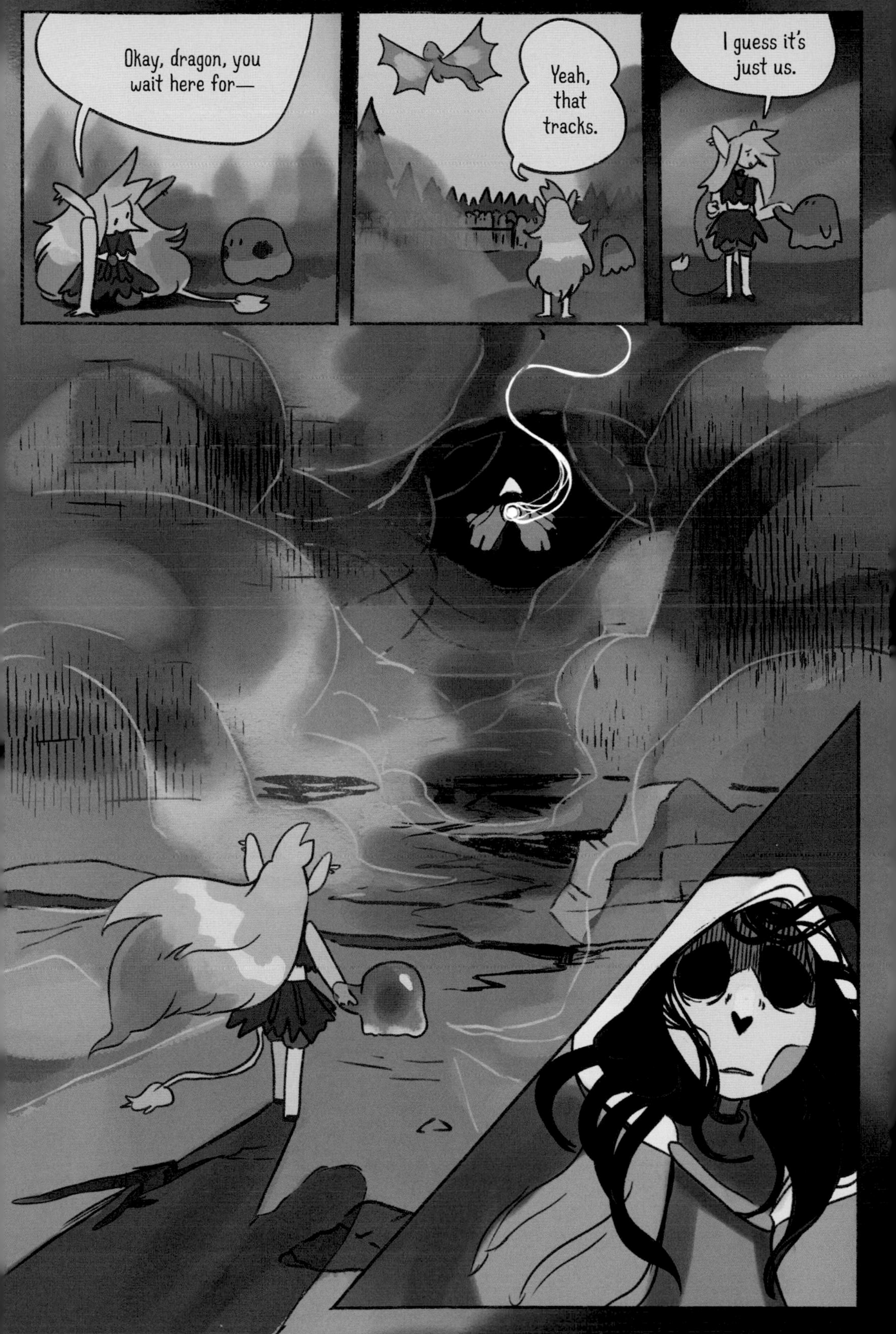
Okay, dragon, you wait here for—
Yeah, that tracks.
I guess it's just us.

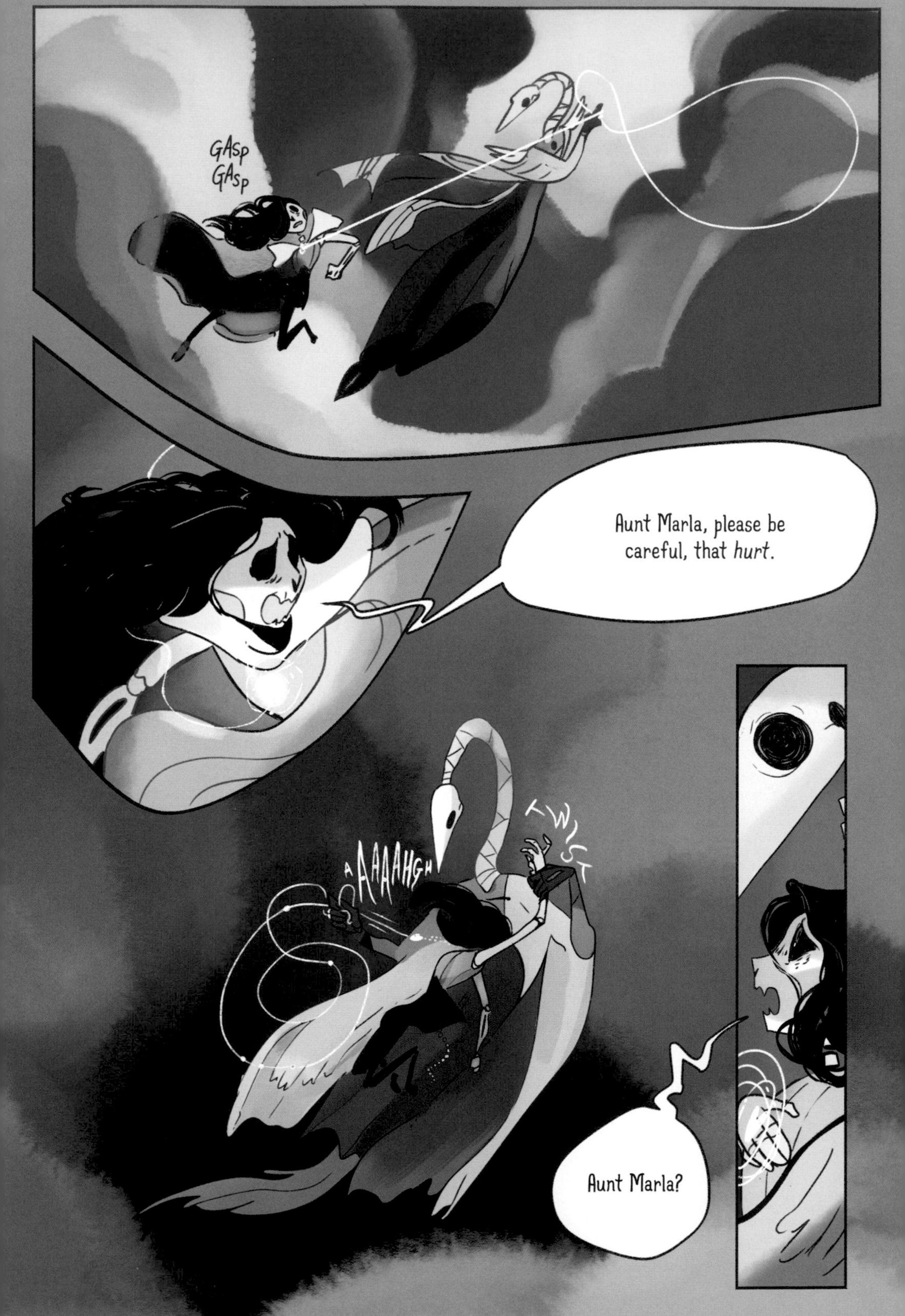
GASP
GASP
Aunt Marla, please be careful, that *hurt*.
AAAAAHGH
TWIST
Aunt Marla?

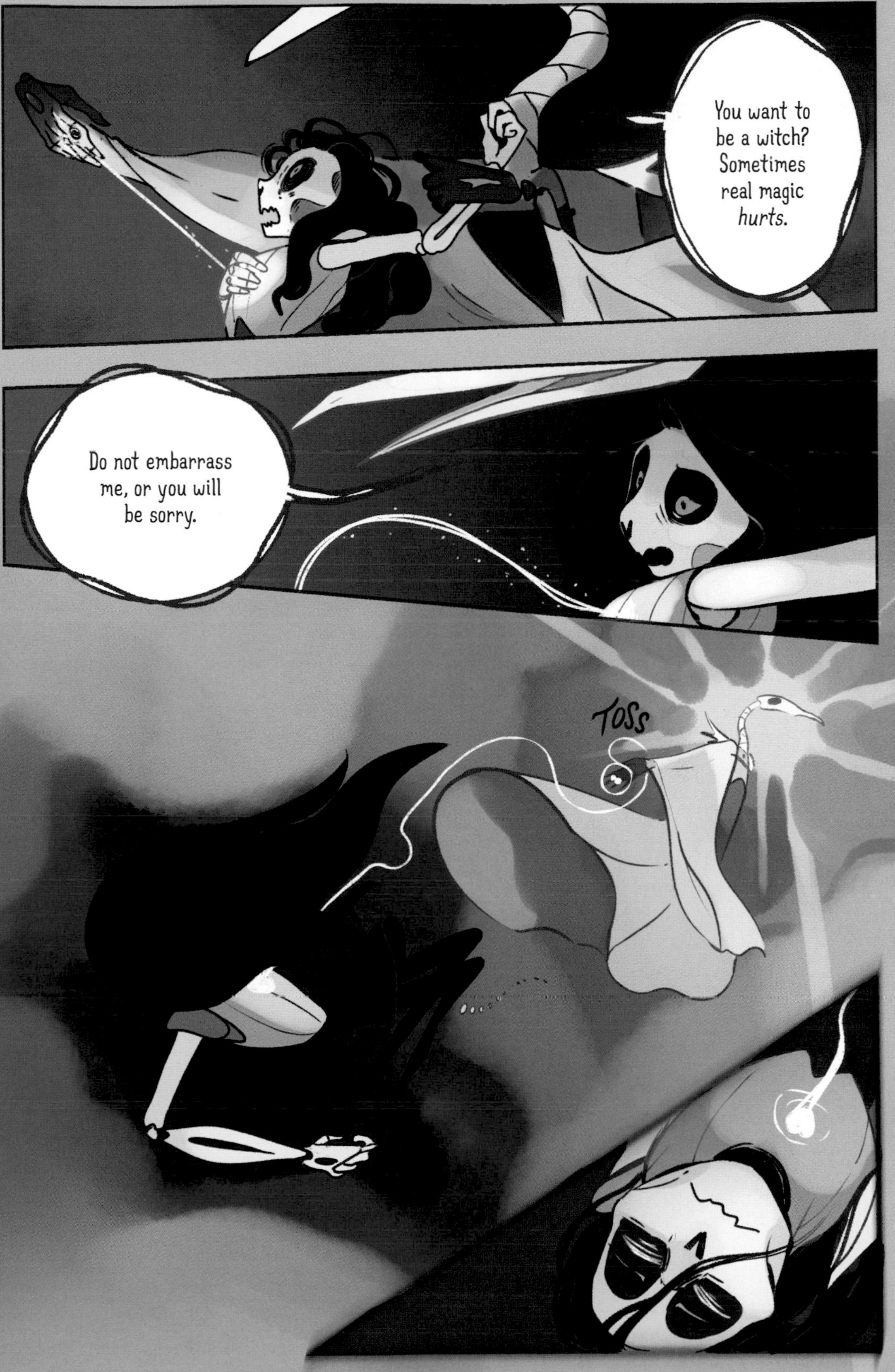
You want to be a witch? Sometimes real magic *hurts*.
Do not embarrass me, or you will be sorry.
TOSS

KAT!!!

KAT!!

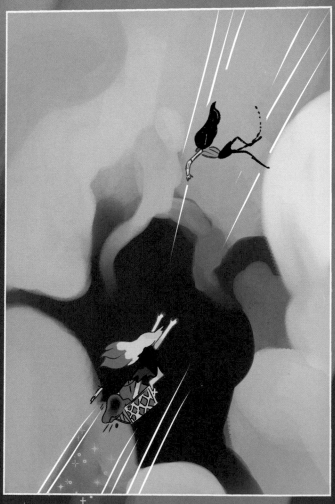

I'VE

GOT YOU!!

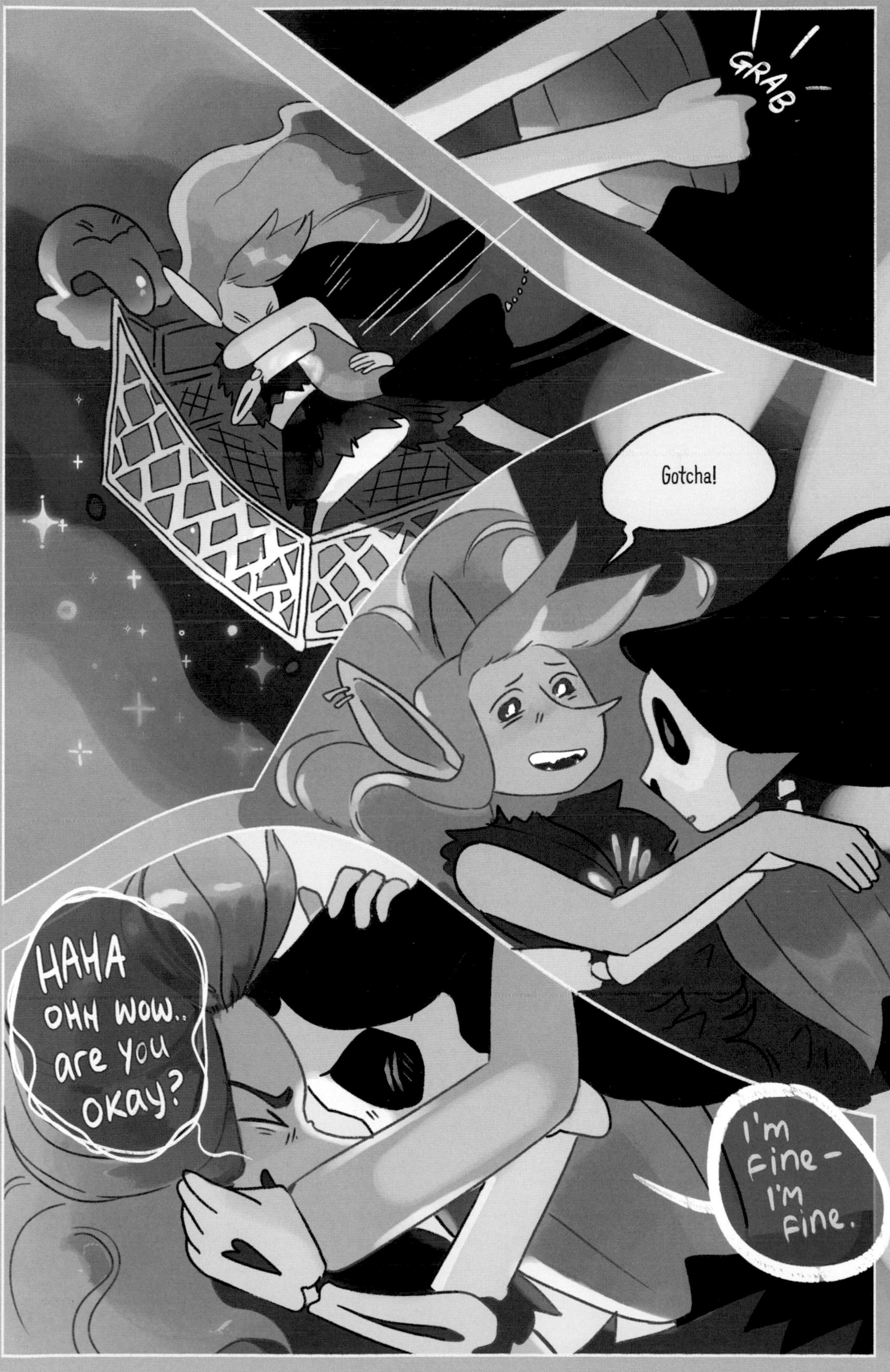
GRAB
Gotcha!
HAHA OHH WOW.. are you okay?
I'm fine- I'm fine.

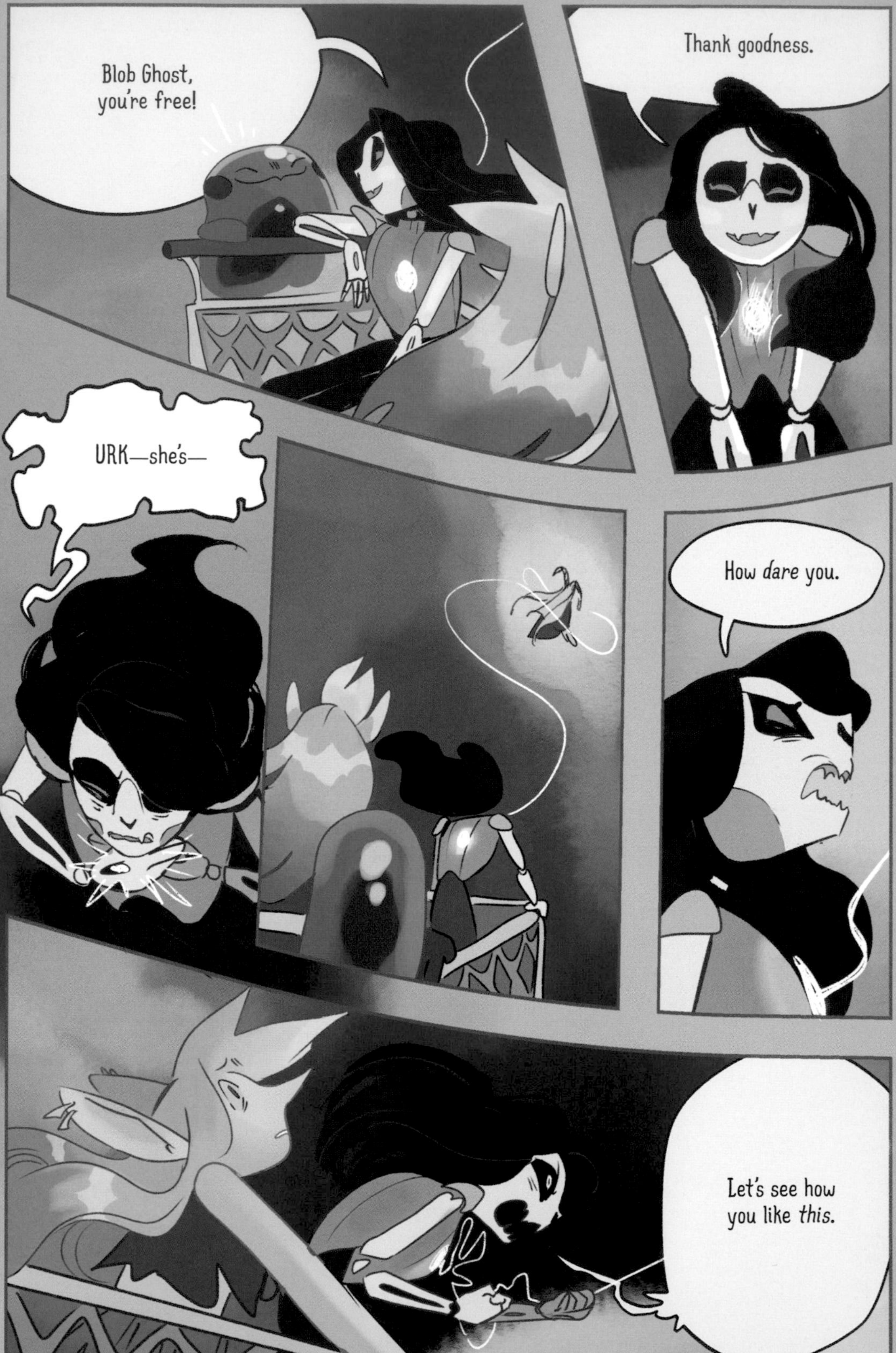
Blob Ghost, you're free!
Thank goodness.
URK—she's—
How *dare* you.
Let's see how you like *this*.

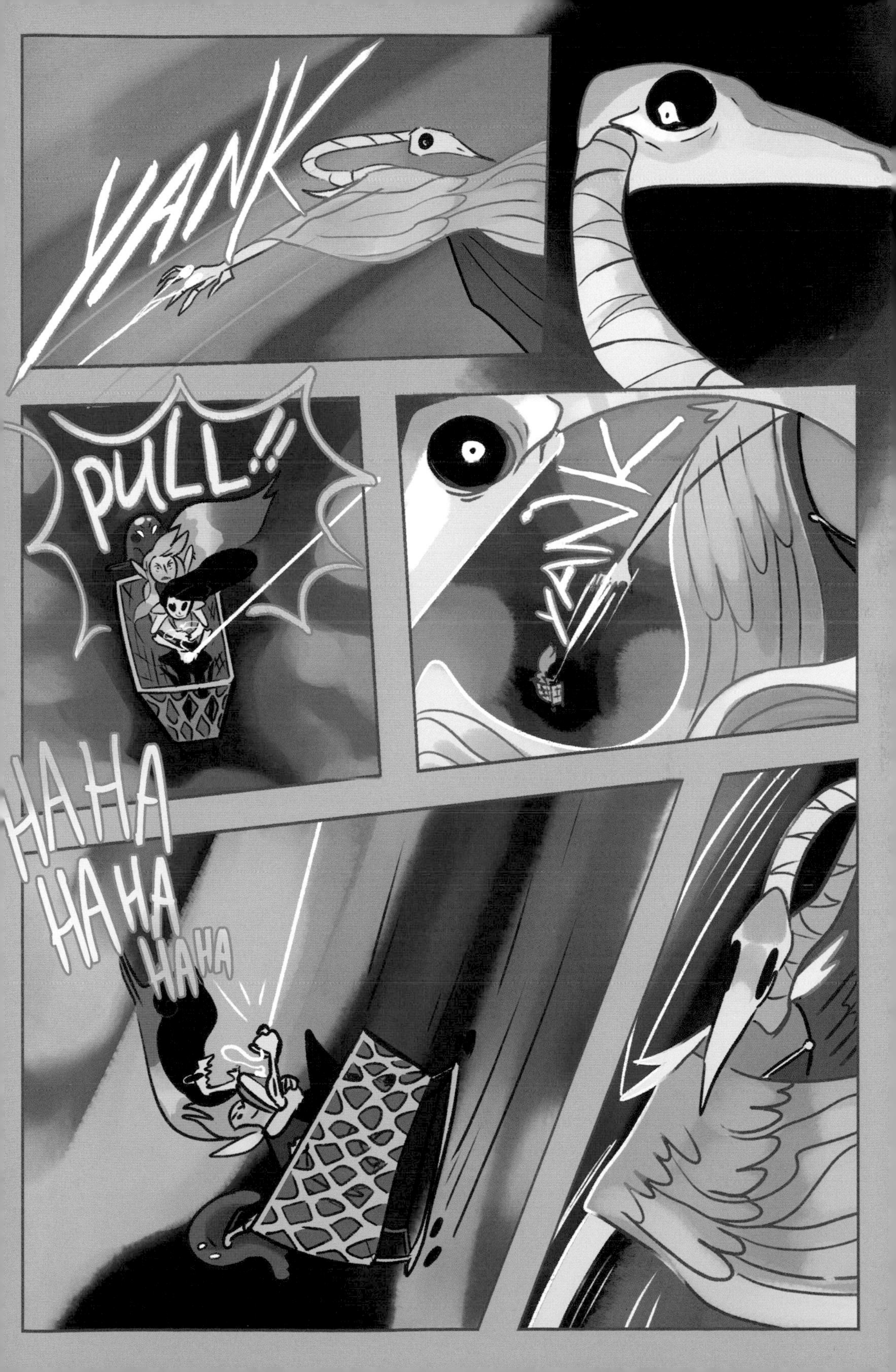
YANK
PULL!!
YANK
HAHA
HAHA
HAHA

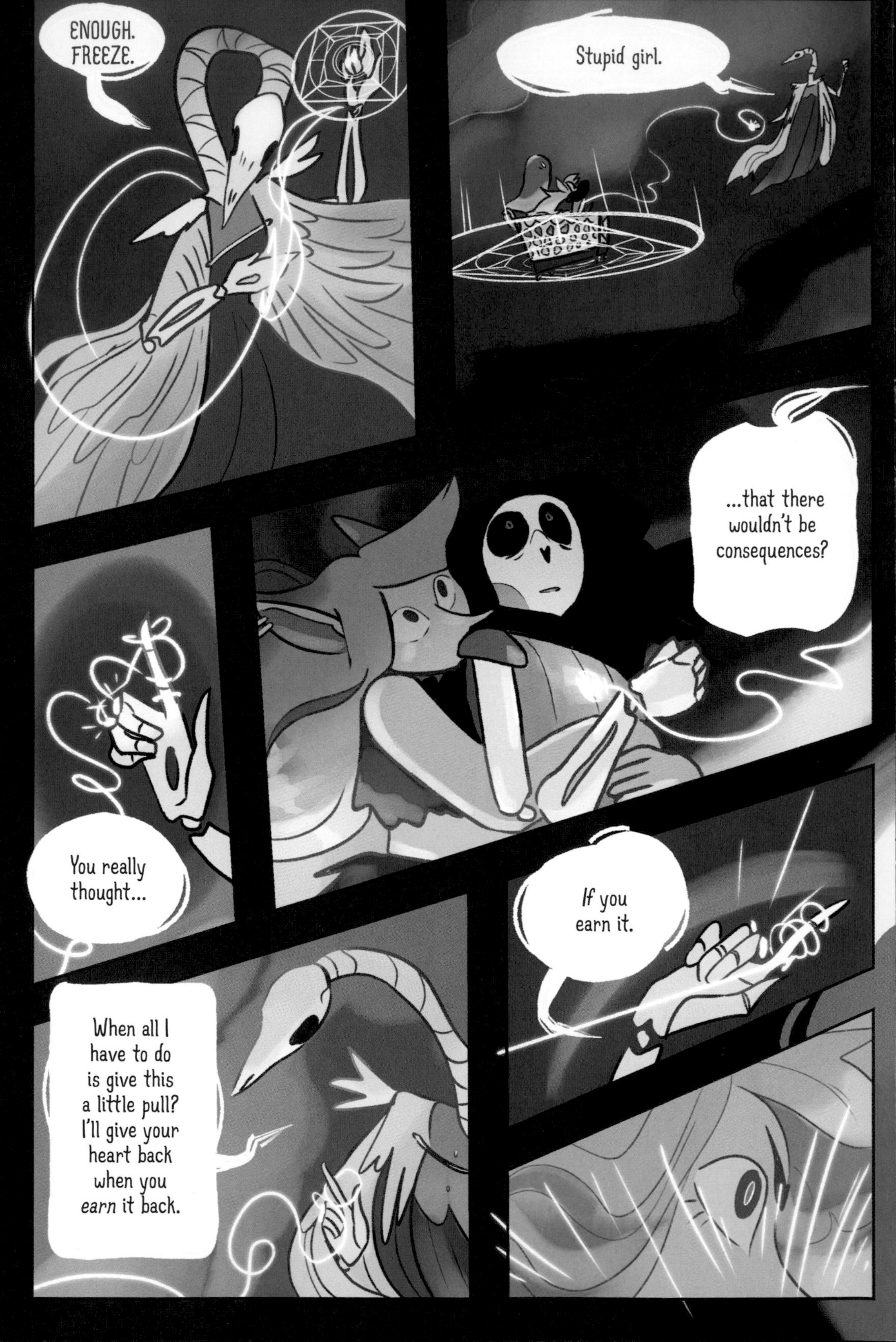
ENOUGH. FREEZE.
Stupid girl.
...that there wouldn't be consequences?
You really thought...
If you earn it.
When all I have to do is give this a little pull? I'll give your heart back when you *earn* it back.

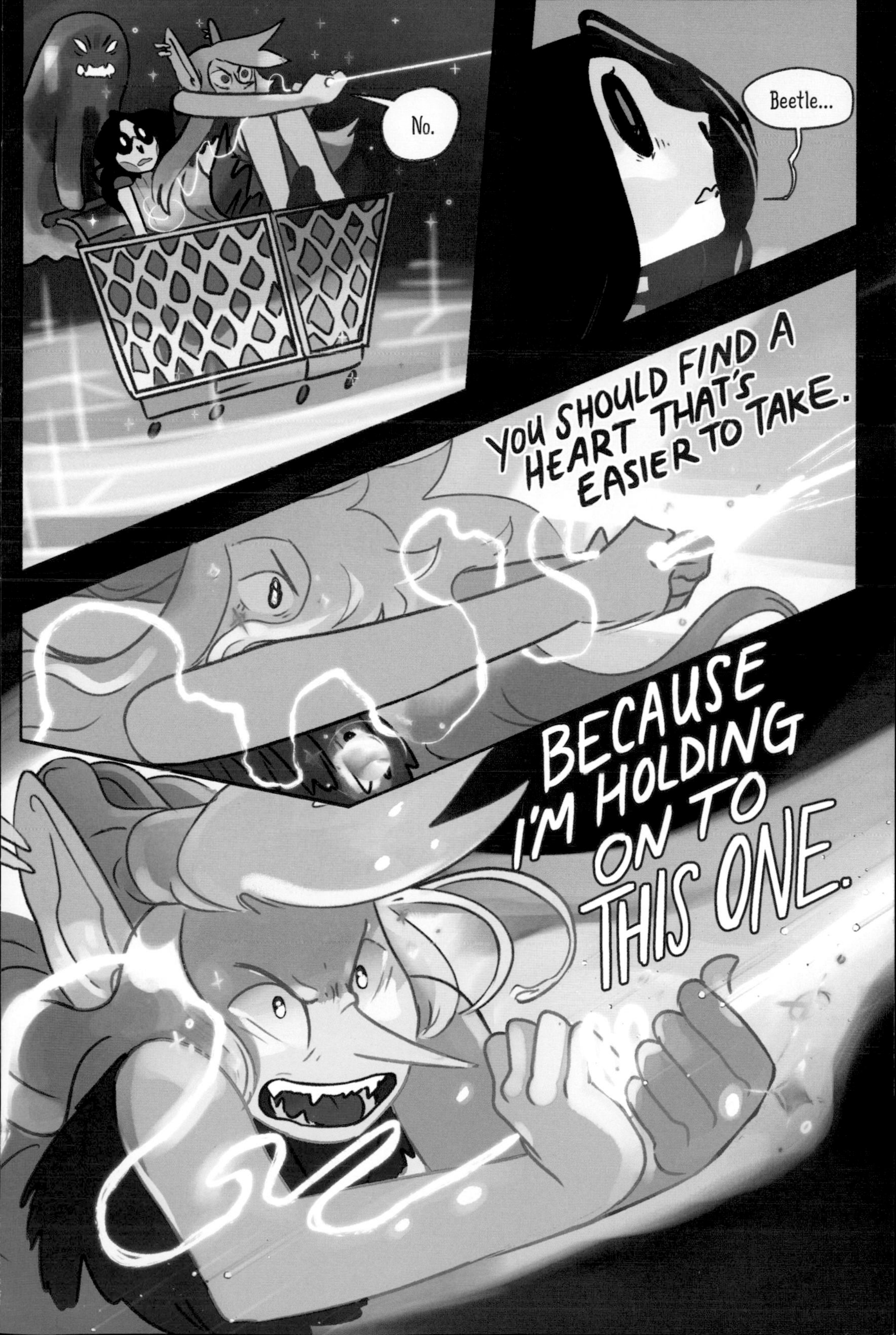
No.
Beetle...
YOU SHOULD FIND A HEART THAT'S EASIER TO TAKE.
BECAUSE I'M HOLDING ON TO THIS ONE.

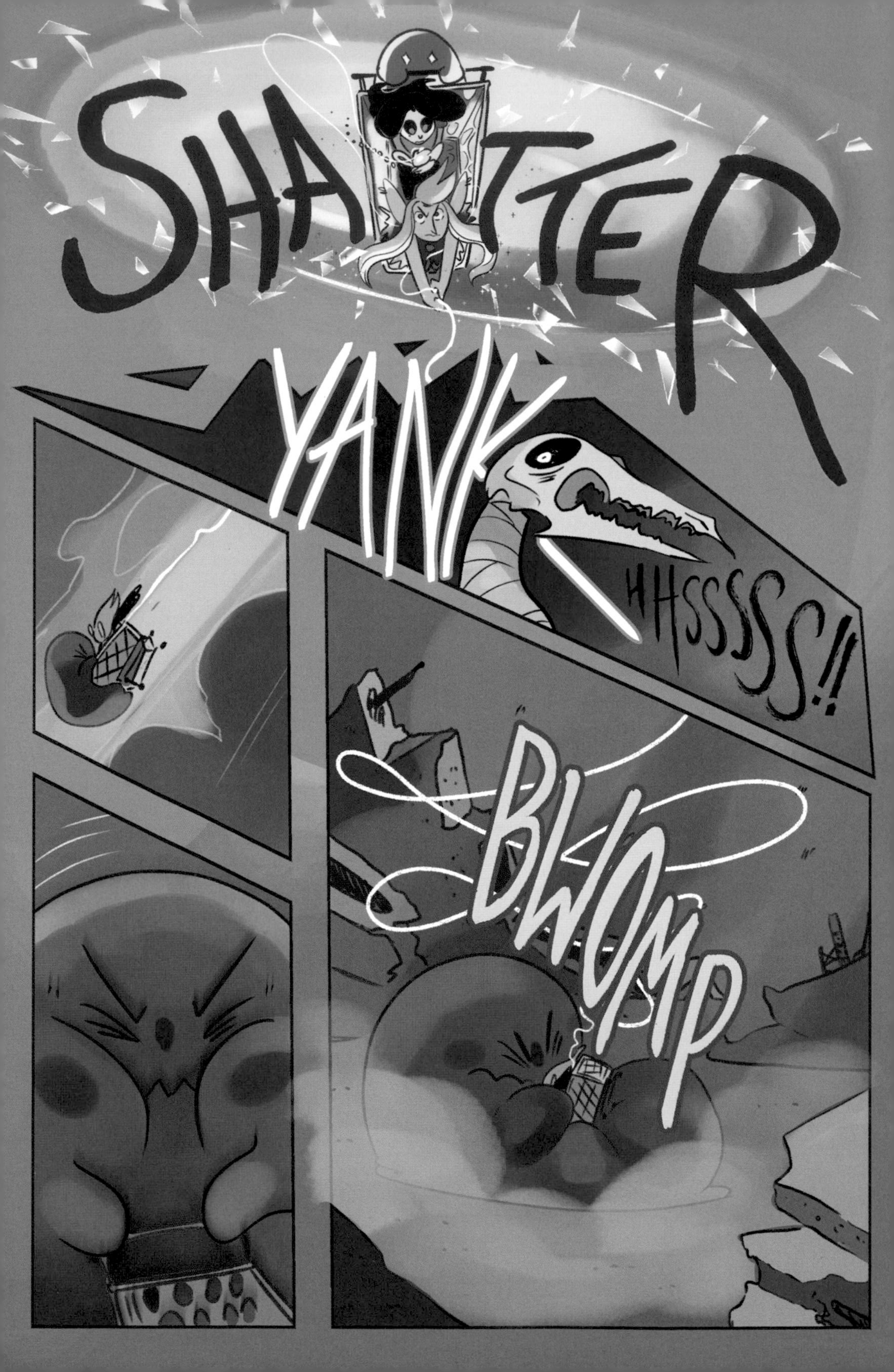
SHATTER
YANK
HHSSSSSS!!
BWOMP

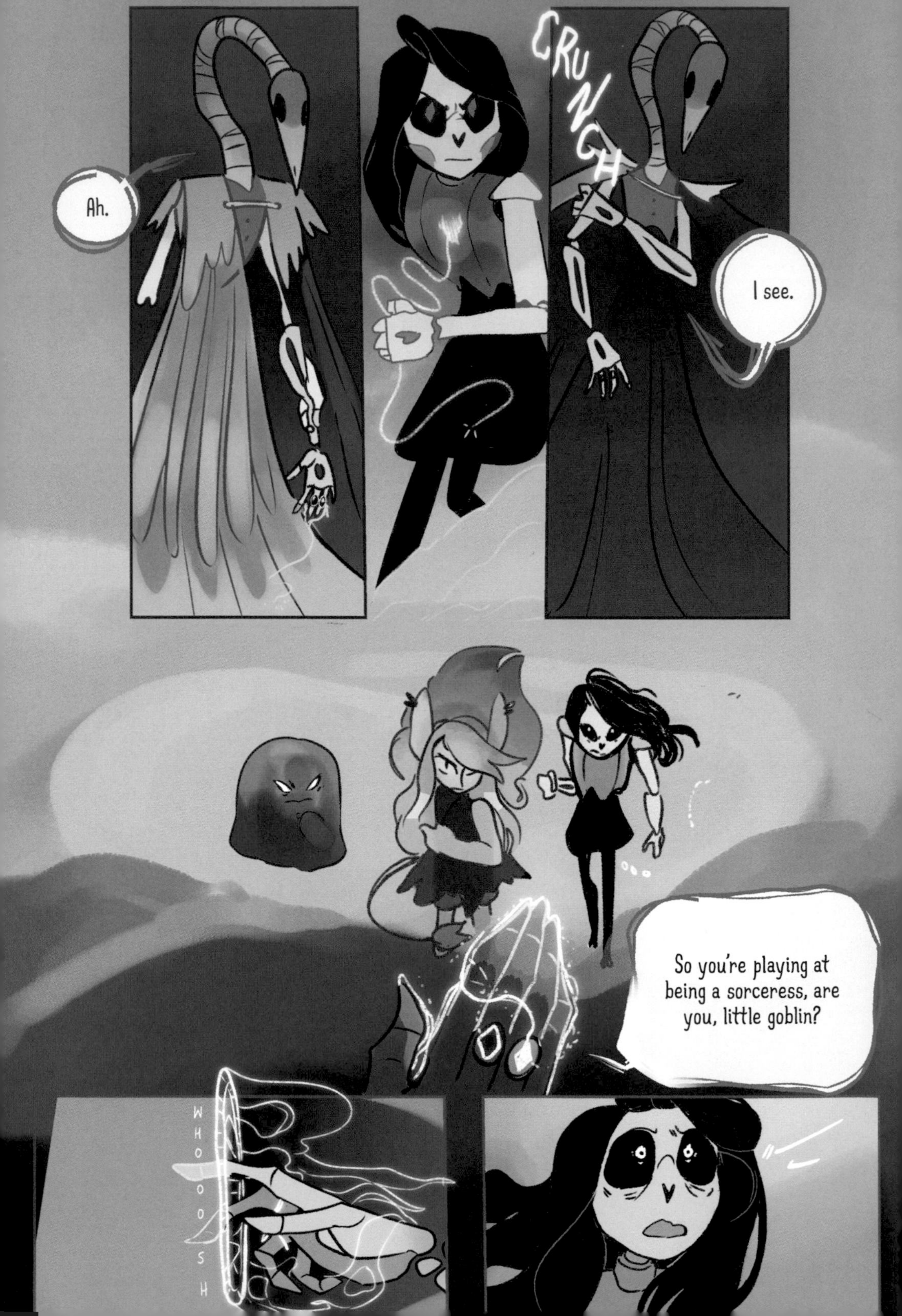
Ah.
CRUNCH
I see.
So you're playing at being a sorceress, are you, little goblin?
WHOOOOSH

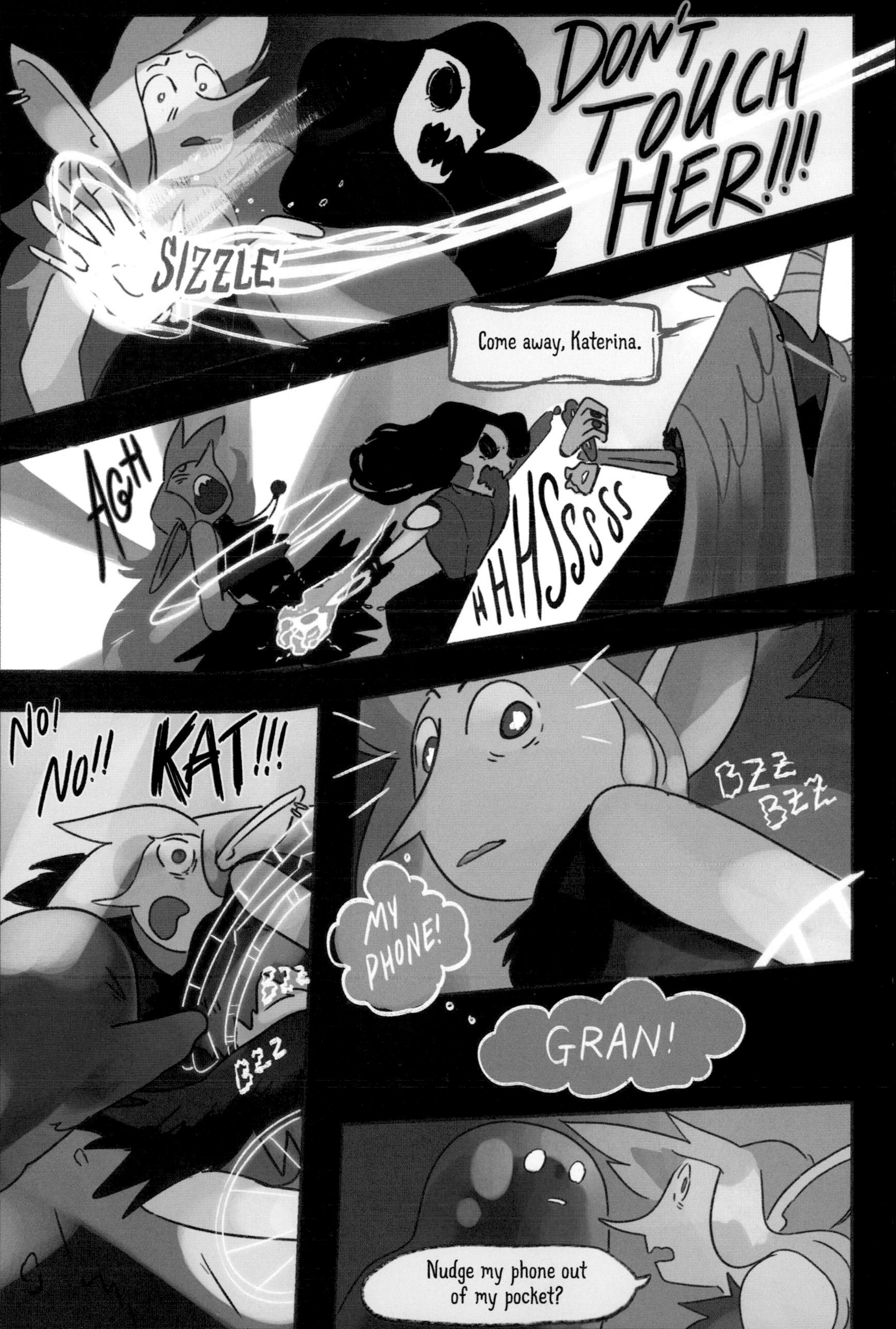
DON'T TOUCH HER!!!
SIZZLE
Come away, Katerina.
AGH
HHSSSSS
No! No!! KAT!!!
BZZ
BZZ
BZZ BZZ
MY PHONE!
GRAN!
Nudge my phone out of my pocket?

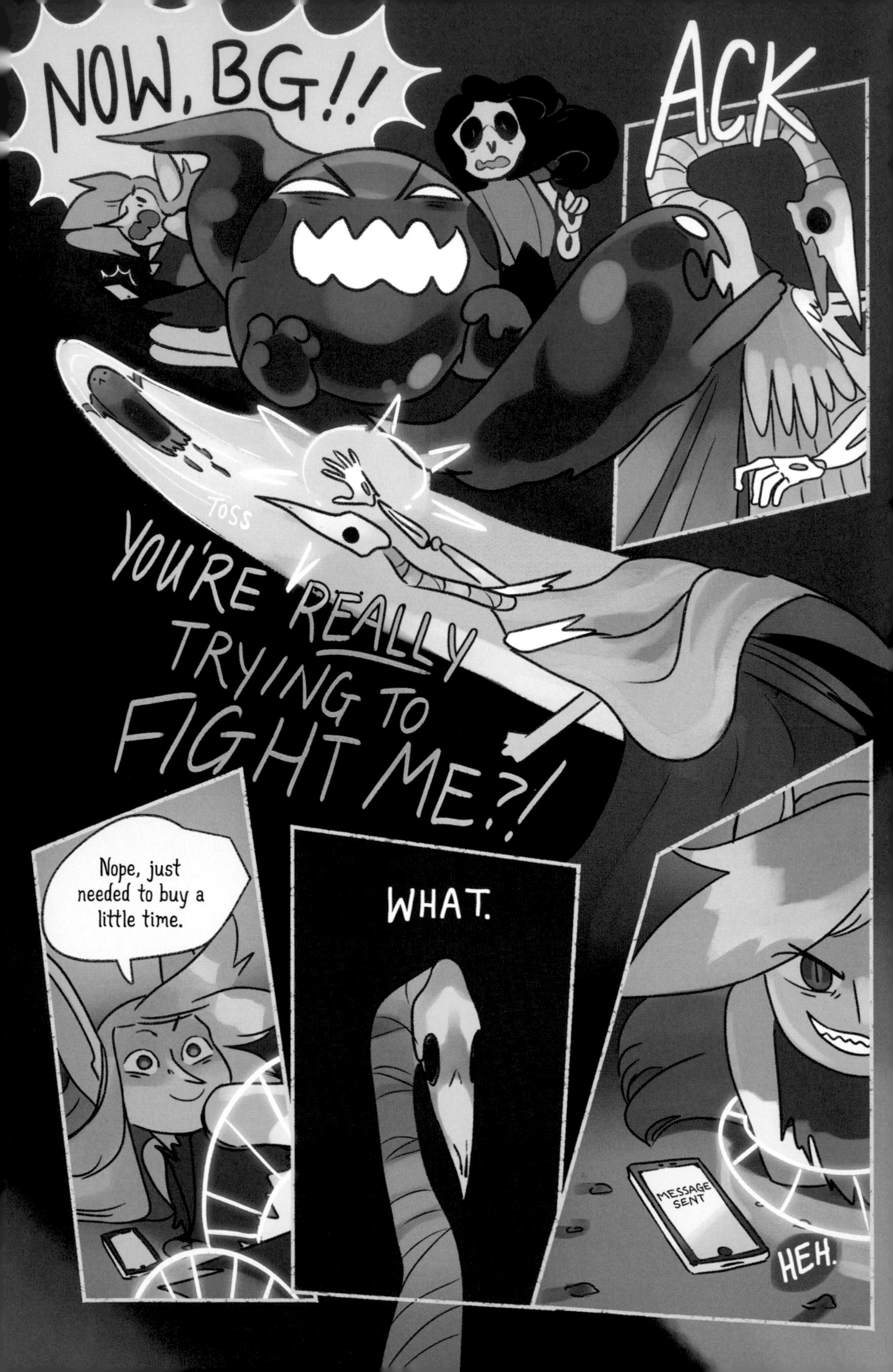
NOW, BG!!
ACK
TOSS
YOU'RE REALLY TRYING TO FIGHT ME?!
Nope, just needed to buy a little time.
WHAT.
MESSAGE SENT
HEH.

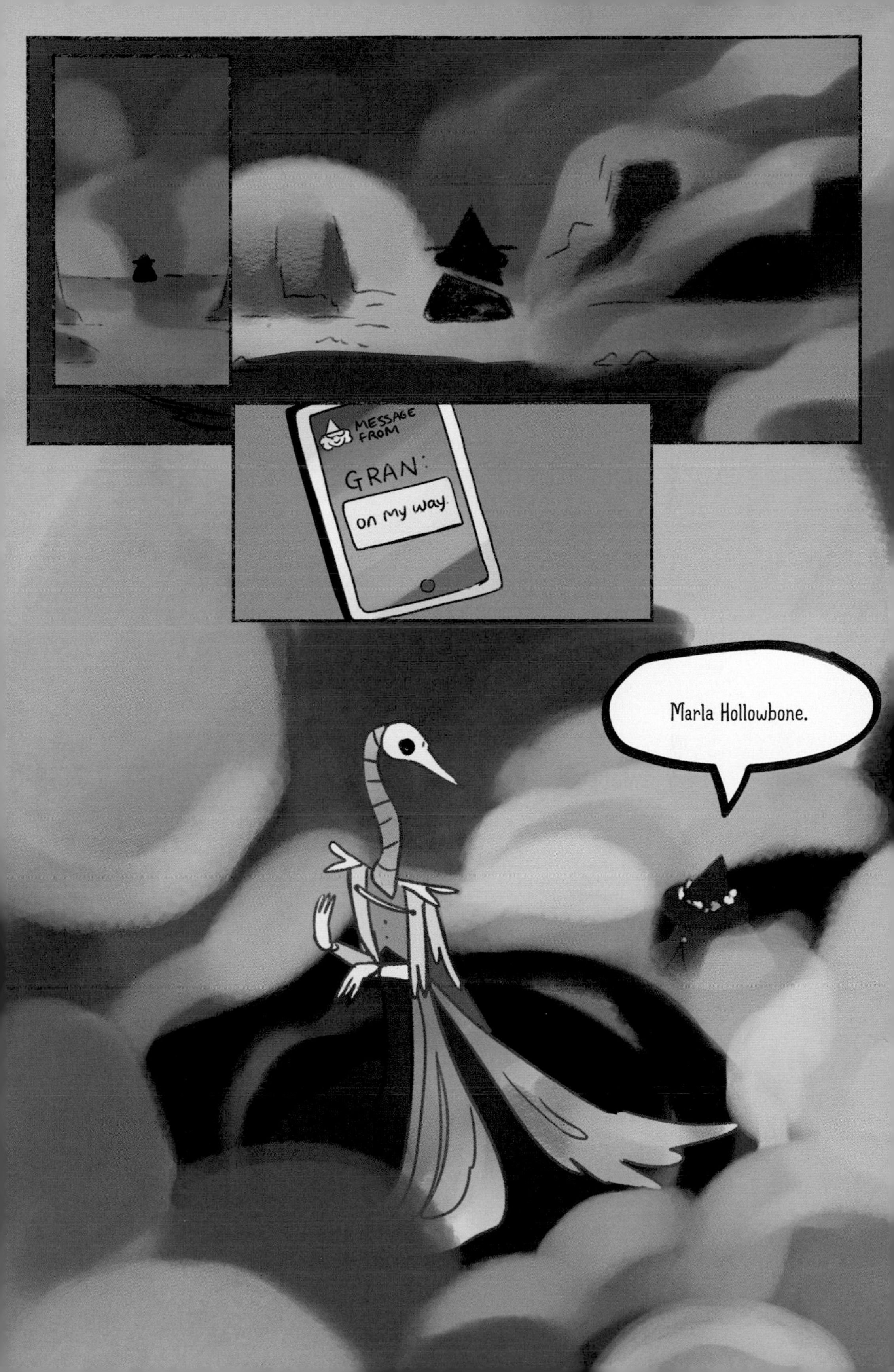
MESSAGE FROM
GRAN:
on my way.
Marla Hollowbone.

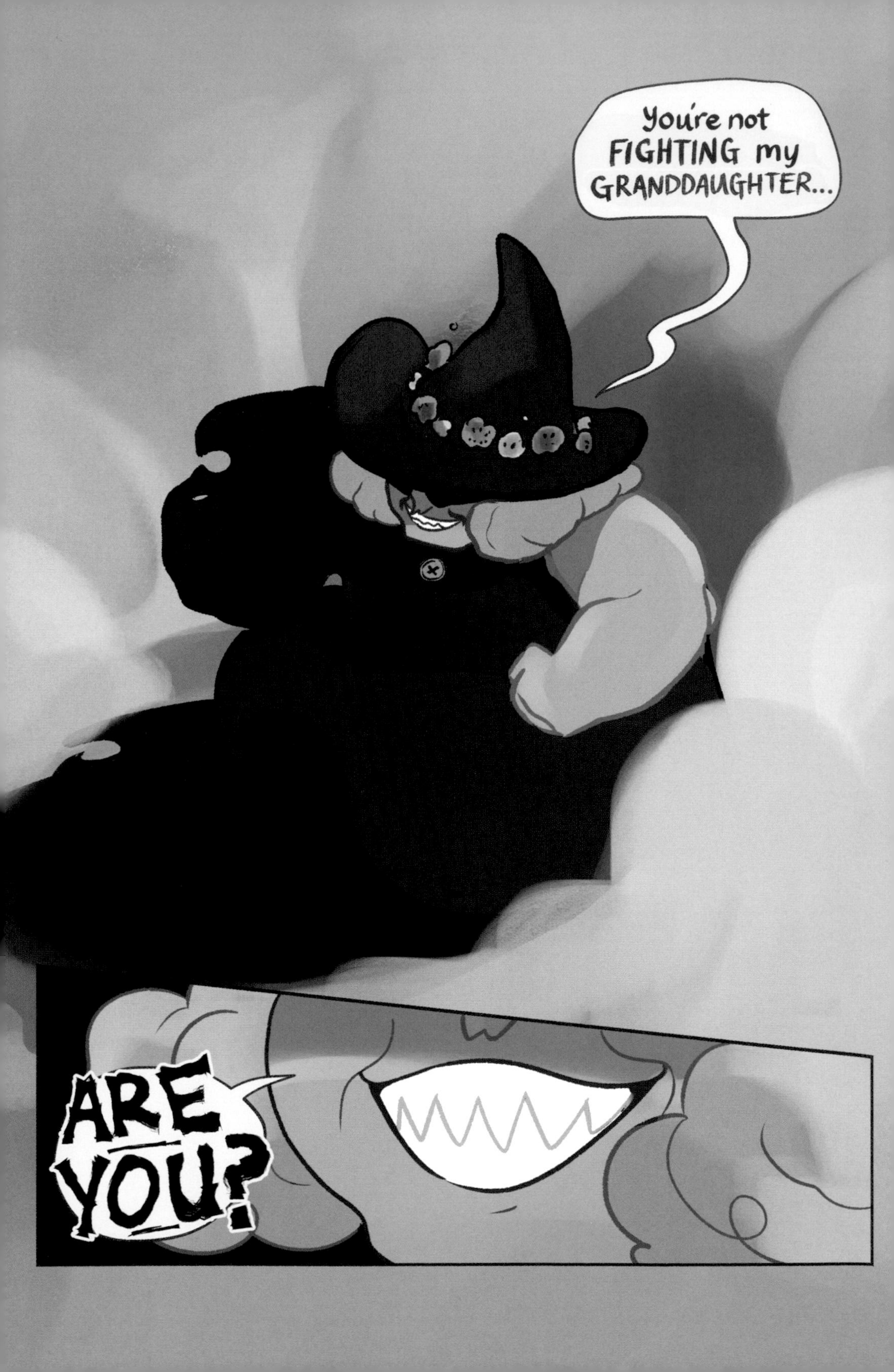
You're not FIGHTING my GRANDDAUGHTER...
ARE YOU?

GOBLIN
MAGIC

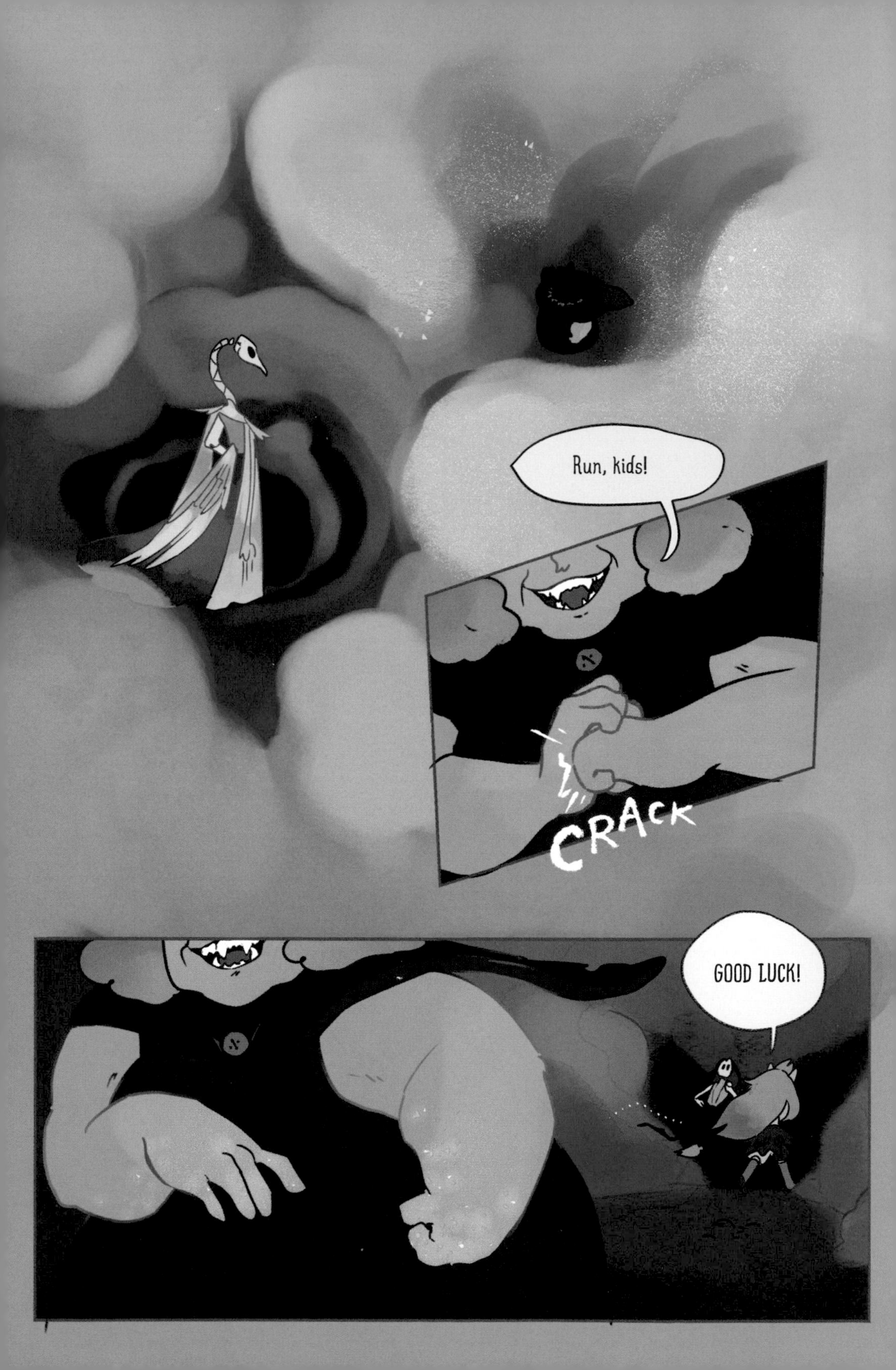
Run, kids!
CRACK
GOOD LUCK!

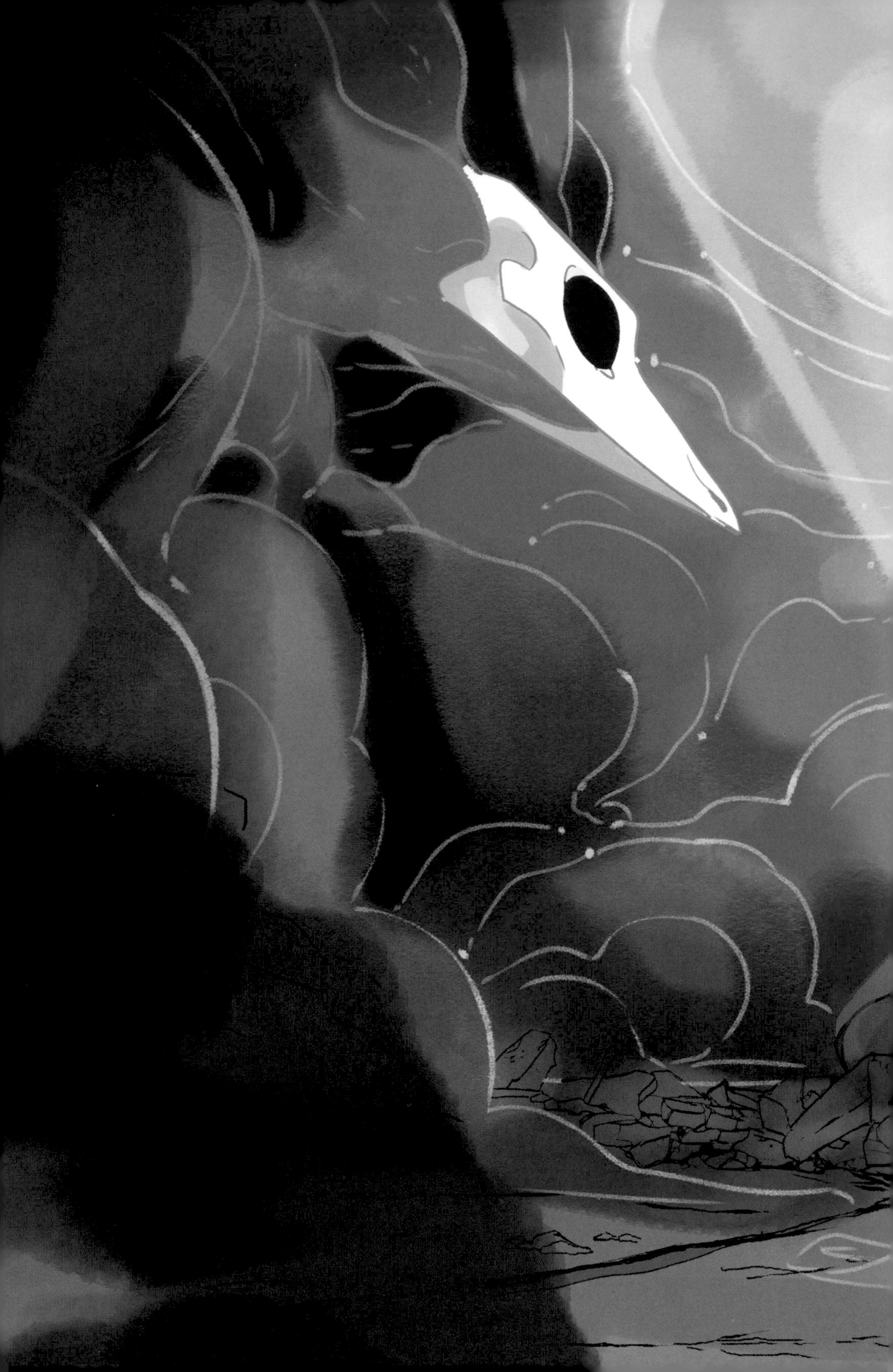

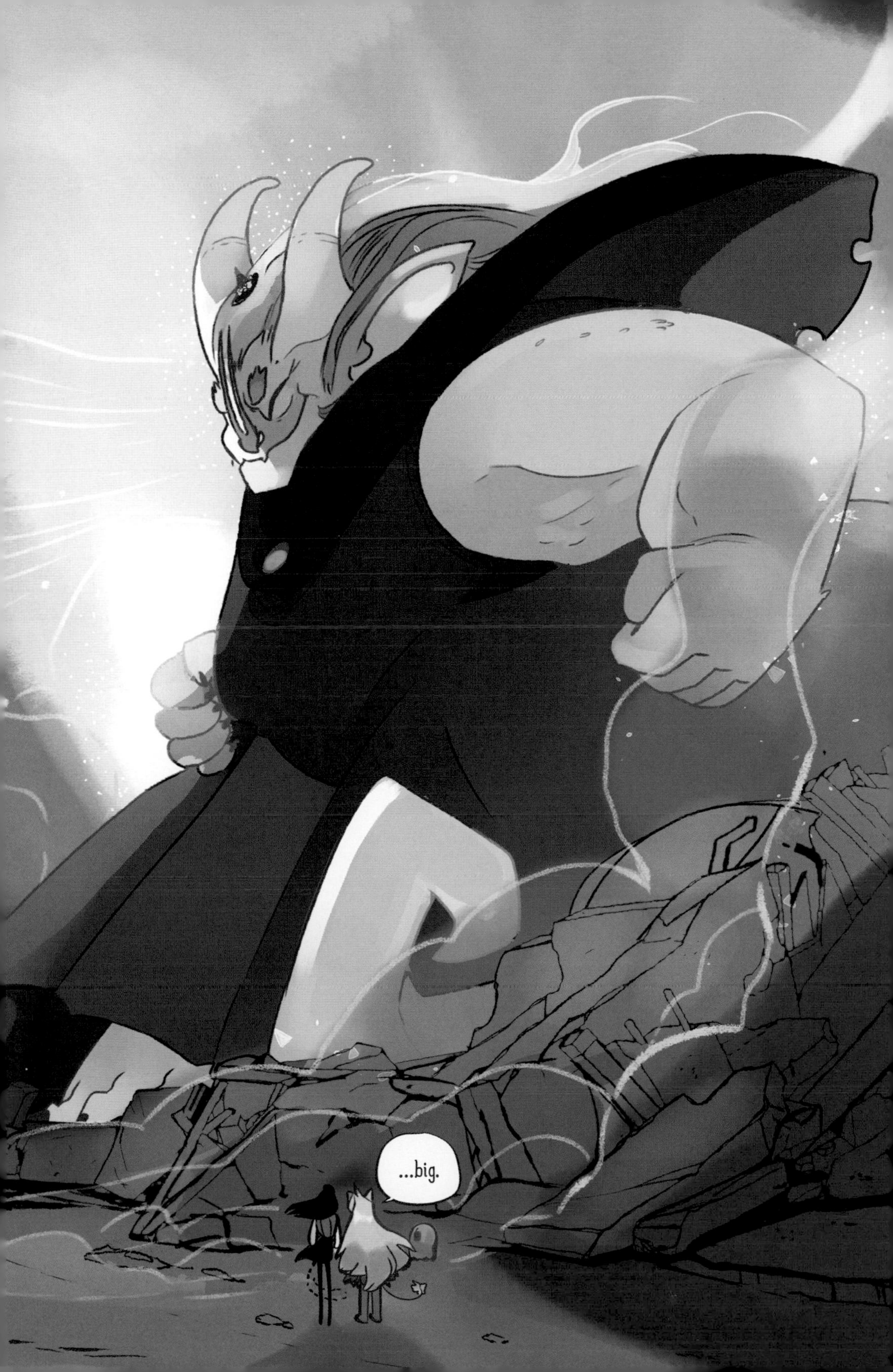
...big.

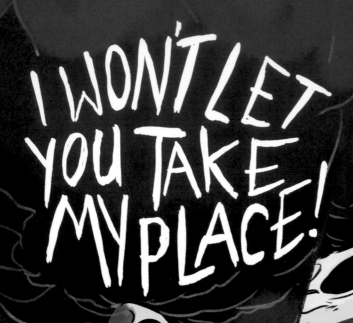

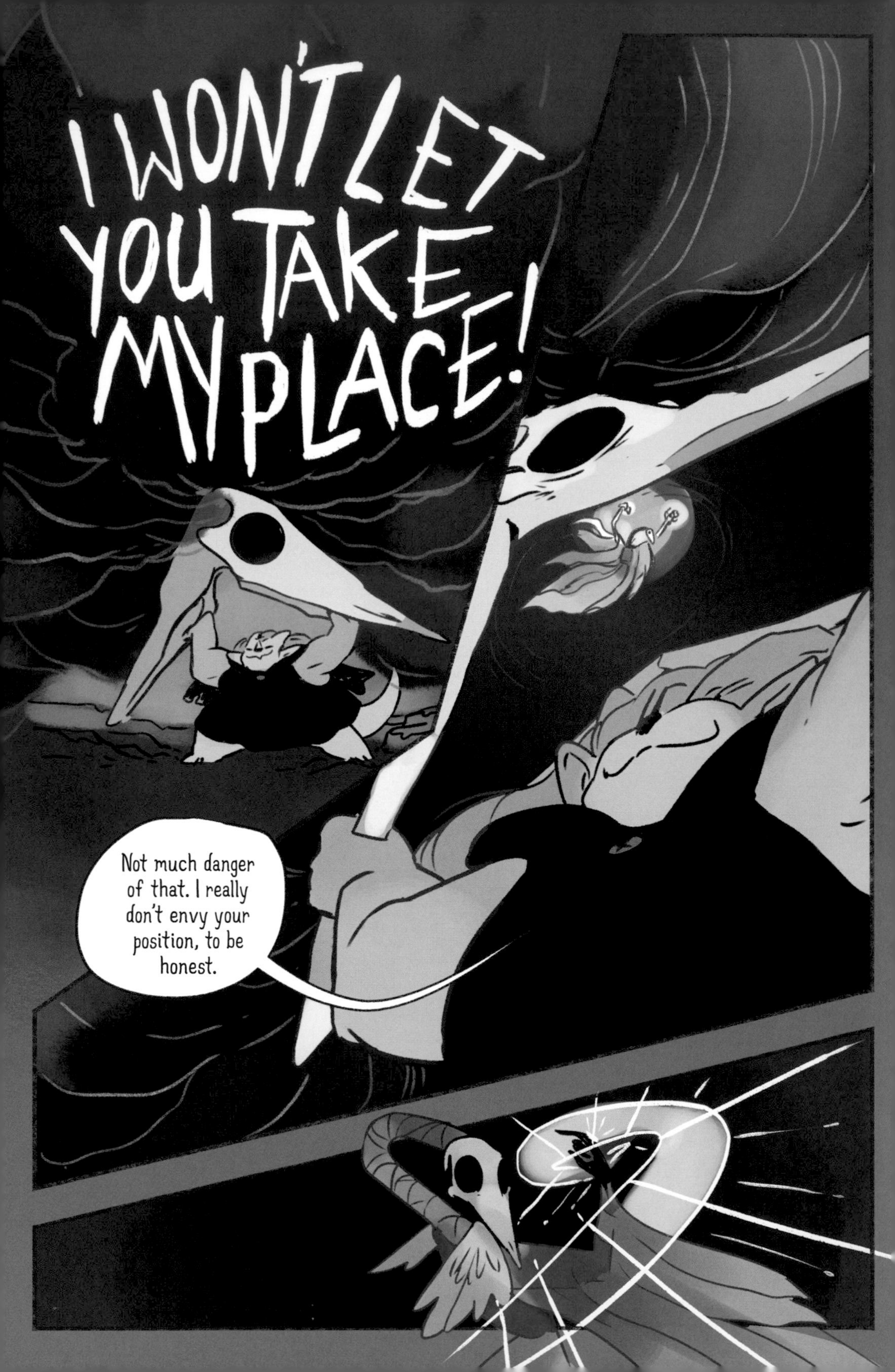
I WON'T LET YOU TAKE MY PLACE!
Not much danger of that. I really don't envy your position, to be honest.

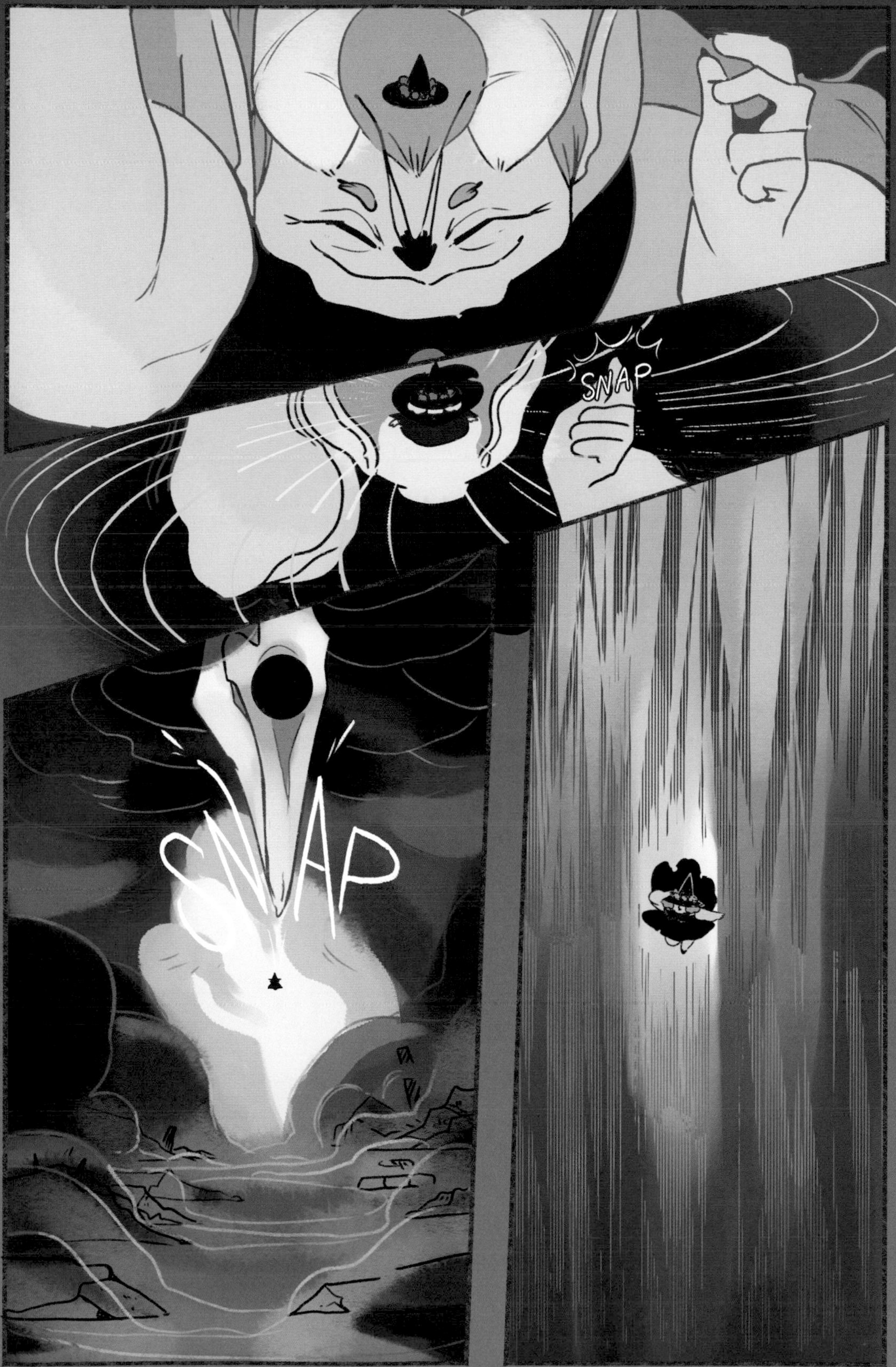
SNAP
SNAP

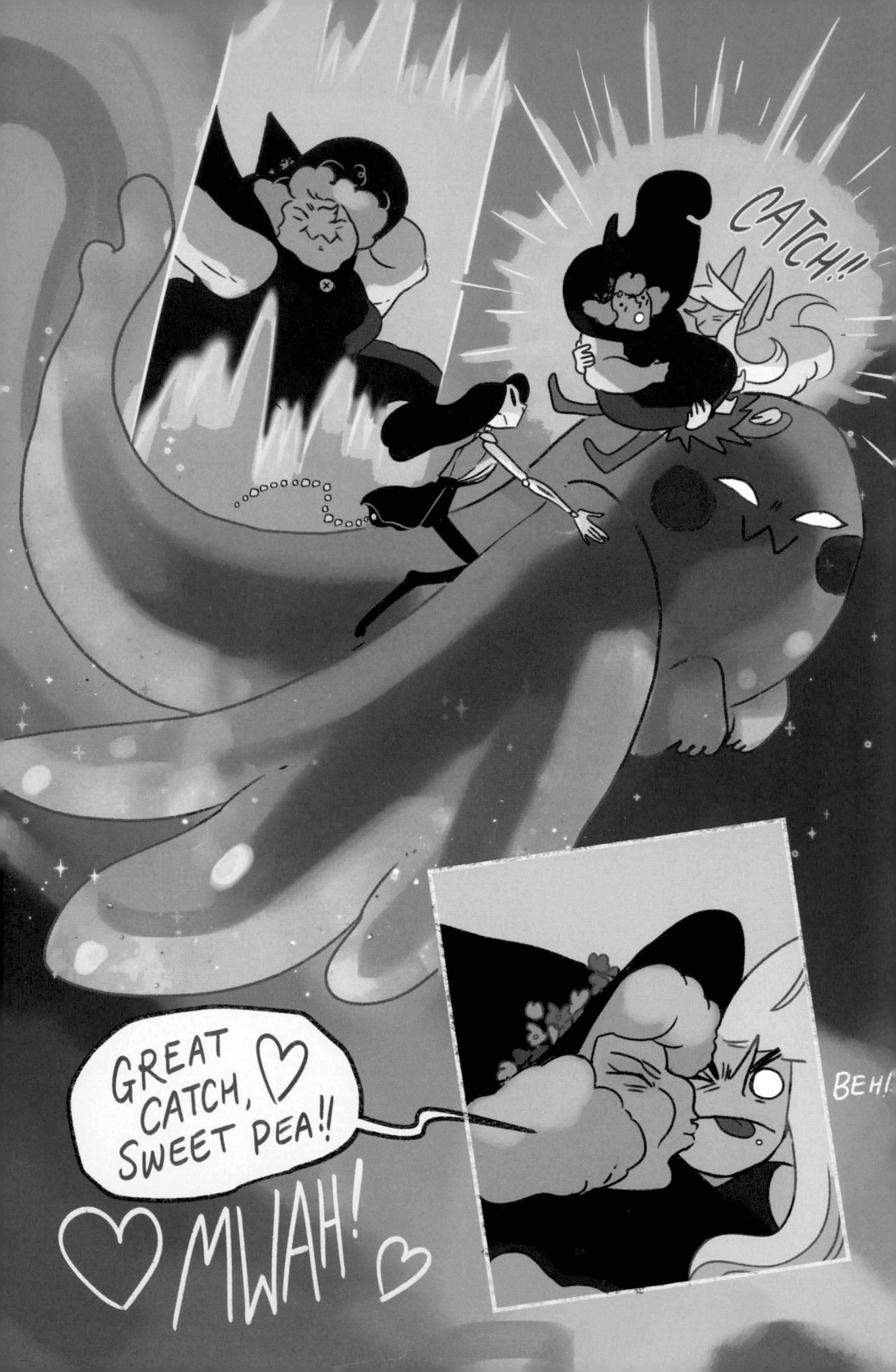
CATCH!!
GREAT CATCH, ♡ SWEET PEA!!
BEH!
♡ MWAH! ♡

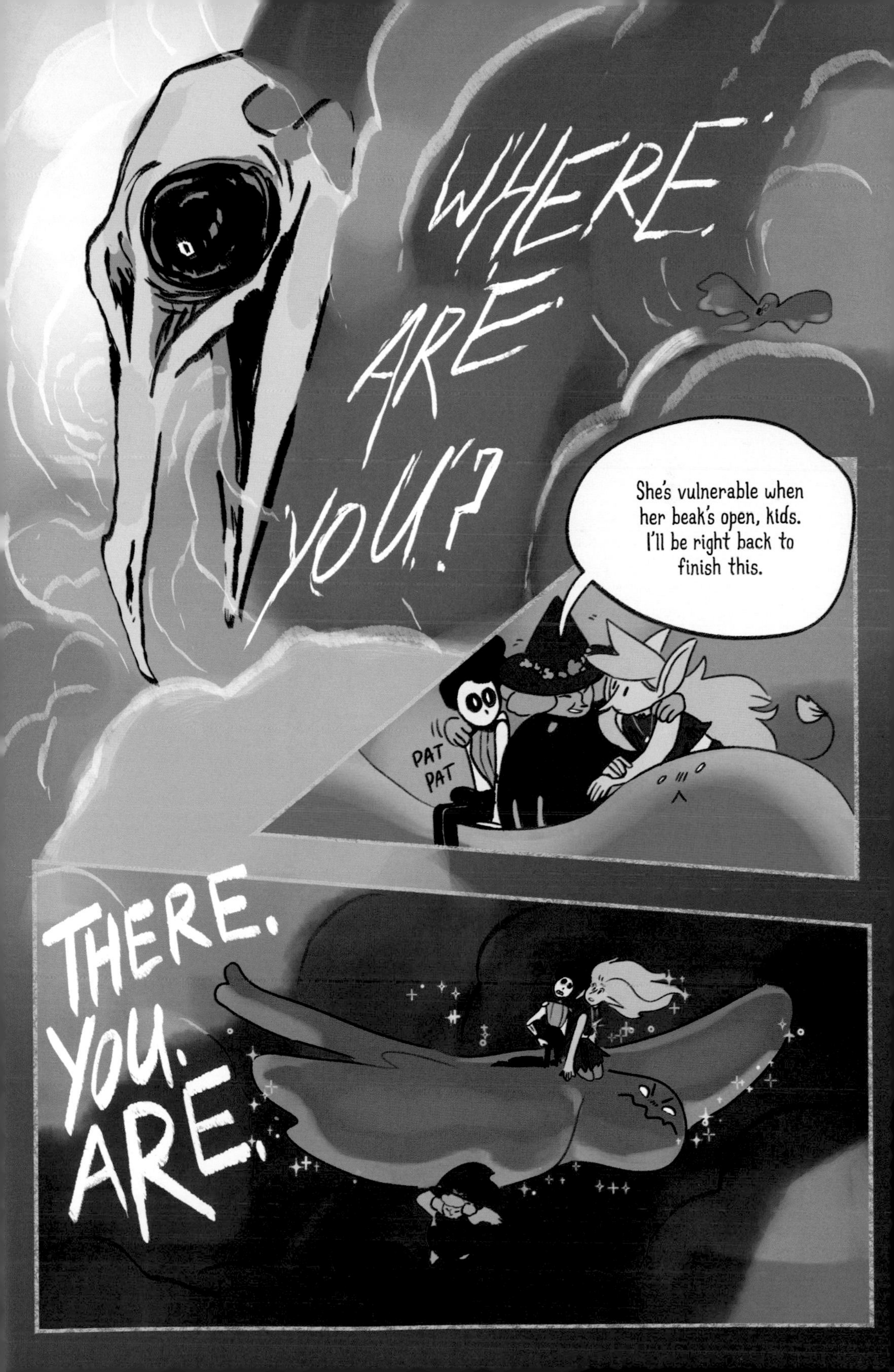
WHERE. ARE. YOU?
She's vulnerable when her beak's open, kids. I'll be right back to finish this.
PAT PAT
THERE. YOU. ARE.

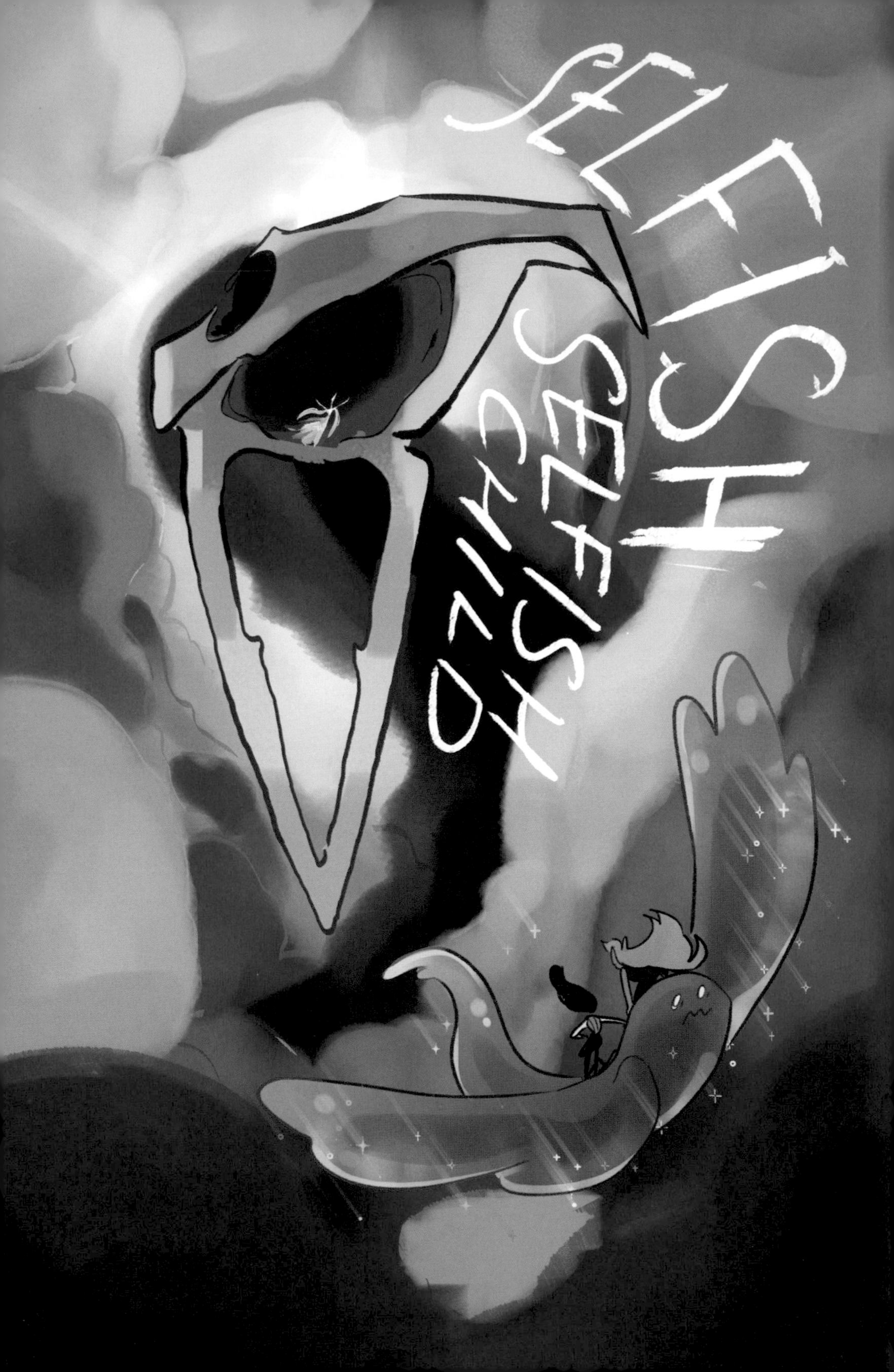
SELFISH
SELFISH
OZZO

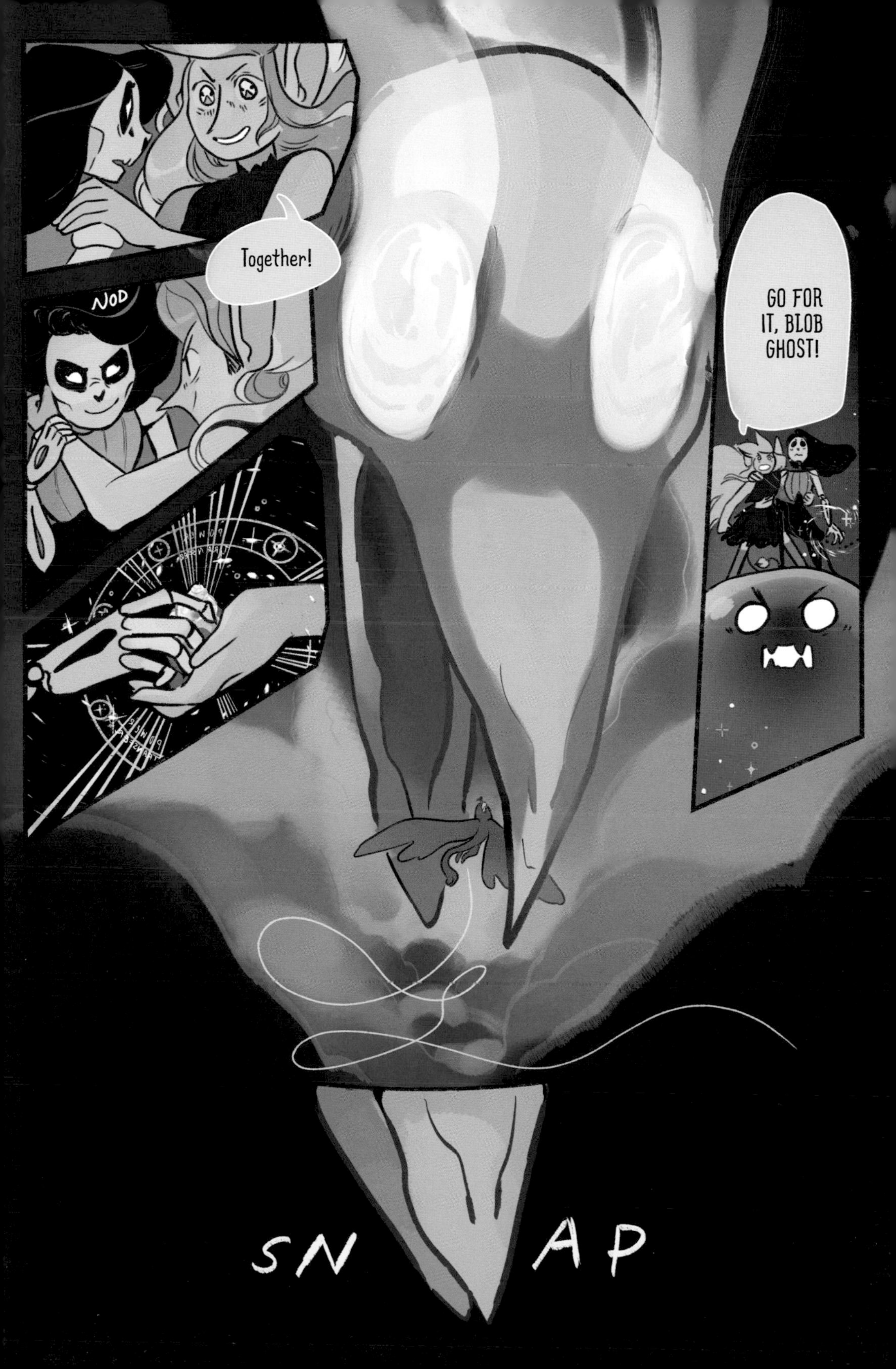
Together!
NOD
GO FOR IT, BLOB GHOST!
SN AP

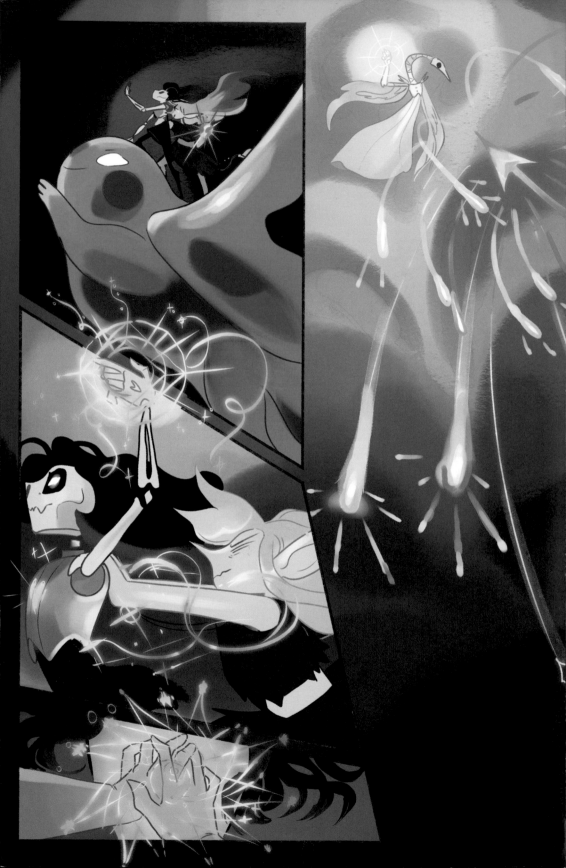

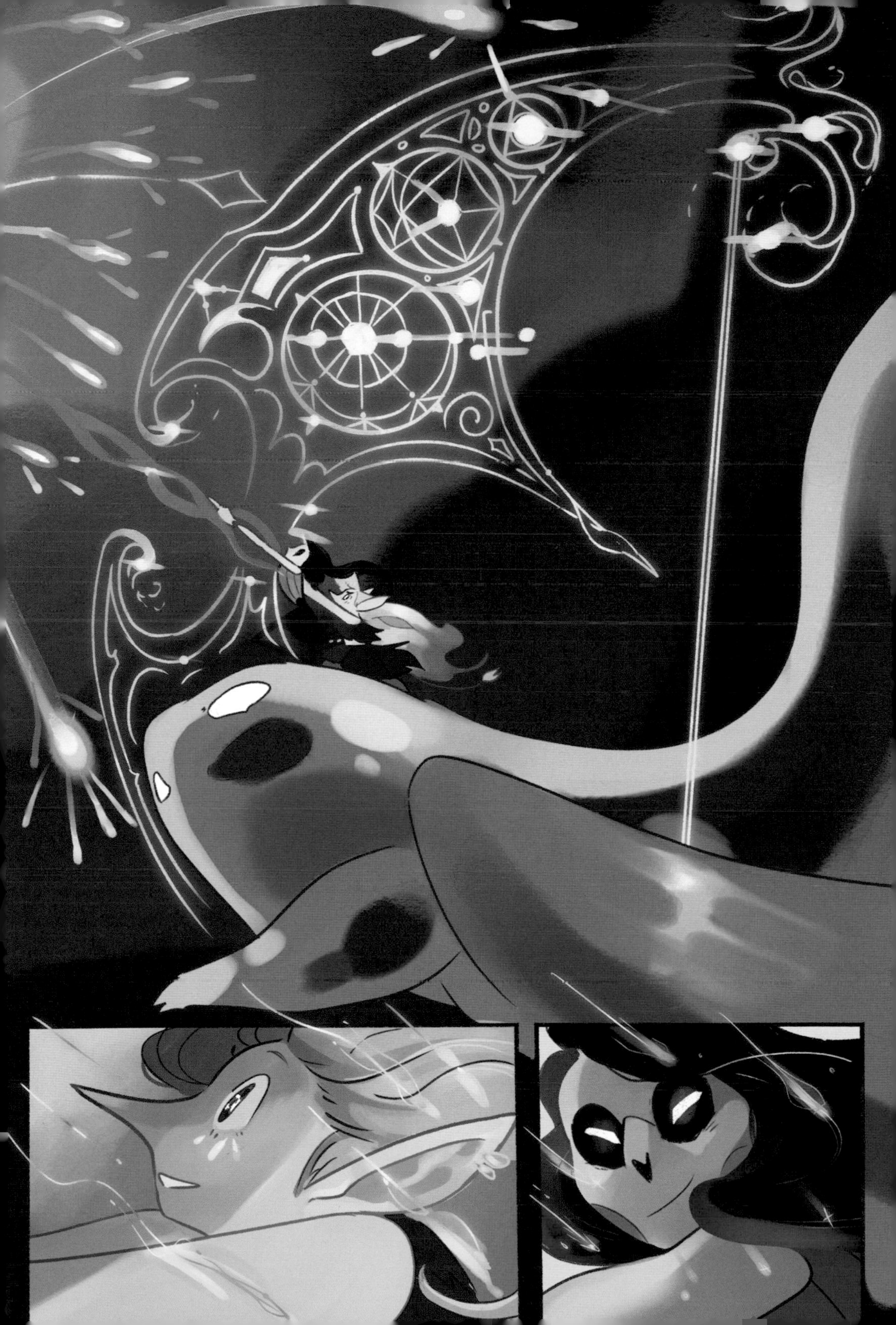

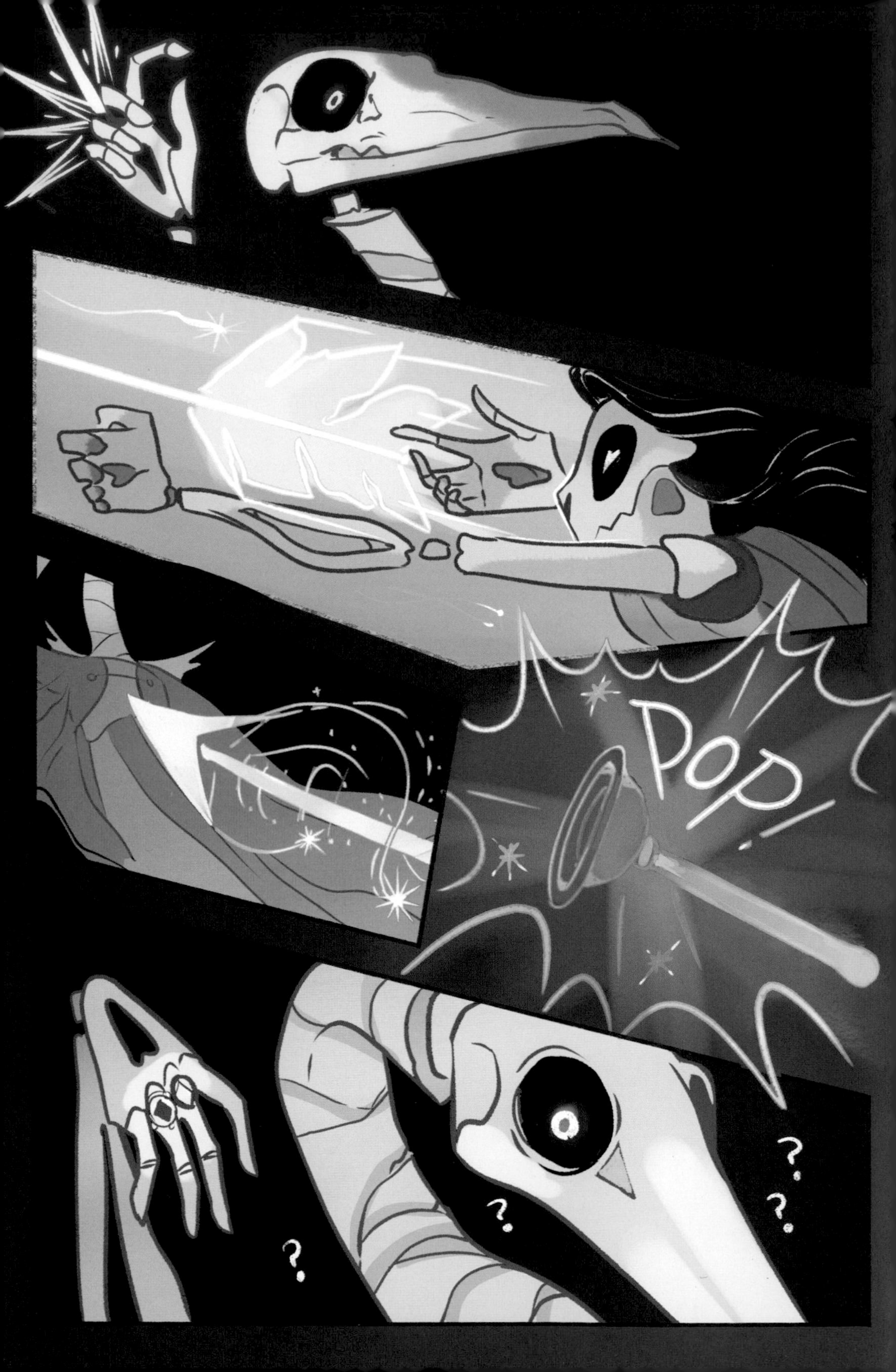

POP!!
?
?
?
?
?

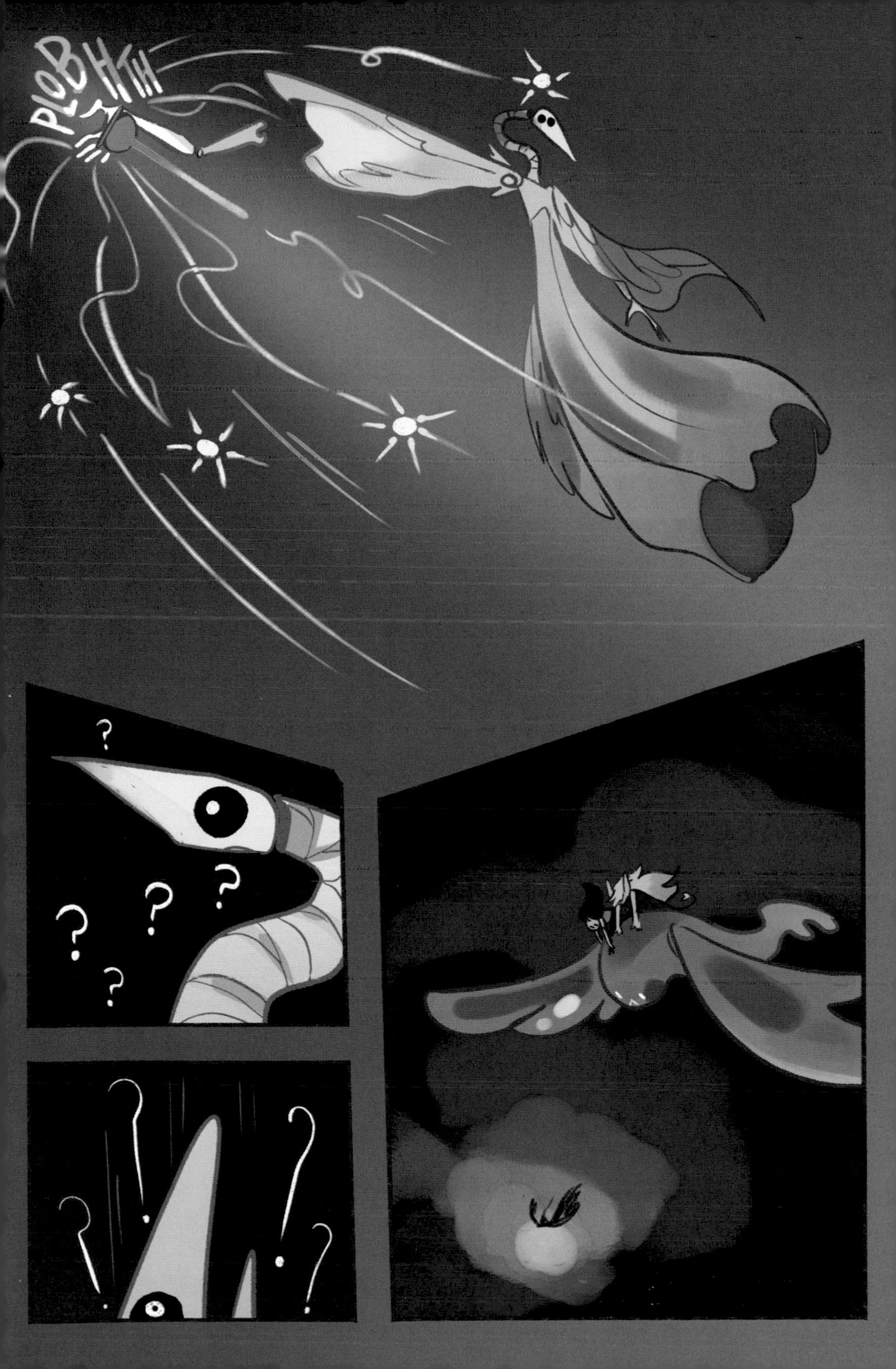
PLOBHTTH
? ? ? ? ?
?! ?! ?

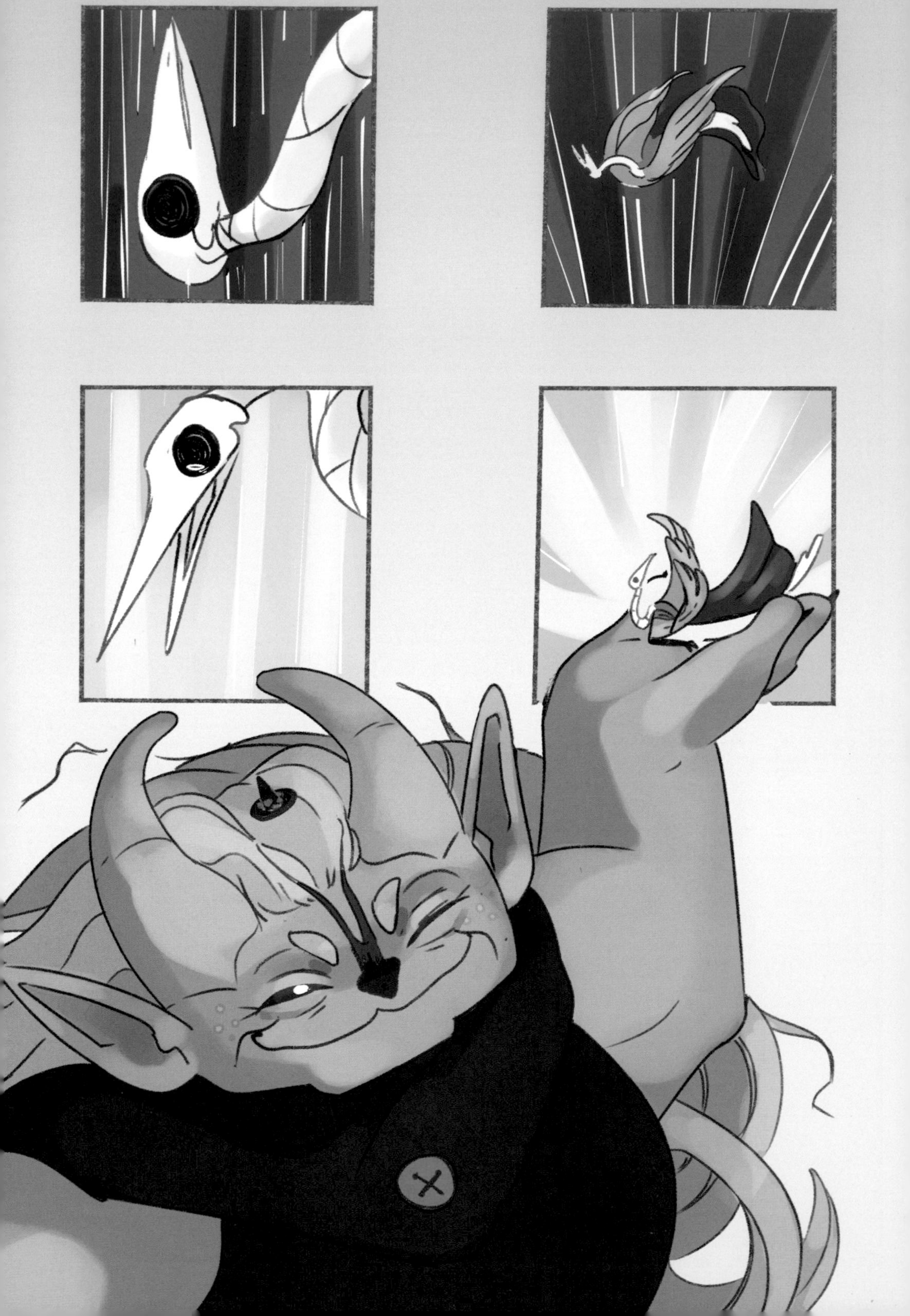

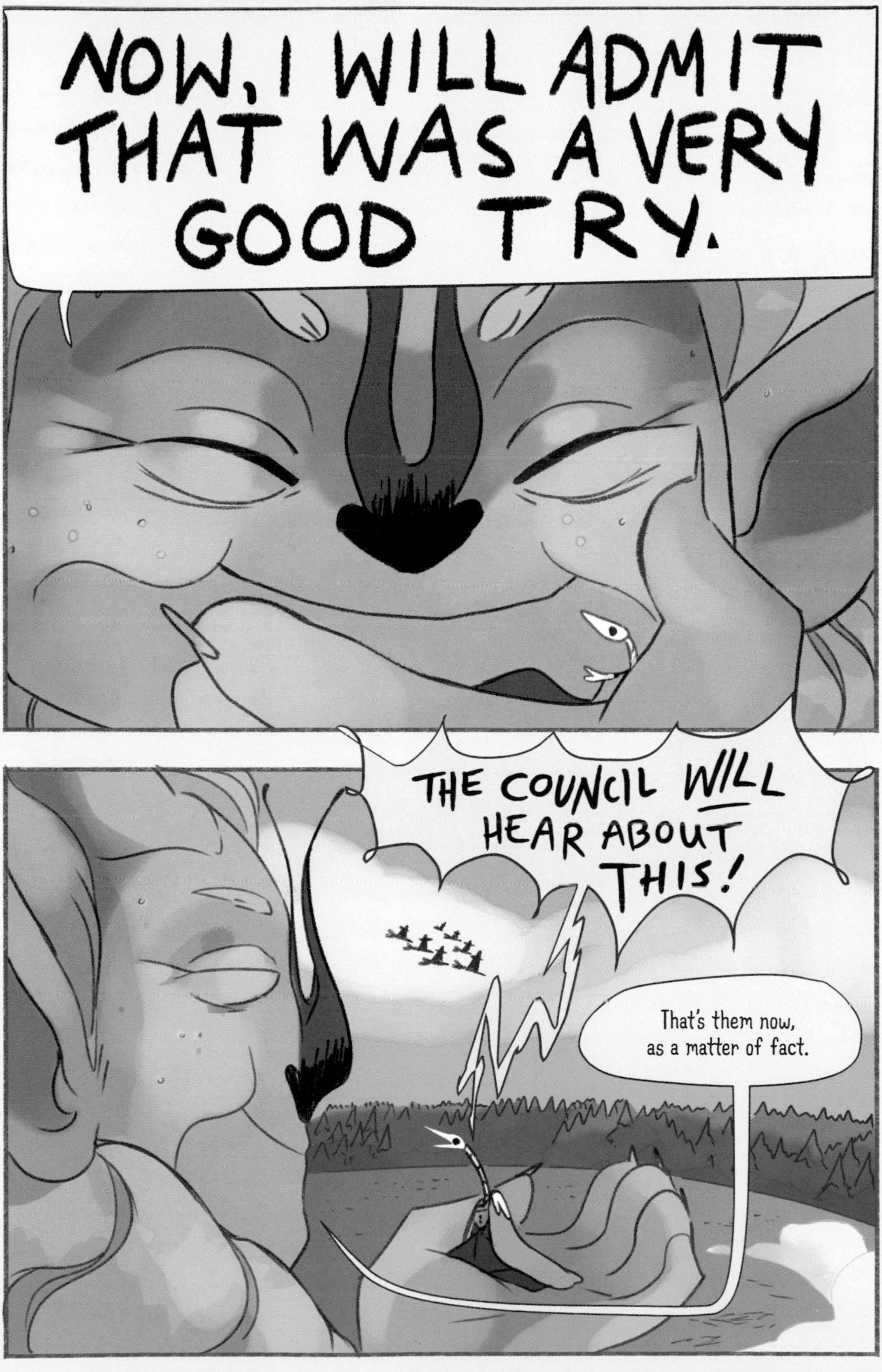
NOW, I WILL ADMIT THAT WAS A VERY GOOD TRY.
THE COUNCIL WILL HEAR ABOUT THIS!
That's them now, as a matter of fact.

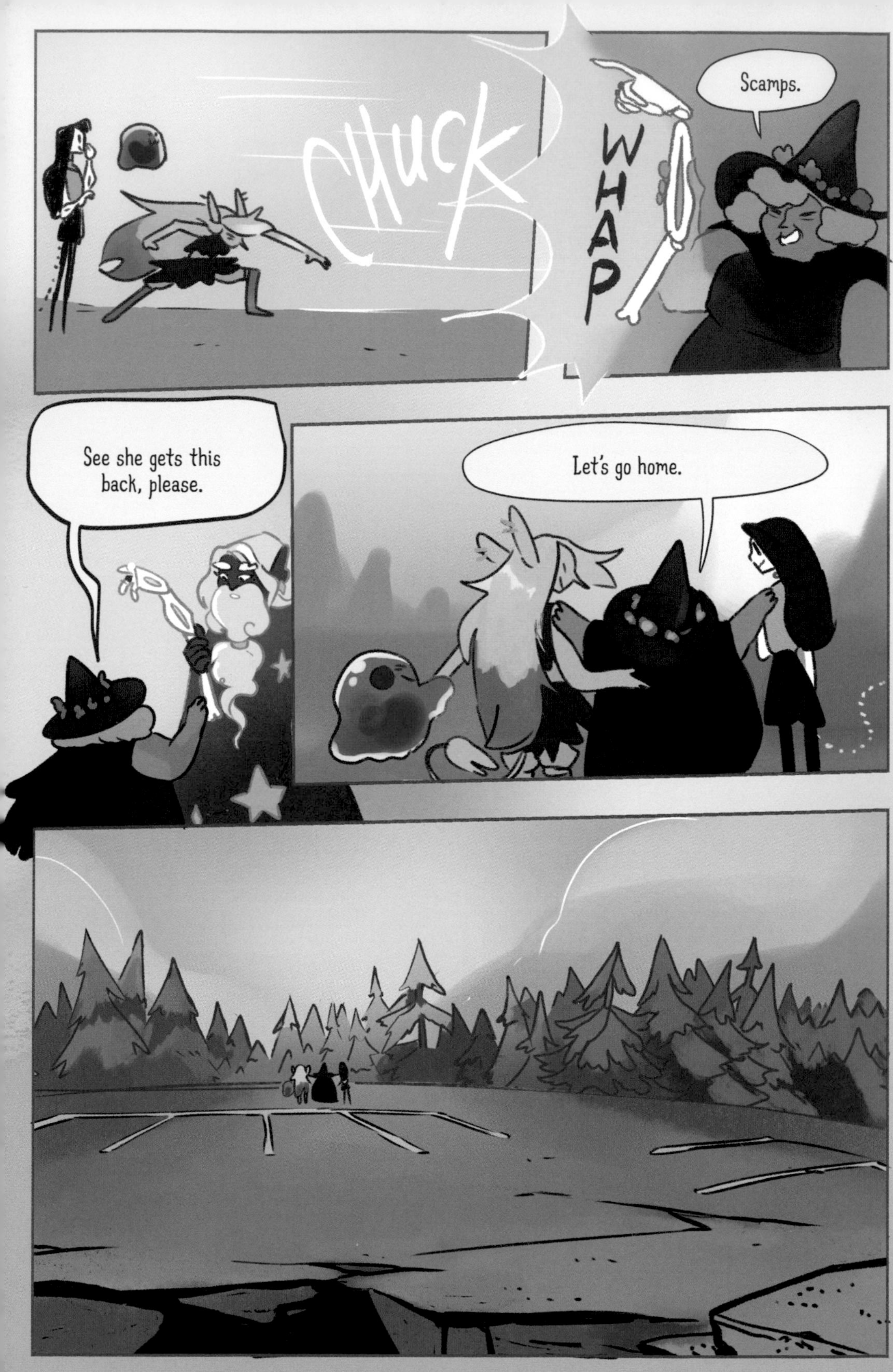
CHUCK
WHAP
Scamps.
See she gets this back, please.
Let's go home.

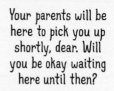

Your parents will be here to pick you up shortly, dear. Will you be okay waiting here until then?

Yes. Thank you.

Oh? Okay.

We're gonna be right back.

Go right ahead. Blob Ghost and I have a lot of catching up to do. I think we're going to get on like a house on fire.

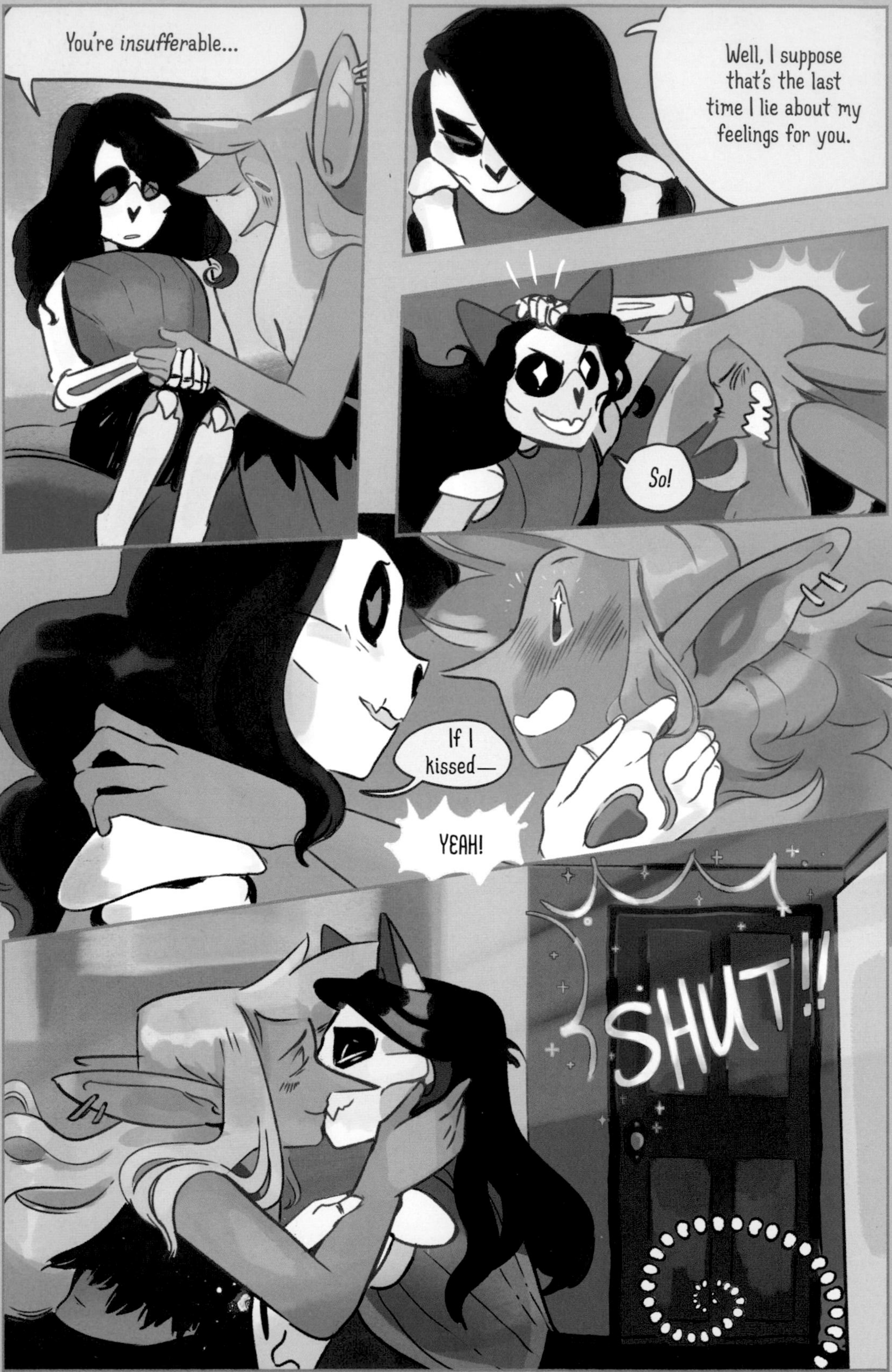
You're *insufferable*...
Well, I suppose that's the last time I lie about my feelings for you.
So!
If I kissed—
YEAH!
SHUT!!

PENNY

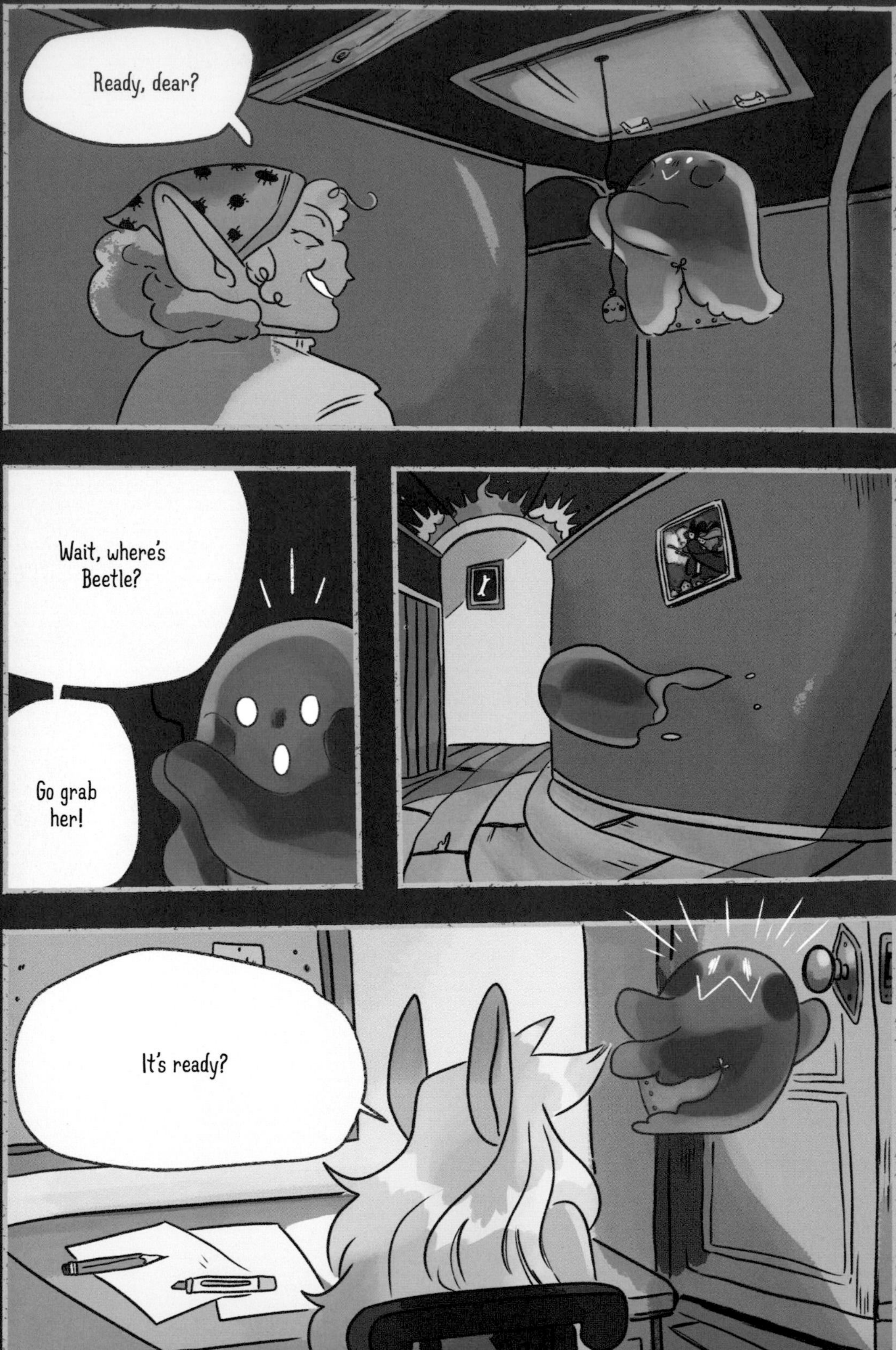
Ready, dear?
Wait, where's Beetle?
Go grab her!
It's ready?

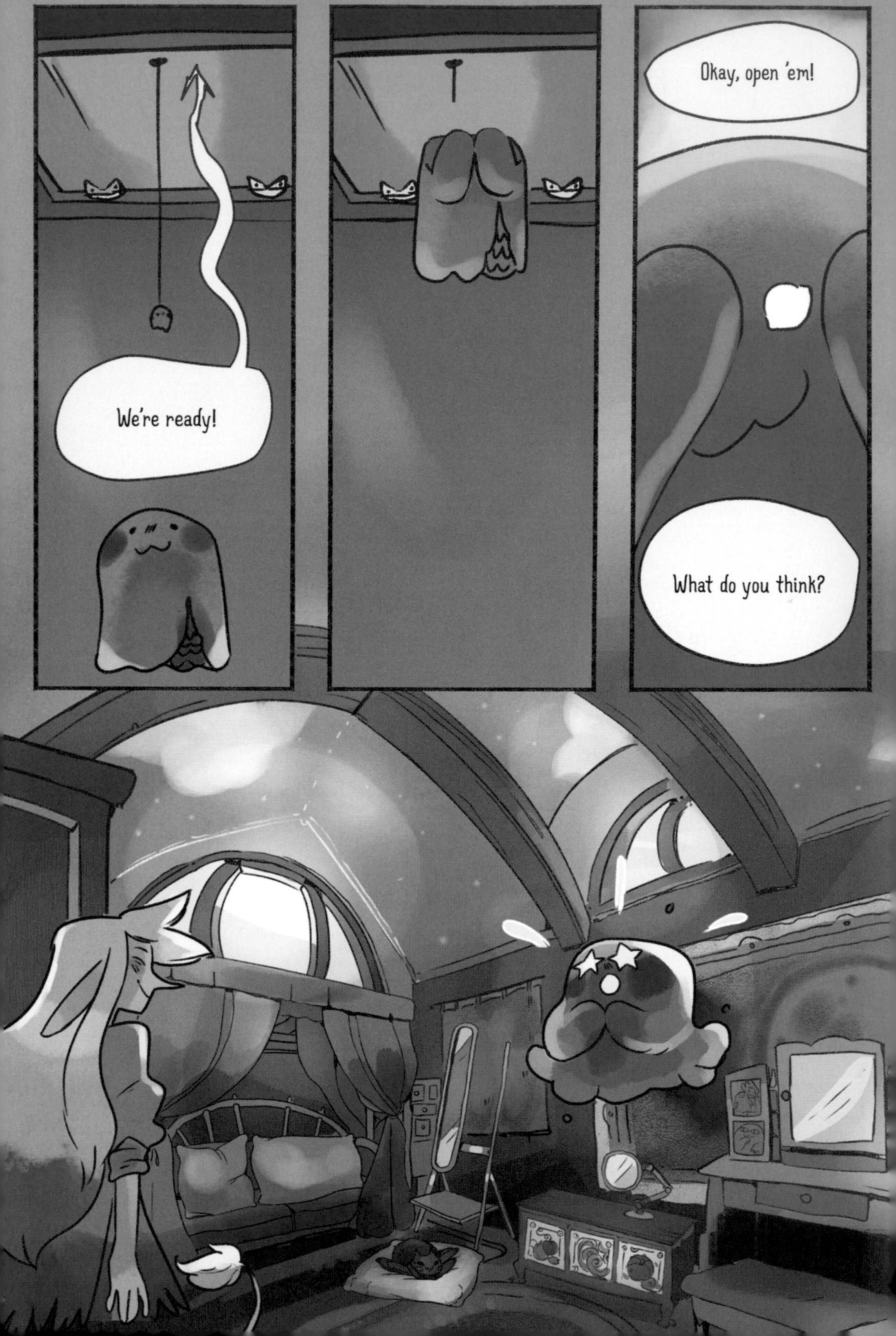
We're ready!
Okay, open 'em!
What do you think?

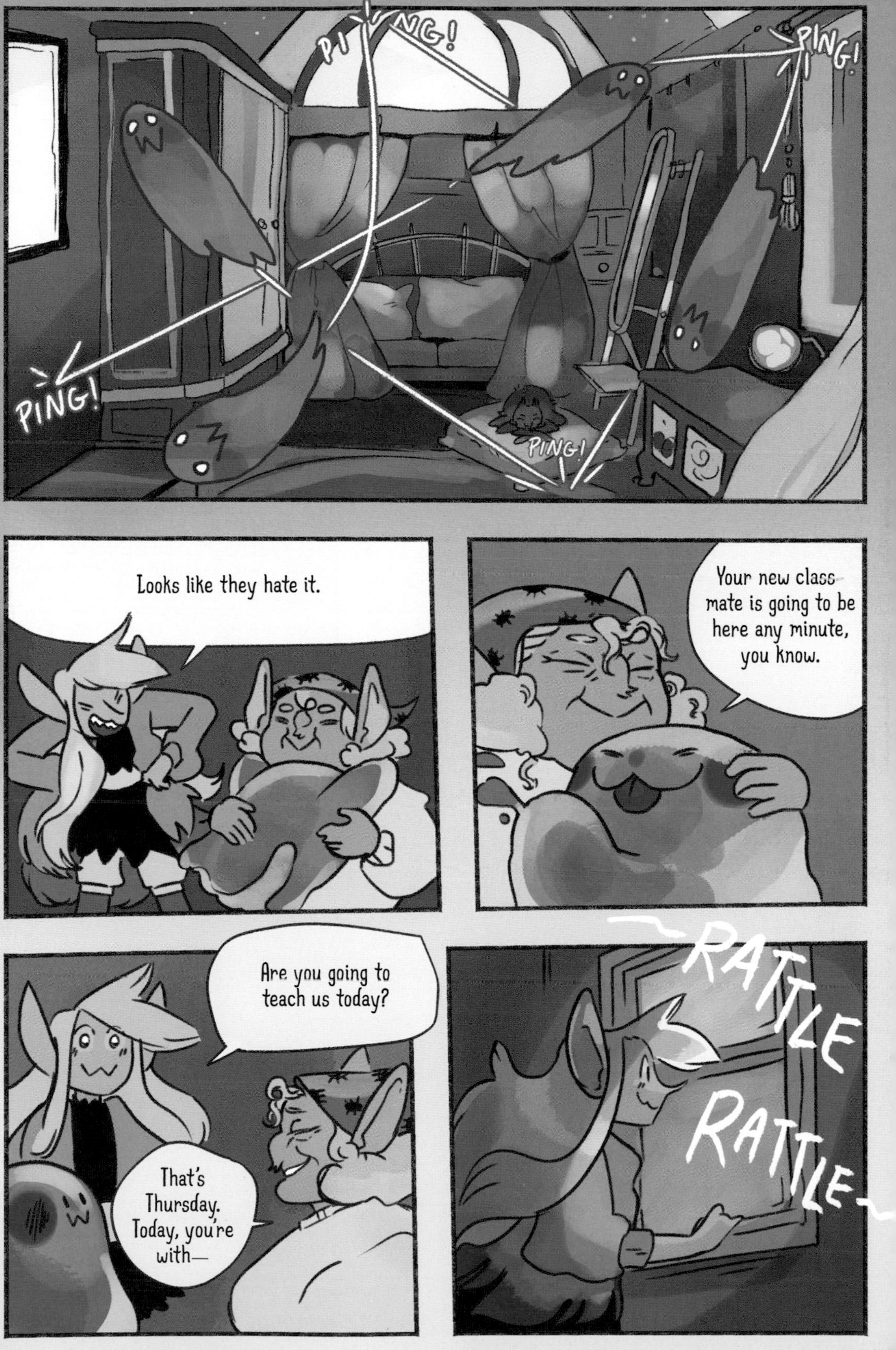
PI-NG!
PING!
PING!
PING!
Looks like they hate it.
Your new classmate is going to be here any minute, you know.
Are you going to teach us today?
That's Thursday. Today, you're with—
~RATTLE RATTLE~

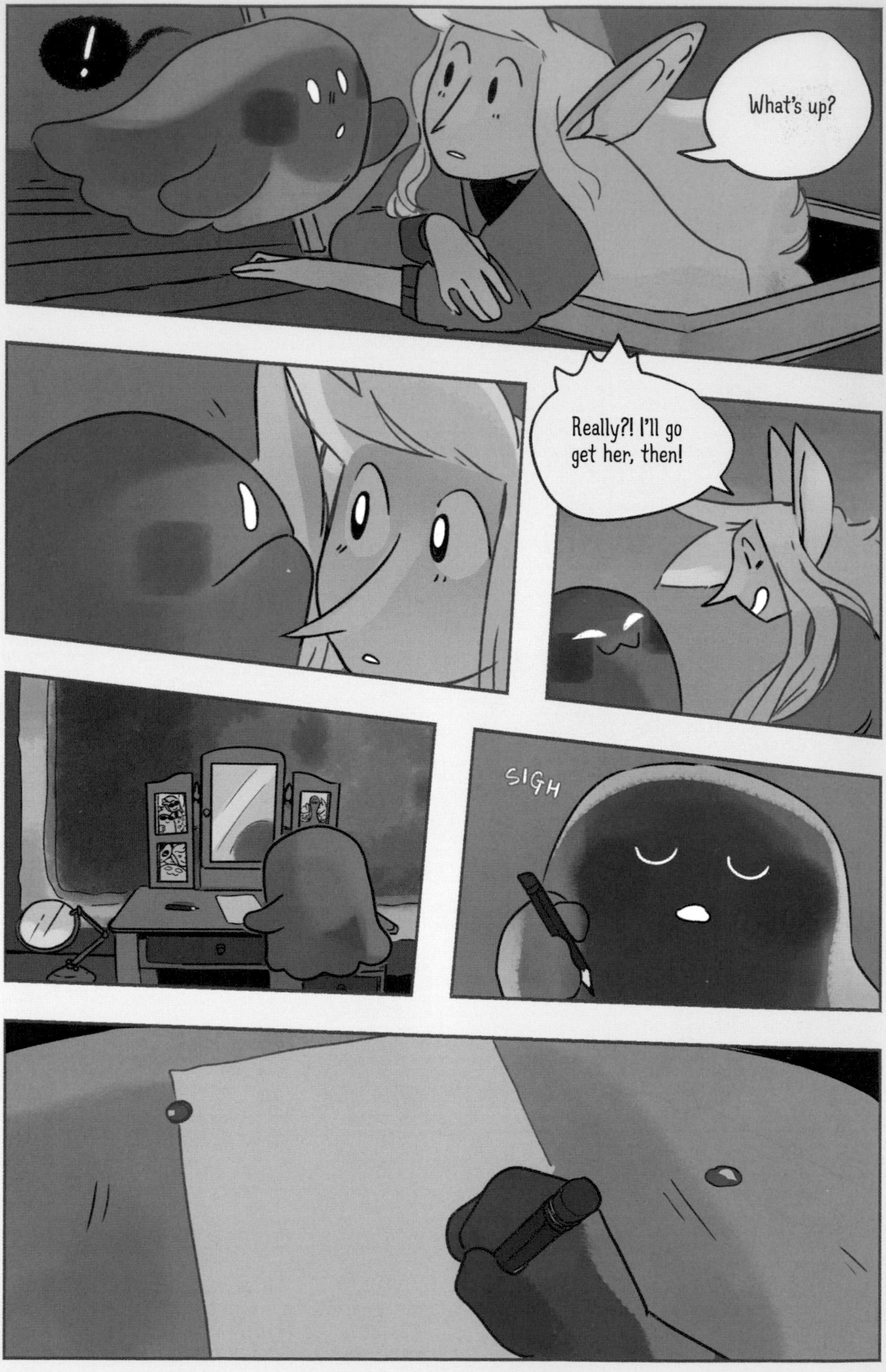
!
What's up?
Really?! I'll go get her, then!
SIGH

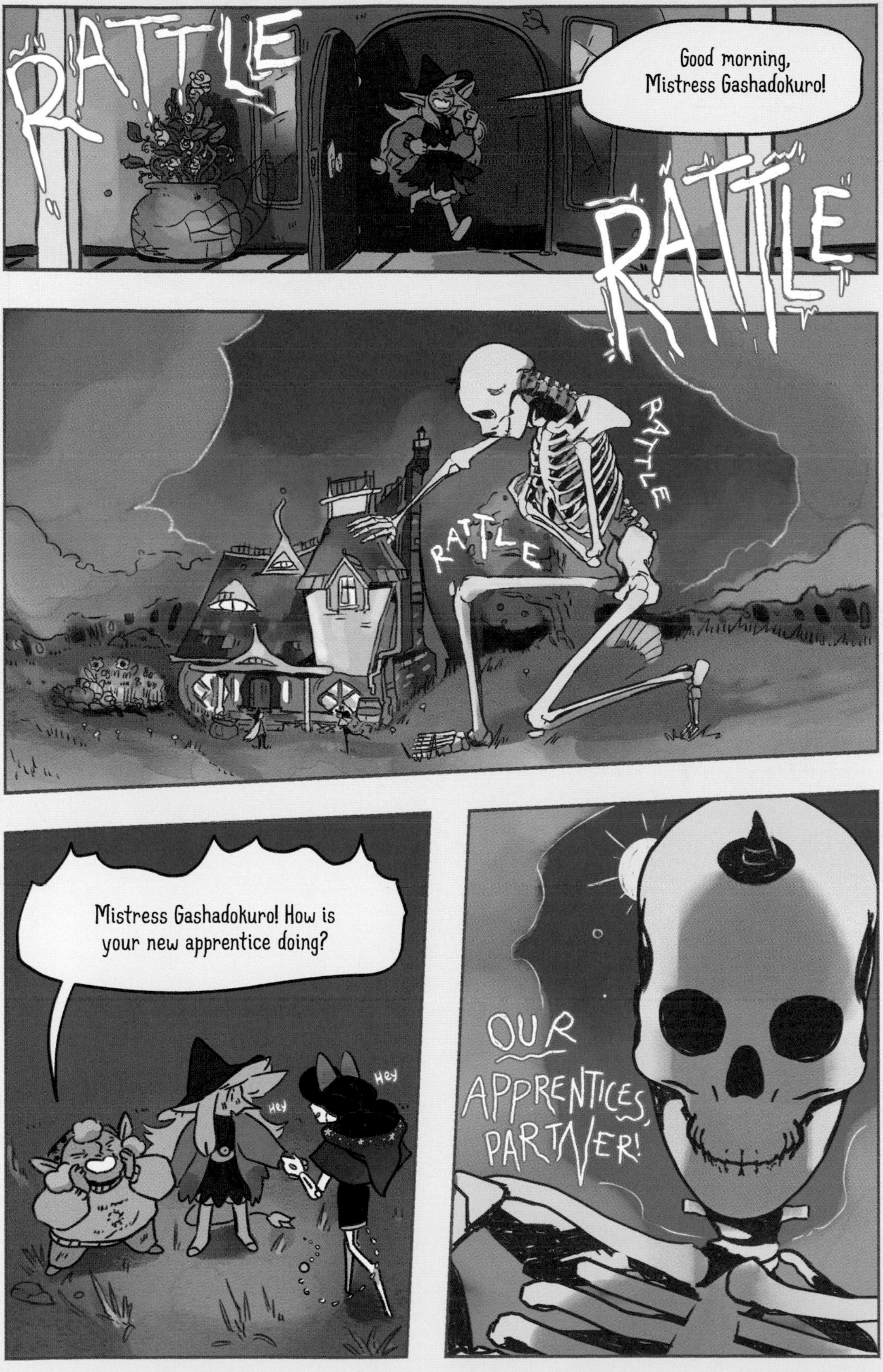
RATTLE
Good morning, Mistress Gashadokuro!
RATTLE
RATTLE
RATTLE
Mistress Gashadokuro! How is your new apprentice doing?
Hey
Hey
OUR APPRENTICES, PARTNER!

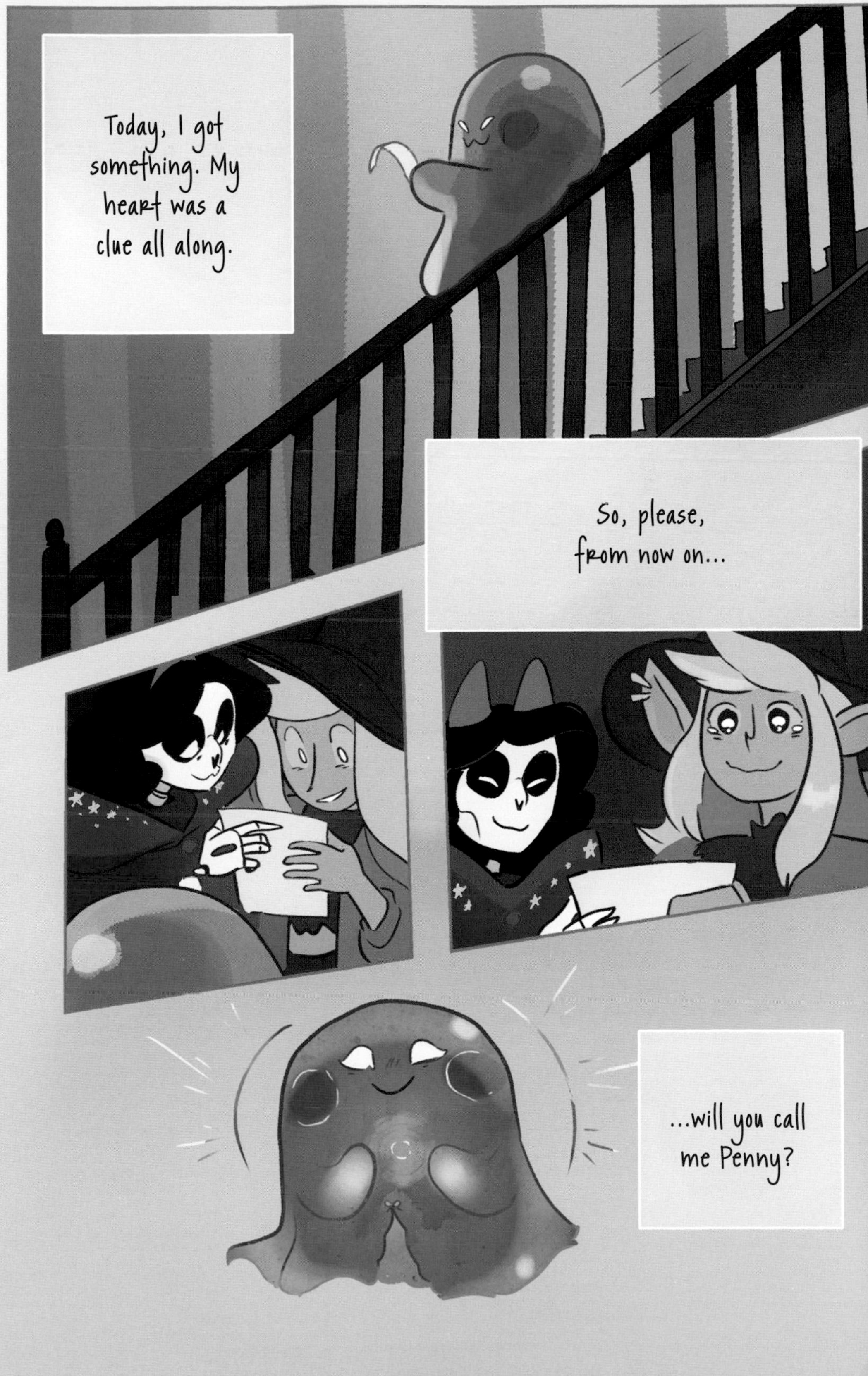
Today, I got something. My heart was a clue all along.
So, please, from now on...
...will you call me Penny?

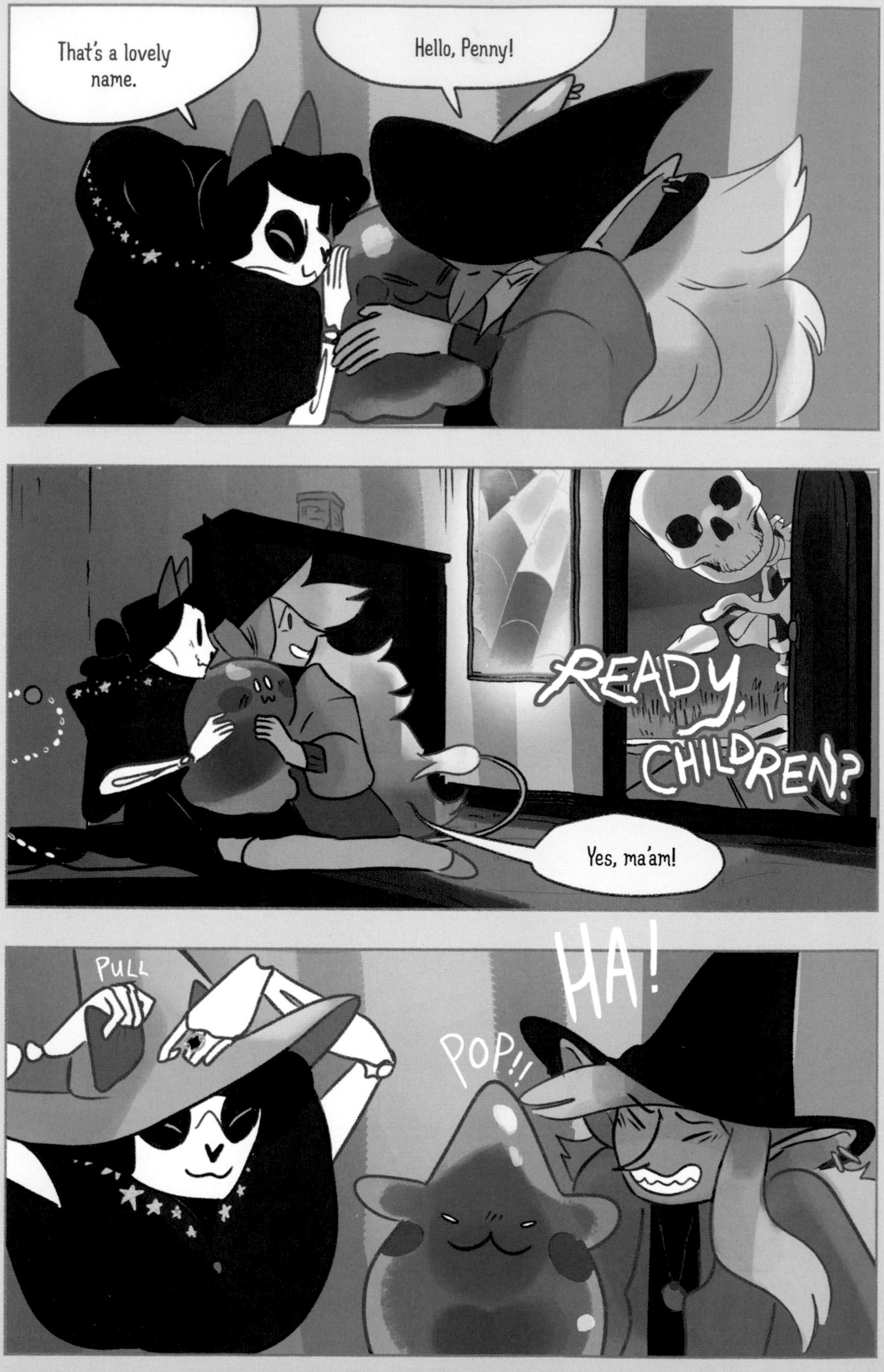
That's a lovely name.
Hello, Penny!
READY, CHILDREN?
Yes, ma'am!
PULL
HA!
POP!!

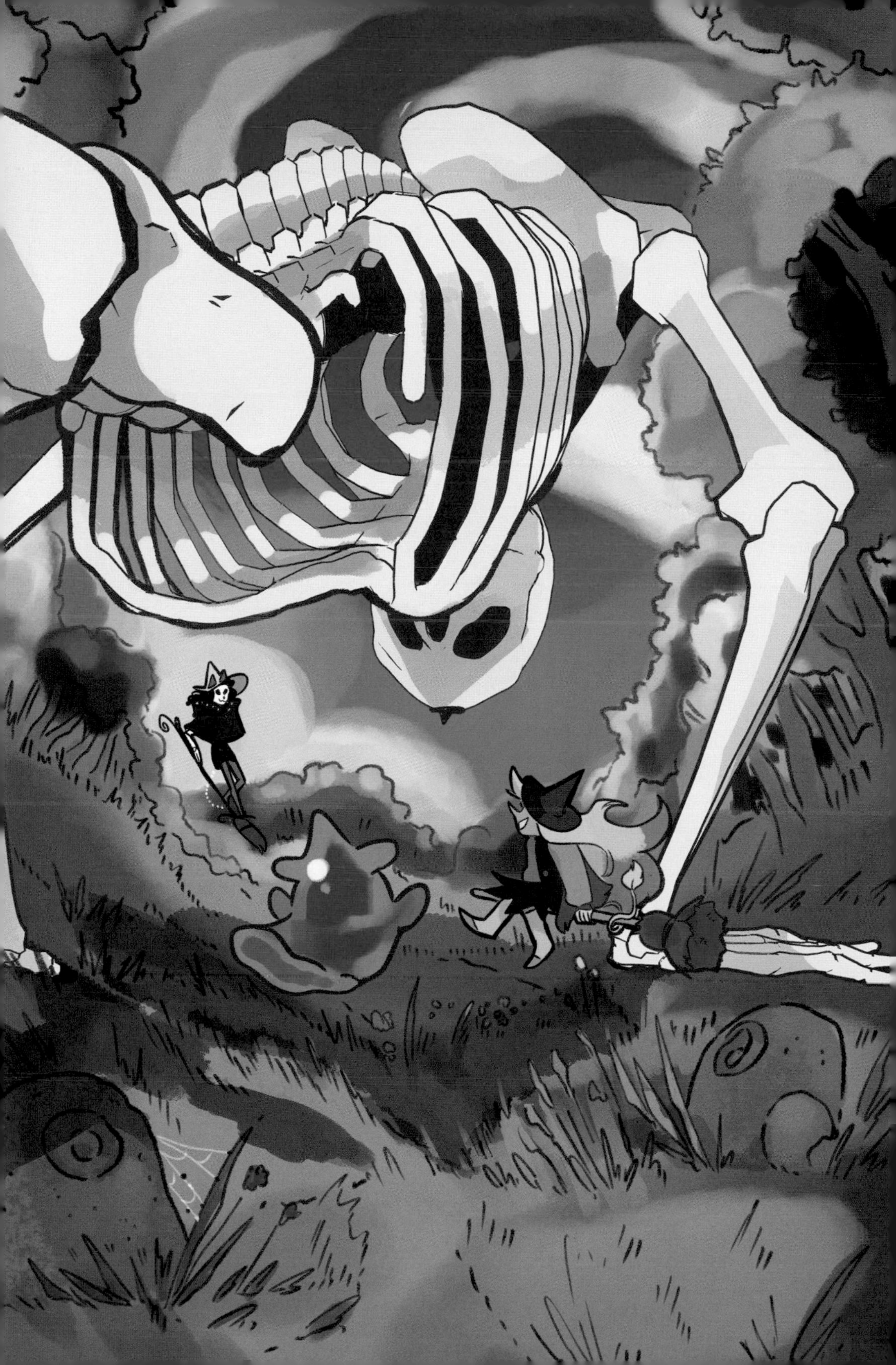

CONCEPT ART

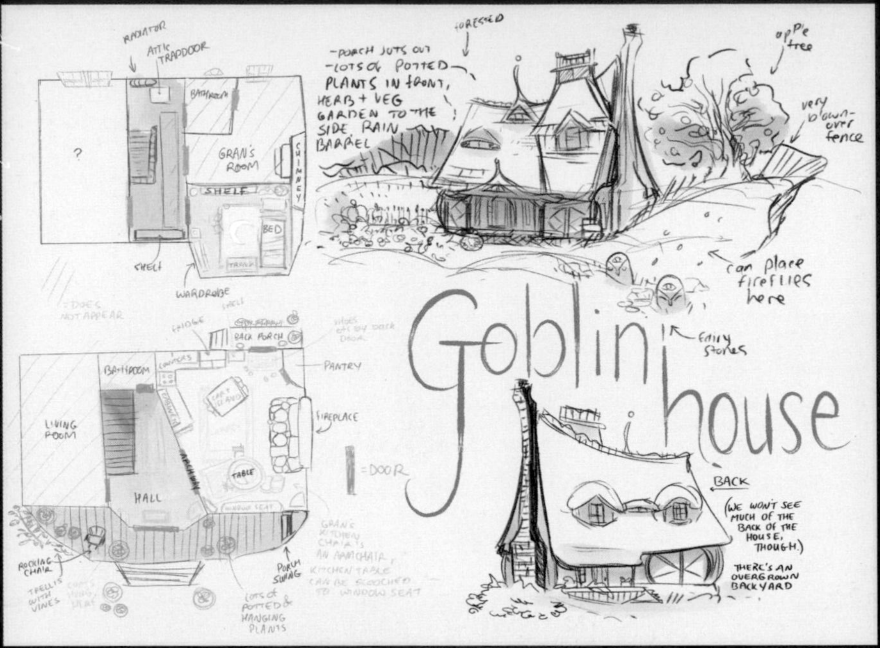
RADIATOR
ATTIC TRAPDOOR
BATHROOM
?
GRAN'S ROOM
CHIMNEY
SHELF
BED
SHELF
WARDROBE
= DOES NOT APPEAR
FRIDGE
SHELF
BACK PORCH
PANTRY
BATHROOM
LIVING ROOM
FIREPLACE
TABLE
HALL
WINDOW SEAT
= DOOR
ROCKING CHAIR
TRELLIS WITH VINES
PORCH SWING
LOTS OF POTTED & HANGING PLANTS
GRAN'S KITCHEN CHAIR IS AN ARMCHAIR, KITCHEN TABLE CAN BE SCOOCHED TO WINDOW SEAT
FORESTED
-PORCH JUTS OUT
-LOTS OF POTTED PLANTS IN FRONT, HERB + VEG GARDEN TO THE SIDE, RAIN BARREL
apple tree
very blown-over fence
can place fireflies here
fairy stones
Goblin house
BACK
(WE WON'T SEE MUCH OF THE BACK OF THE HOUSE, THOUGH.)
THERE'S AN OVERGROWN BACKYARD

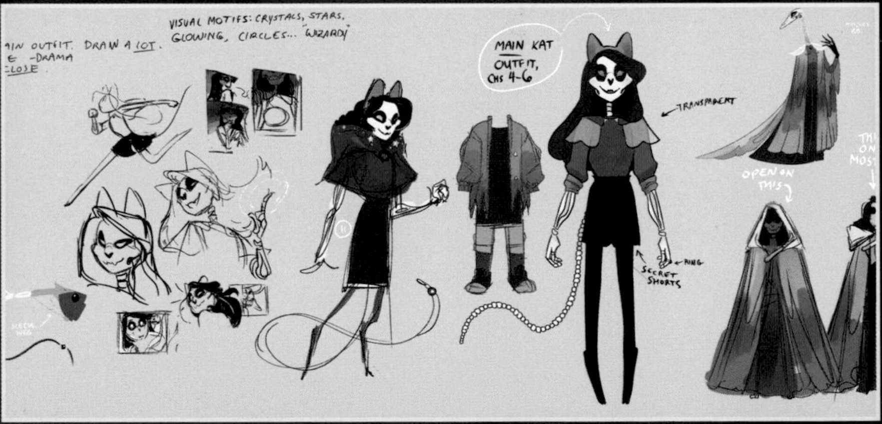
VISUAL MOTIFS: CRYSTALS, STARS, GLOWING, CIRCLES... "WIZARDY"
MAIN KAT OUTFIT, CHS 4-6
TRANSPARENT
SECRET SHORTS
OPEN ON THIS

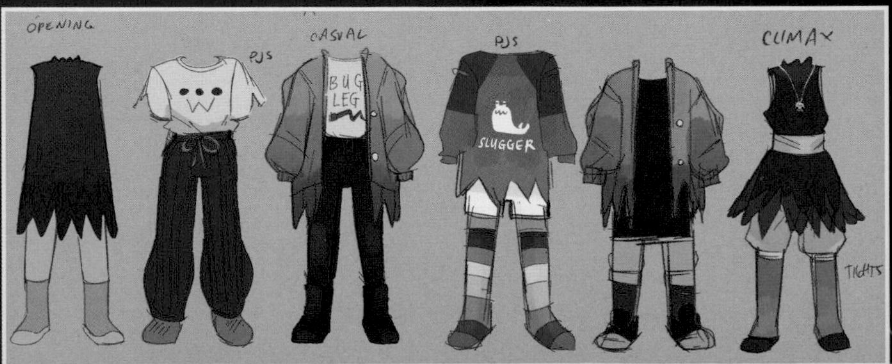
OPENING
PJS
CASUAL
BUG LEG
PJS
SLUGGER
CLIMAX
TIGHTS

Acknowledgments

I'd like to start by thanking my agent, Susan Graham, whose hard work, passion, and great ideas not only shaped this book, but enabled it to exist at all, and for whom I would draw hundreds of chickencats if it meant they'd keep lending me their support. I also owe *Beetle's* existence to the fantastic work of my editor, Julia "Ghoulia" McCarthy, whose excitement over this story and willingness to put up with my antics deserve particular gratitude.

The staff at Simon & Schuster also deserve my boundless thanks, particularly Rebecca Syracuse, *Beetle's* phenomenal designer; Jeannie Ng; Shivani Annirood; Chantal Gersch; Devin MacDonald; Justin Chanda; and Reka Simonsen.

If Natalie Riess and Kristen Acampora had not done the flat colors for this book, my hands would have fallen off. It was a treat to paint their work, and I cannot thank them enough. Natalie has the best bug-and-dragon ideas in the world and has been my fierce and wonderful friend for many years. Kristen is one of the kindest, most uplifting, and most hardworking people I have ever met, and I am so grateful to be her friend.

A special mention is also due to Stacey Friedberg, who workshopped a great deal of this book with me early on.

Tremendous thanks to all my friends and family, especially to Kate Dobson for her mentorship; to Smo for coming up with "Worm of Endearment"; to Deborah, TJ, Angelique, and Nick for their support and good ideas and warrior-cats-role-playing chops; and to all my phenomenal, funny, and absurdly skilled friends for appearing in my life and appearing in this book as background creatures. Thank you for the readers and supporters of my webcomic for also cheering *Beetle* on.

When I first wrote the short comic that *Beetle* is based on, I sent it to Zack Morrison, my rival, and asked if it was any good. Their enthusiasm for these characters lit a fire in my heart. I also showed it to my brother, Luke, who was in middle school himself back then, and *he* laughed at it, so I wrote more for him.

For my friends

ATHENEUM BOOKS FOR YOUNG READERS
An imprint of Simon & Schuster Children's Publishing Division
1230 Avenue of the Americas, New York, New York 10020
This book is a work of fiction. Any references to historical events, real people, or real places are used
fictitiously. Other names, characters, places, and events are products of the author's imagination,
and any resemblance to actual events or places or persons, living or dead, is entirely coincidental.
Copyright © 2020 by Aliza Layne
Illustrations colored by Natalie Riess and Kristen Acampora
All rights reserved, including the right of reproduction in whole or in part in any form.
ATHENEUM BOOKS FOR YOUNG READERS is a registered trademark of Simon & Schuster, Inc.
Atheneum logo is a trademark of Simon & Schuster, Inc.
For information about special discounts for bulk purchases, please contact Simon & Schuster Special
Sales at 1-866-506-1749 or business@simonandschuster.com.
The Simon & Schuster Speakers Bureau can bring authors to your live event. For more information or
to book an event, contact the Simon & Schuster Speakers Bureau at 1-866-248-3049 or visit our
website at www.simonspeakers.com.
Also available in an Atheneum Books for Young Readers paperback edition
Book design by Rebecca Syracuse
The text for this book was set in Prova.
The illustrations for this book were digitally rendered.
Manufactured in China
0420 SCP
First Atheneum Books for Young Readers hardcover edition
2 4 6 8 10 9 7 5 3 1
CIP data for this book is available from the Library of Congress.
ISBN 978-1-5344-4154-5 (paperback)
ISBN 978-1-5344-4153-8 (hardcover)
ISBN 978-1-5344-4155-2 (eBook)